ASHANTI GOLD

Also by Brian Nicholson featuring John Gunn

GWEILO

AL SAMAK

FIRE DRAGON

ASHANTI GOLD

BRIAN NICHOLSON

Trafford
PUBLISHING™

Order this book online at www.trafford.com/07-1274
or email orders@trafford.com

Most Trafford titles are also available at major online book retailers.

Note for Librarians: A cataloguing record for this book is available from Library
and Archives Canada at www.collectionscanada.ca/amicus/index-e.html

Printed in Victoria, BC, Canada.

ISBN: 978-1-4251-3354-2

*We at Trafford believe that it is the responsibility of us all, as both individuals
and corporations, to make choices that are environmentally and socially sound.
You, in turn, are supporting this responsible conduct each time you purchase a
Trafford book, or make use of our publishing services. To find out how you are
helping, please visit www.trafford.com/responsiblepublishing.html*

*Our mission is to efficiently provide the world's finest, most comprehensive
book publishing service, enabling every author to experience success.
To find out how to publish your book, your way, and have it available
worldwide, visit us online at www.trafford.com/10510*

 www.trafford.com

North America & international
toll-free: 1 888 232 4444 (USA & Canada)
phone: 250 383 6864 ♦ fax: 250 383 6804 ♦ email: info@trafford.com

The United Kingdom & Europe
phone: +44 (0)1865 722 113 ♦ local rate: 0845 230 9601
facsimile: +44 (0)1865 722 868 ♦ email: info.uk@trafford.com

10 9 8 7 6 5 4 3

ASHANTI GOLD

To D, Rugs and Basher

FOREWORD

An investigation into the disappearance of an ineffective agent from the now-defunct Secret Intelligence Service at the British High Commission in Accra, reveals a conspiracy to overthrow the governments of countries in West Africa by subversion, terrorism and tribal civil war.

The cruelty and corruption of the 18th century Portugese, Dutch and British slave-traders who raped West Africa of its human and mineral resources, is easily surpassed by that of 21st Century, power-hungry, West African exiles, ruthless arms dealers, diplomats and politicians on both sides of the Atlantic who are involved in the conspiracy.

Governments can be brought down by subversion, terrorism and civil war. Terrorists need weapons which must be bought with money....lots of it. Gold is money......and Ghana possesses the richest gold mine in the world at Sawaba in the Ashanti Region where nuggets as big as walnuts can be illegally panned from the Ofin River and then sold to dealers abroad......just as was done during the 18th Century slave trade.

PROLOGUE

'Enter!'

Daniel Mortimer opened the door and stooping to avoid cracking his head on the low lintel, entered the Captain's cabin. Captain Tremayne was bending over the chart, which had been placed in the best position to get the maximum light from the gimballed oil lamp. A pair of brass dividers, points closed together, was being tapped against the side of his nose as he concentrated on the task of navigating his ship to the anchorage off this hostile coastline which offered no deep water shelter to a ship with the draught of the Royal Trader.

At Latitude 4°47' North of the Equator in the Gulf of Guinea, the temperature in the low-beamed deck-head of the cabin was in the high nineties. The Captain's ruffled white shirt was open to the waist and stained with sweat even though all the aft scuttles were open.

'Where away the Cape, Mister Mortimer?'

'Two points off the port bow, Sir,' and then was added and immediately regretted, 'about two miles off the anchorage, Sir.' The Captain raised his eyes from the chart and studied his First Officer as though he was something that had just crawled out of a weevil-ridden biscuit which was all that was left after the five week voyage from Liverpool.

'Allow me to be the judge of that, Mister; I'll be topside presently. Be good enough to strike the moonraker, skys'l, royals and t'gallants. Have the ledzman stand by in the chains to give the mark and break out both anchors,' and as Daniel made to go, 'oh yes, and make ready the dandy for me to go ashore.'

'Aye, aye, Sir,' and Daniel Mortimer backed out through the door and climbed to the poop deck and the relief of the faint onshore breeze which made the sweltering heat, even at eleven at night in the first watch, marginally more bearable. Daniel gave the orders and the ship's hands swarmed up the ratlins to furl the topmost sails. The ledzman had been expecting the order and climbed nimbly over the side of the ship to the small platform right up in the bow where the

7

martingale stays, which braced the jib and flying jib booms, were secured to cast iron plates in the hull. He tied himself onto the platform with a canvas apron so that both his hands were free to swing the lead and call out the soundings. The whipping on the anchor chains was cut after the chain pins had been loosened so that one blow of a sledgehammer would release the bower anchors hanging on either side of the ship's prow.

The lean-hulled clipper had been carrying the majority of its canvas to minimise the voyage time for the first leg of the triangular run between Liverpool, the Guinea Coast and Charleston. For the middle passage from the Guinea Coast to Charleston, with its cargo of slaves, every square inch of the clipper's canvas would be set, which included her triangular skyscraper sails set above the moonraker and royals. This three quarters of an acre of canvas gave the Royal Trader its maximum speed of 14 knots for the most profitable leg of the voyage when every extra day at sea meant the loss of more slaves and a reduction in the company's profit margin.

Daniel was all too familiar with the routine of the slave-trader's voyage. On the first leg, the ship's cargo would be a worthless collection of poor quality cotton and other fabrics which couldn't be sold on the home market; watered rum, trinkets and muskets which were more lethal to the firer than the target. This cargo would be exchanged for 400 slaves who would be crammed, wrists chained and ankles shackled, into the orlop deck just above the ship's bilges. Then followed the middle passage to Charleston; five weeks, or mercifully, a little less if the south-east trades blew strongly and favourably, with the ship stinking like an open sewer from the slaves' excrement and the putrefying corpses of the lucky ones who managed to die quickly. Three days in Charleston while the ship was cleaned, the slaves were auctioned and the new cargo loaded; then the homeward leg with cotton, tobacco, rum and sugar. Daniel went down the companionway from the poop deck to the main deck and watched the bosun supervising four of the crew who were manoeuvring the small, lug-rigged dandy into the port davits.

Captain Tremayne looked up as the door closed behind his First Officer, shook his head and then seated himself at the table on which the chart was spread and removing a quill from its holder, he wrote, murmuring the words as he added his amendment to the foot of the chart.

'I have noted that along the Guinea Coast there is a current setting from west to east which can increase, and likewise decrease, a ship's passage by as much as five knots. Since I can find no mention of this current in any of my almanacs, I shall name it the Guinea

Current.' He signed this amendment, Howard Tremayne, Captain and then dated it, 'the third day of March, seventeen hundred and six.'

Leaving the ink to dry after sprinkling some fine sand on it, he buttoned his shirt, replaced the cravat and after slipping on his frock coat and retrieving his hat from the bench seat by the aft scuttles, went up to the poop deck.

Daniel glanced up as the Captain arrived on deck and went up to join him, which he knew was expected of him. The beacon lights of the three forts on Cape Three Points were now clearly visible; Akwida to the east, Takrama in the centre and Princess Town to the west. The lantern which had been hoisted to the top of the main mast would now be visible from the fort at Takrama and Daniel knew that the Fort Commandant would have already given the order to embark the slaves into the forty-foot, dug-out canoes which would bring them through the surf, which was clearly visible in the moonlight, and then four cables further to the clipper's anchorage.

The arrival of the Royal Trader had indeed been spotted by the duty lookout on one of the raised turrets of Takrama Fort and the information had been passed to the Commandant, Captain Jeremiah Drysdale. Orders were passed to the wardens of the male and female slave dungeons to prepare their human cargo for transportation out to the ship. The arrival of the ship at this inconvenient hour of the night had spoiled both the Commandant's and the majority of the military garrison's enjoyment of the young and nubile female slaves, who now had to be returned to their cells where the representative of the Royal African Company would check, with meticulous care, their brand numbers against a loading manifest. The reprieve for these women would only be temporary, for as soon as they arrived on board the Royal Trader, all the ships' officers would take their pick of the women and those who were chained down in the orlop deck would have to suffer sexual abuse and rape from the hands of the duty watch who would be sent down to sluice away the excrement and vomit and remove any corpses.

By the time the Commandant reached the foot of the steps which led up to his rooms in the fort, the slaves had left. He climbed into his litter which was immediately lifted to the shoulders of four slaves who carried him over the drawbridge and down the steep track to the fishing harbour of Takrama, where the slaves would be embarked and from where the victualling barges would probably have already left to replenish the Royal Trader. When the Commandant's litter reached the harbour breakwater, both the barges and the canoes with the slaves had gone and were now beyond the surf line on their way to the ship. He spotted Captain Tremayne's dandy moored by the harbour steps; its crew of two ship's hands was carrying a crate up the steps and at the top of the steps stood Tremayne, dwarfed by the huge figure of Caramansa, Mandingo Chief of Eguafo State and the supplier of all the slaves to the Royal African Company.

Drysdale knew that Tremayne had some special deal with Caramansa and the crates being unloaded bore witness to that. He was convinced that Tremayne was being paid in gold; gold stolen from the mines which it was Drysdale's job to protect from theft. The previous year, he had been convinced that he had found the method by which gold was passed to Tremayne and ordered the fort surgeon to make an examination of the slaves' rectums and the female slaves' rectums and vaginas - an examination which he took sadistic pleasure in supervising personally - but with a total lack of success.

Nearly all the gold came from the mines in the gold rich state of Ashanti ruled by the all-powerful King Osei Tutu. What gold didn't come from the mines was panned from the many tributaries which flowed into the River Ofin which, in turn, flowed into the River Pra and thence to the sea. The majority of the slaves would have come from the mines and it was well known that many tried to secrete gold away with which they might eventually be able to buy their freedom. None ever succeeded, because Captain Drysdale was particularly thorough with his task of preventing this as there was a percentage in it for him. He couldn't take the risk of searching Tremayne as that would cost him his commission if he failed to find the gold. He had Tremayne watched for every second of the time he was with Caramansa, but nothing ever changed hands.

Captain Tremayne acknowledged the arrival of the portly little Commandant with a curt nod of his head and continued his discussion with the Mandingo Chief. The two men shook hands - Drysdale could see that Tremayne's right hand was completely empty after it was withdrawn from the enormous paw of the African and the customary click of fingers had taken place. Yet another deal had been struck, but how? Tremayne thanked the Commandant for the revictualling of his ship and returned down the steps to his boat.

Caramansa ignored the Commandant and departed with his retinue of slaves carrying the crates which Drysdale knew contained muskets of far better quality than were issued to the fort. With the pragmatic thought that perhaps he ought to be content with his share of the stolen gold, which he retrieved, Captain Drysdale ordered his litter-bearers to take him back to the fort. He looked at his fob watch; a quarter to two.

Nearly two o'clock; half way through the middle watch. Daniel put his watch back in his pocket and watched the small dandy make short work of the trip back to the clipper. All the slaves were down in the orlop deck and the gridded access hatches in the planks of the lower deck were secured and locked; already the ship stank of rancid sweat and urine and Daniel longed to set sail and get up wind of the overpowering stench. The Captain came up the accommodation ladder which had been rigged flush with the clipper's side and was piped aboard by the bosun as the ship's officers saluted. He went straight down to his cabin. Daniel gave orders to stow the dandy and accommodation ladder and the hands to set the stays'ls, main course and tops'ls. These tasks were all undertaken by the port watch while the starboard watch waited by the two capstans for the order to take in the bower anchors. Daniel went below and tapped on the Captain's cabin door.

'Enter!'

Daniel opened the door and told his Captain that the Royal Trader was ready to set sail. The Captain was in deep conversation with the ship's surgeon, which ceased as soon as Daniel opened the door.

'Very good, Mister Mortimer, proceed please; that'll be all,' and he was dismissed.

'Aye, aye, Sir.' Daniel went back on deck and gave the order to the starboard watch to weigh anchors. The unfurled sails were frapping in the light onshore wind as the clipper lay with her bow pointing to the west, held in that position by the east-going current. Daniel gave the order to take in the le'ward sheets and immediately the frapping ceased. The anchor chains went slack as the clipper heeled to the wind and started to make way. The bosun immediately gave the order to weigh anchors and the five men on each capstan wound in the anchor chains.

'Set the royals and stuns'ls!' Hardly had the order left Daniel's mouth than there was a stifled cry from for'ard. The First Officer hurried forward to find that the younger of the two trainee Midshipmen had injured his foot badly. Daniel dragged him clear of the anchor chain. In the dark, the young Midshipman had failed to see that the anchor chain was lifting and snatching as it came in. His foot had been badly crushed; it didn't seem as though any bones had been broken, but that was for the ship's surgeon to decide. Daniel handed over the deck to the officer of the watch and directed two of the hands to carry the Midshipman down to his cabin, while he went to find the ship's surgeon.

The Royal African Company realised the value of investing in good quality surgeons as their prime task was to minimise the number of slaves who died on the voyage from the Guinea Coast to the Southern States of America. Daniel knocked on the door of the Captain's cabin, which was where he had last seen the surgeon. There was no reply and when he opened the door the cabin was empty. He next tried the surgeon's cabin, but that also was empty so he descended to the surgery on the orlop deck.

There was light coming from under the door and muffled voices from within. Since the surgeon carried warrant rank rather than commissioned rank, without thought of knocking, Daniel opened the door. He stopped in the doorway, stunned by the horror of the scene in front of him. The surgery was brightly lit by four lamps above the wooden operating table on which lay the eviscerated remains of what had been a male slave. There was blood everywhere and it was spattered over the aprons worn by the two men in the room. The surgeon was by the table with a scalpel poised over the gory pulp of intestine, which had been wrenched from the gaping body cavity.

The other occupant of the room was the Captain, who had turned round as the door opened from where he was washing in a tub to one side of the operating table. Daniel had thought that he was washing his hands, but as he turned, Daniel saw that both his hands were cupped in front of him holding, what looked like, six stones each about the size of a walnut. As the light from the lamps fell on the Captain's hands, the colourless stones appeared to come to life and reflected back the light from the bright yellow nuggets of gold.

Daniel felt the bile rising in his throat; he staggered from the room and back up the companionways to the deck where he vomited over the le'ward taffrail of the poop deck. Gradually his gut stopped heaving and he was able to stand up. Still just visible in the distance, astern of the Royal Trader, were the lights of the forts on Cape Three Points.

*

The rusty dredge-bucket plunged back into the turgid water of the rain-swollen river and disappeared below the surface. The steel cables from the pulleys on the tip of the cantilevered boom to the leading edge of the saw-toothed bucket, dragged it deep into the gold-bearing silt on the bed of the Ofin River. Slowly, the dredge rose to the surface with its six cubic metre load of sodden silt and as it broke the surface, brown river water cascaded from every aperture. The boom swung slowly across to the funnel-shaped collector on the dredger; as the bucket reached the collector, the steel cables on the rear came taut and the dredge disgorged its load of silt and water.

12

The boom swung back and the bucket plunged into the river while its previous load was carried by conveyor belt to be washed, ground, pulverised and then chemically treated to extract the gold ore. This process went on day and night as the giant floating dredger was winched up and down the river at Dunkwa to the south of the town of Sawaba in the Ashanti Region.

Two metres before the conveyor belt deposited its load into the washers was a control station where it was Kojo Okyere's job to prevent large foreign objects - usually broken tree trunks - from entering the washing process. He had just stopped the conveyor belt because he had spotted a broken tree branch. On the other side of the belt was a steel platform from which his two assistants retrieved the foreign objects. To do this, they were equipped with an assortment of implements which included a high pressure hose to wash away the silt, poles with barbs on the end for hooking tree trunks, and other poles with scoops and nets to cater for all objects which ranged from electric cookers and car tyres to the tiny bodies of deformed, and therefore unwanted, babies.

The high-pressure water quickly cleared the silt from the object, which turned out to be the body of an adult male. There was nothing unusual about this discovery as many people in the area tried to do their own gold panning despite all the notices warning them of the dangers of doing so. The Canadian Sikafuturu Mining Company, which operated the dredger on the Ofin River at Dunkwa and the mines at Sawaba, on behalf of the Ghanaian National Mining Corporation, had a standard policy that all bodies retrieved from the river were to be taken to the company medical centre. There, they would be examined by the company's doctors, cause of death certified, identity established - a nearly impossible task - and relatives traced, which was an even more impossible task, but one that was undertaken with stoic perseverance by the administrative staff of the medical centre.

There were two doctors at the medical centre; the Canadians provided Dr Adrian Somerskil who had spent his entire working life with the mining company and nearly all of that outside his native state of Alberta. The Ghanaian doctor was Kwesi Azumah, who had graduated from St Luke's Hospital in Toronto and had then stayed on in Canada to complete a mining degree at the University of Alberta in Edmonton where his skills had been recruited by the Sikafuturu Mining Company. Comfort Danso, Kwesi's receptionist, told the doctor that a body had been recovered from the river and was now in the medical centre morgue awaiting an autopsy. She also told him that the man had been easy to identify as he still had the Company's

13

metal identity bracelet on his wrist. The body was that of Kofi Anysombe, a face worker from the deep and very rich Sawaba mine. The mining company's records showed that his recorded next of kin was his daughter, but added that Kofi lived on his own as his daughter had left him in 1996, changed her name and had given no forwarding address.

From its condition, it appeared that the body had been in the water for only a few hours and death would have occurred just a short time before that. Dr Kwesi Azumah established these facts with barely a glance at the body laid out on the table in the chilled autopsy room of the morgue. It was the time of death which puzzled him; why did the corpse smell so awful, even before he had opened the body cavity? He switched on the microphone, which recorded his monologue of the autopsy, picked up his scalpel and opened the corpse from sternum to pelvis. The dreadful stench from the body cavity engulfed Kwesi, making him recoil from a task to which he had thought he was inured. His receptionist, Comfort, was a qualified theatre nurse and acted as an assistant to both doctors during autopsies. She had placed a suture clip over the end of her nose and with a wry smile, offered one to Kwesi who copied her example.

The cause of the smell was immediately evident; just above the rectum, the colon was completely blocked by a large object. The man's faeces had completely filled the large intestine which was grossly distended and had then overflowed into the small intestine. Under the pressure, which the faeces had exerted on the object blocking access to the anal passage, the wall of the colon had ruptured and the waste matter had invaded the body cavity. Death would have been due to a number of causes, least likely of which was drowning. More likely was the unbearable pain of the blocked colon or acute peritonitis caused by the rupture to the intestine. Kwesi had heard from his veterinary colleagues of similar occurrences to horses whose intestines wallowed around loosely and not infrequently became twisted which caused exactly the same effect as the object blocking the dead man's colon.

The Ghanaian doctor asked his assistant to go and get his colleague who examined the cadaver. Kwesi removed the object blocking the colon and passed it to the nurse to wash. 'His back is badly lacerated. At first I thought that would have been caused by the strong river current grinding the body against the rocks, but the lacerations have bled and this man was dead before he went into the river, so they occurred before death,' Kwesi said for the benefit of the microphone and his colleague while Comfort washed the object which had blocked the colon.

'Let's have a look,' and together the two doctors turned the body over. The lacerations were deep and stretched horizontally across the body - at right angles to the backbone - from neck to buttocks. At first glance they resembled the sort of wounds which might have been caused by the body being dragged over sharp, underwater rocks or as if the man had been viciously whipped. There was an exclamation from Comfort Danso at the large wash-up sink and she turned, holding an ore nugget of almost pure gold, the size of a small mango.

'Christ almighty! That must be worth nearly 20,000 dollars,' Kwesi gasped and then switched off the microphone. The three of them stared at the hunk of ore, the thick veins of gold gleaming dully in the fluorescent lighting. Adrian Somerskil had moved back from the autopsy table and broke the silence.

'And those lacerations were no accident; see here both of you,' and they looked, but the Canadian doctor interrupted their examination. 'No, not close to the body; come back here and you'll see right away.' From where he was standing the cause of the lacerations was quite clear. Into the man's back had been carved the word 'CARAMANSA'.

*

Charles Mensah lay motionless in the spacious, air-conditioned rear compartment of the stretched Lincoln limousine as it passed the sign informing east-bound drivers on Route 54 that they were approaching the town of Justice. He was watching a hard-porn video and had no interest in the town of Justice. There was a rack of eight, 180 minute video cassettes beside the TV in the back of the Lincoln; the content of these cassettes ranged from hard-porn to bestiality which helped Mensah while away the three hours which it had taken to drive the 160 miles from Las Vegas to Justice. Beside him, on what would have passed as a reasonable sized double bed, was Letitia Quartey who was also engrossed in the video.

The partition between rear compartment and driver and all rear windows of the Lincoln were double-glazed, one-way mirror glass; this sound-proofed the rear compartment and provided its occupants with complete privacy to imitate and improve on the techniques shown in graphic detail on the small screen in front of them. By this late stage in the journey, both Charles Mensah and Letitia Quartey were naked and soaked in sweat - despite the car's air-conditioning - from their energetic sexual athletics. In spite of the strengthened coil springs and dampers, the driver had great difficulty controlling the large car when the activity in the rear compartment reached a climax.

The intercom between driving compartment, which was occupied by a bodyguard in addition to the driver, buzzed discretely in the rear compartment. The bodyguard informed his employer that they would be arriving at their destination in approximately ten minutes. His instructions were to provide this length of notice of arrival as that was how long it would take Mensah to get washed, towelled dry and dressed in fresh clothes; all the facilities to achieve that freshening-up process were part of the fittings in the rear compartment.

The driver of the Lincoln turned the large car left off the highway a mile to the east of Justice, as directed by the bodyguard. The only sign at the intersection off the highway indicated that the turn-off led to INDUSTRIAL MACHINE TOOLS INC which was a further 12 miles along the road to the north and the town of Adrian one mile to the south. In the gatehouse of Industrial Machine Tools Inc, which resembled a fortified guardhouse - because that's exactly what it was - a warning light and audio alarm attracted Samuel Pickersgill's attention. He reset the alarm, picked up one of three phones in front of him and dialled 100.

'Yea, Boomer here.'

'Sam Pickersgill, Mr Boomer; duty guard at the main gate. A vehicle's turned off the highway an's headed this way.'

'Got it; on m'way,' and the connection was broken. Sam replaced his phone, lifted a pair of high-powered 20x75 glasses off a hook by a door at the rear of the guardhouse and climbed up to the watch-tower. The observation platform was surrounded by bullet-proof glass. Sam slid back a portion of this armoured glass so that refraction didn't impede his view and raised the glasses. He quickly identified the dust cloud despite the shimmering heat haze rising off the baking desert plateau, which lay to the east of the San Juan mountain range.

'Saloon.....big one though,' Sam muttered and went back down to the control room of the guardhouse. Industrial Machine Tools Inc was registered with the Federal Government of the USA as an arms manufacturer and arms dealer. This registration gave the company its legitimate status and about 20% of the sales came from legitimate, government approved deals, both to the domestic and export markets. The huge profit which the company made came from the other 80% of arms sales and deals were the contracts when IMT acted as agent to procure arms for foreign countries. The company had made a killing after the speedy conclusion of Desert Storm in 1991; IMT's recovery vehicles and low-loaders had almost overtaken the

16

rear echelons of the advancing US and British forces in their eagerness to collect all the abandoned Russian tanks, guns and APCs of the retreating Republican Guard of the Iraqi forces. There had been similar pickings after the 2003 invasion of Iraq by the US and British Forces. Some of this equipment had been refurbished and sold to other countries before the first planeload of coalition soldiers was on its way home from the war.

IMT's industrial complex covered an area of some 20 square miles, which didn't include its own ranges, tracked and wheeled vehicle test circuit, airfield and its second-hand aircraft park. IMT's technical and executive staff were all 'bona fide' US citizens, but the large workforce was composed, almost entirely, of illegal immigrants - 'wetbacks' - from Mexico. This fact was well known by both the mayor and the sheriff of Amarillo, under whose jurisdiction IMT's industrial complex came, but likewise, both chose to ignore this because firstly, IMT was a very generous contributor to local government funds and very supportive with election funding. Secondly, all the wetbacks were housed in a fairly reasonable compound, which contained its own shopping centre, amusement park, sports grounds, schools and medical facilities.

What was far more relevant, however, were the two 15 foot wire fences surrounding the compound with the intervening gap patrolled by jeep-borne guards and dogs with their handlers. This made IMT very popular as it confined the wetback problem to an area out of sight of the legitimate community, and even more importantly, out of sight of Washington's prying eyes. For IMT it provided a limitless source of near-slave labour resulting in vast profits which made its president - ex-tank driver, 7th Cavalry corporal, Bradley Tracton - 'Trax' to his senior executives - a multi-billionaire.

'Your security officer on line one, Sir,' the president of IMT was informed by his secretary on his desk intercom.

'Thanks, Joanne,' and he flicked the appropriate switch, 'Tex?'

'Sir, I'm speaking on my mobile on my way to the main gate. Guard reports a vehicle headed this way. I've nothing on the roster. You expecting anyone?' Bradley Tracton glanced at his appointments book and then pressed the intercom while he placed Tex Boomer, his security officer, on 'hold'.

'Yes, Sir.'

'Joanne, I've got no appointments in my book for this time today. Someone's headed this way. You know who it might be?'

'No, Sir; nothing before your poker appointment in Vegas at Caesar's Palace this evening at 2000 hours. Same table and your helicopter will leave at 1845 hours.' All timings in IMT were on the

17

24 hour clock and all spoken in military jargon - 8pm, therefore, became 'twenty hundred hours'. If Joanne had forgotten an appointment, she would have been out of a job.

'Thanks,' and he flicked off the intercom and took his security officer off 'hold'. 'No Tex, no visitors expected. Who've you got with you?'

'Myself and four plus the main gate guard, Sir.'

'Fine; I'll watch it on TV,' and IMT's President put down the phone and switched on the bank of six monitors which could scrutinise a visitor from almost every angle, including the underside of vehicles which were made to park over a recess full of high-intensity lights and CCTV cameras. The president's monitors duplicated only a small portion of those in the control room of the main gate guardhouse.

Around IMT's entire industrial complex were three fences. Starting from the outside, the first two were 15 foot expanded steel mesh and razor wire. The second fence carried enough current to fry 20 humans concurrently. The third fence was there to prevent those on the inside of the compound accidentally coming in contact with the electrified fence. The stretched Lincoln had stopped outside the main gate in the first fence. Both the cameras and explosive sensors in the ground recess under the car came up negative and declared the car to be clean underneath. The car was covered by two, concealed 20mm M61 canons with 300 rounds apiece of armour piercing ammunition.

Tex Boomer picked up the microphone from the console in the guardhouse and asked all the occupants of the car to disembark, leaving all the car doors open, including the hood and the trunk and to stand well clear of the car. 'You have 30 seconds to obey that order or the car and its contents will be destroyed,' his announcement concluded. The driver and bodyguard got out of the car first and each moved to the rear of the Lincoln and opened the two rear doors. From the right-hand door stepped Charles Mensah, dressed in an immaculate light-weight suit; from the left-hand door stepped Letitia Quartey dressed in nothing at all.

'Thank you, lady and gentlemen; now if any of you folks should be carrying any piece, will ya all just lay it down on the ground in front of you...real slow, no, not you lady, we can all see you aint carrying nothing you weren't born with,' Boomer added although Letitia Quartey had made no move and appeared to be totally unconcerned at her nakedness, indeed exactly the opposite, as she seemed to be thoroughly enjoying being the centre of attention. The voice of IMT's President came through the intercom loudspeaker in the guardhouse.

'Take great care, and make your men concentrate on their job, not on that naked black bimbo.'

'Yes, Sir,' and then into the microphone, 'who's in charge of this visiting group.....no Sir, please stand quite still,' this was added by Boomer as Charles Mensah had made to take a step forward. Please state your name, who it is you want to see and the nature of your business. No need to shout because the microphones we have focused on ya'all are very sensitive.'

'My name is Charles Mensah, I wish to see your president, Mr Bradley Tracton, to discuss a business deal worth 200 million dollars. Payment will be in gold and as a gesture of my good faith I have a gift for your president which is on the rear seat of my car.'

'Let him get the gift,' Bradley Tracton instructed over the intercom.

'Mr Mensah, please get the gift from in back of the car,' Boomer instructed, who was having great difficulty taking his eyes off the 'naked bimbo' who was now nonchalantly stroking the black hair of her crotch with her right hand while the left played with the nipple of her right breast.

'Jesus Christ!' Sam Pickersgill whispered, 'she's going to do it right there, I.....'

'Concentrate on the men, damn you!' came from Boomer who was having as much difficulty as all of them in taking his eyes off the woman's libidinous behaviour. Charles Mensah went to the rear of the car, stooped to reach in and brought out a small, square, dark blue jewellery box. Four fingers were eased off triggers from the concealed firing positions. 'Please stand in front of the gates, Mr Mensah, where you can see that white circle painted on the concrete. Fine,' as Mensah halted inside the circle. 'Now hold out the gift in front of you and open the lid.' Mensah did as instructed, opening the hinged jewellery box lid towards himself so that the contents was clearly displayed to the array of cameras around him.

'Zoom in the colour camera, please,' came from the President over the intercom. The powerful 2000 mm zoom lens whirred and the box in Mensah's hands filled the entire screen in front of Bradley Tracton. Set in ruffled royal blue satin was a nugget of pure gold - just about the size of a walnut.

CHAPTER 1

'Get the bimbo into the car before she jerks-off at the gate. The same goes for the driver and the pet gorilla. Tell the driver of the Lincoln to park in slot number 8. They all stay in the limo' until I've finished with Mensah. Arm the detonator of the explosive charge under parking slot 8 and if anyone in the limmo disobeys my instructions, blow it up. I'll see Mensah now; bring him to my office after a full strip search in the guardhouse. Got all that, Tex?'

Yes, Sir.' IMT's president switched off the intercom to the guardhouse and flicked another switch.

'Jo!'

'Yes, Sir,'

'Did y'get all that?'

'Yes, Sir; I've been running a trace on Mensah.......'

'Thanks; beat me to it; anything come up? Can't say the name's familiar.'

'There's a bit on him, which our market research boys've dug up, Sir. They don't seem to miss too much,' Joanne added, who was sharing her apartment - and her bed - with IMT's regional director for Sub-Sahara Africa.

'That's what I pay 'em for. What's there?'

'I'm transferring it to you now, Sir,' and the president's terminal told him that there was electronic mail for him. He tapped the keyboard and the information appeared in front of him.

'What's the stock state?'

'Equipment warehouses are at 83% and munitions and mines at 96%,' Joanne had also predicted that request which was routine whenever a prospective client called.

'Thanks; buzz me when Mensah has been waiting for five minutes.'

'Right, Sir,' and the intercom clicked off.

The instructions issued by IMT's President were repeated to the four people standing in the baking heat outside the main gate. Once the Lincoln had parked in slot 8, the main gate opened and Charles Mensah was told to move forward into the space between the first two fences. As soon as he had passed through the first gate, it closed behind him. When it had closed, the second gate opened and he was told to move forward into the space between the second and third fence. Once the second gate had closed, the third opened and Mensah was directed to the reception room in the guardhouse. Once inside the reception centre, he was told to remove all his clothes, his watch and any other jewellery.

No one came near Mensah and he saw no one. His instructions came through a loudspeaker at each stage of the search, which was monitored in the guardhouse control room by concealed cameras. When he was completely naked, he was instructed to move through the glass door at the other side of the room. The door closed behind him and he found himself in a sealed chamber. In this chamber, sensors and x-rays could pick up the faintest trace of explosives, drugs, weapons or wire-taps. The door on the other side of the chamber opened and the loudspeaker told him that he would find his clothes, shoes and watch in the fitted wardrobe; all of these had been searched. He was told that he could take a shower if he wished and that a car was waiting to take him to the company President for his meeting as soon as he was ready. As a matter of principle, Charles Mensah accepted the offer of the shower, to show that he was in no particular hurry, dressed in his clothes once more and found a car waiting for him as promised.

None of IMT's industrial complex or its offices extended above a ground floor; everything other than the executive offices was housed below ground level and the storage bunkers for the ammunition had been excavated out of the solid rock of the San Juan foothills. Well away from the ammunition bunkers and the 'wetback' compound, but also in the foothills was the housing for IMT's technical and executive personnel. The whole concept was very similar to a US military base in Germany, which was where Bradley Tracton had spent his teenage years as the only son of a top sergeant in the US Cavalry and then a further twelve years as a tank driver in the 7th Cavalry. To the north of the complex, rising from springs in the San Juan Mountains, was Deadman's River which had been dammed; this produced more than enough hydro-electric power for IMT and also provided a superb recreational area for the legitimate workforce around the lake's seven square miles.

The outfall from the hydro-electric power station eventually flowed into the Mississippi via the Canadian River, Lake Meredith, the Eufauld Reservoir in Oklahoma and then the Arkansas River. Raw materials reached IMT on a branch line off the main track between Amarillo and Clayton. The entire complex was almost wholly self-sustaining and considered to be near impregnable other than by a major assault by the US Armed Forces; this had been the conclusion of a congressional inquiry which had investigated the extent of the Pentagon's involvement with IMT. As soon as the US electorate voted Bill Clinton and the Democrats out of office in 2000, the report had disappeared into obscurity with the change of administration and George W Bush's and the Republicans' involvement with terrorism, 9/11, Al Quaeda and Iraq.

The car stopped outside the main entrance to IMT and Mensah was met by another security guard who escorted him to the comfortable waiting room to one side of Joanne's office. This room possessed everything, which a visitor might need in the way of light refreshment, TV screens providing CNN, BBC World News and Reuters' news service and fax, telex, email and photocopier facilities. There was a library, which contained every definitive document on worldwide arms' sales, the latest editions of Janes and an assortment of publications on the world strategic military balance. These were the overt facilities in the waiting room. Every visitor, whether known to the IMT President or not, was required to spend a minimum of five minutes in the room while he was again scrutinised by cameras controlled from the company President's office.

'Please follow me, Sir; Mr Tracton will see you now,' Joanne announced after quietly entering the waiting room. She led the way through her office to Bradley Tracton's office where he was standing at the door waiting to greet his visitor. Joanne closed the door behind Charles Mensah and returned to her office. Bradley Tracton's personal bodyguard, Frank Raubenheimer, appeared from his office to one side of the company President's suite of rooms and joined Joanne in her office where both of them could watch the entire meeting which would be recorded on video.

*

The strength of the Guinea Current and its vicious undertow had accounted for more deaths than any other cause - diseases included - along the southern coast of West Africa. In the latter part of the 15th century, Italian traders from Genoa were encouraged by their discovery of the fabulously rich city of Timbuktu, where even the King of Songhai's dogs wore collars of solid gold, to explore further round the south-west coast of Africa. These voyages identified that, in spite of adverse winds, the west to east voyage was always quicker than east to west and the fair logs of that time were annotated with this 'phenomena'. The Portugese made use of the new navigational techniques developed by Prince Henry, the 'Navigator', to plot the extent of the current, but gave it no name. It wasn't until 1706 that the captain of the British Royal African Company's slave trading clipper, Royal Trader, decided to add his name to nautical posterity by naming it the 'Guinea Current'. Until that nomination had been made, Captain Howard Tremayne's only other claim to notoriety was that of being the Royal African Company's most cruel and, by virtue of his successful profiteering, wealthiest ship's captain.

The west coast of Africa, from Senegal and The Gambia on the western bulge, through seven other countries to Benin, has been provided by nature with thousands of miles of white sand and coconut palms which have been the source material of many front covers of tropical travel brochures. This provision has included deserted sandy beaches, the cooling shade of coconut palms and warm surf, but those who have ignored the warning not to swim beyond their depth have either been drowned or have got into great difficulties, which has often resulted in rescuers also losing their lives.

West Africans have proved their dominance of the world sporting scene in a number of sports from boxing, through athletics to soccer, but not one has even been entered for the swimming or diving events - let alone the synchronised swimming - because there has always been a traditional fear of the sea. This has led to the superstition prohibiting the wearing of a predominantly green garment for fear of offending the sea spirits and no fishing canoe has been seen on the water on a Tuesday - the day dedicated to the sea god.

It was Tuesday and Graham McLean was fishing off Labadi Beach, wearing a bright green T-shirt and knee-length, green Bermuda shorts. It was not the popular part of the beach in front of the hotel which was well-patronised by expatriate children in the school holidays and by wealthy Ghanaians at weekends, but the relatively deserted part to the east of the tidal gully across the beach which filled and emptied the artificial 'African' lagoon. It had been called the 'African Lagoon' because it had been excavated into the shape of Africa for the opening of the adjacent Trade Fair site.

It was 5.45 in the morning and only just getting light. The on-shore breeze still possessed a refreshing quality having been cooled by the comparatively lower night temperature on the sea surface. To the right of the solitary teenager, trying out the new rod, which had been given to him for Easter, the dawn had just illuminated the battlements of Christiansborg Castle, the seat of the nation's government. It had also just touched the tops of the highest buildings in Accra, which spread out in a semicircle from the Castle to the higher ground of Roman Ridge and the ring road which by-passed the city to the north.

Graham had been told by his parents not to fish on his own, but it was only a five minute ride on his multi-geared mountain bike - a Christmas present - from the ex-patriate enclave by the airport to the beach. He was fifteen and his parents and younger sister were still asleep in bed. The only one to see him leave the house had been the night watchman who had been woken as Graham tripped over him in the dark on the front porch. Later that day, when the night watchman thoughtlessly admitted, in the hope of some praise or, better still, a reward that he had seen the young boy leaving the house, he was sacked; and would have been beaten to death by the boy's father had not Mrs McLean intervened.

The line stretched well out into the gentle surf with the rod propped up on a purpose-designed stand. Graham busied himself fitting a plastic bag inside one of the many tyres above the high-water mark on the beach. He had seen the Ghanaian fishermen use these tyres as traps for the beach crabs. His idea was to fit the plastic bag inside the tyre and then fill it with sea water from a small bucket, especially brought along for that purpose. This would then provide an ideal place to keep his catch fresh until he returned home to have it cooked for breakfast. So engrossed had he become in this task that he neither heard nor saw what was approaching him across the beach from out of the sea.

'Pop upstairs, Mo, and get your brother out of bed. He knows we're in a hurry today. If he's sulking about not taking his new rod to Kumasi.......' but Morwena was already half way up the stairs and heard no more of her mother's justification for forbidding the carriage of the fishing rod either in or on the family Nissan Patrol. Mary McLean's husband, Stuart - their friends frequently teased them about the fierceness of the whole family's allegiance to Scotland and everything Scottish (names included) - had left the house at 6.30 am to be at Kotoka Airport, just over a mile away, in time for the Turbo Twin-Pac, 15 seater Bell 212 to take off at 7 am for the hour's flight to the Company's mine at Sawaba, 20 miles to the south of Kumasi.

The family would follow by car later and spend the four days at the company guest house in Kumasi before returning to Accra for the weekend. Kumasi was dead at the weekends and many expats based in that city had guest-houses in Accra so that they could take advantage of Ghana's expatriate social life. This arrangement also allowed Stuart to see more of his children during their holidays from boarding schools - needless to say - in Scotland.

'Not there, Mum.'

'What do you mean, not there?'

'He's not in his bedroom; oh yes, and the fishing rod's not there either.' The first of the alarm bells sounded for Mary McLean.

'Let me look,' she put down her coffee and went up the stairs, trying to remain calm as her ears were assailed by the sound of 'Boyzone' coming from the Hi-Fi in the sitting room. The bedroom was empty, Graham's green T- shirt and shorts weren't in their usual place - thrown on the floor in a heap - so that meant he was wearing them. The rod had gone. She ran back down the stairs and out to the garage; all pretence of calmness had now gone. The bike had gone, as had the small plastic bucket, which he used for bait. Where would he have gone? Should she ring the office in Accra, which in turn would contact the helicopter direct and pass any message to Stuart? No; that was an hysterical act, but Mary felt herself very close to just that. 'Morwena!'

'Yes, Mum,' the inevitable resigned tone which knew that the next command would be,' - turn down that dreadful noise!

'Please turn down that noise, darling, and come here.'

'Alright, Mum, whenawegoing,' the last was droned as all one word as Morwena drooped into the dining room. Suddenly though, everything was different; her Mum was crying. What's wrong, Mum,' her daughter wailed, also breaking into tears as she ran to her mother.

'Listen, sweatheart; think carefully. Where would Graham have gone to do his fishing?'

'Labadi Beach!'

'How can you be so sure, darling?'

'They were all talking about it yesterday afternoon just before you came to collect us from the beach.'

'Talking about what? Who was?'

'How great the fishing was, Mum; you know, the usual crowd,' her daughter snuffled between sobs.

'Please darling, think. Who? so I can ring their Mums and find if they've gone fishing as well.'

'Oh, yes; well, there was Emma and Richard - you know, their Dad's in the army or something.....'

'Yes, darling, I know; go on, who else?' Mary encouraged, as she rushed for the telephone and dialled Penny Briars' number.

'Please, oh please be there, Penny,' Mary pleaded quietly into the mouthpiece of the phone.

'Oh yes, the two Stone brothers.....em, Jeremy and Sacha. Sacha's the older one,' correctness of English forgotten, her mother thought, with another portion of her mind that seemed to be divorced from the reality of what was becoming a nightmare. Her daughter was clearly

25

smitten by the very good looking elder Stone boy - all of 17 and about to take his 'A' levels. 'And the Forest twins - Samantha and Harry......'

'Hello...hello, is that Penny,' and Mary held up her hand to motion for silence as the phones were difficult at the best of times. 'Sorry to disturb you at this hour, Penny, but I'm rather anxious......oh, do I, yes well I've lost Graham and I think he may have gone to the beach to fish and I wondered if Richard had gone too,' this last was said in a rush as she could hold back the tears no longer. 'Oh, thank you, Penny, that would be such a relief, thank you so much. See you in a few minutes, thanks; bye.' Mary turned to her daughter, 'you couldn't get me a tissue from the kitchen, darling please.'

'Sure, Mum, and there's the list of all the friends who were with us,' and Morwena pushed across the telephone scribble pad with the names on it.

'Well done, darling; Mr Briars is going to take the army Landrover and Richard and go and look on the beach. Emma and her Mum are coming here.'

'He isn't a Mister,' from Morwena as she returned with the box of tissues.

'Sorry; what's that?

'Richard's Dad isn't a Mister, he's a Colonel.'

'Yes, of course he is, I must remember that. Let's hope it's just Mummy being silly and then we can thank Colonel Briars for being so kind,' but she wasn't being silly and there was a great deal more heartache she would have to suffer.

John Briars rang the Commander of the British Military Advisory Team and told him what had happened. The Commander suggested that he take his radio and give a call if extra help was needed. His 14 year old son, Richard, jumped into the front seat with the radio as his father backed the Landrover out of the garage onto the red laterite track which ran between the four BMAT bungalows. The bungalows occupied by the Team were on the huge military estate to the east of Accra and less than half-a-mile from Labadi Beach. John swung the Landrover Countryman onto the metalled road, which ran through the military cantonment and paused at the gate where he acknowledged the salute of the sentry.

It was now 7.45 and the main road between Accra and the fishing port of Tema, to the east, was jammed with over-laden lorries and Tro-Tros - the Ghanaian word for the converted Bedford Trojans of 1950s vintage - which carried the workforce from the outlying villages into the capital. John forced a passage through the traffic, over the main road and off it again the other side onto the firing

26

ranges, which lay between the road and the sea. The track that cut across to Labadi Beach was a popular dog walk for all the officers of BMAT and their families and within less than a minute the Landrover was at the beach. John and his son jumped out of the Landrover. 'You stay with me, Richard,' as his father had no wish to add to that morning's crisis.

'There, Dad!' and his father's warning went unheeded as his son's sharp eyes spotted the rod and he went off like a hare across the soft sand. John followed him as fast as possible and reached the spot on the beach where the rod was jammed into the sand and resting on its steel prop. The line still ran out to sea and the beach was deserted.

'Stand still, old fellow,' John cautioned Richard, as he saw that he was about to start searching around the site. 'Don't want to mess up any footprints.'

'Yes, of course, Dad,' and the boy rejoined his father who had seen something which puzzled him and which might well terrify his son who was at that age when monsters, dinosaurs and extra-terrestrial creatures loomed very real. 'Hand me the radio, please, Richard.'

'Can't I do it? Remember, you promised.'

'And you shall, but this time I'll do it.' Richard was about to whine and then saw that his father looked worried.

'What is it, Dad? Has Graham been murdered?'

'Shhh! Enough of that; quiet while I use the radio,' and then he pressed the transmit button and spoke into the integral mike on the front of the hand-held set. 'B-MAT one this is B- MAT two, there's a problem here. Are you in your office? Over.'

'B-MAT one, yes, over,'

'B-MAT two, roger; could you ring the Deputy Chief of Police and ask him and his boys to meet us on Labadi Beach at the point where the track from the range firing point joins the beach. Can you please come here as soon as you've made that call, over.'

'B-MAT one, Lydia's making that call now; serious? Over.'

'B-MAT two, yes, over.'

'B-MAT one, roger, on my way, out.' John handed the radio to his son and motioning him to stay where he was, he walked in a wide detour around the place in the sand from which the cork-handled base of the fishing rod protruded. Of Graham there was no sign, but there were ample signs of his footprints around the rod and leading to and from the sea. What made the hair on John's neck prickle and had prompted the call to the BMAT Commander were the really deep imprints leading from the sea to a churned-up patch of sand. In the centre of the tracks was a shallow, wide trough, which ran from

27

where the waves were breaking to the churned-up patch. On either side of this trough were deep indentations into the sand as though something like an alligator, but of really gigantic proportions, had crawled out of the sea and then retreated backwards into it, dragging the boy with it.

*

'Those steaks smell scrummy. Have you marinated them in something very alcoholic?'

'A little dip in a bowl of red plonk never did a steak any harm. Now, how do you like yours?'

'Rare please; I thought you said you were going fishing today,' Lin Aldridge stated rather than asked while she topped up her glass from the bottle of red wine beside the barbecue. The barbecue party on the lawn in front of the British High Commission's weekend cottage at Ada on the Volta Estuary was a scene being repeated at many of the other cottages owned by commercial companies and diplomatic missions in Accra.

Once the Volta River Authority had dredged away the sand bar at the mouth of the Volta, the seawater flowed into the river and killed the reeds, which contained the Bilharzia-carrying moluscs. As soon as the water was free of Bilharzia, the expatriate community returned after an absence of nearly three years and the social, fishing and water sports life at Ada flourished again. The hydro-electric dam at Akosombo, 35 miles to the north of Ada, held back the waters of the Volta Lake which stretched for a further 200 miles into the north-west of Ghana and provided it with a surplus of electricity which was exported to the neighbouring Francophone country of Togo. The power of the outfall from the dam had been utilised twice and a new dam had been constructed downstream of Akosombo, at Kpong, which further increased the nation's generating capacity.

Ada was a small village, one-and-a-half hours' drive to the east of Accra, at the mouth of the Volta on a very scenic stretch of the river which provided safe swimming, water-skiing and dinghy sailing, sheltered from the clutches of the powerful inshore current. The other popular expatriate beaches were Mile 16 to the west of Accra and Pram Pram to the east. The latter two beaches were only a forty-minute drive from the city so the beach huts were little more than palm frond shelters. The longer drive to Ada led to its development as a weekend resort and the bungalows had all 'mod cons' powered by their own diesel generators, ironically, when they were within a stone's throw of cables carrying thousands of kilowatts of electricity.

Tony Bristow and his wife, Monica, had invited three other couples to join them at the British High Commission's cottage which had four double rooms, a spectacular first floor veranda, on which all meals were taken and a boathouse and servants' quarters on the ground floor complete with speedboat, water skis, Topper dinghy and sailboard. Laurens Fluitman, the general manager of Philips (Ghana) was out on the sailboard while his wife, Marietta, helped Monica with the lunch. Denis Motram, the manager of British Airways, and Roger Aldridge, a second secretary in the commercial section at the High Commission, were out water skiing with the boat boy and the speedboat. Dennis' wife, Caroline, was sunbathing on the diving platform at the end of the wooden jetty while their two children, Pippa and Patrick - aged 10 and 8 - fished from a small canoe which was tied to the platform with a long painter. Roger's wife, Lin, was Korean and had met and married her husband while he was a third secretary in the consular section of the British Embassy in Seoul.

The barbecue area, where the steaks were being grilled by Tony, was out of sight of the veranda where the rest of the meal was being prepared. It was for that reason that Lin had wandered over there because she and Tony were heavily involved in a very physical and sordid affair, unknown - supposedly - to their respective partners. Both marriages were childless and already the gossip had started in the expatriate community as Lin's and Roger's constant bickering excluded them from social functions of one expat' group after another. Tony Bristow was ostensibly a first secretary in the economic section of the High Commission, however his government paymasters weren't in the Foreign and Commonwealth Office in King Charles Street, but operated from the other side of the river in Vauxhall where a 1980s, concrete and green glass hidiosity contained - possibly an inappropriate verb because of the manner in which the building leaked – MI6, the Nation's Secret Intelligence Service.

It was a very hot and humid day. The men wore shorts and the women swimsuits or bikinis. All of those out on the water wore T-shirts and sun hats to protect their skin from a sun temperature of over 40°C. Despite a thatched roof over the brick-built barbecue, which screened it from the sight of those higher up on the veranda, it was stiflingly hot, with only a slight breeze coming off the water to disperse the additional heat rising from the red-grey embers of the charcoal. Tony kept himself in good physical shape with tennis and jogging and like everyone at the cottage, except his wife whose fair skin couldn't take the sun, was well tanned. His torso glistened with sweat from the radiant heat of the charcoal, which hadn't gone unnoticed by Lin, of the glowing golden skin, in her minute bikini,

29

beside him. He took a long drink from the cold can of Heineken, which he replaced in the cool box beside the barbecue.

'We can't be seen from the veranda or river here.'

'It's too risky, wha....'

'Don't be so silly, darling. We're both practically naked and it'll only take about thirty seconds; you know what we're both like the first time; wham, bang, orgasm and finito!'

'Suppose th.....'

'They won't; now stop all the talk and let's have a bit of quick action like you used to be when you wanted me to drop my knickers at every opportunity. Not even those tight shorts can hide that you want it as much as I do. I'll have to go in the water anyway as it's beginning to show on my bikini.' So saying, Lin removed her bikini G-string and bending over, presented herself to Tony. It took less than a minute, as predicted by Lin, and left them both gasping for breath. Temporarily satisfied, Lin replaced her bikini, pulled the bikini bra over hard-nippled breasts, kissed Tony on the nose, ran out to the diving platform and dived into the river. He lent against the barbecue until the smell of burning steak snapped him out of his post-coital lassitude.

'Bugger!' which was an inaccurate description of what had just taken place.

'Lunch is ready!' came from the veranda, followed by a blast on the compressed air hooter to attract those out on the water. There was an answering hoot from the boat and within ten minutes, all were seated on the veranda tucking into their steak and salad.

'How on earth do you keep that figure, Lin, when you eat like a horse?' Marietta laughed as the lithesome Korean had a second helping of both steak and baked potatoes.

'Lots of exercise, Etta.'

'Yes. I saw you swimming. Wh....?

'There's one more bit of ste....'

'Shhh! Tony, don't interrupt,' Monica chided her husband. 'Go on Etta, ignore him.'

'Oh, it was....no, it's no good I've forgotten what I was going to say. Yes. I'll have a bit of that steak if no one else wants it all.'

'Well done; I'll halve it with you,' and Tony sliced the steak in half and held out the plate to her.

'Oh yes! I know what it was; thanks Tony,' as he leaned across with the plate. 'It was talking about swimming that made me think of it; as you ran across from the barbecue to dive into the river, Lin, I could see that flower pattern on your bum and I was sure that I had seen it on the front of your bikini when you were making the salad.'

'Damn! sorry folks,' Tony apologised as the plate slipped onto the table.

'Probably put it on the wrong way round after going to the loo,' was her husband's contribution. 'Any more of that wine?'

'Yes, masses, pass your glass and I'll work the tap on the box,' Monica offered quickly, hoping that there wouldn't be another Aldridge row. The children came in spot on cue and asked if they could go for a run in the speedboat with the boat boy.

'Is that OK, Tony?' their father asked.

'Sure, go ahead.'

'OK, off you go and do up your life jackets,' came from Caroline who had contributed little so far that day to the conversation while she concentrated single-mindedly on her sun tan and at the table on filling herself with food. More than one action undertaken concurrently was a bit of a strain on Caroline's grey matter, which was why she possessed a reputation as a rather simple bimbo. How she had ever qualified as a BA air-stewardess - where she had met her future husband - mystified everyone.

'Yes Mum,' in chorus and the awkward moment passed, much to Tony Bristow's relief. He glanced quickly across at Lin who was totally unconcerned about the whole incident and seemed to be enjoying it.

'Dear God,' he thought, 'what the hell am I doing. I've got to stop this,' but he knew he wouldn't be able to do that without the whole sordid business doing the rounds of the expat community. He probably wouldn't lose his job, but it would cost him his marriage and Monica's substantial private income from her very wealthy parents. 'What a bloody mess,' he almost said out loud.

'You alright, darling?' his wife asked with genuine concern at seeing the anguish reflected on her husband's face.

'Yes fine, thanks. Spot of indigestion; think I'll just take the canoe out and do a bit of fishing while everyone's having a siesta.'

'Alright; take care won't you,' his wife cautioned as the weekend house party prepared to sleep off the effects of the food and wine. Lin was on the verge of asking if she could join Tony in the canoe as it would offer the ideal opportunity for the two of them to continue where they had left off before lunch. He had made no offer and was avoiding looking at her. She realised that that would be pushing her rampant libido too far, particularly with the hawk-eyed Etta who had spotted that she had put on her bikini, back-to-front, after the pre-prandial fuck at the barbecue.

She watched Marietta Fluitman go down the steps to the boathouse carrying the plastic rubbish bag; the dustbin was kept down there and if either Monica or Marietta had been down there before lunch they would have had a perfect view of Tony and her fornicating at the barbecue. Lin shrugged with indifference as she settled down on one of the rattan sofas with her Jackie Collins novel. She had started life as a disco hostess and whore in the red light district of Seoul and it wouldn't have been the first time - nor the last, and she smiled - that she had been caught 'in flagrante' by a cuckolded wife.

Tony Bristow loaded his fishing gear and coolbox into the canoe, threw a life-jacket in after it and with his sun hat pulled well down over his eyes, paddled slowly across the river towards the bend upstream and the shade where he had caught his last 30lb barracuda.

It was nearly two hours later that Monica was brought wide-awake by the shouts of the Motram children who had run to the house from the jetty where the boat boy was standing up in the speedboat. She glanced at her watch; gracious, I've been asleep for over an hour,' she thought as she looked over to where everyone was standing around the wooden jetty. The canoe was tied to the stern of the speedboat. There was nothing in the canoe and no sign of Tony. Monica could hear a roaring sound in her head and she felt as though she was walking on a sponge. Lin Aldridge was sobbing hysterically for some reason. Everyone was looking at her... nothing was making sense... this was a nightmare and then, mercifully, oblivion released her from her misery and confusion.

The children had spotted the canoe right out by the sand bar; it had been floating, capsized, in the surf breaking over the bar. They had searched for twenty minutes and then with no trace of Tony Bristow or of any of the equipment, which he had taken with him, the boat boy had returned to the bungalow. All the people who owned boats at Ada joined in the search, but nothing was found. Tony Bristow had vanished.

*

The motorbike patrolman of the RCMP did a careful U-turn on the icy road and returned to the Dodge station wagon parked on the side of the road. Front and rear doors were open onto the pavement, the car was empty and the engine was running. The policeman looked around, but there was no one in sight so he walked back to the bike, unclipped the mike from the radio and put through a vehicle registration plate check to the computer.

The car was on Cedar Drive less than 400 yards from the Mount Cedar Nursery School in the expensive residential area of Jasper Place on the north bank of the Sascatchewan River. Even burglaries were rare in such a well-patrolled area because Cedar Park Estate was where the Mayor of Edmonton had his house. It was more than the police chief's job was worth to let lawlessness invade the wealthy and influential residents' tranquillity.

'The car's registered to a JB Mackenzie of 8, Riverside Drive, Cedar Park Estate. That's old man Mackenzie's son; what's the problem, Dave?' and before RCMP patrolman Dave Taplow could answer, 'if it's a parking violation for crissakes forget it. His old man owns Sikafuturu - and most of the city too.' Dave Taplow explained the problem and within a minute, two police cars left Edmonton City Central Police Station and in doing so also left a fair amount of tyre rubber on the road surface.

'Mary?'

'Yes, it's Mary Mackenzie here.'

'Oh, hi, it's Jean,' no immediate response, 'Jean Henshaw at the nursery school.'

'Sorry Jean, yes, my mind was miles away on a shopping list; you know how it is.'

'Sure; is Ian coming to school today?'

'Yes Jean; he should be there by now,' a tightening of the gut as instant anxiety gripped the mother. Visions of icy roads and a crashed car spun into focus in her mind's eye.

'Oh, that's fine, I'm sure he'll be here any minute. Is that nice driver of yours bringing him?'

'Yes, I......hold on; a car's just pulled into the drive. Oh God! it's a police car.......'

'Mary!....Mary!....' but the phone swung at the end of its cable as Mary Mackenzie rushed from the house as the police car drew up outside the house.

'Old man', Duncan Mackenzie, the president of Canadian Sikafuturu Mining Company Ltd, one time Governor of Alberta and owner of the single richest gold mine in the world at Sawaba in Ghana, was told an hour later, by his son John, that his grandson Ian had vanished. The driver had also vanished; there were no signs of a struggle, no footprints, tyre marks, witnesses.....nothing.

CHAPTER 2

'Continental or cholesterol?'

'What?

'Breakfast.'

'Oh, continental, please; when in Guernsey do as the French do, I suppose,' John Gunn sleepily answered Claudine's query from the kitchen.

'No really, there's masses of eggs, bacon, sausages, tomatoes and so on if you want it. I stocked up as the sea air gives everyone an appetite,' and Claudine appeared in the doorway wearing only a T-shirt which emphasized rather than concealed every part of her figure.

'Go on then; I'll have the full cholesterol, but it's not only the sea air which gives me an appetite. You in a tiny T-shirt has whetted another appetite; may I have you for starters, please.'

'Oh no you don't,' but he did and so breakfast was delayed for another twenty minutes. 'Randy bugger,' she whispered as she looked down at him.

'It's just like you said; it's the sea air and if you walk around in that tiny T-shirt I'm never going to get to the breakfast table.'

The white-painted de Cartaret cottage stood on its own at the end of the track which led to the lighthouse on St Martin's Point at the southernmost tip of the island of Guernsey. Claudine de Cartaret's father, Jean, was a fisherman who had acquired a new 53 foot boat from the insurance claim on the one he had lost when it had sunk after a collision with another ship to the south of Sardrière Island. That had all been in the summer before the Gulf War in 2003, when Claudine's search for her missing father brought her into contact with John Gunn. Gunn had been tasked by the British Intelligence Directorate to investigate the connection between ten missing Russian nuclear missiles and the disfigured Iraqi arms dealer who owned Sardrière Island and its medieval castle. All that remained of the island after Gunn blew up the arsenal of ammunition beneath it was a gaunt memorial rock protruding from the sea which was home to a handful of gannets and cormorants.

Jean de Cartaret was away from his home base of St Peter Port for three weeks in the area of the Îles d'Ouessant with the other boats of the port's ocean-going fleet. His daughter had taken advantage of the empty cottage to invite Gunn for a long Easter weekend away from London. After their joint involvement in the successful Anglo-American operation to prevent Saddam Hussein's acquisition of Russian nuclear weapons, the British Intelligence Directorate had recruited Claudine as a field operative. Her ingenuity, stamina and resourcefulness in the pre-Gulf War operation, together with her fluency in French and Spanish, her PPL and Yachtmaster qualifications had greatly impressed Simon Peters, the BID Assistant Director for South-East Asia. The offer and acceptance of a job and the tearful farewell with her father, for whom she had been daughter, first mate, crew and cook, was followed by six months of rigorous training with BID which she had just completed.

This training not only tested human tissue, muscle and ligament as exhaustively as that devised by the SAS - for indeed, that aspect of the training was run by an ex-squadron commander from 22 SAS Regiment - but it trained and developed 'the little grey cells' so beloved by Agatha Christie's little Belgian private detective, Hercule Poirot. In addition to her previous qualifications, she was now adept in unarmed combat, communications, cyphers, hostile driving - taught by a retired Commander of the Metropolitan Police Flying Squad - breaking, entering and safe-cracking - taught by a reformed inmate of 'the Scrubs' - and had become an outstanding shot, even with large calibre handguns. This latter ability had surprised BID's ex-Small Arms School Corps instructors. Claudine had explained that living on her father's boat, since her mother's death when she was a baby, and acting as his crew when she was barely out of nappies, had required her to heave warps and ropes of all sizes resulting in a pair of wrists which could more than restrain the kick of a .375 or .45 magnum calibre handgun.

The British Intelligence Directorate had been created on the instructions of the Prime Minister in 1988 shortly after the publication of Peter Wright's book 'Spycatcher'. Whilst there was no specific connection between the decision to reorganise Britain's intelligence effort and Wright's book, the revelations which it contained finally exploded the myth of British intelligence expertise, so long kept alive by Ian Flemming's James Bond. The revelations about Burgess, Maclean, Philby, Blunt and the unknown fifth member of the communist core of MI5 and many other leaks, defections and major international blunders, revealed MI5 and MI6 to be a bunch of incompetent amateurs, riddled with archaic 'old-school-tie' anachronisms. The task of reorganising Britain's intelligence services had been given to a young and recently promoted Army General who had resigned in the mid 80s when thwarted by the Ministry of Defence and Treasury in his efforts to maintain the quality of conditions of service of the British soldiers based in Germany.

Jeremy Hammond had dropped his military rank on leaving the Army, was head-hunted by Stroud Porchester, leading City business consultants, and in the space of three years restored two ailing companies to profitability. He had accepted the task given to him by the Prime Minister and had achieved it six months inside the target date. A knighthood was followed by his appointment as the first Director of the British Intelligence Directorate. During the transition from one system to another, MI5 and MI6 were retained in their buildings at Millbank and Vauxhall, fulfilling a purely clerical function, while purpose-designed premises were built for BID.

Kingsroad House was the legitimate head office of Express Delivery Services plc. The company had been created by Jeremy Hammond with government funding. Once the Post Office lost its monopoly on mail delivery, Express Delivery Services was but one of many mail, telegram and parcel delivery services which competed in a free market. EDS' transport fleet included two Airbus A 300s, four British Aerospace 146/300s, two Westland Super Lynxes and two Aerospatiale Gazelles in addition to motorbikes, vans, container haulage and two, 40,000 ton container ships. All of this transport could communicate either by radio or cellnet telephone with both each other and head office. It provided the ideal cover for the comings and goings of the BID workforce to Kingsroad House or anywhere else in the world and the considerable profit, which it made offset the cost of BID to the British taxpayer.

This policy of making the British intelligence effort partially self-funding was reflected in all BID overseas stations. The SIS officers in Embassies and High Commissions were gradually made redundant; the very best were recruited into BID, but that was less than a handful and not one member of MI5, or Box 500 - the sobriquet from its internal postal code - passed the rigorous security vetting which started where the previous positive vetting finished. All major overseas stations operated from commercial premises, well-distanced from the 'leaky' embassies and high commissions and undeclared to the ambassadors, high commissioners and staff of those establishments and their well-documented breaches of physical and personal security. They had a remit to plough-back all profits to fund the intelligence effort and the intelligence which they gathered was fed to the appropriate embassy or high commission from Kingsroad House.

Both espionage and counter-espionage departments of BID were under the same roof in Kingsroad House and worked in conjunction rather than in conflict with each other. BID had its own training centre at Maidenhead, which was collocated with its own clinic and convalescent wing. Kingsroad House had a medical centre, which had an intensive care unit, an operating theatre and four rooms where patients could be stabilised until strong enough to travel to Maidenhead. The whole operation in Kingsroad House could be moved to two other premises in London within three hours and to another building in Southampton in 24 hours.

Claudine had completed her training at Maidenhead just before Easter and had been accepted into BID by its Director in a very informal interview in his office in Kingsroad House. He had gone through every detail of the reports from her instructors and had amazed her with his knowledge of every aspect of her training high spots and not-so-high spots. At the end of the interview, she had been told that she had achieved the standard required and was given the chance to comment on any aspect of the training or anything else. Her reply was to confess her surprise at the personal interest which he, the Director, took in every detail of her training and previous life with her father, some of which wasn't even recorded in the reports.

Sir Jeremy Hammand had smiled and then told her that the explanation of her observation necessitated an understanding of the British perspective of intelligence gathering. He had suggested an analogy between BID and the Olympic Games. He had gone on to elaborate on this analogy by explaining that after the revival of the Games in 1896 by the Frenchman, Baron Pierre de Coubertin, competitive athletics in Britain had been treated in almost the same way as the acquisition of intelligence about an enemy. It was the privileged occupation or pastime of the wealthy and well-educated who managed to complete their education at either Oxford or Cambridge.

Claudine had felt completely at ease in the comfortable, but uncluttered office of the Director. He wasn't a tall man, probably no taller than 5'10" or 11", slim with piercingly dark eyes and short, neat grey hair. With a smile, he had gone on to develop his analogy further by explaining that as short a time ago as the Crimean War and the disastrous Charge of the Light Brigade, any form of spying on the enemy had been considered ungentlemanly and unsportsmanlike by the British War Office. This, Sir Jeremy had continued, was one of the reasons that the Light Brigade had charged down the wrong valley. If the British Army had had proper intelligence it would have known that the entire Russian Artillery was deployed on the sides and end of the valley through which the cavalry was about to charge.

Whilst the British steadfastly continued to treat war on the same terms as a game of cricket, the enemy used every spying trick in the book to gain an advantage. The fact that it didn't defeat the British Army, Sir Jeremy remarked, was not because of superiority of numbers or any ability of the British Generals, but because of the incredible aggressiveness and bravery of the British soldiers and the heroism of their young officers. Sir Jeremy had attributed the aggressiveness of the British to the Anglo-Saxon heritage, which had been well-spiced with both Norman and Viking blood. Sir Jeremy considered that the amateur status of the British Olympic effort, both before and after the two world wars, was well matched by that of the intelligence services. Whereas the Olympic effort had progressed in professionalism and competitiveness, British intelligence had stagnated after a glimmer of professionalism in the Second World War, and had finally lost all direction and morale after successful penetration by the KGB and its own, in-house squabbles between MI5 and MI6. Nothing but a completely clean sweep could cleanse the British intelligence malaise, so he had been told by the Prime Minister.

The Director had concluded his analogy by saying that if the nation wanted to win gold then it had to have dedicated professional athletes trained by dedicated professional coaches. He told Claudine that the only way he could live with himself, sending young men and women out on highly dangerous missions, from which some might not return, was to train them into the best intelligence operatives in the world; winners of gold.

Claudine had asked Gunn if he had had the same interview with the Director when he had been recruited after the Daya Bay incident in Hong Kong. He said that he had and, yes, he had felt a bit special after his talk with Sir Jeremy, but he went on to tell Claudine that as a Divisional Commander, Sir Jeremy Hammond was reputed to have known the name of every soldier in that Division. That wasn't true of course, Gunn had told her, but the soldiers believed it, boasted about it and worshipped the man. When he resigned from the Army, a whole tranche of his Division had left with him and quite a few were working for BID.

Now dressed in jeans and an over-sized sweat-shirt, Claudine turned as Gunn came into the kitchen. Dressed almost identically to her, his sheer size made the cottage's kitchen look small. Nearly six foot three inches and with a body closer in shape to Arnold Schwarzenneger than the bean-pole figures of male models, Gunn

38

was always noticed which was a distinct disadvantage in his profession. He went over to Claudine, slipped his hands underneath the sweat-shirt, gave her a hug and kissed the tawny mane of ash-blonde hair.

'Go and sit down at the breakfast bar before I ruin your eggs and bacon. Fruit juice is in the fridge; no, in the bottom shelf in the door,' as he looked inside. 'I've just poured the boiling water into the caftière so let it brew for a couple of minutes before you push down the plunger.

'What's the plan for today?'

'Dan Treuniert, who owns one of the charter companies operating out of the North Marina, has said we can have one of his Princess power boats.'

'How much will that set us back?' Gunn asked while depressing the plunger on the caftière.

'Nothing, he said; he's a very old friend of Dad's and he told me he owes us one for the very generous compensation he was given by the government for the damage done to the boat Alan Paxton used to get out to Sardrière Island.'

'Yes, I'd heard that; the explosion blew out the glass and wrote off all the nav' and radar kit. You're right, the sea air does make everything taste better,' and an empty cereal bowl was pushed to one side. 'Where were you planning to go in this high-speed runabout?'

'Well, they are lovely boats even if they are a bit plasticy and as we have to be back in London tomorrow, it seemed pointless to sail - particularly as there's so little wind,' and Claudine placed a plate piled with eggs, bacon and everything else harmful to the human body, but which had sustained the British Nation for a couple of hundred years, in front of Gunn and then paused by the windows over the double sink. 'The forecast is only for ones and twos from the north-east, which is little use to us and makes it very chilly unless we can get out of what wind there is. I'd thought of a picnic lunch in Derrible Bay on the other side of Sark.' Claudine poured herself a coffee and joined Gunn at the breakfast bar.

'Is that the bay below the Dixcart Hotel?'

'No, that's Dixcart Bay but the two are beside each other...here,' and she slipped off the stool and picked up a chart, which had already been folded to show the Island of Sark. She put it between them and placed her finger on the chart. 'Those are the two bays. You can easily get down to Dixcart Bay by a path, which runs through a gap in the cliffs from the hotel. Derrible Bay is a different matter; look at all the heavy hachuring,' and a slim finger traced the hydrographer's illustration of rocks and cliffs. 'You can get down to the beach, but it's dangerous; one slip and you're dead - or very seriously injured.' Gunn's plate was empty; he took it and the cereal bowl to the sink and returned to the breakfast bar. 'Your Mum trained you well.'

'That was Ah See, our amah in Hong Kong, who ruled me, in particular, and my two elder sisters to a lesser extent, with a rod of iron. Can't say I've ever regretted it. That really does look daunting, even on this chart. What's the height of those cliffs?'

'It should say....yes, there's a ring contour at the top of the cliff..180 feet.'

'It's a perfectly sheltered anchorage for anything other than a sou-westerly. Excellent idea; can I do anything to help?'

'Yes; throw anything you want to take into the bag in the hall and then you could carry these two cool boxes,' and she indicated with a sweep of one leg towards two blue-lidded containers, 'out to the jeep. We probably don't even need the food I've put in the cool boxes as the boat usually comes for a day's charter with chilled oysters and champagne included.'

'Right; washing up?'

'No, go on; you've proved that you're house trained. I'll do that while you load the jeep.' The small, pink Suzuki jeep was soon loaded and Gunn lent on it as he looked at the uncluttered view of sea and sky. The sky was mostly pale washed-out blue with only a small amount of high altitude wisps of cirrostratus, which could have been the first indications of an approaching warm front. Gunn glanced up at the sun; it was surrounded by blue with no cloudy halo so there was probably no prospect of a major increase in wind for the next twelve hours or so. There was a really sharp chill in the air, despite the sun and the sea was almost mill-pond calm, clearly showing the small gusts of wind which darkened the blue shading of the surface.

'Brrrr....my blood's too bloody thin,' he muttered, zipping up his anorak as Claudine locked the front door and then came across the lawn to the jeep. She climbed in behind the wheel, started the small but nippy 1100 cc engine and with a spurt of gravel they set off up the track past the lighthouse to the main road into St Peter Port.

At 9.30 on an Easter Monday, St Peter Port was well-crowded with tourists, but only a fraction of the number that would throng the harbour-side streets on the May and Summer bank holidays. The new and old marinas were both well filled with visiting boats, as were the buoys in the outer harbour; many of the boats bore clear evidence of their owner's care over the winter months and the smell of fresh varnish and polyurethane paint wafted across to the open

40

jeep as Claudine turned off into the North Marina car park. She parked it in a reserved space by the offices of Guernsey Yacht Charter and both of them jumped out of the doorless jeep and went into the reception area of the yacht charter company.

'Hello Claudine, how ya' goin?'

'Good thanks, Noelene. Have you met John? I'm sorry, I can't remember how long you've worked for Dan.'

'No and just over a year, in that order.'

'Right, Noelene, this is John Gunn; John, Noelene Jones from Brisbane,' and the two shook hands.

'Keys are there, Claudine,' and Noelene pointed to a bunch of keys attached to a large cork floater. 'Dan says could you sign the form so that he can keep the insurers right. He's handing over one of our 500s to a character in yachting hat and blazer - the whole bit! - who can hardly tell the difference between his arse and his elbow let alone the sharp and blunt end.'

'Thanks Noelene,' and Claudine picked up the keys. The wall to one side of the reception desk was decorated with framed pictures of the company's charter fleet of Princess power boats. Each picture showed the dimensions and performance of the boat, which Gunn was studying while he waited for Claudine to sign for their boat. The Princess which they had been lent for free was the 470 fitted with twin Volvo Penta TAMD 72 engines of 430hp each which gave the boat - so the information said - a top speed of between 31 and 34 knots. Gunn glanced across at the performance of the 500; almost identical performance, but the larger boat needed two, 480hp engines to achieve the same speed as the 470. The informative Noelene had been studying Gunn's back while Claudine signed the boat charter papers. They both thanked her again and turned to leave.

'Claudine,' she stopped and turned.

'Yes?'

'Sorry to be nosey, but Dan said that if you had a large man with you, could I ask you to bring back the boat in one piece as he needs it tomorrow.'

'That's OK Noelene; yes, Dan does mean this large man and I promise we won't damage the boat,' and the two of them left the office. It had been prudent of Dan to get the insurance form signed. .

Dan waved to Claudine from the fly bridge of a gleaming Princess 500 from the stern of which came pleasant and powerful diesel rumbling and gurgling noises. The moment he saw Gunn he covered his eyes with one hand and shook his head while Gunn waved cheerfully back with a broad grin. Beside Dan was a vision of what fashion magazines imagined was worn by the boating set. It was a shade over five-and-a-half feet high and came complete with pipe, which was being cleaned out and the dottle discarded on the pristine white deck of the bridge. Claudine and Gunn left Dan to his private misery and continued to the end of the pontoon where their equally-gleaming Princess 470 was moored.

Claudine jumped aboard and Gunn handed her the cool boxes and squashy bag with their clothes, books and bits and pieces from the trolley which he had pushed along the pontoon. He was saved the chore of returning the trolley to the car park by someone who had spotted his empty one and took it off his hands. As he turned, he heard the first of the Volva-Penta TAMD 72 diesels burst into life. Claudine was on the fly bridge running a finger over the dials as she checked engine revs, oil pressure, coolant temperature and pressure and charge level on the ammeter. Once satisfied, she first pressed the heater button for the six cylinders of the second engine and when the light extinguished, the start button; more satisfying noises from the stern of their Princess.

'Ready for me to cast off?'

'No John; you're much better than me with these things. Would you take her out. I'll come down and do the springs and warps.'

'Sure? I've no hang-ups about being ordered around. What happens if I disobey an order? Will you promise to punish me!'

'Oh! Shut up you sex maniac,' which caused the man on the next boat to look up expectantly for which he was rewarded by a dazzling smile from Claudine and a frozen stare from the female in the stern of his boat. 'I'm much more at home with a yacht and besides, it's your name on the hire agreement....'

'You rat! Wait 'til I get on that fly bridge,' but she didn't and nimbly climbed over the side of the fly bridge down to the deck and onto the pontoon.

'Ready to cast off, skipper,' Claudine grinned from the relative safety of the pontoon.

'If I could cook I'd leave you behind, you cunning little hussy, now look lively with those springs before I come down and administer punishment.'

'It's all cold and you know it's not for that reason you wouldn't leave me behind. Springs and for'ard warp clear! Can you manage or would you like me to cast off aft and then come up there and help you?'

'Come up here and you'll get that very neat arse of yours spanked.'

'On my way!' and Claudine joined Gunn on the bridge as he eased the Princess gently out of her berth. The man on the boat had given up all pretence of stowing his spinnaker into its turtle - the connical-shaped container in which it was kept in the pulpit ready for hoisting - and gazed whimsically after the departing Princess, unaware that 'she of the freezing stare' was making her way for'ard from the stern. Claudine put her arms round Gunn and squeezed hard. 'This is fun; when do I get my spanking?'

'As soon as I can find how to put this bloody machine onto autopilot. Now, go and sit over there,' and he indicated the upholstered bench seat which surrounded the starboard and rear quadrant of the fly bridge. 'You know I can't concentrate when you're close to me - at least not on anything else.' Claudine did as ordered, while Gunn took the Princess out of the North Marina into the Little Russell channel and turned the sharp bow to the south-east. The note of the diesels turned to a well-muffled roar, the bow lifted momentarily and then settled as Gunn adjusted the electro-hydraulic trim tabs on the stern and the Princess carved a path across the calm sea to the guano-encrusted rock where two years before had been Sardrière Island and its medieval castle. Had Gunn turned as he brought the motorboat onto a course of 120°, he might have spotted the sun's reflection from the binocular prisms, which followed the course of the white Princess towards Sardrière Rock and the Island of Sark beyond.

*

In some ways Las Vegas was as unreal a place as Disneyland where fantasy was the order of the day and humans - certainly adults - seemed out of place. The entertainment capital of the world was selected by Caramansa because the world of gambling and fantasy provided ideal cover for the group of fugitives from West Africa and the laundering of huge sums of money.

The Caramansa's aim was to bring down all the legitimate or quasi-legitimate governments of Sub-Saharan West Africa and unite the ensuing chaos, willingly or not, into UROWAS - The United Republic of West African States – which would be governed by the thirteen strong security council. The security council had one representative from each of the countries represented in the conspiracy. The 'government in exile' of the embryo UROWAS had drawn up its constitution, which bore a strong resemblance to the UN Charter. The President of UROWAS would be elected from the Security Council by the 13 other delegates for a term of five years; no President could do two consecutive terms in office and so on.

The UROWAS Assembly was 130 strong; exiled fugitives of each country were allowed ten members in the assembly, no matter how small or large the country. This rule had already caused bloodshed when the Nigerian delegate to the Security Council had insulted the Gambian delegate. The latter had drawn an automatic and shot the former. The Nigerian had been running away when the shot was fired and so the bullet had hit him in the largest target area visible to the Gambian - his arse. All members of the Assembly and delegates to the Security Council received a salary; Charles Mensah had set up the International Credit Bank in Las Vegas to fund these salaries, while he was a senior member of his country's delegation to the United Nations, and to buy arms for his 'freedom fighters' in West Africa.

The bank was started with perfect timing on the crest of the banking boom, using embezzled funds intended for aid programmes in his country. Mensah's next appointment was as a counsellor in the Ghanaian High Commission in Ottawa, where once again he had the ideal opportunity to misappropriate aid to his country until his greed came to the notice of the High Commissioner and Charles Mensah then vanished; an exile from his country and with a price on his head.

Because of worldwide greed in the nineties and unbelievable stupidity shown by erstwhile reliable banks which rashly over-extended themselves with loans, ICB and its directors made a fortune - in fact, several fortunes. Ludicrous rates of interest were offered which were eagerly grasped with little thought for checking the banks liquidity. A steady stream of stolen gold trickled out of West Africa, and Ghana in particular, which ended up as bars of .999 fine purity in the vaults of ICB's head branch in Las Vegas. ICB's income grew rapidly from laundering drug money from Columbia, Panama and the Golden Triangle in South-East Asia, handling the funding of terrorism against the USA, UK, France, Germany and Italy and world banking's insatiable avarice.

When the G8 countries finally admitted that their economies were going into recession, Caramansa's International Credit Bank had suffered a series of body blows which would inevitably lead to its closure by the US Treasury. An investigation into ICB's liquidity and assets had been orderd by Congress, which would quickly reveal its bankruptcy unless vast amounts of new income were made available. Closure of the head branch in Las Vegas would be followed in minutes, worldwide, by the closure of all its branches. In other words, the end of the Caramansa Conspiracy and Charles Mensah's dream of achieving his destiny of becoming supreme chief of 200 million West Africans.

The Bank's trouble had started when the Caramansa-funded coup to remove Sergeant Sam Doe from the presidency of Liberia was defeated by a combined Nigerian/Ghanaian intervention force under the auspices of ECOWAS - the Economic Community of West African States. What at first had seemed to be a highly successful civil war, planned to coincide with Iraq's invasion of Kuwait to keep Western attention away from West Africa, had dragged on interminably and vastly exceeded the budget allocated to it. Caramansa could have coped with this if it hadn't been exacerbated by another major loss of ICB's revenue.

ICB had laundered the majority of President Noriega's drug money, which had provided the Bank with its main income. Noriega's capture by US Forces and his subsequent imprisonment, followed by a series of US DEA successes in halting the flow of cocaine from Columbia to the USA, dried up all but an insignificant quantity of the Bank's drug racket income. The highly successful US F 111 bombing of Gadaffi's residence dried up ICB's income from Libya. Coincident with these disasters for Caramansa, the executive vice-president of ICB had completely failed to understand the severity of recession creeping up on the industrialised countries. Caramansa's launch of its ICB-funded coups in Nigeria, Togo, Mali, Côte d'Ivoire, Burkina Faso and Guinea coincided to the day with the collapse of the Bank of Credit and Commerce International.

Private and corporate investment drained out of ICB, worldwide, as banks, pension funds and building societies attempted to limit the damage. The rush of withdrawals turned into a flood as the world teetered on the brink of crisis with the chaotic disintegration of the former Soviet Union and the genocidal ethnic bloodbath in Bosnia. Caramansa was bankrupt and hence the summons to all members and delegates to the fortress-like ICB headquarters in Las Vegas. Funding for the purchase of arms for the civil wars and coups which were to bring about the downfall of the West African governments had dried up. Charles Mensah, the architect of the Caramnasa Conspiracy and the self-elected President of UROWAS had been told by Bradley Tracton, the president of International Machine Tools Inc, that his shopping list for arms and ammunition would cost, not 200 million US dollars as he'd thought, but 400 million US dollars. The majority of this money would be required for bribes to US senators and congressmen to obtain export licences to get the arms out of the USA. Caramansa didn't have that sort of money, in fact, the executive vice-president of ICB had just informed him that there were insufficient funds to meet the monthly paycheck of UROWAS members.

The General Assembly of UROWAS convened in an auditorium, which was almost as capacious as that of the UN. It was on the 30th floor of the ICB building in Las Vegas. Security was germane to the continued existence of this exiled organisation as nearly every person in it had a price on his or her head. All were wanted for crimes against the governments and people of the countries from which they had fled. Some of their numbers had been depleted or had just vanished in circumstances which suggested that some form of summary justice, ordered by the government of their country, had been carried out by proxy in the USA. Caramansa had a private army guarding the inside and outside of the building and the interior of the auditorium was surrounded by guards armed with the .45 calibre-upgraded version of the 9 mm Uzi carbine.

The auditorium was semi-circular with the traditional Supreme Chief's throne stool at the top of the straight edge, the stool for the executive vice-president of ICB was positioned below that and still further down, the thirteen stools of the Security Council delegates. Nearer the base of the straight edge of the semi-circle, was the raised podium and lectern with a bank of microphones at the front of it. No press conferences were ever held in this most securely guarded of places so the reason for more than one microphone was not immediately apparent; possibly, they awaited the day of triumph when the new United Republic of West African States would be announced to the world. In front of the podium, the seating for the members of the General Assembly radiated out in concentric semi-circles, rising gradually towards the rear of the auditorium.

All the members were seated and all wore the full robes and headress of their native countries. National dress was mandatory in the General Assembly for everyone except the guards. The lights dimmed and floods came on, picking out the thirteen seats of the Security Council. In a remarkable stereo effect, the beating of the 'Donno' drums heralded the arrival of the thirteen delegates of the Security Council while all members of the Assembly remained seated. The floods went out and a single spot picked out the stool of the executive vice-president of ICB. Another spot picked out three drummers holding the 'Antumpans' or talking drums. These were carved from the tweneboa tree and the membranes were made from elephants' ears. These drums could only be carved by a Chief's proclamation and heralded the arrival of a person of royal family status.

Letitia Quartey was Caramansa's mistress in addition to being executive vice-president of ICB and therefore considered herself to be of royal blood. From Harvard she had been awarded with an honours degree in accountancy and from the Almighty she had been awarded with an insatiable sexual appetite and the athletic physique necessary to sustain it. In recent years, this affliction, or attribute, had become known as sexaholism; it was a well-reported malady of the occupants of Beverley Hills, and according to accounts in the tabloid press was an affliction shared by John Kennedy, Marilyn Monroe and Bill Clinton. A single spot picked out her entrance to the auditorium and illuminated her path until it merged with the spot lighting the stool.

Her bizarre choice of costume was not included in the UROWAS Constitution as it would have made a mockery of traditions, which were still closely observed in West Africa. She wore the costume of the 'virgin initiate' for the Akan 'Obra' ceremony, which consisted of nothing more than a simple loin-cloth and necklace and bangles. The initiation ceremony was still observed in the countries of West Africa under different tribal titles and took place at the time when the young girls of the tribe had their first menstrual period. In some tribes, this ceremony still concluded with the circumcision - removal of the female clitoris - of the young maidens. This, fortunately, was not the case in Letitia's native country of Ghana, otherwise the Almighty's gift to her would have been wasted.

The young maidens were presented to the village by the chief and then lots of food and good fun was had by everyone, particularly the young maidens - provided, of course, they did not belong to a tribe which still practised circumcision. As soon as Letitia Quartey was seated, all lights went out. At this moment in the convening ceremony, the guards raised their Uzi carbines and kept the auditorium under surveillance through the image-intensifying sights, which showed every detail of the darkened room in a pale green light.

As though the sound was coming from thousands of miles away across the Atlantic Ocean, electronic audio-wizardry filled the auditorium with the unmistakeable sound of the 'Etwie' or leopard drum - so called because it was said to resemble the sound of that most revered of West African creatures. For hundreds of years, the warring Ashanti Tribes had used the drum to terrorise their enemies. The 'Etwie' drum could only be sounded to announce the arrival of a supreme chief and a single spot lanced down from the lofty arch above the auditorium to reveal Caramansa on his golden throne stool.

The auditorium was flooded by concealed lighting, rotating panels in the fifty metre by twenty metre wall space behind Caramansa changed the whole backdrop into the UROWAS flag - top left quadrant, gold with thirteen black stars; the other three quadrants filled with thirteen horizontal stripes in sequence from the top, black, gold, green and red. The opening bars of the UROWAS anthem brought the Assembly to its feet and then they all bowed towards Caramansa. The twentfirst session of the UROWAS General Assembly had begun.

CHAPTER 3

'What's the tide doing?'

'Still falling for another couple of hours. Keep clear of the rocks immediately to the south of L'Etac de Sark - that's there....where you can see those overfalls and then go to the east of Les Vingt Clos...those are the two visible rocks beyond. You can go in between, especially with a boat like this which can't draw more than a metre at most, but there's a very strong current which can force even something like the Princess onto the rocks.'

'Right, thanks for that,' and Gunn eased the two throttles back to the central position and the power boat settled into the water off its planing hull. Both of them were well wrapped up against the chilling slipstream of the boat's passage through the water. It was still very early in the season and the only boats which they had seen had been the small fishing boats out from Creux Harbour collecting the lobsters from the pots which would have been baited the previous evening. Although there were so few boats around, Gunn glanced over his shoulder before changing the Princess's course in a sweeping turn to the north which headed it towards Point Derrible and the entrance to the bay. The only boat in the otherwise empty sea astern of them was heading towards Le Bec du Nez on the northern tip of Sark and as Gunn started his turn, it disappeared behind the island of Brecqhou.

'I'll get the anchor ready,' and Claudine slid down the stainless steel handrails of the fly-bridge companionway and then shouted back to Gunn, 'what's the depth?'

'Chart datum's two where we want to anchor. With another two hours to go to low water, allow for 4.'

'OK,' and Claudine moved sure-footedly along the foredeck of the motorboat to the Simpson-Lawrence power windlass at the bow. The boat's Delta anchor was in self-stowing rollers on the stemhead of the boat and once the locking split pin had been removed was ready to run. Claudine pulled up the anchor chain from the locker in the forepeak and laid out 15 metres of it on the teak deck, concertinered in two metre loops. Once that was done, she took the tension off the locking pin and pulled it clear. By the time the anchor was ready and she had given a 'thumbs up' to the fly-bridge the boat was approaching Point Chateau on the eastern side of the bay.

Rising out of the bracken and gorse on the cliffs above the bay was an old ruined folly which was marked on the chart in front of Gunn as 'conspic'. Using the ruin as his leading mark, Gunn brought the Princess into the bay on a heading of 31°, which would keep it clear of the submerged rocks around the point. The sun was now astern of the boat and as soon as the steep sides of the bay sheltered the boat from the wind, Gunn could feel some of its warmth and undid the zip on his anorak. He pushed both throttles into neutral and with barely a murmur from the big diesels the sleek white motorboat drifted into the calm, clear water of the bay. The digital depth display showed 2.5 metres below the boat's keel.

'Let it go!' Standing clear of the prepared chain, Claudine let the anchor plunge into the sea. The way had come right off the boat, but the tide was still drifting it towards the shingled beach. Gunn put both engines astern and gave them a touch of throttle. The forward motion stopped and the boat started to make way astern. Gunn put both engines into neutral and operated the decompressors. The muffled sound of the diesels ceased and was replaced by that of the waves breaking onto the beach 150 yards away and the cries of the gulls which immediately circled the boat to assess its potential as a source of tit-bits.

'Lovely; the sun really has got some warmth when you're out of the wind,' and Claudine shed her anorak and polo-neck sweater as she came aft to the stern well-deck. 'There's champagne in the fridge and if you believe that aphrodisiac bit about oysters and want to top up after this morning's exercise, you'll find them there as well! I'm going to have a quick sunbathe on the bridge. I'll have my champagne up there please.'

'Oysters?'

'Why not,' and she disappeared up the companionway shedding clothes as she went.

Sheltered from the wind, the motorboat swung to the effect of the tide and the stern slowly came round until it pointed towards the perpendicular rockface of Point Derrible on the east side of the bay. Gunn went into the saloon and then down the couple of steps into the galley on the port side of the boat. He opened the fridge and removed one of two red-ribboned bottles of champagne and a cardboard box, packed with crushed ice and seaweed, from which he removed the oysters.

'Knife; now where would they keep the knives? Ah!' and a drawer revealed a whole selection of knives from which to choose an oyster-splitter. Gunn split open a dozen oysters and then laid out the opened shells on a serving plate of crushed ice. He removed a tray from the rack above the sink, spread a cloth over it and arranged the oysters, champagne, glasses, sliced lemon, tabasco sauce, salt and pepper and then stood back and admired his handiwork. 'Not too bad for an amateur chef,' and he carried his handiwork up to the bridge.

'Where've you been? The oysters were in the fridge not on the sea bed, I....ouch!' the large lump of ice had landed accurately as aimed in Claudine's cleavage. She leapt from the fitted seat at the rear of the bridge clutching the ice and bent on retribution.

'Ah...ah, you can't attack a defenceless waiter, besides, I shall spill the champagne.'

'So when did the close season for waiters begin?'

'Today; now sit down while I pour the champagne. You know how difficult it is for me to concentrate when you've got hardly any clothes on.'

'That any better?' and with a deft movement, Claudine removed the skimpy bikini.

'Much, but I can't stand warm champagne and oysters. Hang on a sec,' and Gunn and the tray returned to the galley. He forced the cork back into the bottle and replaced it and the oysters in the fridge. There was a loud thump on the saloon coachroof. Gunn opened the scuttle above the galley sink. 'Patience, patience....I won't be a sec,' but unusually, there was no repartee in response. Gunn closed the fridge door and then paused...listening. He moved quickly out of the saloon and up the companionway to the bridge. Claudine lay on the bridge deck with an appalling wound to the side of her head and a pool of blood spreading out on the deck under the blonde hair.

For a split second, Gunn froze and then the deck beside him erupted in splinters of fibreglass and a neat hole appeared. He scooped Claudine up in his arms, turned and scrambled back down the companionway as the fibreglass bridge-coaming beside his hand burst into fragments. Once back inside the saloon, he lowered Claudine onto the fitted, upholstered seating and then collected a blanket out of the for'ard cabin which he wrapped around her. Whilst his body was going through these motions, his brain was racing to make sure he did everything humanly possible to save Claudine....if she wasn't dead already. He touched the pulse in the side of her neck; nothing. Another bullet drilled through the coachroof and bounced, spent, onto the saloon carpet.

'Bloody sniper's up on the cliff,' Gunn muttered. 'We're sitting like clay ducks in a shooting gallery.' He went to the for'ard steering position in the saloon, reached up to the radio fitted into the coachroof above the steering position, punched up channel 16 and

51

picked up the mike. 'Pan! Pan! Pan!' ......a pause and then again, 'Pan! Pan! Pan! Guernsey Coastguard, Guernsey Coastguard, Guernsey Coastguard, this is motorboat Princess Five, Princess Five, Princess Five. My position is Derrible Bay, I repeat, Derrible Bay on east side of Sark.... wait...wait,' and Gunn glanced at the Brookes and Gatehouse GPS satnav digital dispaly, '2°21' West, 49°26' North. I have a passenger critically injured with a gunshot wound. SAR helicopter required immediately if life is to be saved. I repeat SAR helicopter required immediately if life is to be saved; over.'

'Princess Five, this is Guernsey Coastguard; roger to your Pan call; SAR helicopter leaving shortly. All other ships, repeat, all other ships clear this channel. Confirm Derrible Bay on east side of Sark, over.'

'Guernsey Coastguard this is Princess Five, Derrible Bay confirmed. I'll fire red smoke when I spot the helicopter. I must move my position as gunman with sniper rifle on cliffs is still firing at my boat. Tell the Police on Sark what's happening. Do you roger this, over.'

'Princess Five this is Guernsey Coastguard, that's a roger. Keep this channel open. There's only one policeman on Sark and he's not equipped to take on a gunman; Guernsey Police are dealing with it. We'll leave you to move your boat. Good luck, out.'

Not only every boat in VHF range had picked up Gunn's Pan call, but so had the radio in the reception area of Guernsey Yacht Charter in the North Marina. Noelene Jones turned up the volume while Dan Treuniert switched his big HF radio to the frequency used by the port's fishing fleet and spoke to Jean de Cartaret. He then rang the helicopter charter company at the airport and hired a machine to go out and get Jean from his boat. He was told that there would be no question of a charge for the machine and the pilot and winch operator were on their way to start up the helicopter.

Gunn went back to Claudine and was horrified by her deathly pallor. 'For crissake don't die.......you bastard,' directed at the unknown assassin. The starboard windscreen shattered into fragments. He reached across to the control panel of the inside steering position and switched on the engine heaters..... throttle buttons in neutral....throttles half open.....heater lights off. He pressed both starters together and without hesitation the big six cylinder diesels fired and settled to a steady rhythm. The scuttle on his right burst, casting shards of safety glass across the control panel. He was about to operate the electric windlass when he noticed that Claudine had put a turn of the chain around the hefty steel cleat on the starboard bow. Years of anchoring sailing yachts had developed habits, which were difficult to change. In a detached way, Gunn noticed the blood on his right hand as he made his way aft out of the saloon.

The port side of the boat had to be marginally less in the sniper's view, Gunn reckoned as he left the saloon crouched low. His rage and grief at losing Claudine and his frustration at being used for target practice by the cliff-top sniper caused him no concern for the target he would present when he went for'ard to loose off the anchor chain. He paused momentarily as he reached the front of the coachroof and the last vestige of cover before the open foredeck of the motorboat. In the fractions of seconds before he moved, he wondered if the sniper's rifle was a self-loader or bolt-action. If it was the latter, he might have a chance.....say eight seconds to get there, loose off the chain from the cleat and back; fire, reload, fire.....two rounds snap shooting at a moving target with a slant range of about 200 yards. Marksman standard shooting for a professional; he had to assume that that's what the sniper was because all his training had taught him to assume the worst and never under-estimate the enemy. If the weapon was a self-loader and anything like the Belgian FN or the Enfield SA 80 then it would be one round a second....eight rounds. Even 'sod's law' said that one of those eight would hit him, Gunn reckoned. The thought of being hit worried him not at all, it was the thought of screwing up the recovery of Claudine to the nearest intensive care unit and life-saving surgery - if that wasn't already too late - that made him pause for those fractions of a second to make sure he didn't foul it up by getting himself killed.

He dashed forward, still in a crouch, to the cleat at the bow of the boat. There was a 'plop' sound and a spout of water jumped out of the sea on the port side. No crack and thump which meant the weapon was silenced; that meant less muzzle velocity, but again, that was no help as there was more than enough muzzle velocity to drive the bullet through a half inch of fibreglass. Irrelevant data; now at the cleat and the turn of chain thrown clear. He turned for the rush back to the shelter of the saloon superstructure, but was hurled back from the cleat and sprawled across the foredeck. There was a red-hot numbing sensation in his right side. 'Bugger this!' and Gunn crawled back at best speed into the shelter of the saloon coachroof, rose to a crouch and winced at the needle sharp pain. He pulled himself into the saloon as another chunk of fibreglass flew from the aft deck moulding.

Beside the door from the saloon out to the aft well-deck was a plastic container with all the emergency flares. He removed two of them and peeled off the paper protection over the base firing trigger and dropped them on the seat beside Claudine. He didn't dare look at Claudine, but limped for'ard to the steering position, sat in the swivel seat and operated the windlass. The Delta anchor flipped over the bow and self- stowed in the stemhead rollers as Gunn rammed both throttles as far forward as posssible. The Princess trembled and the water boiled beneath the stern as both 16", four-bladed alu-bronze screws drove the boat forward. By the time the sleek powerboat had completed its tight turn out of the bay it was already racing through the water at 20 knots.

As the boat reached the calm, half-metre swell of the open sea, Gunn spotted the fluorescent orange SAR helicopter approaching from the west. He locked in the autopilot and turned, wincing at the sharp jab of pain from the bullet wound in his right side, went aft to the flares on the seat beside Claudine, picked them up, fired both triggers and pushed them into the fishing rod brackets on each side of the aft well- deck. Back again into the saloon where he noticed, with disinterest, the mess his blood was making of the fitted carpet, then over to the engine throttles where he reduced the boat's speed until it was just making headway and with his left hand turned it into the wind as the helicopter arrived overhead. The winchman was hanging below the chopper with the stretcher as it reached the boat and was met by Gunn holding Claudine, wrapped up in her blanket, whom he'd carried out, held tightly in his left arm. Claudine was strapped into the stretcher and the winchman held her as he spoke into the throat mike to the winch operator. Claudine and her rescuer rose up as the helicopter banked and turned towards Guernsey.

If the boat had stayed behind the high wall of the mole which formed Maseline Harbour's breakwater about half-a-mile to the north of the Princess' position, Gunn would have left the task of finding the gunman until he had at least found out how badly he had been hit. As it was, his attention was drawn to the small harbour mole because a large white motorboat, similar to his own, appeared from behind it at full throttle. Leaving a harbour at that speed was the performance of a complete idiot or someone who needed to be as far away as possible as soon as possible. Coincidence? Gunn reckoned not and heaved himself, with his left arm, up the companionway to the fly-bridge.

He disengaged the autopilot and pulled the chart closer before attempting to chase the other boat. The moment the other boat had emerged from Maseline harbour and had seen the Princess and the SAR helicopter, it had turned sharply to port and headed north. 'Where?' Gunn asked himself, feeling slightly light-headed from the loss of blood. North was Alderney some 15 miles away which seemed an unlikely destination. Where had the boat come from? Could it have been the boat he had spotted earlier following the proscribed route from St Peter Port to Maseline Harbour? As Gunn considered these possibilities, an idea was taking shape and still studying the chart, he once again pushed the throttles to maximum speed and the Princess surged ahead in a starboard turn to the south.

The boat, which had followed them out from St Peter Port had been a white one like the one which had exited at great speed from Maseline, but then as most motorboats were white, that line of deduction was unlikely to be much use. Then again, Dan Treuniert had been handing over a white Princess 500 as he and Claudine had taken out their Princess. Coincidence again? Possibly, Gunn answered his own thoughts. Whilst there was no doubt about the sniper's marksmanship - and his blood-sodden T-shirt and slacks bore witness to that - what was his standard of seamanship and knowledge of these islands which were surrounded by some of the most treacherous waters in the world? Gunn ceased the conjecture and decided; the boat was the Princess 500 and it would be heading back for St Peter Port. There had been time for that boat to berth in Maseline Harbour and for the sniper to reach a vantage point by the ruin above Derrible Bay from which he could shoot down at their boat below. Even if the boat had nothing to do with the sniper, he had to get back to St Peter Port to be with Claudine and before he lost consciousness.

Gunn focused with difficulty at the figures on his watch; nearly dead low water and Springs at that. There was no difference in speed between the Princess 500 and the 470; the 500 had the bigger TAMD 122 diesels but also had another two or three feet of hull and half a ton more of engines to push through the water. Without any thought of the risk, he took the Princess inside Les Vingt Clos and the rocks off the tip of L'Etac de Sark and swung the wheel to starboard, bringing the boat onto a north-westerly course towards the islands of Jethou and Herm. Sure enough, around the northern tip of Sark's Bec du Nez appeared the other Princess on a course due west for St Peter Port. Gunn put the boat into autopilot and pulled the chart towards him, holding it tightly against the slipstream as the motorboat's log registered 33 knots. In the top right corner of the chart was the graphic display of the tidal streams. He checked his watch again; at Springs, nearly four knots of north-going tide. That meant four knots under his keel as a plus and four knots on the port beam of the Princess 500 pushing it towards the treacherous waters to the south of Jethou Island and ship's graveyard around the Goubinière Rock.

There was no question of doing any calculations to see if he would be able to achieve his plan. Whether it worked or not largely depended the level of knowledge of navigation and boat handling of the person at the wheel of the other boat and whether he knew the local waters. The two boats were on a slant collision course with an intercept speed of some fifty plus knots. Gunn fought off a surge of dizziness and lassitude brought on by his loss of blood and cursed as he fought to concentrate on what he was doing. With the boat still in autopilot, he forced himself to go back down to the saloon. Every jar as the Princess bounced over the low swell sent needles of pain into his right side. From the plastic container in the saloon, he removed all the flares and took them back to the fly-bridge. These would be his only weapon if one was needed. He looked at the closing gap between the two boats. No, he'd misjudged it. There must have been less tidal stream then he had thought. Gunn swore loudly into the eye-watering slip-stream. If he held his course for much longer, he'd be dashed to smithereens on either Grosse Ferri or the rock beyond it, La Platte.

Gunn eased the wheel a shade to port, which brought his Princess on a course which would shave the west side of Grosse Ferri where the chart indicated 5 metres of water at chart datum. North of Grosse Ferri was a deep, but very narrow east/west channel which twisted and turned through rocks and submerged wrecks to the south of La Platte. Four hundred yards apart....200....100, a bullet splintered the plexiglass windscreen of the fly-bridge. The other boat couldn't make the southern side of Grosse Ferri, it was committed to the narrow, twisting channel to the north of it and south of La Platte. Fifty yards, and then the two boats were momentarily hidden from each other as they passed either side of Grosse Ferri.

La Platte had been given its name because it was flat - like a dish. Gunn swung the wheel over to port to prevent his boat riding straight up onto this 'dish'. The rocks of Blanche and Aiguillons to the west of La Platte hurtled past his starboard side, almost within touching distance, but no other boat. Then he saw the Princess 500 - airborne - before crashing, bow up/stern down, into the saw-toothed rocks of Aiguillons, where it was shredded and then engulfed in flames. Gunn pulled the throttles back to stops in the centre and turned his boat as the air was filled with another deafening sound. He looked up as the SAR helicopter banked steeply over the boat. The deck felt slightly spongy beneath his feet and he gripped the wheel hard to stop himself losing consciousness. Two men were hanging at the end of the winch rope as it was lowered towards the fly bridge.

He presumed that the person driving the Princess 500 had suddenly realised, but too late, the trap into which he'd been forced and turned to starboard for the flat rock of La Platte rather than port and into the solid rock face of Grosse Ferri. La Platte had acted like a water-ski ramp, hurling the Princess 500 into the air after ripping open its hull from stem to stern. One of the men from the helicopter was now down on the bridge and carefully strapped Gunn into the stretcher. The light-headedness had returned and he was trying to insist that he take the boat back. One man stayed on the boat while the other held Gunn as the two of them were winched up into the helicopter. He was just aware of the winch operator lifting him into the helicopter and then he lost consciousness.

*

Caramansa followed the spotlight down from his throne stool to the lectern on the podium. He climbed the two steps up to the lectern and switched on the microphones.

'Loyal men and women of the government in exile of UROWAS; it is with much excitement and pleasure that I speak to you at this 21st meeting of our assembly. I bring good news to all of you. The illegitimate governments of West Africa will shortly be overthrown and our glorious revolution will unite our oppressed people into the most powerful nation in Africa.' Caramansa's prepared speech continued for forty-three minutes and the cheers grew louder as the promises of what the future held for UROWAS grew more and more outrageous. At the conclusion of the speech, Caramansa received the customary standing ovation, which lasted for five minutes. Attendance at the monthly assembly was mandatory and failure to show enthusiastic support for everything said by Caramansa or the delegates of the security council guaranteed the loss of the monthly pay check.

Video cameras monitored the members of every nation of the assembly and the delegates would study the recording of the meeting in the minutest detail before issuing the pay check. On completion of Caramansa's speech, all the assembly members left the auditorium and reconvened in the banqueting hall where food and alcohol flowed in abundance. Once the members were clear of the room they were followed by the guards who locked all the doors and stood guard over them. When the captain of the guards was satisfied that the Security Council had complete privacy he pressed a button by his station at the main entrance to the hall and a green light lit up on the lectern.

Caramansa left the lectern and descended the steps in the central aisle to the large round table in front of the Security Council stools. As he took his seat at the table the delegates followed suit until only one seat was left on Caramansa's right which was taken by the bare-breasted Letitia. No one was called by their real name; Charles Mensah was Caramansa and Letitia was Kisi - the traditional Akan name for a girl child born on Sunday. Seated around the table from Caramansa's left were Monday's children, Kojo (Senegal) and Kwajo (Mali), Tuesday's children, Kwabena (The Gambia) and Kobina (Guinea Bissau), Wednesday's children, Kwaku (Guinea) and Kuuku (Sierra Leone), Thursday's children, Yaw (Liberia) and Ekow (Cote d'Ivoire), Friday's children, Kofi (Ghana) and Fiifi (Togo) and Saturday's children, Kwame (Benin), Kwamena (Nigeria) and Ato (Burkina Faso). Now the real business of the monthly meeting began.

'We will start with a statement by Delegate Kisi,' Caramansa announced.

'Today, Congress directed the Treasury to conduct an investigation into ICB. That investigation, so our informant in Congress has told us, will start in three weeks' time. Unless new funding is found for ICB, that investigation will find that ICB is bankrupt and will also discover the source of our funding over the last two years. Everyone round this table will go to prison for anything between 15 years and life, depending on the charges against us and the skill of our lawyers. However, lawyers need to be paid and we don't even have the money for that. We might all flee from the USA, but remember please fellow delegates,' she added as several heads nodded at the suggestion of flight, 'that we all possess illegal passports and are already on all the undesirable alien lists of Africa, every country in the developed world and most of those in the undeveloped one.' Those that had nodded at the thought of fleeing from the USA looked glumly at the table in front of them. It seemed that the sweet life of the past two years and promises of great riches in the utopia of UROWAS was only a dream that was not to be realised. 'That,' continued Kisi, 'is the situation. Now our Supreme Chief will tell you how we will restore our previous fortunes and the funding for our freedom struggle.'

'We need money, fellow delegates; buckets and buckets of it and we need it within two weeks and three at the outside. Unless any of you have developed a fool-proof way of working the gambling machines of this city, there is only one way to get the millions of dollars which we require. Steal it. At the end of this meeting, each of you will be issued with a casette on which is recorded the instructions for your task. These tasks vary from bank robberies, through kidnap and extortion to the removal of Burma's entire year's production of heroine and cocaine. Kofi', and the Ghanaian delegate immediately got to his feet, 'in your country the operation will be run by our colleague, Kisi, and you will have two tasks: your first one is to remove the 53 gold bars from the Bank of Ghana which were found in the sealed cell at the old fort in Kumasi in 1965. These gold bars contain a minimum of 500 ounces each of .999 fine gold and at its current value of $440.50 an ounce are worth 11½ million US dollars. Our second task is to kidnap the grandson of the president of Canadian Sikafuturu Mining Company from his home in Edmonton, Alberta and the son of the general manager of the company in Ghana. Sikafuturu owns the single richest gold mine in the world at Sawaba in our Ashanti Region of Ghana. The ransom for the safe return of those children is one hundred million US dollars.'

'That is an example of your tasks, fellow delegates, and the detailed instructions are on your tapes. Please pick up the tape, which is in the plastic cassette on the table in front of you. Take it to your delegation room now, summon your ten members and brief them. You will leave the tape and the case in your delegation room. It is not to leave this building and is security coded to show up on the beam through which you all pass on leaving our national assembly. It will show up wherever you try and hide it. Failure to obey this instruction will be punished by death for the culprit. Failure to achieve your task will receive the same punishment. You were all aware of the price of membership and all of you have taken your monthly salary for two and a quarter years. The sweet life is over; now we must earn our place in history and stand beside the freedom fighters of UROWAS. The meeting is closed.' Not a word was said as the thirteen delegates left the auditorium.

When all of them were clear of the room, Charles Mensah turned to Letitia. 'Phase 1 of your second task is complete. Both children have been kidnapped and we will now let the parents' anxiety climb to desperation level before they are contacted with the ransom note. Let Kofi do the gold job at the main branch of the Bank of Ghana in Accra. I want you to handle the Sikafuturu Gold Mine. It will need very careful handling as it seems that two of our Ivorian brothers were unable to keep their mouths shut and some information has leaked to the British SIS agent. Both brothers and the agent have been eliminated, but we don't know if the agent managed to get a report back to London. The agent and our brothers died after some rather clumsy interrogation. Go on; you'd better be on your way as your flight to London leaves in less than an hour.' She turned to leave and he remarked, 'don't forget to put on some clothes,' but she gave no indication of having heard the advice as she left the auditorium.

*

The red laterite earth of Sub-Sahara Africa was like concrete in the dry season and tomato soup in the wet. In most of the countries, the laterite roads were merely graded at irregular intervals and left to the discretion of those who needed to use them at any other time than the dry season. Elsewhere, particularly in cities and towns, the practice was to lay tarmac straight onto the laterite; this was quick and gave the impression of civilisation until the first rains arrived and then great chunks of tarmac were washed away leaving the sealed roads 100% worse than the laterite ones, with really treacherous pot holes which could - and did - snap axles as easily as Italian bread sticks.

Penny Briars was negotiating just such a road in the expatriate area of Accra by the airport, in the Briars' battered old short wheel base Nissan Patrol. Beside her sat her daughter, Emma, and they were making their way slowly along Sankara Road to the McLean's house. It was early April and the end of the dry season so the laterite which had been squeezed like toothpaste through the fractured tarmac in the last rains had set like concrete into immovable obstacles, around and over which the large, wide profile tyres of the Nissan bounced and graunched.

Once upon a time, the Nissan had looked quite respectable - that would have been the day that its previous owner, the out-going Lt Colonel on the British Military Team had sold it to his successor, John Briars. John was a large officer - in every way. His battered frame bore many similarities to that of his car; broken nose, cauliflower ear and a deceptive cast in one eye gave ample proof of twenty years dedicated to a small oval ball. As a sportsman on the rugger field he had played for the army, the combined services and his country and on the cricket pitch he had played for his county. As a soldier he had been decorated twice for bravery. He had played as a prop-forward and looked like and was built like a brick shit-house. He possessed a gorgeous sense of humour, was kind and gentle and in a large and hairless head kept a needle sharp brain for figures which could calculate the odds at the races or the blackjack tables in milli-seconds. John Briars drove his car as he had played rugger, bouncing off the opposition, until both driver and machine looked much alike.

'Oh, buggeration!' The Nissan had just leapt over a mini tank obstacle and the jolt back onto the road had shaken off the fabric head-lining of the car roof which had fallen over Penny's head, completely blinding her. She pushed it up with one hand and like

60

that, turned into Number 24, Sankara Road, the home of the McLeans. Like many such marriages, Penny Briars was almost the exact opposite of her husband in every possible way except for her sense of humour and kindness. Small, neat, tidy and calm were descriptive adjectives which all of their friends in Accra would have used, but she possessed kindness in abundance which was why everything had been put aside that morning to go and comfort Mary McLean. John had taken a day off work to take Penny, Emma and Richard to the Shai Hills game reserve on the Akosombo road, but that plan had been instantly discarded on receipt of Mary's phone call.

Mary rushed out of the house as she saw the battered Nissan turn through the gates and as soon as Penny had extracted herself from the driver's seat and the fabric off the car roof, the two women embraced. 'Thanks so much for coming, Penny. I'm sorry to be in such a state and it's sure to be me making a mountain of a molehill. As soon as I put the phone down, I remembered that you told us last night when we were having drinks at the Stone's that you were all off to Shai Hills game reserve. I promise I'll be OK and you mustn't ruin your day.'

'Don't be silly; we can go to Shai Hills any day. It's only an hour up the road and anyway it'll be very hot and that red laterite dust gets everywhere, so I'm delighted with an excuse not to go. Sorry, that sounds awful, but I'm sure John will find Graham and we'll get a call any minute.....damn, I've left the radio in the car. Emma!'

'Yes, Mum', from right behind her.

'Oh! I didn't see you there Em, could you.....'

'Yea, sure; shall I bring it into the house.'

'Yes please.'

'Come in and have some coffee while we wait to hear from your John. I haven't phoned Stuart yet as he gets so tetchy if I bother him when he's got an important meeting and today's meeting in Kumasi is particularly important I've been told.'

There was a burst of static and then a heavy carrier signal from Penny's radio, which had been dropped into an embroidered sling bag. Penny leapt from her armchair in the McLean's drawing room, rummaged in her bag until she found the Japanese Cleartone radio and then hurried from the room to the drive outside. Although the High Commission radio system worked through repeaters which boosted the signal and range of the radios, they were highly directional and did not function very well inside buildings - particularly those in the expatriate area which were built with an excess of reinforced concrete. Mary and the two girls followed

Penny, to her dismay, as she was convinced something awful would be said over the radio about Graham and Mary and the girls would hear it.

More static and then perfectly clearly, 'Hello B-MAT 2 Alpha this is B-MAT 2, over,' the number designated the husband's radio and his appointment and the 'Alpha' his wife's radio. Penny usually became flustered when called on the radio and this morning she had an audience and so was even more so.

'B-MAT 2 Alpha, send over.' Nothing in response.

'Are you pressing the transmit switch, Mum?' came the helpful suggestion from Emma.

'Of course I am!' and Penny's cheeks reddened with frustration. 'Oh damn, no I'm not, I'm pressing the battery test switch. Sorry folks, let's try again. B-MAT 2 Alpha send, over.'

'B-MAT 2 Alpha, this B-MAT 2, so you've found the right button at last,' Penny's face went puce with anger and if she could have flown along the radio waves and punched her husband's smug, grinning face she would have done so. Emma smiled, but Mary and Morwena were too overwrought to notice the badinage.

'Where are you? over.'

Penny concentrated hard and made sure her thumb was on the transmit switch; 'B-MAT 2, this B-MAT 2 Alpha, at the McLean's house, over.'

'B-MAT 2 Alpha, this is B-MAT 2, roger; be with you in five , out.' Penny's mouth opened as if to say something and then closed.

'Five what?' Mary asked.

'That means he'll be here in five minutes, Mrs McLean,' Emma explained. Dad'll never say anything on the radio that's personal. He usually gets hold of people on the radio and then asks them to ring him. As he can't get at a telephone, he's coming here, probably with Graham.'

'Thank you Emma; tell me something, if your father uses the radio to get hold of people and then tells them to ring him, why doesn't he use the telephone in the first instance?'

'Cos he's a soldier, Mrs McLean.'

'Ah, I see,' but Mary McLean clearly didn't and when she shot an inquisitive glance at Penny, the slight shrug of shoulders indicated similar bewilderment. The subject was to remain a mystery because at that moment the Landrover appeared at the gates and came into the gravelled driveway. John Briars and his son, Richard jumped out, but no sign of Graham. Penny was watching her husband's face and instantly picked up the signal from his eyes to go to Mary. She put her arms round her friend who was already weeping. John Briars went up to Mary and put his arm on her shoulders.

'Mary, my dear, we can't find Graham at the moment, but I promise we are doing everything we possibly can to put that right. The police are combing the area of the beach where we found his fishing rod and Miles Stockwell has managed to get the CO of 5 Battalion to get all his soldiers to join in the search. I think we'd better get in touch with Stuart. Come on, let's go into the house.' John Briars ushered the sad little group into the house and then picked up the phone, dialled Stuart's office number in Kumasi and left a message with his secretary. He assured Mary that Stuart would be on his way to Accra by helicopter as soon as the message was delivered. Morwena was comforting her mother and John suggested that Penny arrange for some tea to be made. Penny went to the kitchen and asked the cook to produce tea; before she could return to the drawing room, her husband joined her. He explained what he and Richard had found on the beach. 'It seems there's something odd going on,' he continued,

'What do you mean? Isn't Graham's disappearance odd enough?'

'That's just it; yes it is and when Miles arrived at the beach with the CO of 5 Battalion, he told me that Tony Bristow's disappeared as well.'

'That's no loss; serves him right for cheating on Monica. Is.....wasn't he one of those secret thingummies we're not supposed to know about, but everybody does?'

'Yes he is...or was, as you rightly used the past tense.'

'What happened?'

'There was the usual crowd at the BHC cottage at Ada yesterday and he went fishing by himself and vanished.'

'What, no sign of anything?'

'Well, they found the canoe; you know, it's the one the children muck about in when we get the use of the cottage.'

'Where was it?'

'Right out in the big waves over the bar and that was odd too because he had set off up-river to do his fishing.'

'Oh dear, I hope this isn't another series of disasters that come in threes like the car accidents last year.' A forlorn hope, as they would all discover within the next 24 hours.

CHAPTER 4

'Morning John; mind if I help myself to some of your grapes? It's high time you were back in the office. We've got a mountain of work for you.'

Where the hell was he? Gunn could hear this voice talking to him, but nothing seemed to make sense. What office? He didn't have an office. He was one of BID's field operat.... the mist began to clear a little and the face of Simon Peters, the AD for SE Asia started to come into focus. He'd been lifted into a helicopter.....from a boat, a princess.....damn, why wouldn't the mist clear? A princess? what had a princess got to do with anything.....Claudine, and then the room and its occupants came into sharper focus. Simon Peters on the left of his bed... yes bed, and Gunn tried to sit up, but Simon restrained him. Bloody hell! who was this on his right? It was the Director, Sir Jeremy Hammond. He must be in a bad way if the Director was at his hospital bedside. He felt as though he had a mouth full of cotton wool and tried to spit it out. Nothing happened, but it felt better. 'Wher....' God was that croak his voice? Better try again, 'where's Cla....' a little better, but still the voice of an old man and he was sure it wasn't his.

'She's fine.' Who said that? and then someone bent towards him and he felt the slightest of pricks in his left arm. A pause and then the mist started to clear rapidly and the room and faces came into sharp focus.

'Where's Claudine?' now that was his own voice.

'She's in the next room to you, and she's fine, thanks to you and the amazing strength of the human skull,' it was the Director talking and Gunn turned his head to the right and forced himself to concentrate.

'Promise....'

'Yes I promise, stop me if I'm making you tired. The surgeon says we can have a few more minutes with you. The sniper's bullet should have killed Claudine, but she must have a skull like a rhino as it was deflected and travelled round the side of the cranium and then exited. She lost quite a bit of blood, but all she's suffering from is a little mild concussion. You're the one we're worried about; you lost over four pints of blood. How're you feeling?

64

'Bit groggy, Sir, but better by the second to hear about Claudine. Where is this hospital?'

'It's our own clinic at Maidenhead. They did a superb job on you and Claudine in the intensive care unit at St Mary's Hospital on Guernsey and then we flew you both direct to our clinic. The......' but the surgeon lent forward and put a hand on the Director's shoulder. 'Let you get some sleep.'

'Thanks Sir. I .....' but he was already asleep.

The next morning, Gunn awoke refreshed and with a clear head. The conversation of the previous day was still a bit hazy, but the part about Claudine wasn't. The door opened and one of the many gorgeous nurses at the Maidenhead clinic came in. It was rumoured that they were chosen for their looks by the Director because he had a theory about pretty girls speeding up the male recovery time. Probably all rumour, but who then chose the male nurses for the female patients? 'Ah, the sleeping beauty's awake; feel like breakfast, John?'

'Yes I do, please, and who are you?'

'Melissa; I came on duty at eight and I'm off at four and yes, I'd love to have dinner when you're stronger.'

'Have I asked you that while I've been here?'

'Oh, many times, but so do all the others. Now let me help you sit up.'

'Yes please.'

'Behave, or I'll get your girl friend to help me. What an intelligent woman like that sees in a great...ouch! That was silly of me to get within reach of your hands.' The door opened and a trolley with a breakfast which would have done credit to any ten star hotel was wheeled in. 'Keep your distance, Tracy, he's all hands this morning and recovering far too quickly.'

'Goody, are you going to leave him to me...'

'Wait a minute...can I join in this conversation. I mean...'

'No you can't,' as Melissa moved efficiently around the room doing things which nurses do in hospital rooms, managing to make even the unpleasant task of delivering a urine bottle match the panache of the head wine waiter at the Dorchester and then she approached Gunn. 'Now keep your hands to yourself and stuff that under your tongue and cook it for a minute,' and the thermometer was placed in his mouth and his lips firmly closed by Melissa's slender and slightly scented fingers. There was no doubt about it, Gunn thought, there was certainly something in this bit about surrounding patients with pretty and provocative nurses.

Tracy had placed a tray on the table which she swung over his bed at the same time succeeding in showing Gunn that she was wearing very little under the crisp and tight fitting uniform other than a bra and whatever was holding up the sheer black stockings which were guaranteed to raise any male blood pressure. She was then chivvied out of the room by Melissa who removed the thermometer. 'You're fine.'

'Is that a medically qualified statement about the state of my health or your opinion of me?'

'Hark at the conceit of it; eat your breakfast before I recommend an enema every hour on the hour,' and with that Parthian shot, Melissa left Gunn to his breakfast.

'Hello John.' Gunn hadn't even heard the door open. Claudine stood just inside the door and he was quick enough to see the painted nails of Melissa's hand quietly close the door behind her. Claudine had the looks and body that made even a sack draped over her look rather better than a Versace frock. Even the bandage round her head looked as though it had been styled to make the best of the hairstyle after the surgeons had had to remove some of the hair to suture the wound in her skull. Indeed, all of this had happened and Melissa had spent quite half-an-hour preparing Claudine for her visit to Gunn.

'You are beautiful; can I kiss you?'

'What the hell do you think I'm here for, you great moo!' and so he did and then she said very quietly, 'thanks; I'm told I owe my life to you. I'm not sure how you thank a person for that,' and she held tightly to his hands as though trying to impart some form of healing current into his body to repay the favour.

'You've done it already by not dying on me. Not sure I could've coped with that. Now come on, lets dry away those tears and you can tell me how long I've been here and how much you remember. I'll fill you in on what I remember and with a bit of luck someone like Simon will fill in the gaps.'

'He's done that already; I'll tell you what happened after you were picked up by the chopper and then you can tell me what happened after you removed those oysters.'

'That sounds fair; off you go then.'

'This is your second day here and the third since our motorboat trip to Sark. There were two men on the Princess 500 which was the one we saw Dan handing over on the jetty in the North Marina. The man driving the boat was an insignificant little creep with a record a mile long who'd been hired by Yacoub - the other man.'

'Wher...'

'Shhh, listen; your turn next.'

'Sorry, go on.'

'Yacoub was the brother of Idrissu, Hassan's security chief on Al Samak Island. Idrissu was beheaded by Hassan after his failure to prevent my escape from the house which led to my discovery of the hangar where I found those aircraft. The gruesome irony was that he met with the same death as his brother. His head was severed from his body by the broken windscreen on the Princess' fly-bridge when the boat was smashed to pieces on the Aiguillons rocks. They found the headless body, badly burned, in the remnants of the boat with the body of the other man. His head was found nearly a hundred yards away in the Blanche rocks. They also recovered the rifle; it was a British Army issue Lee Enfield .303 sniper's rifle with a times six Leupold sight.'

'That's about it, except to say from Dan - who's been to see you incidentally - get better soon and please don't ever charter another of his boats! The police told Simon that Yacoub had followed me to Guernsey and witnesses who were shown a photofit of the man had seen him up on the cliffs at St Martin and above the harbour.' Gunn then explained what had happened after the removal of the bikini until he'd lost consciousness.

'Now,' Gunn continued, 'can you tell me what's wrong with me as no one else will.'

'You mean apart from your inordinate conceit and infuriating confidence.'

'You're very evidently cured; yes.'

'The steel-nosed .303 bullet went clean through you without damaging any of your innards, but it scored one of your ribs which the surgeon said must have been painful. You lost pints of blood, which I hope hasn't drained your sexual libido completely. Apart from that, a blood change and a thorough servicing, there's not much that a hot woman can't put right. No! you'll have to wait or you'll burst your stitches,' and Claudine moved out of reach further along the bed.

'Has Jean been to see you?'

'Yes, and you, although you were still under the effect of sedatives. He had a room here for two nights, but once he realised that I was out of danger, he went back to his boat. The charter company at Guernsey airport sent a helicopter out to his boat which dropped him off at St Mary's Hospital. Dan arranged that and the company said that he didn't have to pay. Your surgeon has said that we can both leave the clinic today and BID has offered us one of their Gazelle choppers to take us to Guernsey. The Director wants you

67

back at Kingsroad House on Monday where you are to see Mike Parker, the Assistant Director for Sub-Sahara Africa.'

'Wonder what that's about; apart from a holiday in Kenya, my knowledge of that continent is next to nil. What about you?'

'The doctors say that you'll be as right as rain after they remove your stitches next week. Boringly, I've got to be kept under observation for the next month, so I've offered to stand in for Louise, as Simon's PA, so that she can take some leave. If you're happy to spend the weekend at our cottage, I'll come back with you on Sunday.'

'Yes I would and on Sunday night you stay at my house in Elm Park Lane where Mrs Charlesworth will cluck around you like a mother hen. Please stay as long as you want.'

'Thanks, that's great and I'll take you up on Sunday night, but I want to get back to my little house in Richmond as I've still got masses of work to do there and I've already put the builders off twice.'

'That was a good buy; that little house in Friars Lane overlooking the river.'

'The couple who owned it was desperate to sell as he'd lost his job in a merchant bank and the only income was hers as a teacher. I felt awful when my solicitor haggled over the price, but I suppose that's the way it goes. You're right, it was a bargain.' Claudine looked at her watch. 'Come on, we'd better get some clothes on as the chopper will be here in half-an-hour. I believe it lands on the roof and there's a lift access straight down to the operating theatre for emergency stretcher cases.'

'Wouldn't surprise me,' Gunn said, easing himself gingerly out of bed. 'Sounds just like the Director's usual efficiency ....ouch!'

'You alright? Can I.....'

'Thanks, but I must do this. If 'they' say I'm fit to do this then I'm sure 'they' are right. Ah, that's better,' he had both feet on the floor and stood up. The door opened and Melissa appeared. 'Better and better, have you come to dress me?'

'No I haven't; lot of fuss about nothing, as usual from a man. Most women have more stitches than you've had every time they have a baby. Your clothes are in the cupboard and the helicopter will be here in twenty minutes. We have a patient coming in from Sarajevo with far worse injuries than you, John Gunn, and your room is needed. So look sharp while I change the sheets.' Claudine had gone as soon as the nurse entered.

'Don't I get any privacy.....'

'No, you silly man; as usual you're leaving far too soon and it's my job to make sure you don't die on government property.' Gunn realised that the efficient Melissa was very close to tears and the banter was a cover for her anxiety. 'Come on, I'll help you with that,' and so she helped him on with his clothes. When he was ready and turned to say goodbye, she put her arms round him taking great care to avoid the wounds on his right side and burst into tears, all pretence of the hardened professional nurse gone. Gunn bent and kissed her and then slipped out of the room closing the door behind him. Claudine's door was open and as soon as she saw him, left her room and the two of them went to the lift and up to the helipad on the roof of the clinic.

Gunn and Claudine returned to London on the Sunday night and on Monday morning he reported to Mike Parker's office on the eleventh floor of Kingsroad House. The eleventh floor was shared by all the Assistant Directors and their PA's, together with the Controllers and a spare office if the current field operative allocated to that AD needed to do any paper work. Right at the top of the building was a mini heliport on the roof, then Cyphers and Communications on the 14th floor, no 13th floor, Director and Deputy Director with all the conference and briefing rooms on the 12th floor and the main access to the building on the 10th floor via the adjacent multi-storey car park. The 10th floor was all Administration and Finance while below that on the 9th, 8th, 7th and 6th floors was BID's counter-espionage department which had replaced MI5.

Ground floor to the 5th floor was the Express Delivery Service, which possessed its own lift shafts. Kingsroad House had many unique aspects to its design and construction. So that the inquisitive client visiting EDS wouldn't speculate why the numbers in the lift which he used only went to 5 in a 14 storey building, they also went to 14. If the client's inquisitiveness persisted and he pressed button 14, he would end up on that floor and would find the offices shown on the panel beside the buttons. Not only was Kingsroad House divided horizontally to separate BID and EDS, but also vertically - like a sandwich - leaving a thin layer of a corridor and one room on the north side of the building for EDS and two corridors and four room-widths on the south side of the building for BID.

There were three basement floors, which contained BID's medical centre, extensive transport department, stores, armoury and shooting range. The third level of the basement also gave access to the four exit tunnels which were used to leave the building. Anyone who was tailed to Kingsroad House could guarantee to shed that tail; the majority of these tails were easily identifiable because of the length of time which they spent hanging around outside the building.

'Hello John, I'm Cilla - Mike's PA - he's expecting you. How are you?' was how Mike Parker's PA, Cilla, welcomed Gunn into the Directorate for Sub-Sahara Africa.

'Fine and improving daily, thanks Cilla.'

'Coffee?

'Please; white, no sugar.'

'Right, I'll take you straight in to Mike's office. Your controller, Christine Dupré, is with him and will remain for your briefing,' Cilla informed Gunn as she knocked on and then opened the door to the AD's office. A woman controller, Gunn thought, as the door opened. Well, the RAF now had women as combat fast-jet pilots, the Army had employed women in combat jobs since the Second World War when they performed extremely effectively and heroically as crews on anti-aircraft guns and the Navy had allowed women into its ships with some reasonably predictable disasters and bad PR. So why not BID?

'Why not indeed,' Gunn muttered to himself as he spotted the one woman in the AD's room whom he assumed had to be Christine Dupré.

'Mike, this is John Gunn,' and Cilla left the office closing the door behind her. All the AD offices were identical; the only variation was where the occupant positioned the desk, armchairs, coffee table and other incidental furniture. Gunn reckoned that a psychiatrist would have a field day analysing that subject.

'How do you do, John; we haven't met before, but I'm well briefed by Simon,' as he shook hands with Gunn. 'Have you met Christine before?'

'No, can't say I have.'

'Right, Christine Dupré, John Gunn,' and Gunn took the hand which was offered by the fashionably dressed Christine seated in the armchair on his left. Mike indicated the armchair beside Christine, into which Gunn lowered himself gently - noted by the other two - and Mike Parker sat facing both of them. 'Just a very brief introduction, I think, would help and then I'll get on with the business in hand. Christine is British and was married to a French diplomat, Jean-Louis Dupré. She and her husband spent twelve years in the Francophone countries of Cote d'Ivoire, Togo, Benin and Mali before Jean-Louis was murdered in Abidjan by five men who broke into their house. Having murdered her husband, the men attempted to rape Christine; she shot four of them dead and using the fifth man's own panga, beheaded him. Needless to say, perhaps,

Christine speaks fluent French and a selection of dialects of the Akan language including Gha, Eve and Twi - sorry John,' as Mike realised Gunn was about to interrupt; 'three of the main tribes of Ghana. She has also travelled extensively into every country of West Africa. Christine was on her first overseas posting with the SIS when she met her husband.'

'For you Christine, John was brought up in Hong Kong, but went to school and university in England. He speaks Mandarin, Cantonese, French and German. He has a BSc in civil engineering, served with the Royal Artillery in their Commando and Parachute Regiments and on active service in the Balkans. He has passed the SAS selection test and would have served with 22 SAS if he hadn't been recruited by BID. His particular area of experience is SE Asia and, to a lesser degree, the Middle East but he has no experience of West Africa. It is our Director's decision to combine your wealth of knowledge of the area and John's effectiveness as a field operative to produce a solution to our current problem.'

What was it, Gunn asked himself, as Mike Parker was telling Christine about his background, that made French women or those who were French by adoption, so good at putting on clothes; and equally as good at taking them off! The thought made him smile and he realised that Mike Parker was still talking and he was being closely studied by Christine. She had long, very dark hair, which was done in a chignon on the back of her head and her small features and slimness bore a strong resemblance to those of the late Audrey Hepburn. The door opened and Cilla appeared with a tray of cups. Once the coffee had been distributed, Mike Parker turned his chair towards Gunn.

'It won't come as any surprise if I tell you, that the whole of Africa is a mess, from west to east and north to south - particularly south. What chance has a continent got with a lunatic like Gadaffi in the north, the madness of Sam Doe and Charles Taylor in the west, the depraved lunacy of Mugabe in the south and the bloodthirsty warlords of Somalia, Eritrea and the Sudan in the east. The Mercator projection of the world, which we're all used to, is very deceptive because the illustration it gives of land masses close to the poles is so misleading. Greenland looks to be larger than India when in fact it is a quarter its size and North America appears to be larger than Africa when in reality it is only a shade over half its size. A much more accurate portrayal of relative landmass is shown on the maps designed by the German historian, Arno Peters. Africa is the largest single inhabitable landmass in the world and it is also the biggest, bloody mess - and that adjective is used correctly, not as an expletive!

Hundreds of thousands of Africans are dying needlessly every single day.'

'Of its 52 nations, about 40 are involved in or are about to be involved in civil war, military coups, terrorism of one form or another or some other variety of fanatical tribal or religious genocide. The sufferers are the innocent, the women and the children; the benefitters are the corrupt politicians and exploiting industrialists from both inside Africa and the industrialised world of the north and ruthless militarists seeking nothing but to augment their own wealth and power.'

'Of the remaining 12 nations, nearly all but one are teetering on starvation, the unstoppable spread of Aids or some other endemic disease. That one nation is Ghana - the old Gold Coast. The only country to progress, albeit with a few slips on the way, from independence to multi-party democracy via fair elections and relatively little bloodshed; the one shining hope of Africa. Now, even that country is threatened and that is the reason for this briefing.' Cilla appeared at this point and removed their cups. 'Any more coffee?' but both Gunn and Christine Dupré declined.

'Not much more from me now, before you hear what we want you to do,' Mike continued. 'Since Charles Taylor's failed attempt to usurp the Presidency from that crackpot, ex-Sergeant Sam Doe, in Liberia in 1991, there have been a whole series of apparently motiveless conflicts - motiveless even for Africa where facile tribal quarrels can be the root cause of genocide. Sierra Leone, Burkina Faso, Mali, Togo, Benin and Nigeria have all erupted with coups or attempted coups. The breakdown of law and order in Cote d'Ivoire and reports of subversion in Guinea Bissau, Guinea and Senegal all seem to be orchestrated, but from where? Even the tiny nation of The Gambia, which relies on tourism as its main source of foreign currency, has reported an influx of racketeers and a phenomenal escalation of street muggings which is driving away the source of the nation's main income and threatening the stability of its government.'

'Throughout all of this, Ghana has remained serenely stable and a safe place for tourists and commercial investment. The country has achieved a steady rate of growth in its economy, firm financial control of its budget and thoroughly commendable internal investment to improve the standard of living of its people. A week ago, we received a report from the SIS man at the High Commission in Accra. He claimed to have stumbled on some information from one of his sources that said that all of this unrest in West Africa was being orchestrated by some extra-continental form of mafiosa and the name 'Caramansa' had surfaced. The SIS man was Tony Bristow......'

'Past tense?' Gunn interjected.

'Yes; missing believed dead, but more of that in a moment.'

'Sorry to interrupt.'

'No, you were quite right to. Please stop me at any time. I've become absorbed in my area of the world and it's very easy to forget that others know less about it than I do and far more than me about other parts of the world. We were just about to position our BID, in-country agent in Ghana to replace Tony Bristow when he disappeared. For some time now he's been having a very public and sordid affair with the Korean wife of a second secretary at the High Commission. For most of the time he's been in the appointment, his CX reports have been found to be completely useless and we get more accurate information from buying copies of the Accra Times and Daily Graphic.'

'The new BID in-country agent is Dina Gbedemah - she was born on a Saturday so her Akan name is Ama and her surname is spelt exactly as it sounds except for the first letter, 'G', which is silent - you will meet her in the first floor Italian restaurant of the Park Lane Hyatt for lunch. Like all our in-country agents, she has never been to Kingsroad House and all her information is routed through Vauxhall. We have set Dina up with a dressmaking business - she is a very talented designer - with the main branch in Accra, which also makes men's clothes, and subsidiary branches in Kumasi, Takoradi, Tema, Sunyani in the west and Tamale in the north. Don't worry about these names, you'll pick them up later on from the written 'Instant Guide to Ghana' which Christine has prepared for you.'

'I regret to say that the only thing which made us take this last report of Bristow's seriously was the fact that he disappeared 24 hours after sending it to Century House at Vauxhall, from where it found its way to us. We got the report last Saturday week and he disappeared the next day while fishing in the Volta Estuary. We still have no proof whether he was gobbled up by a barracuda, murdered or is still alive and being kept locked up somewhere. That is your first task; find him or find out what happened to him. Your second task is to find out if there is any veracity in his CX report. I've been told by the Director that you are not to get involved in any rough-housing as you are in no physical condition for that. I gather that you were used as a target for some sniping practice less than a week ago and I'm amazed to see you looking so fit. I've said enough; probably banged on far too much. Your turn now; anything you want to ask me?'

'Not at the moment, Mike. I'd like to read and absorb Christine's brief first. Do you mind if I stand for a bit? Forgive the cliché, but the old wound begins to ache a bit when I'm sitting,' and Gunn stood up. 'On second thoughts, perhaps just two questions before I'm unstitched and go to meet Dina. When do I go, what's my cover and what does Caramansa mean?...sorry that's three.'

'The answer to the first question is Wednesday, but subject to your medical report after the stitches come out and the answer to the second will come from Christine who'll do your assignment prep' and brief tomorrow. The answer to the third is that it was the name of a great Akan Chief in the 18th Century whose rule extended over most of West Africa. He not only sold his people into slavery, but also exchanged gold for arms, which were eventually used by the Ashanti Nation to defeat the British Army. I've been told that you have an appointment at the Medical Centre after this when the stitches come out. You have the remainder of today and this evening to study Christine's brief. Your prep' starts at 08.30 tomorrow and you leave Gatwick for Kotoka Airport in Accra on the BA flight on Wednesday evening at 2100 hours.'

*

The co-pilot of the Turbo Twin-Pac Bell 212 helicopter removed the radio headset, undid his seatbelt and climbed out of the left-hand seat. Both he and the pilot had heard the news about the General Manager's son and now a phone call to the office in Sawaba from the Company's main office in Edmonton had been patched through via Intelsat to the helicopter. The general manager sat on his own in the 15 seat passenger compartment, staring blankly out of the toughened glass windows as the pilot pushed the chopper to its maximum speed of 150 mph on the flight from Kumasi to Accra. The co-pilot carried a headset and boom mike with jack-plugged extension lead, which he plugged into the socket above the General Manager. 'Mr McLean, Sir,' and then louder as there was no response, 'Mr Mclean, Sir,' who turned in a dazed fashion towards the co-pilot. 'Sir, I'm sorry to trouble you, but Mr Mackenzie, the Company President is on the line from Edmonton.' Stuart McLean took the headset and placed it over his head and thumbed the toggle switch as the co-pilot returned to his seat. The two pilots exchanged glances; both would hear the patched-through call.

'Stuart McLean speaking.'

'Stuart, its Duncan here. Don't begin to know what to say to express the sympathy of everyone here about young Graham.'

'Thank you, Sir, for coming back so quickly,' he looked at his watch, 'and at such a miserable hour of the morning in Alberta.' It would have been shortly after 2 am in western Canada, Stuart calculated with one part of his mind as another grappled with the news about his son and yet another tried to concentrate on the telephone conversation.

'Stuart, I'm sorry to be the bearer of yet more bad news, but a sadness shared sometimes makes it a little more bearable. I know it's grasping at straws, but it's just possible that there's a glimmer of good news in what I'm about to tell you.' Stuart Mclean restrained himself from urging the old man to get on with it and stop waffling, but he knew that the waffle was motivated by kindness and he bit back the retort.

'Let's hear it then, Sir, as things couldn't be much worse.'

'My grandson's vanished, Stuart,' and the old President was unable to keep the emotion out of his voice.' Stuart was struck dumb; his uncharitable thoughts of a few seconds earlier made him cringe with self-loathing.

'Dear God, Sir, I'm so sorry. What happened?'

'Little Ian was being taken to school by John's chauffeur and never got there. The police found the car abandoned, with engine still running, about a quarter of a mile from the school. No sign of a struggle, no sign of anything; Mary's in hospital under sedation and my John and me're feeling much like you must be right now.'

'What's this mean, Sir? You mentioned earlier about clutching at straws and possibly some good news.' With one part of his mind, Stuart realised that the helicopter was descending towards Kotoka Airport. They would be on the ground in a couple of minutes.

'Yes, well perhaps this idea of mine's a bit far-fetched, but it seems the disappearance of two children belonging to the three most senior members of Sikafuturu which is the sole owner of the richest gold mine in the world, goes beyond happenstance. It's my belief that they've been kidnapped and it won't be long before we get the ransom note.'

'I'm sorry, Sir, my brain's not functioning as well as usual today; where's the good news in that theory?'

'Dammit Stuart, don't you see; it means that they're alive! When we heard that Graham had gone missing while fishing by himself along a coast with one of the worst reputations in the world for drownings, we all feared the worst. In the case of young Ian, unless it was some visitation from outer space, a man and a boy don't just vanish without leaving signs of a scuffle or footprints or something. It has to be a kidnap, Stuart, and don't you worry, son; I'll sell everything I own to get those boys back.'

'Thank you, Sir. That has provided a certain measure of comfort and like you, I'll grasp at any straw at the moment. Perhaps you'll excuse me if I break the connection now as we are about to land and I must get to my Mary and Morwena. I'll get back to you as soon as I hear anything and perhaps you would do the same from your end.'

'Sure, son; take care and my love to Mary and Morwena. Goodbye.'

'Goddbye Sir,' and the co-pilot cancelled the satellite hook-up.

*

'B-MAT 2, this B-MAT 1, over.'

'Daddy, the boss is calling you,' Emma announced as she grabbed the radio and gave it to her father. Another of John Briar's post-rugger-playing afflictions was almost complete deafness in his left ear after one of his more excitable opponents, having failed to hook the ball in the set scrums on seven consecutive put-ins by his own scrum-half, punched John's ear and when that didn't change his hooking fortune, tried to bite it off. The punch severely damaged the eardrum and bomb blasts on the streets of Crossmaglen in Armagh had completed the damage. The radio had been sitting on the piecrust-edged circular table on John's left, next to the deaf ear.

'Damn, thanks, love; B-MAT 1, this is B-MAT 2, send, over,' and John Briars left the drawing room to go out to the driveway.

'B-MAT 1, can you get away to come and meet me at my house? over.'

'B-MAT 2, yes; B-MAT 2A in control of the situation here. Be with you in five, over.'

'B-MAT 1, thanks, out.' John Briars went back into the drawing room and told Penny that Miles Stockwell, the BMAT Commander, had asked him to come to his house. 'That means more bad news, love,' he whispered to Penny, out of Mary's hearing in the hall. 'I can always tell; when Miles gives no hint what he wants me for, it's bad news. The last time this happened it was when our poor old dog got run over.'

'Don't John; take Richard with you as he'll soon become bored here and make a nuisance of himself. Emma is a great help to me and can distract Morwena until Stuart arrives.....speaking of which,' and Penny went to the open front door,' that's Stuart now. You go with Richard, and I'll follow when I've handed over to Stuart.'

'Righto, bye love; c'mon Richard,' and they left the house. Stuart thanked John Briars briefly as he got out of the company Mercedes and then ran into the house to his wife. Penny and Emma retired discreetly into the garden until they might be needed.

John Briars drove the Landrover to his house where he dropped Richard and then he walked back the 50 yards or so to Miles Stockwell's bungalow where he was greeted by the daft and loveable

Shemma of doubtful African Collie pedigree. 'You silly girl,' John greeted the affectionate Shemma who was nibbling at the toes protruding from his flip-flops which was one of her many neurotic habits. 'Where's your master?' and in answer to that question addressed to Shemma, Miles Stockwell appeared at the front door.

'Hello John; thanks for getting here so promptly. How are things up at the Stuart's house?' and before John could answer, 'come on through to the veranda.' That definitely meant bad news - or very sensitive news - John reckoned, because all of them discussed those things outside the bungalows as it had to be assumed that their houses were bugged. John had always thought that this procedure, whilst thoroughly sensible, was a little over cautious because if the electronic bugs were anything like the telephones then there was no possibility of any eavesdropping. 'Coffee, John?' and then Miles looked at his watch with the usual British reticence to consume alcohol before the now ceased 'opening time', 'or a cold beer?'

'Cold beer would do nicely, thanks.'

'Yes, I'll join you,' and he pressed the bell in the hall. 'I don't know where the hell the morning's gone; I saw the Commandant and all the Staff College students off on their flight to Harare this morning after meeting you on the beach..... ah! Cephas, could we have two cold Heinekens, please?' and the ever-smiling house steward disappeared to pour the beers. The two beers arrived in silver tankards on a silver salver and were placed on the rattan table on the veranda. 'Many thanks, Cephas,' and when Cephas had returned to the kitchen, Miles spoke. 'You were aware of Tony Bristow's affair with Lin Aldridge, John,' it was a statement rather than a question.

'Sure, and so is the entire expatriate community in Accra.'

'I told you earlier that he had disappeared, but the mystery surrounding that disappearance becomes more bizarre by the minute.'

'How do you mean.....bizarre? I admit I was thinking of other things, but I thought he had drowned which is fairly commonplace in these parts.'

'That is the obvious explanation while he was out fishing by himself, but it doesn't tie in with where the boat was found. It was his weekend for the cottage and he and Monica had invited the Aldridges - inevitably, the Motrams and the Fluitmans - you know, the MD of Philips.'

'Yes, sure, we know them. Are there suspicious circumstances? I can hardly see poor old Monica doing it. She's the original cuckold or just pretends to ignore the whole affair. Anyway, she'd be far more likely to do away with Lin than Tony, whom I think she still loves - God knows why.'

'My sentiments exactly; yes, in answer to your query, there are highly suspicious circumstances. You know that information which you picked up in the casino at Black Caesar's Palace from that little croupier who's always been in your debt since you paid for his wife's operation at the Military Hospital?'

'Little Eddie Twintoh.'

'That's the guy; you'll remember the decision I made after he'd told you that he'd overheard two very drunk Ivorians, with a great deal more money than gambling ability, discussing something called 'Kamchatka'....'

'Caramansa.'

'Caramansa, that's it and a grand plot to overthrow all the West African regimes and unite the countries in some form of extension of ECOWAS.'

'Yes sure; I strongly advised against saying anything to that bone-headed, be-kilted defence attaché in the High Commission, to which you agreed. You decided that it was worth passing on because old Eddie has produced some very accurate information in the past and I agreed.'

'That's exactly as I recall it. That was only on Thursday because you usually go to the casino on a Wednesday night, correct?'

'Correct; we had a very similar discussion to the one we're having now in exactly the same place, after which you went to the High Commission and spoke with that fool Bristow. Sorry, that wasn't meant to sound derogatory, but who else could you have spoken to? The DA's never progressed beyond the stage of playing with toy soldiers and the High Commissioner won't listen to anything unless it furthers his quest for a 'K' to add to his CMG.'

'I've never known you mince your words, but again that's exactly as I remember it. That fool - as you so accurately describe Bristow - must have talked to someone about that information; probably Lin, who talked to someone else - you told me she spends all her time in the evenings, when she's not being screwed by Bristow, drinking and dancing at Afrikiko, Blow Up or the Red Onion.'

'That's right; seen her there myself,' John said with a chuckle, 'crawling all over the less-desirable expatriates and Ghanaians. That woman's got a real nympho problem and if she hasn't picked up Aids in the year she's been here, then I'm a Dutchman. What happens now?'

'That's why I called you on the radio. I've just had a most extraordinary phone call from London.'

'Who from?'

'Donald Hastings; you know him. He spent all his time in Southern Arabia and was the youngest Brigadier in the Army when he was promoted. I was one of his company commanders when he was commanding the Muscat Regiment.'

'He left the army and disappeared into the make-believe world of James Bond, didn't he?'

'I'm glad you said that because that was exactly my reaction to the phone call; straight out of a James Bond film. He told me on the phone that his 'insurance company was very concerned about the fishing accident and would be sending out an investigator who would be in touch with me'. Those were his exact words.'

'Bloody hell! we're in for a visit from '007' himself!

CHAPTER 5

The lift stopped at the first floor and Gunn stepped out into into the foyer of the Park Lane Hyatt's Italian restaurant. His stitches had been removed an hour earlier and the BID doctor had told him that the entry and exit wounds had healed satisfactorily, but he would need to take it steady for a week or two. In a slim briefcase, he carried the briefing pack which Christine Dupré had prepared for him.

'Yes Sir; on your own or are you meeting someone?' Gunn's attention was drawn by the maître d'.

'Thanks, I'm meeting someone; a Miss Gbedemah.'

'Just a moment, Sir,' and an ornate reservation book on a lectern by the entrance to the restaurant was checked. 'Here we are; would you follow me please, Sir?'

'Thank you......... Dina Gbedemah?'

'Yes, I'm Dina and you must be John Gunn,' the voice was about the purest, accentless English Gunn had ever heard. They shook hands and Gunn sat opposite Dina. 'Here's my card, John, which gives you the addresses of all my shops in Ghana and also my private address,' and she raised her hand, which produced a waitress at their table. 'We'll order now please. What will you have to drink, John?'

'I'd very much like a cold Frascati, the antipasto and the garlic prawns please.'

'I'll join you on the Frascati,' and she turned to the waitress, 'a bottle please and for me the smoked salmon followed by the garlic prawns.'

'Where and how did you achieve such perfect English, Dina?'

'I have dual nationality; my father's English and my mother Ghanaian. We have homes in both countries. I was brought up in this country and finished my education at Oxford, before going to Paris and then Naples to complete my training in dress design. My father is a doctor who works for UNICEF and he is currently out of the country in Yogoslavia or whatever it's called today, trying to sort out the misery of the orphans of that mess. There, that's me, I know enough about you, so cheers,' and she held up a slim glass of the clear, chilled Italian wine. The meal was a success and to any casual or interested observer looked exactly like what it was - a business lunch.

Gunn returned to his house in Chelsea and spent the rest of the day studying Christine's briefing pack. At 7.35, he walked to his local, The Cavalier, where he had a lager and the steak and kidney pie, peas and potatoes. The pub was fairly empty so he was brought up to date on the dreadful state of the nation by Harry, the publican, after which he walked home and went on reading until one in the morning. That same morning he was in Christine Dupré's office punctually at 08.30.

'Morning John, what's your knowledge of West Africa like now?'

'I would love to say, greatly improved, but that would suggest I possessed some previous knowledge which would be a lie. I really am woefully ignorant on that part of the world, but considerably less so after reading that brief of yours. May I keep it or do I give it back to you?'

'No, please keep it. This is your programme for today,' and Christine handed Gunn a single sheet of paper with a series of timings and his appointments with the various departments which had to be visited for his 'preparation' prior to a mission. 'How was lunch?'

'A most impressive person and a pleasant lunch.'

'Good; now let's sort out your cover for this mission,' and Christine came round from behind her desk and sat opposite Gunn. The hair was done in the same style and the slim wrists and hands holding the thick file were evidently much stronger than they seemed if they could behead a man with one blow from a panga. There was no jewellery on either hand, only a minute gold watch on the left wrist. 'Because of your lack of knowledge of West Africa, generally, and Ghana, in particular, I've decided to put you back in the army.' Gunn smiled. 'Does that bother you?'

'Not in the slightest, on the contrary; I was smiling because of the worn old joke about soldiers only visiting other countries to meet interesting people and then kill them. It's an excellent cover.'

'When I was preparing your cover, having been told that you knew very little about Africa, I went and saw Donald Hastings, the AD for the Middle East. You probably know him.'

'Yes, well; he was the Deputy Commander of the British Forces in Hong Kong and I saw quite a bit of him on my last assignment.'

'Yes, so he said. He's arranged your cover with Major General Spratley who, I'm told, is the Assistant Chief of Defence Staff responsible for the UK's overseas commitments. His directorate is divided into two sub-directorates, headed up by a couple of

81

Brigadiers. These two Brigadiers divide up the world into four areas; west, far-east, middle-east and Africa, of which each takes two. Your Brigadier is a Peter Swindels and the other is a Charles Pomeroy. Your immediate boss is a Colonel Mike Dalaby. All of these officers have been briefed with the minimum of information necessary to authenticate your cover if there should be any enquiries. Colonel Dalaby is responsible for managing the FCO and MOD-funded training of officers from Africa and he, or a member of his staff - ie you, visits all the countries where the UK has military training teams on a regular basis.'

'You will be a Lieutenant Colonel and your appointment is designated MEA 5 - the desk responsible for West Africa. Your arrival in Accra and your lack of 'hands on' experience of the country will cause no suspicions. Donald told me that when he was in Hong Kong, there was always a stream of officers who would visit in the dry season between October and December, on the feeblest of excuses and at the taxpayer's expense, to do their Christmas shopping. Their ignorance of Hong Kong's people, culture, geography and history was only surpassed by their unscrupulous greed in claiming full allowances while living free in other people's houses. So your ignorance of Ghana should cause no suspicion.'

'How much will the BMAT officers know of my cover?'

'That's been dealt with already. The commander of the team knows that you're from BID. The BMAT officers aren't the problem, in fact they'll provide you with unlimited access to the military hierarchy of the Ghana Armed Forces, should you need it. No, the problem we've had to sort out was the Defence Attaché.'

'Blimey, why? I thought DAs were there to help in situations like this.'

'Do you know Hamish Graham?'

'Never heard of him.'

'Donald described him as "short, fat, bald, myopic - physically and mentally - and with uninterrupted bone in his cranium from one ear to the other". Donald was in a Scottish Regiment, as is this character, and apparently knows him well.'

'So what's this character likely to do?'

'Just about anything stupid you care to think of, according to Donald, so we've removed him out of the way. Very conveniently, there's some sort of annual conference, which the army has at Warminster each year at this time.'

'The Director of Infantry's Conference...'

'Oh, that's it, is it; anyway, Hamish Graham has been told that he's to return to UK and present a paper at that conference on some subject, which I was told, but for the moment escapes me. He's been told that he can take his wife, Barbara, with him and they both, with their two children, left Accra,' and Christine looked at the small calendar on her desk, 'yesterday. You will be met at the airport by BMAT and taken to the Labadi Beach Hotel. The Commander of BMAT will make a show of introducing you to some of the senior Ghanaian officers in their military training organisation and will let it be known that you have decided to take your annual leave touring around Ghana and its neighbouring countries. On this sheet of paper,' which was passed over to Gunn, 'is a diagram of the directorate for which you work in the MOD with all the names of your colleagues and a summary of the current training in UK for the Ghana Armed Forces, that proposed for next year and what has been done in the last five years.'

'It would be perfectly normal for you to visit Dina's shop in Accra as she has advertisements and boutiques in all the major hotels. Make contact with her, with Tony Bristow's SIS secretary - Amanda Routledge - and, of course, BMAT. That's it; I've run slightly over time, but there're a few minutes for questions.'

'Will you be controlling me from London or in-country?'

'From London, unless you require help, in which case I will stay at the Labadi Beach Hotel and can be there within 12 hours of your request.'

'Fine, Christine; nothing else, thanks,' and Gunn looked at his programme. 'Communications and Cyphers followed by Finance and Administration; bye,' and he left Christine's office.

Gunn spent an hour with Terry Holt, the head of Comms and Cyphers, another hour with Mary Panter of Finance and Admin and then went down to the basement for his appointment with the Armourer. Tony Taylor asked him for his gun and took it into his workshop,which smelled of gun oil, leather and metal swarf. 'You keep this in excellent condition, John,' he pronounced after a very thorough examination of the 9 mm Polish Radom. You still happy with this handgun?'

'Yes, thanks, Tony; it's never given me any trouble.'

'Would you be prepared to try another for me?'

'Of course; what's special about this other gun?'

'Only one thing; it's identical in every way with your Radom, including the high muzzle velocity. It's a shade lighter because it's made of an alloy, but what appeals to me is its 15 shot magazine. With one in the chamber that gives you 16 rounds; two more rounds than your Radom can hold. Those two rounds could mean the difference between life and death'

'You got shares in this gun?' but he took the proffered weapon and examined it. 'Who makes it?'

'Tanarmi of Italy; it's an improved version of the Czech original. That's the Tanarmi TA 90. Want to try it?'

'Yes, let's give it a go,' and Gunn picked up a set of ear defenders and took the Tanarmi through to the range. Tony Taylor came and stood behind him and handed Gunn two, 15 round magazines. Gunn cocked the weapon and fired all 15 rounds at the target. Behind him, the Armourer pressed a button and the target came forward from the butts to the firing point. The 15 holes were clustered in an area the size of an orange in the centre of the Figure 11, male silhouette, target.

'D'you like it?'

'Haven't made up my mind. Wind it back and I'll have another go.' As soon as the target reached stops in the butts, Gunn raised the Tanarmi and fired it in bursts of two and three rounds until the magazine was empty. The target reappeared in front of them. In the centre of the helmeted head was a hole the size of a tennis ball.

'I'll take it, please.'

'Thought you might. Shall I wrap it or will you wear it!'

'Usual routine I suppose; is the Queen's Messenger on the same flight as me?'

'He is and you can collect the gun from the High Commission when you call in on your way from the airport to your hotel. Best of luck.'

'Thanks,' and after washing his hands thoroughly in white spirit to remove the powder traces and then in soap, Gunn left Kingsroad House and walked back to his mews house to finish his packing.

*

'They're all in the conference room now, Sir.'

'Thanks Jo; is Nat Cohn there?'

'Yes, Sir; he got back from Africa last night.' Nathanial Cohn, a third generation citizen of the States whose family of German Jews had fled from Berlin in 1938, was the Regional Director for Sub-Sahara Africa. His had been the task to find out what Charles Mensah was going to do with the long shopping list of arms and ammunition which he had presented to International Machine Tools Inc just before Easter. His trip to Africa had made him cancel a five day Easter break with Joanne - PA to the President of IMT - at a cabin he owned in the San Juan mountains.

'He in good shape?' Bradley Tracton's PA coloured.

'Yes, Sir, he's fine.' The Company President made it his business to know everything about his employees, as they well knew. He

84

strongly approved, and encouraged, in-company liaisons as it kept it all in the 'family'.

'Kay, let's get this show on the road,' and the President left his office, followed by his PA and his bodyguard, Frank Raubenheimer, who had appeared immediately he came out of the office. The three entered the conference room, which was filled by a superb, polished rectangular ebony table. In fact, it wasn't rectangular because the two long sides were convex and thus allowed the President, who sat in the middle of one of the convex sides, to see all of the people at the table. It also made it easier for his bodyguard to see everyone. Frank sat on an upholstered bar stool on a dais to the left rear of his boss, from where he could see everyone in the room and his hands were unimpeded should he need to use the Scarab Scorpion 9 mm auto-pistol with its two, taped, 32 round magazines.

All the heads of departments were present; small arms, armoured and soft-skinned vehicles, guns and tanks, munitions, aircraft and ships, PR, finance and the appropriate Regional Director; today it was Nat Cohn. 'Kay, everyone,' Bradley Tracton began without wasting any time on procedural frills. 'Y'all know the agenda for this meeting. Item one of that agenda is to decide if we're to go ahead with the arms deal for this guy who calls himself 'Caramansa'. If the deal works, there's a clear $50 million profit in it for IMT. That's enough from me; Nat, let's hear what you've got.'

'In the last eight days, I've seen eleven of our agents in West Africa; five of those guys we keep on a retainer and the other six get commission. All of them have good to excellent contacts with the governments of their countries. None of these agents know each other, but all have given me similar information. What all this indicates is co-ordinated subversion and terrorism to overthrow legitimate and quasi-legitimate governments of thirteen countries in West Africa.'

'Only one of the agents, in Côte d'Ivoire, could give me a name and he was scared shitless as two of his contacts had been found in a monsoon sewer in Accra with their tongues cut out. The name, we already know, is Caramansa. This guy, Charles Mensah, who came to see us before Easter, is using the name of a great warrior chief who ruled most of West Africa about a couple of hundred years ago when the Limeys, Frogs, Cloggies and Spics were grabbing up handfuls of Africa and shipping the black slaves out here. Caramansa was the sole exporter of his own people into slavery in America.'

'Will this plot succeed? It's got a chance, if for no other reason, because the US of A and other industrialised countries are all looking the other way – at Iraq, Iran, North Korea and Afganistan. We get our money if it succeeds or not. The daily death toll in Africa, other than by natural causes, ranges between 10,000 and 100,000 per day. I doubt if the total death toll of this conspiracy, win or lose, will exceed 100,000. So who cares? Certainly not the US of A and there's no shortage of congressmen lining up to take our bribes to provide export licences. It's the same old story; if we don't sell him the arms, there're a hundred others who will. If this Caramansa's got the gold, I have advised our President to take it. That's it,' and Nat Cohn sat down.

Bradley Tracton asked for any comments from around the table. The only comments or suggestions were all of a practical nature on the provision of the items on Caramansa's shopping list. He turned to Nat Cohn on his left. 'Kay, that's decided; before we move on to discuss the shopping lists sent in by Burma, Bosnia, Libya, the IRA and the Palestinians, can you tell us, Nat, how this whole container-ship-load of arms gets to where this Caramansa character wants it?'

'Sure, Trax;' executive directors and above were allowed to call the company President by his nickname. 'Please turn your chairs around, gentlemen,' this was directed at those members of the board sitting opposite Nat Cohn. All of them were used to this procedure as the screen, which filled the entire wall behind them was frequently used at meetings. Nat Cohn dimmed the lights using the array of switches set into the arm of his chair and then the screen was filled with a map of Northern Africa from the Mediterranean to the Equator. From a slot beside the switches he removed a slim pencil-like projector on the end of a fibre-optic cable. This laser projector placed an intense spot of brilliant light on the screen.

'In these West African countries,' and Cohn swept the spot of light in a lozenge shape to embrace all the countries from Senegal to Nigeria, 'the population tends to be concentrated on the coast with the obvious exception of Mali and Burkina Faso which have no coastline. In the south of these countries, the soil is fertile, the climate is tropical and the vegetation is lush. As you get closer to the Sahara, the soil dries up, the climate gets hotter and drier and the population thins out. No one wants to know about the northern parts, so it's from these parts that Caramansa wants to distribute his arms. This is how we've set it up for him. The arms will be taken by one of our 80,000 ton container ships - in this case Texas Star - from Galveston to the port of Banjul in The Gambia - here,' and the spot of light rested on the port of Banjul at the mouth of the Gambia River Estuary.

'From here it will be unloaded into lighters which will be towed 200 miles up river to a railhead at Mara - here. Mara is the first distribution point and the Gambia shipment will be removed here.

All the other containers will go by rail to Tambacounda, in Senegal - here, where the branch line joins the main one. Here, the shipment for Senegal will be dropped off. The train continues from west to east dropping off containers at Kita in Mali, Siguiri in Guinea, Tingrela in Côte d'Ivoire, Banfora in Burkina Faso, Navrongo in Ghana, Mango in Togo and Gaya - here - on the border between Benin and Nigeria on the Niger River. In Nigeria, the weapons'll be brought down the Niger to Baro - here, just to the south of Nigeria's new capital, Abuja - where they're to be collected by General Sam Tampona - no prizes at this meeting for guessing what his nickname is! - who'll be Caramansa's Governor of Nigeria if this crazy UROWAS conspiracy succeeds.'

'That's it, except to say that IMT's responsibility for these arms ends here,' and the spot of light identified the port of Banjul. 'From here on, Caramansa's guys take over. Payment will be in two parts; one third within ten days of the decision by this board to supply Caramansa and the remaining two thirds when the shipment reaches Banjul. Any questions?' There were none; the lights came up and Bradley Tracton pulled a folder towards him and opened it. 'Right, next item gentlemen; the Burmese military junta's request for nerve gas.'

*

The KLM Airbus 300 touched down on the runway at Kotoka Airport at 7.40 pm after the short flight from Kano in Nigeria. Kisi had left Heathrow the night before on a KLM feeder flight to Schipol in Amsterdam where she had stayed the night in the Kraznapolski Hotel in the centre of the city. To her delight, she had discovered that channel 20 on the hotel's TV produced non-stop porn. After an hour and a half of porngraphic movies, she had rung for room service, which had, fortuitously, sent up a 21 year-old male trainee in hotel management. With much practice and expertise she had raped him, although he probably reckoned that he had seduced her, and then, libido temporarily subdued, she had gone out for a large steak. This was followed by a large black male she picked up in Kanal Straat and took back to the hotel. This kept her busy until 3 am when she kicked him out of her room and went to sleep. The flight from Schipol to Kotoka via Kano had left almost on time at 10.07 the next morning. Kisi travelled first class.

Kisi's false American passport was in the name of Anita Asmah and her profession was stated as business consultant, which, arguably, was not that far from the truth. Because the customs official was jealous of a fellow countrywoman who had clearly achieved great wealth, he insisted on opening all of Kisi's three suitcases and purposely handled all her underwear while he watched for a reaction. There was none, but the man had never done a more stupid act in his life. Kisi seethed with impotent fury, carefully noting his rank, the number displayed on his shoulder and his name on a plastic card on his right shirt pocket. The rumpled and untidied cases were pushed to one side when the official was unable to find anything which might produce a bribe for him to overlook and nonchalantly dismissed Kisi with a wave of his hand to go and tidy her own cases and close them. Showing no emotion, Kisi closed the cases, replaced them on her trolley and left the customs hall. Kofi was waiting at the meeting point with his chauffeur.

'Good evening, Anita, have you had a good flight?' Kofi greeted Kisi with deference.

'No! I fu......' but even the expletive was drowned by the roar of the reverse thrust of the Aeroflot Tupelov TU-154 as it landed. Kofi's chauffeur, Kojo Blood-Dzraku, was Caramansa's head enforcer in Accra and once Kisi's cases had been loaded into the back of the Mercedes, she beckoned to him and pointed through the plate glass partition between them and the customs hall. The official who had turned over her cases was in the process of doing the same with a large, string-tied cardboard box belonging to another Ghanaian returning to Accra from London which had revealed a wealth of bribe-worthy material. A shiver ran down the customs official's spine as though someone had walked over his grave and he looked up. On the other side of the glass partition, beside the uppitty black American woman, was the largest man he'd ever seen staring straight at him and while he stared, the woman handed him a piece of paper and then pointed through the partition at him. His mouth went dry and sweat burst onto his forehead. The Ghanaian woman was talking to him, but he waved her away, left his counter and went out airside into the darkness as the needle thin landing lights of the Aeroflot Tupelov TU-154 swung across the concrete apron in front of the terminal.

'Are the plans for the Bank of Ghana finalised?' Kisi asked Kofi as soon as they were both in the car and Kojo had received his instructions regarding the customs official. Kofi was petrified of Kisi because it was rumoured in his Evé village of Kpando, from which both of then came, that she was a witch.

'Yes, Kisi, I have followed Caramansa's instructions to the letter and we are ready to do it the day after tomorrow.'

'Kofi, you must obey instructions; this is the last time I remind you. I am to be called by the name on my passport; no one is to mention the name Caramansa.'

'I'm sorry Ki.....Anita, but you make me nervous. I won't make the mistake again.'

'Right; did you have any difficulty in bribing the bank official who will open the vault for us.'

'None at all; he couldn't believe that we would give him so much money. He has asked us to make sure that he is knocked unconscious during the raid so that no suspicion will fall on him. We have also removed his entire family who are locked up in the house on Independence Avenue. He has been told that if he wishes to see his wife and children again, he must do exactly as instructed by us.'

'The McLean boy?'

'He is also in the house and has given us no trouble. Kojo is to be congratulated for the efficient manner in which he carried out that kidnap.'

'Why? it's not very difficult to kidnap a child. Our team in Edmonton was just as efficient.'

'Agreed, but Kojo's patience paid dividends. He had decided to remove him from Labadi beach because most of the expatriate children go there every day. The parents take it in turns to fetch and carry them and leave them there unsupervised. Kojo had been watching the house in Sankara Road and when the boy slipped out of the house at 5.30 on Monday morning with his fishing rod, Kojo put his plan into action. He had three of our men with him and an inflatable dinghy with outboard in the back of a lorry. They followed the boy to the beach, launched the dinghy from the cover of the rocks by the military firing range and approached the boy directly from the sea. Kojo told me that the boy never noticed them until they dragged the dinghy up onto the beach and grabbed him.'

'The ransom instructions?'

'We have the tape ready for you. The McLeans have an answerphone in their house which they switch from 'delay' to 'immediate' when they go to bed; that's usually at about 10 pm or shortly after. As soon as we are sure that the answerphone is functioning, you can play the tape which gives the instructions where to find the ransom note tape. That must be done tonight.' Their car had just gone round the Thomas Sankara roundabout; the traffic was fairly heavy and progress was slow, but after passing the Canadian High Commission and the American Ambassador's Residence, the Mercedes turned left off Independence Avenue, a hundred yards further on, through the gates of one of the old colonial-style houses. These houses had been built on pillars which raised them off the ground to prevent the ingress of damp and creepy-crawlies and had wide, shady verandas, high-ceilinged rooms and marble floors. As soon as the chauffeur Kojo had dropped them and unloaded Kisi's suitcases into the house, he returned to the airport to deal with the customs official.

In the centre of the ground floor of the house was the entrance to the cellar. The house sat on a plinth about ten feet above the ground; there were wide, double steps which curved up to the front door and some much smaller wooden ones at the back of the house for the servants' use. In the centre of this plinth was the stairwell which led down to the cellar, below ground level, which was the only place in the house's colonial era where anything could be kept at a temperature remotely close to cool. There were four large rooms in the cellar with ventilation ducts from ground level outside. These ventilation ducts, which kept the air circulating in the cellars, were covered with steel grilles set in concrete and wire mesh mosquito netting. Because these cellars had contained all the food and stores when the house had been built, all the rooms were fitted with steel doors making them ideally suited for their present function as cells for Graham McLaren and the bank employee's family.

Servants took Kisi's cases to her room while she walked through to the spacious drawing room where she helped herself to a gin and freshly-squeezed lime juice. For years the house had been let to BP (Ghana) Ltd as the residence for its general manager, but that lease had been terminated at the end of the previous month so that the house could be used as the in-country centre of operations for the final phase of the Caramansa conspiracy.

'How's our little bird in the British High Commission? Still singing well?'

'Very well; however Kojo's enthusiastic interrogation of Bristow and the two Ivorians has cut off our source of information to discover if the SIS had found out about our plans.'

'Didn't Bristow have an assistant or secretary or something?'

'I've no idea; that wasn't my task,' Kofi now felt threatened. 'I was told not to get involved in anything else, but to remove the gold from the bank and get it back to the USA.'

'Quite right; you leave the brainwork to me. Now, the arrangements for getting the gold out of Ghana; any problems?'

'None; the removal of the gold will take place at 1000 hours tomorrow morning. At that time the traffic is always grid-locked and even if someone got a message to the police, there is no way a car could respond to the call. We have hired our helicopter; it's one of the Bell 206s leased by Offshore Exploration which operates out of Kotoka Airport. Its maximum lift capacity is 1,700 lbs with a full fuel load. We don't need the full fuel load as the chopper only has to fly as far as the salt pans on the west side of the city. There, the gold will be lowered through the roof of a specially modified panel lorry, which will bring the gold back to the airport. The helicopter is fitted with an autopilot and will be set on a course back out to sea at wave top height and well below radar coverage. The pilot will jump into the sea, swim ashore - if he's lucky - and disappear with the $50,000 he's been paid.'

'In the back of the lorry, the gold will be redistributed into 20 wooden crates containing damaged or unserviceable offshore drilling equipment being returned for repair - which is a bona fide cargo. The damaged equipment is going by air-freight to IMT in Texas on one of its own 747 freight carriers. That load manifest has already been cleared through customs; incidentally, the official we bribed is the one who gave you a hard time. His death at the hands of Kojo will merely be brought forward by 24 hours. The flight will clear US Customs at Dallas and then fly direct to the company airfield at Amarillo the next morning. By only using a quarter of the fuel load we increase the lift to 3,000 lbs. The 53 bars should weigh 1,658.28 lbs and the remainder of the lift capability is for the winchman, me and my two assistants.'

'What do you mean, 'should'? Don't you know the exact weight?'

'Bear with me, Ki...Anita; if the gold bars had been poured since the last war and to the British assay then I would know their exact weight, but no one, I believe, knows exactly when these bars were poured, even if it was during this century. I have had to make assumptions and err on the heavy side to make sure that the chopper can take off.'

'My apologies; you've clearly done your work well. Now what about this helicopter?'

'As I've said, the machine's ideal as its avionics include an autopilot and it has double doors on the port side of the cabin which give an access width of 1.52 metres. It also has a winch and under-slung load carrier.'

'And the pilot?'

'No problem; we have our own pilot who is perfectly happy to do the job for the money he's been given. As soon as the crew boards the helicopter, which has been chartered for a flight to Takoradi, the Offshore Exploration pilot will be removed and our pilot will take over. We will be in radio communication with the helicopter from the bank. The gold bars will be removed from the vault by our team in security guard uniforms and taken out to the car park on the Thorpe Road side of the bank on two trolleys. As soon as the trolleys reach the car park, the helicopter will come in with the net and strop lowered. The trolleys will be pushed into the net and the helicopter will immediately winch them up as it heads south over High Street and out to sea. The whole idea is to make the authorities believe that the gold has been taken offshore to some waiting ship or yacht, whereas it will be sitting right under their noses at the airport. The more time the navy spend rushing around in their patrol craft and the air force in their Aermacchis looking for non-existent ships the better.'

'That all sounds to be thoroughly well planned; well done. Now, I'm going down the road to the Afrikiko to see who's there and let my eyes and ears have a little exercise. It's just possible that there might be some people from the British High Commission there as their residential compound is right opposite on the other side of the road. I'll take the beetle which is inconspicuous.'

'OK, but remember you're well known and that bar is always watched by the security police. If you're identified, that's the end of our plans.'

'I'll be careful, and if I'm identified it'll be the end of me, but not our plan. I trust you have your pills?'

'Damn right; I'm certainly not going back inside that BNI building on the other side of this avenue.'

Kisi left the drawing room and went to her room. She reappeared twenty minutes later and even Kofi had difficulty recognising her. He handed her the keys to the Volkswagen and she drove out of the gates and turned right onto Independence Avenue.

Kisi drove back round the roundabout towards the airport and took the first turning to the left into Afrikiko's car park. She turned the little car round and parked it next to a large banyan tree by the road in a position where it couldn't be blocked in by another car. The open air seating of the beer garden-cum-disco was festooned with coloured lights, the music was loud and there was much laughter. The waiters moved among the tables with trays of litre glasses of cold, frothing Club Beer. The majority of people at the nightspot were young, teenage expatriates on holiday from school in Europe and America. With them were the Ghanaian hangers-on, benefiting from the plentiful supply of beer. On the periphery and watching the young expatriates were the wary-eyed drug pushers and watching the drug pushers were the plain clothes police and the security police from the Bureau of National Intelligence.

Kisi was in luck; to the right of the teenagers' table was another one filled with young people who were unmistakably British. They could only be from the British High Commission and Kisi collected a beer from a passing waiter and wandered over. Yes, she was right; as she came closer she could pick up snatches of conversation. Were there any Americans in the group? No; no American accents. Kisi picked her target and went up to the young man closest to her. 'Excuse me,' the conversation stopped; 'I've just arrived in Accra tonight to work on one of the US Peace Corps projects. I don't know anyone and I wondered if I might join you?'

'Of course, here, grab this seat. Go on Dave, you go and find another one, there're plenty over there,' and her gallant and slightly drunk target waved vaguely towards the bars. 'I'm Don and on your left is Amanda.' The conversation had regained its previous volume as the new arrival was welcomed into the fold. 'We're all from the British High Commission and are having a bit of a wake to-night.'

'Shhh Don, careful what you're saying,' Amanda cautioned and Kisi pretended not to notice the exchange.

'Rubbish, Amanda, Yanks and Brits are all on the same side. Look at the Gulf War.'

'What's this wake thing, Don?' Kisi asked in wide-eyed innocence. Bloody hell, Don thought drunkenly, noticing Kisi's superb cleavage and figure and striking good looks. Could be onto a good thing here tonight if I play my cards right, his mildly befuddled thought process assessed and then he went hot and cold all over as he felt her thigh press up against his leg.

'A wake.... well,' Amanda was chatting to Dave so he was alright. 'We Brits have wakes er....what did you say your name was?'

'I didn't, Don, and Kisi's right hand rested gently but firmly on his thigh; Anita.....Anita Asmah.'

'Great name......' Don was now having great difficulty remembering his own name, what the hell he was talking about or, indeed, anything else. Embarrassed at his arousal, he crossed his legs, ensuring that he didn't disturb Kisi's hand.

'You were talking about wakes, Don.'

'Ah.. yes, well a wake is a sort of party to cheer everyone up when someone has died.'

'Oh dear, how awful! Has someone died?'

'Well. not exactly,' Amanda was still engrossed in her conversation with Dave. 'Her boss,' and he nodded in Amanda's direction, 'was drowned in a boating accident last weekend. The body was never found, but that's not unusual along this coast.'

'How dreadful!' Bullseye! Tony Bristow's secretary - Amanda; an excellent evening's work and if this drunken juvenile prick next to her wasn't incapable, she'd teach him a thing or two tonight that would make his thinning hair curl. Kisi laughed to herself and squeezed Don's thigh allowing her hand to move closer to his groin.

CHAPTER 6

'You useless faggot!' Kisi climbed off the inert form of Don Peasmarsh and started to put her clothes on. After the drinks at Afrikiko, Don had asked her if she would like to come back to his flat for coffee. This had been said with a lear and a wink, so theatrically juvenile that Kisi had the greatest difficulty in not laughing. She had followed him back to his flat in the British High Commission compound, just to the south of Independence Avenue. She made a point of stopping beside the guard on the gate and speaking to him; on another night, he might well let her through with no fuss.

Kisi parked her Volkswagen beside Don's Peugeot 206 - even his choice of car was boring, she thought, as he fell out of it, tried to put his arm round her, missed his footing and fell at the foot of the stairs up to his first floor flat. She helped him to his feet and then up the stairs. After three attempts, he found the key and after four more, managed to get it into the lock and the door open. She led him through to the bedroom, pushed him back onto the bed and removed his clothes. She then did her seductive striptease routine which produced not a flicker of arousel from the supine Don; the only thing she could raise was a silly grin on his face.

At this point in Don's adventurous love life, he rolled off the bed, staggered into the bathroom and vomited, successfully missing the lavatory bowl and doing it all over the floor. After a drink of water, Don returned to his bed and passed out. Not even Kisi's energetic attempts produced a flicker of life and at that point, if not brain dead, Kisi pronounced Don Peasmarsh groin dead.

In frustrated fury, Kisi filled a bucket full of water in the kitchen, poured it over Don and walked out of his flat after removing one of the flat keys from his keyring. Later that morning, Don Peasmarsh, Third Secretary, Grade 9, in the High Commission's Consular Section, would wake up with an appalling hangover and not the slightest recollection of the events of the previous evening. Don was no faggot, but just very unworldly and rather naive. It would be some 48 hours before he would discover that his chronic case of 'brewer's droop' had saved him from being infected by the HIV virus on his first attempt at a one-night stand.

Kisi didn't go down the stairs, but went up the stairwell, reading the names on each of the doors. Success came at the top left flat which belonged to Amanda Routledge. Kisi now had name, location and - from the calling card helpfully displayed outside the flat - Amanda's flat and office telephone number.

Back down to the bottom of the stairs and then Kisi did a thorough reconnaissance of the whole compound which included the two accommodation blocks of flats, the High Commission Club, swimming pool and tennis court and a building works compound which was locked. From her handbag, Kisi took a small notebook and drew a diagram of the compound with approximate distances. She then went back to the stairwells of both blocks and made a note of all the names, telephone numbers and a diagram of where everyone lived.

Not a completely wasted evening, she reckoned as she climbed into the car and drove out of the compound. It was 1.40 in the morning. Kisi went round the Thomas Sankara roundabout and straight on round the ringroad to Kwame Nkrumah Circle and turned left and then left again into the car park in front of the Blow Up disco. She went into the darkened disco with its brain-numbing noise and strobe lighting, picked the largest Ghanaian youth she could find and led him out to the car park. Ten minutes later she dismissed him and drove out of the car park, libido temporarily assuaged.

Her next call was at 24 Sankara Drive, the home of the McLeans, where it seemed that everyone had gone to bed. Kisi took the mobile phone and the small tape recorder out of the glove compartment. She dialled the McLean's number; sure enough, it was the answerphone which took the call and after the tone, she pressed the 'play' button on the tape recorder. As soon as the message had finished, she broke the connection and then drove back to the house on Independence Avenue. On arrival back at the house, she checked the inmates of the rooms in the cellar and then went to bed.

*

'Presumably, he'll be from Century House in Vauxhall, John?' Miles Stockwell asked as the two of them were driven to the airport by Commander BMAT's driver, Corporal Badu, in the aged Datsun Bluebird staff car.

'No, I don't think so, Miles. Not much has been said about it all, but I believe that the entire MI5 and 6 set-up was completely changed a short while ago.'

'That must be about the only thing that has been kept secret; how did you hear of this?'

'Well, I have a very close friend, in fact he's godfather to Richard, who received one of those redundancy envelopes some years ago. He'd spent nearly all his service in the SAS. He was absolutely gob-smacked to be told that he was to be made redundant, particularly as he said he knew of any number of sloths - his description, not mine - who had escaped the axe. Two days after receiving his redundancy notice, he had a telephone call from Donald Hastings. All I know is that two days after that he waved two fingers at the Army and vanished; not literally, because we still keep in touch. The only slip of tongue he's made to me in the last two years is to mention the word 'Directorate'.'

'Perhaps you're right; have you been able to jack up a programme for him to visit a few people to authenticate his cover as a desk officer from Peter Swindels' outfit?' The staff car had just turned off Independence Avenue into Kotoka Airport; it was 06.50 and the BA flight from Gatwick via Abidjan in Côte d'Ivoire was due in at 07.00.

'Yes, no problem; here, I've got a copy of his programme for you,' and he opened his briefcase and passed over a single sheet of A4. 'We were told that his visa is all in order and the Ghanaian MOD in Burma Camp is perfectly happy about him taking a holiday here after his two day official visit is finished. Mike Peterson, the manager of Landrover - whom I play golf with every week - has very kindly agreed to lease him a Landrover Discovery.'

'Bloody hell! wish the FCO would let us have one of those. What's his name?'

'Mike Peter.......'

'No, sorry; our 007 character.'

'Oh, John Gunn; for this visit a rather young, Lt Colonel John Gunn.'

'Was he genuinely in the army?'

'Sorry, I've no idea; never heard of him.'

'I think I may have.....that is, of course if it's the same man and not an alias.'

'Where d'you think you knew him?'

'The first Gulf war in 91; I was on the staff of 5 Brigade. The Gunners had a very effective forward observer from 29 Commando Regiment. His highly accurate adjustment of fire onto the Republican Guard contributed considerably to the quick Iraqi surrender. I can remember hearing him on the Brigade fire control net. He got an MC after that operation. That was a John Gunn.....I wonder if it's the same man. Oh well, we'll soon know. Here we are,' and the staff car

96

pulled into the parking area reserved for military and diplomatic cars.

Wearing their airside passes, the two British officers walked through the terminal to the gate which let them out onto the concrete apron in front of the terminal. John Briars paused at the newspaper kiosk and bought a copy of the Daily Graphic, before they both went through the gate. The British Airways 767 touched down as they came out of the terminal and the two of them walked over to where Dennis Motram, the BA Manager, was waiting beside the pre-positioned steps. The 767 turned off the runway and started the slow journey back along the taxiway to the terminal.

'Morning, Miles... John; meeting someone off the flight or just checking on BA's punctuality,' they were greeted by Dennis Motram.

'Just another visitor from MOD, Dennis; Caroline and the kids well?' Miles Stockwell asked.

'Fine thanks....'

'Hey, have you seen this, Dennis?' John interrupted, looking at his Daily Graphic. 'The bit about the Aeroflot plane last night?'

'Oh yes, I was called up to the airport late last night. A somewhat macabre business and no explanation at all at the moment.' The 767 was now turning towards the apron and they had to raise their voices to be heard.

'Just after taking off,' Dennis explained, 'the captain of the Tupelov 154 spoke to the tower and said that he couldn't get his nose wheel to retract and asked for permission to return to Kotoka. The airport went onto a full scale alert, which was why I was called out, while the Tupelov circled over the sea dumping fuel. When it came into land, the captain said he had all the right indications of lock-down of the nose wheel, but he was afraid it might be a false indication and the wheel would fold up under the aircraft.' Dennis was shouting to make himself heard and then the engines were cut, the noise subsided and he lowered his voice.

'The Tupelov stopped at the end of the runway, over there,' and he pointed, 'and the emergency vehicle with Alexei Korjavin, the Aeroflot manager, went out to inspect the nose wheel before letting the aircraft taxi to the terminal. They found the remains of one of the airport's customs officials tied to the struts, which carry the dual nose wheels. As the nose wheel was retracted on takeoff, the legs had been severed and the skull squashed to pulp. It's not immediately clear if it was an accident or murder. We've had two or three stowaways climb into the wheel recesses before; one fell out over the sea and another was discovered back at Gatwick frozen to death and as stiff as a board. Ah, here come the passengers and the start of today's set of problems.'

Gunn had travelled World Traveller Class, which was a nice way of saying 'Economy'. Fortunately the girl at the check-in desk at Gatwick had managed to get him a seat by one of the emergency exits which had provided him with plenty of legroom. He removed his briefcase from the overhead container slung the jacket of his lightweight suit over his arm and joined the queue of large Ghanaian women jostling to get off the 767. From the top of the steps, Gunn immediately spotted the two, Army officers in stone-coloured slacks and shirts and when he reached the bottom of the steps walked over to them.

'Colonel Stockwell?' Gunn enquired of the officer wearing red aiguillettes on either side of his collar.

'John Gunn; nice to meet you. I'm Miles and this is John Briars. In a team as small as ours we don't have time to mess about with ranks.'

'Thank you Miles; nice to meet you John,' and they joined the next queue to clear immigration, from there to the baggage claim, no halt at customs - perhaps not surprisingly, the customs officials were not stopping anyone, which was remarked on by John Briars - and finally out onto the front concourse where Corporal Badu was waiting to take the trolley.

'Is there a problem with customs?' Gunn asked.

'Very rarely, if ever, for us, but they can be real bastards to their own people if that's the mood there in; much like customs officers the world over. No, last night one of them was dispatched in a particularly bloody way,' and John Briars pointed to the article in the paper.'

'What we're planning to do, John, is to take you back to my house now,' this came from Miles Stockwell, 'for some coffee and breakfast and then we've a very short programme for you to visit the commandants of the various training establishments here. After that we will leave you to your own devices. Here's a copy of your programme,' and Corporal Badu held the car door as Gunn got into the back seat. Gunn glanced at the programme.

'Thanks, that looks fine. Would the High Commission be open at this hour?'

'Should be; we've got you down for a courtesy call on the High Commissioner later today. The hours of work are from 7.30 to 14.30.'

'Yes, I saw that I was due to visit him; no, the Queen's Messenger was on the same flight and was carrying some documents for me which he was taking straight to the High Commission.'

'Of course, no problem,' and Miles gave the necessary instructions to the driver. At the High Commission, the receptionist handed over the package to Gunn and little more was said until they arrived at Miles Stockwell's bungalow where he was greeted first by Shemma the dog and then by Miles' pretty, blonde-haired wife, Bobbie, and his two daughters, Sarah and Anna, out from the UK for the school holidays. The three men went through to the veranda where Gunn readily accepted a large cup of freshly filtered coffee. As they went onto the veranda, the phone rang and was picked up by Bobbie. The three of them sat at the table on the veranda.

'Were you involved in the first Gulf war, John?' Miles asked.

'Yes I was, and if I remember rightly you were a staff officer with the headquarters of 5 Brigade.'

'Yes, I.....' but the door opened and Bobbie stuck her head out. 'Sorry to interrupt, but that was your Penny, John. Something's happened at the McLean's house and she's on her way there now. Richard and Emma are coming over here and I thought we would all go up to the pool at the Shangri La.'

'Fine, darling; don't forget the radio.'

'I never do; it's always you who forgets it! Sorry to desert you, John, when you've only just arrived, but this is all to do with an expat family that is in a spot of bother at the moment; bye everyone,' and Bobbie's head disappeared back through the door.

'Is it alright to talk here?' Gunn directed the question at Miles Stockwell.

'Yes it is; is there anything that we can to do to help or any information you need?'

'The answer is yes, to both of those offers, but can I start with the second one first.'

'Sure, go ahead.'

'Do you know how or from where Tony Bristow got hold of that information about orchestrated subversion and terrorism in all the countries of West Africa?'

'Yes, I told him,' John Briars replied.

'And where did you get that information?'

'From a croupier in the casino at Black Caesar's Palace.'

'Didn't we pass that near a roundabout on the way here?'

'Yes we did; it's just south of the Danquah roundabout. I think a quick bit of background would help here.' John Briars explained about his weekly visit to the casino and his friendship with the croupier Eddy Twintoh.

'How reliable is Eddy's information?'

99

'We must leave you to make a judgement of that,' Miles answered. 'Neither John nor I are qualified to make an objective assessment of the information Eddy's passed to us. What I will say is this. Eddy has given John two pieces of information before; both were accurate to the last detail. Eddy's wife, Patience, certainly owes her life to John's generosity in paying for her operation at the Military Hospital. John wouldn't mind me telling you that the operation and hospital fees were funded by a highly successful night on the blackjack table! Eddy says he overheard the information from two Ivorians who were playing the tables and who had had far too much to drink. In that casino or very shortly after, someone else must have overheard them because both men were found in the deep monsoon ditch, which runs on either side of that road, the next morning. They were both dead and the murder was reported in both the local papers. What the papers didn't say was that both men had had their tongues cut out.'

'Silly buggers, silly buggers!' Gunn turned round to find a large African Grey parrot marking time from one foot to the other on the branch of a frangipani tree. His head was cocked on one side as he studied Gunn.

'Sorry, John; I forgot to introduce you to Arnold, which has clearly upset him. John, this is Arnold; Arnold this is John Gunn who is visiting, so try and be polite if that's possible.'

'I trust he's been positively vetted,' Gunn smiled as he studied the handsome pale grey parrot with the vivid red trimmings to tail and wing.

'No, 'fraid not; the only vetting he gets is from our Scottish vet, who works for Overseas Development Aid, and incidentally, takes care of all the BMAT pets.'

'Why the name Arnold?'

'Ah, well you see he was a present from the armed forces supremo, some years ago, whose first name was Arnold.'

'Doesn't he fly away?'

'No he doesn't; he's obviously been a pet all this life and seems to prefer hanging around humans being thoroughly rude to them and having a good nip when they least expect it. Keep an eye on him, John, as he'd managed to get quite close to you before you spotted him. Sorry, back to business.'

'Right, tell me about Tony Bristow,' Gunn prompted after moving his chair so that he could keep a watchful eye on Arnold.

'Who's going to go first?' Miles Stockwell looked enquiringly at John Briars.

'Go on, Miles; your views on that character will be less vitriolic than mine. I couldn't stand the sight of the pompous ass or his thespian-struck wife.'

'There's not much to say, really; when I first arrived here a year ago he seemed pleasant enough and certainly Monica, his wife, has always been very hospitable, but then so she is to everyone. Tony rabbited on about everything; he loved the sound of his own voice and always banged on at great length at any conference boring the pants off everyone. Most of the information he sent back to Century House was absolute rubbish and I think he just made it up by extemporising around articles in the national press. He always made a great play of his close links with the SAS and appeared to have some Walter Mittian fantasy by encouraging me to think that he had been closely involved in some of the SAS's more clandestine operations. The affair with Lin Aldridge started about a couple of months after Bobbie and I arrived here. Both of them were appallingly indiscreet - Tony and Lin, I mean - but Monica either didn't realise what was happening or didn't want to realise. I gather from John that at any party where both couples were invited, Tony and Lin would be off to the car to bonk each other within the first hour.....'

'That's no exaggeration,' John Briars chipped in, 'the rest of us used to have bets on how long it would be before they vanished. At one party, less than a month ago I suppose, both had arrived on their own and never even made it to the front door. I regret to say that it became quite a game and we took it in turns to nominate the duty bonking witness.'

'John, come on.....'

'No Miles, you know it's true, and John must know what was going on.'

'You've mentioned Monica, but what was Lin's husband's reaction to all of this,' Gunn asked.

'Complete indifference,' came from John Briars. 'The man's a zombie; I honestly think he's on drugs or something.'

'Steady John,' Miles Stockwell cautioned, 'although I tend to agree with you.'

'What's his job in the High Commission?' Gunn brought them both back to facts rather than conjecture.

'He's head of the commercial section; a Grade 6 in FCO terminology,' Miles answered.

'And what's this Lin been up to since Tony Bristow disappeared last Sunday?'

'She appears to have given up all pretence of being a wife and spends all her time in the seediest bars and discos looking for men who'll screw her. Jack Forest - he's the deputy manager of the Chase Manhattan bank here in Ghana - took two single men to 'Blow Up' the night before last and they saw her pay a teenaged expat to bonk her out in the car park. Now this is a rumour, but very believable after the turn of recent events; Roger is supposed to have picked up Lin in a girlie bar in Seoul on a previous tour, perhaps old habits.......' but John Briars tit-bit of scandal was interrupted by a shriek from the kitchen which was quickly followed by the appearance of Cephas - the house steward - on the veranda. Gunn could have sworn, if it hadn't been medically impossible with his skin pigmentation, that the smiling and cheerful steward had turned grey with fright.

'Sir! Sir! Cobra, come quickly please!'

'Damn, alright Cephas; watch it, but keep well clear. Is it another spitting cobra?'

'Yes Sir, spit already but no harm done.'

'Come on, John..... sorry it's a bit confusing with two Johns. We seem to have a family of these wretched spitting cobras here.' Miles and John went through the drawing room towards the kitchen while Gunn opened the large Jiffy envelope and removed the 9mm Tanarmi and a full magazine. He loaded the magazine, worked the slide and chambered the first round. He then released the ring hammer slowly to half-cock which put the automatic on safe, slipped it into his ankle holster and followed the other two out to the back yard

Maggie, the cook, who had found the snake lurking under the communal sink, had had hysterics and was sobbing somewhere amongst the sugar cane in the back garden by the servants' vegetable patch. Cephas's wife, Florence, had grabbed their little boy and had disappeared after Maggie, leaving Cephas with a 15 foot long bamboo, and looking rather like a pole vaulter with a severe attack of ants in his pants, to take on the cobra. As Gunn came out into the back yard he was cautioned by Miles Stockwell; 'be careful, John, it's a real daddy of a spitting cobra; they can spit over 20 feet and the venom will blind you.'

In the corner of the yard was a thick black snake about seven or eight feet in length with the first part of its body raised to the vertical and hood spread. Its belly was marked with bright orange stripes across the body. Miles Stockwell was holding another bamboo and told the steward to go round the other side of the backyard wall to the front drive in case the snake escaped through one of the many holes in the wall. John Briars was looking for something to throw at the cobra.

102

There was a sharp report and the cobra's head disintegrated. Gunn quickly replaced the automatic in its holster and went back into the kitchen. There was a stunned silence in the backyard while Miles Stockwell and John Briars stared at each other. 'It's alright, Cephas, the cobra's dead,' Miles shouted. Bamboo and brick were put down and the two men followed Gunn back into the house.

*

'Thanks very much for coming so quickly, Penny,' was Mary's effusive greeting as Penny Briars climbed out of the Nissan in front of the McLean's house. 'Stuart's inside with Mo; I know it sounds silly, but can you give me a lift down to your house?'

'Yes....of course, but...'

'Please, Penny.'

'Yes, right; jump in, Mary.' Penny was mystified; there were no less than three cars outside the McLean house - the company Mercedes, their big long-wheelbase Nissan Patrol and Mary's small Honda Civic. Penny started her battered old Nissan and drove back out of the gates onto the pot-holed Sankara Road.

'Thanks; the reason we have to be in your car is that we've received a ransom note about Graham.'

'What!'

'We didn't say anything on Monday to you because we were so terrified that the kidnappers might do something awful to the boys.'

'What are you talking about? Which boys?'

'Sorry, my mind's in a turmoil. Bear with me,' and Mary took a deep breath.

'Mary, take as long as you want. Do you still want me to go to Teshie?'

'Yes please; right, I'm ready. On the way back from the mine on Monday, Stuart was contacted by old man Mackenzie; he's ....'

'Yes, I know who he is.'

'His grandson, Ian, has also vanished and he told Stuart to be ready for a ransom note.'

'Dear God, but ....'

'Wait, let me finish. That ransom note came today.....or more likely last night as it was on our answerphone. We've got to go and collect another tape tomorrow which will give us all the details of how much is to be paid and so on. The tape also said that if we got in touch with the police they would cut off bits of the children's bodies and send them to us. No prizes for guessing the first bit they'll chop off two boys......'

'No!.....'

103

'Yes; that's the sort of creatures we're up against. The tape also said that they have a bug on our phone and can hear everything we say in the house and garden. That's why we're in your car and why I've asked you to go to your bungalow in the military camp at Teshie, because they won't be able to follow us into the camp.... I hope.'

'When do you get this other tape?' Penny was finding it very hard to concentrate on her driving as she grappled with the enormity of the McLean's problem.

'Stuart has to do that; it's out at the Shai Hills game reserve. The tape had very detailed instructions; at the gate Stuart has to set the digital kilometre trip to zero and then has to follow that route which takes you to where all the baboons gather.... you know, below that rock escarpment.'

'Yes, I think I remember it.'

'The tape said that when his kilometre thing reads 3.4 kms, there will be a large flat rock on the left of the Nissan. Apparently, so the instructions on the tape said, there will be a small bolder on top of this flat rock and in a crevice on the side of the bolder furthest away from the track will be a package containing the tape. There were one or two more instructions which followed, but basically he has to collect the tape at 7.30 am precisely tomorrow. Stuart says that he's bound to be followed and watched from somewhere on that rock escarpment. Stuart also said that all the monolithic outcrops of rock along that road make it ideal to watch him and see if he takes anyone with him. How Stuart's managing to think so clearly, I don't know, as he's beside himself with worry about what to do. He also said that this kidnapping was extremely cleverly planned to have abducted two hostages simultaneously, some seven thousand miles apart. Police action by either us or the Mackenzies in Canada will result in immediate retribution against both boys. Because of that, neither of us dare do anything for fear of the awful consequences, not only for our child, but the Mackenzies' as well.'

'I just can't believe that this is all happening to you... to us, Mary. It's just like some of those silly things that John and Richard watch on those dreadful video tapes which he hires from the shop at the Danquah roundabout. Here we are; anyone following us, Mary?' and Penny turned through the castellated arch at the entrance to the military camp.

'Ther're about twenty cars behind us. How is one meant to know which one's following us?'

'God knows; we'll stop at the Stockwell's house because John'll be there. The BMAT team has a visitor from MOD. As if we haven't got enough on our plates without one of those boring old farts wanting to be entertained everywhere at our expense.' With that succinct summary of her views on MOD visitors, Penny turned the old Nissan off the road onto the laterite track and then left again into the driveway of the Stockwell's bungalow.

Outside the bungalow was Miles's staff car and Miles and John beside a tall and well-built young man in slacks, open-necked shirt and carrying a jacket. Cephas was hovering in the background and Shemma was trying to nibble the visitor's toes. 'Your visitor may be boring, Penny, but he certainly doesn't look like an old fart,' Mary remarked as the Nissan pulled up in the shade of a large nim tree.

'No, you're right; John said he was a Lt Colonel, but he looks jolly young for that or perhaps it's just that I'm getting older; same as that business with policemen - you know - when they start to look young you know you're getting old.' Penny and Mary got out of the car and went towards the three men.

'Hello Penny, Mary; meet our guest from London who's just arrived. John Gunn this is Penny, our John's better half and this is Mary McLean; Mary's husband, Stuart, is the general manager of Sikafituru Mining. After Miles had completed the introduction, Penny caught his eye and interrupted.

'I'm sorry to interrupt things, Miles, but could Mary and I just have a word - privately,' and she glanced at John Gunn who wasn't paying the least bit of attention and was engrossed in watching the Stockwell's chickens scraping around under the umbrella trees.

'Really darling,' this came from her husband, 'can't it wai...'

'No John, it can't.'

'Of course, Penny...Mary, come on through to the veranda. John won't mind waiting a couple of minutes.' Gunn seemed not in the slightest concerned as he and Shemma had wandered off for a closer inspection of the chickens' activities. The four of them went into the bungalow. 'Please sit down, ladies,' Miles indicated the armchairs. 'Now, apart from our anxiety about Graham, what's new?'

'He's been kidnapped and a ransom demand's been sent to Mary and Stuart,' came from Penny.

'What! John, just make sure that Cephas or Margaret aren't in the kitchen, would you.'

'Sure,' and he left the room.

'When did this happen,' Miles asked.

'This morning,' Mary answered and then gave him a brief account as John Briars came back into the room.

'Stop for moment, Mary,' and she did so, slightly surprised. 'The one person who should be listening to this, isn't in the room.'

105

'What do you mean, Miles? If there's the slightest hint of police involvement, they've said they'll cut off bits of his body and send then to us,' and Mary started to sob quietly.

'No Mary; no police. The man we left outside on our driveway, John Gunn.'

'Oh Miles, what can he, an army officer do to help us,' Mary sobbed as Penny comforted her.

'He's not an army officer.' The crying stopped.

'Well what is he then, Miles .....superman or something?'

'From what we've seen this morning, the next best thing. I think the only way I can describe what he does is to say that you've just met the real-life version of James Bond.'

'You're joking,' but Penny went into the drawing room and looked out of the window, which faced onto the driveway. Gunn was still by the umbrella tree; Shemma had rolled on her back and was having her tummy tickled and she and Gunn were surrounded by the Miles' chickens and guinea fowl. She walked back out to the verandah. 'Well, he's certainly got a way with the women - if that's the criteria for secret agents,' she announced as she went back through the French windows onto the veranda. 'Are we - that is, Mary and me - allowed to ask what he's doing here, or is all of that covered by some wretched thing like the Official Secrets Act or whatever it's called?'

'John Gunn is out here to investigate the disappearance of Tony Bristow.......'

'Of course!' Penny interrupted Miles, 'I'd forgotten he was one of those people....'

'Do stop interrupting, darling, and let Miles finish,' Penny was chided by her husband.

'I'm sorry Miles, but this whole thing gets more and more like...er...well, I suppose a James Bond film, by the minute. Shall I go and ask him to come and join us?'

'Yes, why not,' Miles agreed.

'Oh gawd!' John Briars muttered as Penny hurried from the veranda, 'we're never going to hear the end of this in the Briars' house. You know what Penny's like with her romantic novels. She'll fantasise about this for years. Sorry, Mary, I don't mean to be frivolous.'

'I know, John; it's quite a relief really, and if this man is so good......incidentally, if he's all so secret, how do you know he's so good and the next best thing to superman?'

'We hadn't got round to telling you girls about that,' John Briars chipped in, 'but just before you two turned up at the house, the

Stockwells had another cobra in the back yard and old Cephas was prancing around like a demented dervish while Margaret, the cook, and Florence - that's Cephas' wife - had hysterics out in the back garden. Needless to say, old Nuher, the gardener, had vanished as they all conveniently do when there are snakes around. While Miles and I were pratting around with sticks and things, this John Gunn produces a bloody great pistol out of thin air and blows the cobra's head off. Honestly, it was the most amazing shot - the more so to someone like me as I've never been able to fire a pistol and couldn't even've hit the bloody wall behind the snake, let alone take its head off at twenty yards.'

'I think nearer ten, John, but I agree, it was an amazing shot and done with such speed and lack of fuss. I don't know if he has any other.......ah! John, please join us again. I think what the girls wanted to tell me is related to your visit here. Sorry if I've spilled the beans about what you do, but I think the girls have to know.' Miles' comment about any further talents which Gunn might or might not have possessed had been interrupted by the latter's return to the veranda, preceded by Penny and followed by the faithful Shemma who had evidently decided that the sole purpose of Gunn's visit to Ghana was to devote himself to her.

'Doesn't matter in the slightest, Miles; there are many more who'll have to know before this business has been dealt with. What's this about and who's going to tell me?' Gunn asked looking from Mary to Penny.'

'I'll.....' started Penny.

'Hush, darling; let Mary tell John,' her husband interrupted.

'Yes, alright,' Mary started and then the phone just inside the French windows rang.

'Excuse me,' and Miles went inside and picked up the phone, while Mary started to tell Gunn the whole sorry saga of Graham's disappearance and the ransom note. Miles was on the phone for about seven or eight minutes and then reappeared with a perplexed expression on his face.

'Not more bad news?' John Briars asked.

'Well, the answer to that's yes and no, I think; that was General Amanfo. He's the Head of the Armed Forces, John. He was ringing to say that they must postpone your meetings today and hopefully will set them up for tomorrow. The old man was very cagey, but something's gone wrong or there's an alert or something and they're putting every unit on stand-by. That means that you're free for the rest of today, John, except for your meeting with the High

Commissioner at 10.30 this morning......' Miles looked at his watch, 'in 25 minutes.'

CHAPTER 7

'Tower, this is Nine Golf Five Five Zero, ready to taxi.'

'9G550, you are clear to taxi, runway 175.

'Runway 175, 9G550,' the whine of the 420 shaft horsepower Allison turboshaft on the Bell Long Ranger rose a few decibels, the pilot released the brakes and the helicopter taxied out from the concrete apron in front of the commercial air services hangar at Kotoka Airport towards runway 175. Ahead of the helicopter was a Swissair 737 turning onto the runway. The helicopter stopped at the waiting position. The man in the seat behind the pilot stood up, removed a thin-bladed knife from inside the sleeve of his work overalls and plunged it up to the hilt in the back of the pilot's neck. The man in the co-pilot's seat leant over and undid the safety harness and the pilot was lifted into the passenger compartment. The co-pilot took over the helicopter with the dual controls as the Swissair 737 started its takeoff. The Bell helicopter turned onto runway 175 behind the departing 737.

'9G550, tower, clear for take off.'

'9G550,' went the acknowledgement and the helicopter moved forward and then rose rapidly, gaining altitude as it banked to starboard and headed west for Takoradi as indicated in the filed flight plan. The dead pilot was removed to a seat at the back of the passenger compartment. The man in the passenger compartment opened the duffle bag which he'd been carrying and removed a flying helmet and safety strop. He buckled the safety strop round his waist and hooked the snap shackle onto the strong point on the starboard side of the passenger compartment. Once his helmet was on, he plugged the hanging lead and jack-plug into the extension lead, swung the boom mike in front of his mouth and tested communications with the pilot. Satisfied, he pulled back the sliding door on the port side of the helicopter and connected the netting of the load-carrier to its strop and the strop to the winch. It was 09.54.

In the Bank of Ghana, Kofi had kept his appointment with the bank employee who had been allowed to speak to his wife on the phone, before being told to open the Bank's vault. The circular door swung open and Kofi's two assistants pushed their trolleys into the gleaming steel interior. The 53 bars of gold gleamed dully from the steel shelving in front of them. Kofi watched the bank employee while his assistants loaded the bars from the shelves onto the two trolleys. In his left hand, Kofi held the radio to communicate to the helicopter; his right hand was inside his traditional Ghanaian robes holding an Encom .45 calibre machine pistol with a 30 round magazine. It was 10.03.

'Who gave authority for this unscheduled vault opening?' The Bank's security guard was standing outside the vault with a pump-action shotgun held across his chest. Kofi fired from underneath his robes and three, heavy, soft-nosed .45 slugs hurled the guard back five yards and onto his back. The three of them stopped loading the gold while the guard was dragged inside the vault. There were shouts from the main banking hall and the sound of people running towards the vault.

Kofi's men, in their security guard uniforms, pushed the two trolleys out of the vault and turned to the right heading for the Bank's Thorpe Street exit. The bank employee who had opened the vault never knew what killed him; he was shot point-blank in the back of the head and fell inside the vault door. The shouts were getting closer as Kofi swung the perfectly balanced door closed, spun the locking wheels and combination dials and then wrapped a fistful of pliable PE around the central locking wheel. The first person had now appeared at the other end of the corridor and there was a shout.

Kofi waved back to the man who seemed temporarily reassured and then transferring the radio from his left hand to under his right arm, very carefully removed the thin glass fulminate of mercury detonator from the left pocket of the shorts which he wore under his robes. He pushed the tip of the detonator into the PE, snapped the top off it to start the corrosive acid timer, turned to his right and walked unhurriedly towards the exit. There was another shout behind him followed by a deafening explosion; it would now take days, if not weeks, to open the vault. As he reached the door, Kofi spoke into the radio. The message was acknowledged with a transmission blip rather than voice and he saw the Bell Long Ranger coming in low from the sea.

Kofi's men were now in the car park with their two trolleys which had loose covers thrown over the bars of gold. Chaos and bedlam were beginning to errupt in the Bank of Ghana behind him as Kofi walked over to the car park. The whine of the turbine and beat of the rotor blades drowned out all coherent thought as the helicopter went into a low hover. The net spread itself out on the tarmac and the two security men pushed the trolleys in and then climbed onto the netting.

Not a second had been wasted and no one had panicked; Kofi reached the under-slung net as the loading was completed and joined his two assistants by climbing onto the net and taking a firm handhold. The engine note changed, the beat of the blades became deafening as they bit into the hot thin air to get lift and the winch lifted the gold and the three men clear of the car park. People were now running across to the car park from the Bank, waving their arms and shouting. Six feet.....twenty feet......a hundred feet and then the helicopter dipped its nose and started to pick up speed as it crossed the High Street and headed out to sea. Kofi hung on with his right hand having let go of the machine pistol, which was slung around his neck. He still held the radio in his left hand and twisted his wrist over. It was 10.12.

Once over the sea, the chopper sank to its minimum height; the under-slung load of gold and men skimmed only feet above the waves as the helicopter raced westwards at a best speed of 95 mph with its 'un-clean' aerodynamic shape. Once clear of the city, which was left behind in 45 seconds, the beaches were deserted and soon the blinding white glare of the salt pans came into view. It had been most important, in the planning of the robbery, to select a load-transfer point which was inside the police check points on all roads leading into Accra. Whilst Kofi and his team wouldn't have hesitated to shoot an over-zealous policeman looking for a potential bribe, it was a delay he had wished to avoid. Coming up ahead of them was the outfall of the River Korle, which ran in a steep-sided gully. The chopper banked to starboard and the under-slung load swung out as the pilot brought the machine in low along the gully. It was most unlikely that anyone had seen them.

A quarter of a mile from the main Accra/Takoradi road by the side of the river was an abandoned concrete-building-block factory; parked beside this was the panel lorry. Kofi saw the roof panels of the lorry open as the chopper banked again to starboard and the heavy beat of the blades indicated that the machine was slowing into the hover. The opening in the lorry roof was now right below them and the winch whined as it lowered its cargo through the aperture. The sudden change from the blinding glare reflected off the salt pans to the relative dark of the lorry, left the men with no vision and they had to be helped from the net by the lorry crew. Last came the winch operator who climbed down the strop and once in the lorry, unhooked the net and then tapped Kofi on the back.

Kofi spoke into the radio and the helicopter lifted clear and sped, unencumbered, towards the sea. The pilot undid his harness, inflated his life jacket and hooked on the small, survival inflatable dinghy. He reduced speed and engaged the autopilot. The Bell Long Ranger cruised slowly towards the sea. The pilot's last task before leaving was to carry out Kofi's final instruction to him which was to pull the red toggle on the CO2 bottle which would inflate the plastic doll inside the aircrew overalls. The pilot had considered this to be a masterpiece of attention to detail. He placed the overalls in the right-hand seat with their attached shoes and helmet and fastened the harness across the deflated dummy. The chopper was approaching the sea; the pilot was by no means an expert swimmer and therefore had every intention of jumping from the machine as close to the shore as possible. He knocked out the hinge pins from his door, which fell away below the Long Ranger and then leant across and pulled the red toggle on the CO2 bottle. The helicopter erupted in a ball of flame before crashing into the sea and sinking in thirty feet of water.

The Magirus-Deutz panel truck turned right onto the Accra/Takoradi road and headed for Accra. In the back, Kofi and the three men from the helicopter plus two more who had been waiting in the lorry, set to work to distribute the gold bars amongst the twenty crates of unserviceable drilling equipment. All the unserviceable parts were large valves and pump-heads from offshore drilling rigs, which provided ideal apertures into which the gold was placed. Everything had been rehearsed carefully before. One man removed the bars from the trolleys and passed them, in turn, to two others who wrapped them in bubble-foam packaging. Each of the wrappers then handed them to the fourth member of the team who placed the wrapped bars into the crates. The fifth member of the team nailed down the crates, steel-banded them and then crimped on the customs seal with the crimping tool bought off the customs official whose life had come to an abrupt end in the nose wheel compartment of a Tupelov 154.

A large truck had been selected so that the men could move around with ease inside. At the front end of the load container was a large crate, almost the full width of the truck and some five feet square in which all their equipment had been packed. None of the crates needed to be moved and all of this was supervised by Kofi with a stopwatch and his radio. The truck turned left off the road leading into the centre of Accra onto the outer ring road which by-passed the city to the north. The journey to the airport had been driven three times at exactly the correct time on the Thursdays of the three previous weeks using three different trucks. It would take 21 minutes for the truck to reach the airport entrance. Any traffic delays would be a bonus, but could not be taken into Kofi's calculations.

112

The truck ground down through the gears as it climbed the long hill towards North Ridge. Kofi knew every yard of the road even though they were in an enclosed truck; the only illumination came from three interior lights, which had been fitted for the task of crating the gold. The truck reached the crest of the North Ridge and the driver went up through the box as they cruised down the gradient to the major junction with the northbound Kumasi road. Seven crates were nailed, banded and sealed. The men were stripped to nothing more than shorts and the sweat poured from their bodies in the oven-like interior of the metal container.

Now the truck had reached the bottom of the gradient and changed down for the short climb up to the Achimota crossroads; three miles to go to the airport; eleven crates sealed. At the back of the truck were two large cool-boxes packed with ice, beer and Coca-Cola, but none of it could be touched until the task was finished. Over the crossroads and down the mile run to the Tettie-Quarshie roundabout where they would turn right onto the airport road; 14 crates sealed. The man unloading the bars from the netting collapsed to the floor, completely dehydrated. Kofi stepped into his place and the bars kept moving along the work gang. The truck had slowed for the roundabout and then swung to the right as it joined the traffic into Accra from the Tema highway; 500 yards to the airport turn-off; 17 crates sealed. The second wrapper collapsed, but his companion merely increased the speed of his task.

Kofi was now bathed in sweat and the interior of the unventilated truck stank horribly of stale male sweat. The truck was slowing again; they had reached the left turn to the airport; 400 yards to the entrance to the cargo area and one more crate. The last three gold bars went into the crate, the lid slammed shut, the steel binding was pulled tight, clamped and severed and the seals crimped into place.

The brakes squealed as the truck pulled up at the gates; two minutes passed while all the paperwork was checked. The Magirus-Deutz was driven onto the apron where two fork-lift trucks were waiting to off-load the crates. Another three minutes passed, which gave Kofi just enough time to remove the panel between the container and the cab and climb in beside the driver. He then replaced the panel, gave the driver an ice-cold Coke and jumped out of the cab, went round to the rear of the truck and broke the seals on the doors. The doors were opened and the cargo ground-handling crew jumped into the back and dragged each of the crates to the rear where they were removed by the fork-lift trucks and taken over to the air-freight aluminium pallets.

113

When the last of the crates had been removed, Kofi closed the rear doors of the truck and then watched as the aluminium pallets were loaded into the IMT Boeing 747-400. The cargo doors were closed, the four General Electric turbofans were started and the aircraft taxied out to runway 175. Six minutes later, the engines built up to full thrust and the Boeing and $11 million of gold bars left Kotoka Airport.

Kofi went round to the truck's cab and climbed into the right-hand passenger seat. The driver had died within seconds of drinking the cyanide-laced Coke. He dragged the dead body of the driver out of the left-hand seat and onto the middle one, got out of the cab and walked round to the left side where he climbed in behind the wheel. He pushed the dead driver into the righthand corner of the cab and strapped the body into the seat with the safety harness. The Magirus-Deutz was driven to the lorry park at the junction with the ring road and the Kumasi Road, where Kofi parked it up and then went and collected his small Nissan open-backed truck. Using the winch behind the cab of this truck, he pulled the large, seven-foot long crate from the back of the Magirus onto the Nissan. He then dragged the driver from the cab and, once again, with the use of the winch he joined his colleagues in the seven foot crate. That task complete, Kofi left the keys of the vehicle in the ignition and drove away in the Nissan to Tema Port, nine miles east along the coast, where his crate was loaded onto a dilapidated fishing vessel which he'd chartered.

He cast off the seaweed-choked warps from the old boat and took it round from the fishing harbour to the commercial port where he came alongside the public jetty long enough to take the painter of the outboard motorboat from the man who had been paid - what he considered - was a small fortune for guarding the boat and which was then tied to the stern of the fishing boat. Kofi took the old boat out through the gap in the breakwaters and at the painfully slow pace of 7½ knots headed out into the Gulf of Guinea.

One hour later, with no other boat in sight, he opened the sea-cocks of the fishing boat with its engine still running, climbed into the motorboat and started the 85 horsepower Mariner outboard. Kofi undid the painter, depressed the buttton to engage gear on the combined throttle and gear control and drove clear of the fishing boat.

Three minutes later the waves broke over the stern of the boat and it disappeared below the surface in 600 feet of water carrying with it the crate filled with bodies and cyanide-laced bottles of beer and Coke. Kofi was back at the public jetty 15 minutes later where he tied up the motorboat, collected his Datsun van from the car park in the fishing harbour and then drove back along the Tema highway to Accra and the house on Independence Avenue.

*

'I'll take you to the High Commission now, John, and then after you've met the High Commissioner, we'll drop your case at the Labadi Beach Hotel. Bobbie's got the children at the Shangri La and I suggest that Mary, Penny and her John join them there and I'll take you there, John, after we've checked in at the hotel. I expect there's much more you'll want to talk to Mary about. Does that make sense?' Miles asked Gunn.

'Fine; ready when you are. Bye Mary.....Penny... John, I'll see you all a little later,' and Gunn went with Miles Stockwell through the house to the driveway and got into the back of the staff car with him. 'Anything I ought to know about the High Commissioner, Miles, before we meet?'

'Not really; I suppose he's fairly typical of that level of diplomat. Having said that, I've little or no experience of diplomats as I've never done an attaché appointment. He's obviously clever - both he and his wife got Firsts at Oxford which is where they met, I believe. Perhaps unkindly, but I've heard it said a marriage of intellects rather than bodies as the union has produced no children. He's desperately ambitious; picked up a CMG in his previous job as a commercial counsellor at the High Commission in Ottawa and it's a standing joke in the High Commission here that everything is done to add a 'K' to that CMG.

'Is he effective in the appointment?'

'I suppose so; you see.....' and Miles paused while he chose the right words. 'The FCO is exactly the opposite to everything we've been taught in the Army. For us, our first and last priorities are our soldiers..... their morale, their training, efficiency, fitness, job satisfaction, their families, their problems and so on. In an embassy or high commission, there's only one person that matters and that's the ambassador; everything else is subordinate to that. I very much doubt if the man here even knows how many people are employed in the High Commission and couldn't care less if there are problems with housing, families and so on. I can never fathom out these men who possess no sense of humour, can talk about nothing except their work, whether on or off duty, are quite unable to delegate anything to subordinates without constantly interfering and nit-picking over completely unimportant detail, can't relax and don't want their all-consuming ambition cluttered by children.'

115

'That's sad; is that planned or what?'

'What the children?'

'Yes...'

'God knows; all sorts of rumours inevitably, but it's a subject to avoid if invited to the Residence.'

'No discussion about children?'

'Damn right; not unless you want to kill the conversation stone dead.'

'Well, thanks for the warning, not that I'm likely to be invited.'

The car followed the coast road into Accra through the shanty suburb of Labadi Village to its junction with the dual carriageway ring-road where the car turned right. As they turned onto the ring-road, three police cars with sirens wailing passed them on the other side of the carriage way and with squealing tyres turned right onto the coast road which ran through Christianborg and Victoriaborg to the city centre.

'There's definitely something going on,' Miles muttered as he turned to watch the police cars. 'I hope to God there hasn't been an attempted coup or something.' As they reached the Danquah roundabout, Miles' radio came to life.

'B-MAT 1, this is CHARLIE zero five, over.'

'BMAT 1, send over.'

'CHARLIE 05, can you contact me by telephone asp, over.'

'B-MAT 1, I'll be with you in 4 minutes, I have visitor for CHARLIE 01, over.'

'CHARLIE 05, understood, out.'

'That was Ian Maskell, the second secretary for information at the High Commission. An excellent man; there's obviously something quite serious going on so the sooner we reach the High Commission the better. Corporal Badu.'

'Yes Sir.'

'Quick as possible please.'

'Right Sir,' and the driver changed down and coaxed a little more speed out of the ancient Datsun. Two hundred yards beyond the roundabout, on their right, was the headquarters of the Ghana Police, which was a hive of activity. In the road in front of them were motorcycle police on both sides of the dual carriageway controlling the traffic. Their flag-flying staff car was allowed through the police control and made the turn across the central reservation into the Osu Link road, which led to the High Commission. The staff car turned in through the high, steel gates, past the barrier, which prevented car bombs being driven into the High Commission and stopped in front of the main entrance.

116

Miles Stockwell led the way into the High Commission and the receptionist pressed the switch to release the locking mechanism on the door into the chancery side of the building. The two men went up the broad staircase and then turned left through another door with a five number-coded lock. Ian Maskell was in the corridor outside his office and greeted Miles who introduced Gunn. The three of them went into the second secretary's office.

'Welcome to Ghana, John; please sit down. Coffee?'

'Yes please.'

'You Miles? When's your appointment with the High Commissioner?'

'Yes please and in six minutes,' Miles answered after glancing up at the wall clock.

'Right..... Maggie!' and a dark-haired girl came in from the PA's office, 'could we have three coffees please. I called you on the radio, Miles, because we've just heard that there has been a major robbery at the Bank of Ghana.'

'Oh, that's what it is,' Miles said with unmistakable relief in his voice. 'I knew something had happened because the GOC has postponed all John's appointments at MOD in Burma Camp. 'I was worried that it might be something more serious than that.'

'I think this is pretty serious,' Ian Maskell corrected the BMAT Commander. 'The accounts so far are inevitably very garbled, but this was a big operation, very well funded - a helicopter was used to remove the gold....'

'What!' Miles interjected.

'They've blown the locks on the vault, which has sealed it. From witnesses who saw them making their escape from the bank, they reckon they've taken the Ashanti gold bars which were found in the old fort in Kumasi.'

'Oh, no; that's a tragedy...'

'Right; their face value must be something in the region of ten million dollars, but as a collector's item they must be worth five or ten times that figure.'

'Casualties?'

'Yes, 'fraid so; one security guard shot dead and a bank employee missing. They think he's dead and sealed inside the vault. Come on, it's time for you to see the old man. Thought you ought to know asp as this may make the armed forces a bit jittery.'

'Quite right; thanks Ian. Come on, John, we'd better go and see Humphrey Winfield.'

'Sure,' from Ian Maskell, 'grab your coffees after you've seen him.'

Miles and Gunn left the second secretary's office and went next door where they were met by a pleasaant and very plain lady who introduced herself as June Baker, the High Commissioner's PA. The two men went straight in to meet Humphrey Winfield.

The High Commissioner was politeness itself, somewhat understandably assumed that Gunn was from the MOD and gave both men ten minutes of his views on Ghana, its economy, politics, armed forces and culture. That completed, they shook hands again and left the High Commissioner's office.

'Well, that was pretty painless; rather like my last visit to the dentist,' and Miles took Gunn first to Ian's office where they had their coffee and then to his hotel where he waited while Gunn changed into uniform. Even though the military appointments had been cancelled for that morning, Miles had suggested and Gunn readily agreed that it made a lot of sense for him to be seen in uniform. As they were leaving the hotel, Gunn paused at reception and after making an enquiry was given a small card with the directions to Dina Gbedemah's shop and was given the keys to his Landrover Discovery, which he was told was out in the car park.

The Shangri La was a hotel-cum-country club in the city. It was 400 yards beyond the airport on Independence Avenue and had tennis and squash courts, self-torturing exercise rooms and saunas, a large, heart-shaped pool, barbecued food and cold beer. It also had the added attraction of a constant selection of KLM stewardesses draped around the pool as the airline used the Shangri La for its lay-overs in Accra. Thatched roofed tables surrounded the pool and at one of these was Miles' wife, Bobbie, who had been joined by John and Penny Briars and Mary McLean. The younger children were in the pool while the elder Stockwell and Briars girls were stretched out on the loungers concentrating on their suntans. Miles and Gunn joined John Briars and the three women and ordered two bottles of Club Beer from the waiter.

There was a tangible aura of uncertainty around the table as none of them knew whether they ought to say anything about the real reason for Gunn's visit to Accra. Gunn knew that he would get nowhere while this uncertainty existed and it was up to him to get rid of it. 'What I'd like to do,' Gunn started as soon as their beers had been poured, 'is to go over what I know and then anything that I've missed out, perhaps one or all of you will fill in for me.' Relief showed on all the faces.

'Back in London, we heard from Bristow that there was a whisper around Accra of co-ordinated subversion and terrorism amongst the countries of West Africa to overthrow the legitimate governments and unite all the countries into a republic under one supreme ruler.

118

Since my arrival, I've learnt that that information was passed to John who quite rightly passed it to Bristow who quite incorrectly failed to tell us his source. It was Bristow's subsequent disappearance, which led to me being briefed to come out here under the guise of an MOD visitor and to check the validity of Bristow's report. Since my arrival, I've learnt of the kidnapping of your Graham, Mary, and little Ian Mackenzie in Canada. Miles and I've also just heard that all the Ashanti gold has been stolen from the Bank of Ghana.' This bit of information produced gasps from around the table.

'For a country which has achieved such political and economic stability, this sudden turn-around to rumours of terrorism and subversion, disappearances of diplomats and kidnapping of children can only be the first stage of a conspiracy to discredit the government and police and terrorise the population. This terrorist activity has reached far more advanced stages in most of the other West African countries, as you will all know. Terrorism needs money; money to bribe politicians and money to buy weapons. As in the old joke, what do you do if you want money? You rob a bank.' No one around the table spoke and the laughter of the children in the pool seemed distorted as though coming from far away.

*

'Brad Tracton;' the president of IMT had picked up the secure telephone after his PA, Joanne, had alerted him that a call was imminent.

'Hello Sir, this is the captain of Victor Romeo Charlie 748, in-bound to IMT via Dallas International. I have Puerto Rica under my port winglet and estimate Dallas at 1610 hours local time. The cargo is intact and was delivered right on schedule.' All of IMT's aircraft were registered in the Cayman Islands and so carried the national designator of VRC. IMT operated three Boeing 747-400s and two Lockheed C5 Galaxies; the latter, with their payload of nearly 100 tons and 11,000 mile range, were used to get either large quantities of weapons, quickly, to where they were required or for transporting urgently needed tanks or self-propelled guns. All the aircraft communicated with IMT via secure satellite links and through an additional scrambler process, which was re-coded every 24 hours. The CIA was well aware of this, but not even their resources had been able to break IMT's communication codes.

'Thanks, Al; any trouble in Accra?'

'Not that we could pick up, Sir. We monitored their police radios for an hour after the withdrawal from the bank and the whole scene was a shambles. Seems a lot of heads will roll as it took the first

119

police car 16 minutes to cover the half mile from police headquarters to the bank after they'd been alerted. As planned, there can be no possible connection to our flight departure, which had been scheduled for over a week.'

'That sounds good; speak to me again when you're in-bound to IMT.'

'That's a roger, Sir; we have to lay-over at Dallas for the night - FAA regulations - but we'll be on our way at 0900 hours tomorrow and at Amarillo 45 minutes later; bye.'

'Bye, Al,' and Brad Tracton replaced his phone, glanced at his watch and then buzzed his PA.

'Yes Sir.'

'Jo, get me that Charles Mensah guy would you. I need to know if he's raised the down payment for the arms. I'm going to Vegas this evening to play poker, but if I go a half hour earlier, Mensah could come to Caesar's Palace and give me a run down on how much cash he's raised so far. Say, about 1900 hours in the Brutus Suite. See what you can fix.'

'Got that, Sir; call you back when it's fixed.'

'Thanks, and warn Nat of the change in timings as he's coming with me to brief me on Caramansa's shipment and then play poker.'

'Will do, Sir,' and when the phone was back in its cradle Joanne cursed quietly to herself; the poker would go on all night so she would have an empty bed. Brad Tracton replaced the phone and buzzed for Frank Raubenheimer, his bodyguard.

'Sir.'

'Step into the office, Frank, would you.'

'On my way, Sir.' The door to the president's office opened seconds later and the bodyguard came in. Frank Raubenheimer was a professional, in every sense of the word. His family came from South Africa, which they had left in disgust at the increasingly liberal attitude towards the blacks. They were Boers through and through and in their view apartheid was the only way to treat blacks. Brad Tracton knew of his bodyguard's racist views, but had hired him because he was little more or less than a programmed humanoid killing machine. Killing people meant as much to Frank Raubenheimer as swatting a fly might to any reasonably normal person; nothing.

Frank had emigrated from South Africa to the States two years ahead of his parents so that he could enlist in the US Marines and fight in the first Gulf War. He had succeeded and arrived in Saudi Arabia a week before the invasion as a young, 21year-old marine. Five years later in 1996 he was in Bosnia and by then a sergeant. He had twice been awarded the Congressional Medal of Honour and a slack handful of purple hearts.

He kept his employer's office under constant surveillance from cameras concealed and positioned to leave no blind spots. His entire life was dedicated to the task of ensuring that his employer lived to draw his old age pension. Frank was a shade over six foot in height, weighed 200 pounds, shaved his head, as he had done for five years in Vietnam, and possessed not a spare ounce of flesh on his body. Every moment that he wasn't performing the function of a bodyguard, he was working out and his 'office', next to Brad Tracton's was a mini-gymnasium. To him, sex was a necessary bodily function like eating or defecating. A woman was provided for him three times a week as part of his terms of employment. His parents had both died in a car crash while he was in Iraq and he had no relatives.

'Poker as usual this evening, Frank, but I'll be leaving a half hour earlier so that I can meet with this Charles Mensah character. He's certain to bring one of his gorillas, but I'm not expecting trouble. Nat Cohn's coming with me. Any problems?'

'None Sir.'

'Thanks; see you later.' Frank left the office and Brad Tracton shook his head. Frank Raubenheimer was not the talkative type.

The helicopter left IMT at 1759 hours and landed in the grounds of Caesar's Palace at 1854 hours. Brad Tracton walked the fifty yards to the casino hotel and was shown up to the Brutus Suite. He waited outside while Frank checked out the room and then took his usual seat at the round, royal blue, baize-covered table facing the double doors. At precisely 7pm, there was a knock at the door and his guest was announced followed by his bodyguard. Brad Tracton waved towards a chair and the waiter.

'A glass of water, please.'

'Whisky, malt, neat no ice; right Mr Mensah, I'm ready to load your shipment. Time's come for the first payment; I have the gold from Accra and I've agreed that it represents the first 10 million dollars of the 135 million down payment. Now, where's the other 125 million?'

'I have it here for you, Mr Tracton.'

'What, right here?'

'Yes indeed, right here, as you say,' and Charles Mensah snapped his fingers. His bodyguard moved forward and lifted the bulky brief case into plain view. Frank Raubenheimer's eyes had never left the brief case since the moment it had entered the room. The brief case opened into two compartments; from one was removed a set of

121

electronic jewellers' scales with digital readout, from the other a leather case about the same size as a box file. The lid of the case was opened to reveal that it was packed to the brim with uncut diamonds.

'Please, Mr Tracton; perhaps you would care to weigh the diamonds.' He did and then removed a slim calculator from his jacket pocket and fed in the data. He looked up at Mensah.

'I reckon you're 18½ carats short, Mr Mensah.'

'Your reputation does you justice, Mr Tracton,' and Charles Mensah produced a small, inch-square leather case from his pocket which he placed on the blue baize in front of Brad Tracton who opened it, removed the single diamond from inside and placed it on the scale. 'I think you will find that that will suffice and comes with my best wishes for the special lady in your life. It is original and I had it cut myself and so is untraceable, Mr Tracton.' The stone registered 20 carats and sparkled with a brillant fire. The down payment was complete.

*

'Any problems?'

'None at all. Gold's on its way and all witnesses disposed of.'

'Not quite all, but you've done well, Kofi, and I shall report as such to Charles Mensah. 'I'll deal with the bank man's family,' and Kisi went down the steps to the cellar. She opened the heavy steel door of the cell occupied by the wife and children of the now deceased bank employee who had supplied the vault combination. The cell was pleasantly decorated, air-conditioned, had an en-suite bathroom and lavatory and a well-stocked mini-kitchenette. The woman had been told that her husband had been involved in a very important transfer of funds from the World Bank to the Bank of Ghana and that she and her three children had been kept in this secure room in one of the bank residences to ensure their safety until the transaction was complete. It had never crossed the woman's mind to question this ludicrous explanation, particularly when she saw the house where she and her children were to stay, the nice room and - luxury! a colour TV. The story had been believed without hesitation as the husband had frequently exaggerated the importance of his job in the bank.

Kisi went into the room where the children were already watching the TV as they had done for the entire time of their captivity. 'Time to go home everyone,' she announced and led them out of the house to where her car was parked at the back. The buxom wife squeezed into the front seat and the children climbed into the back. The family had a small house in the Kanda area, which bordered the large slum of Nima. Kisi pulled up outside the house and the family returned to their home. Kisi opened the bonnet of the Volkswagen and removed the crate of Coca Cola and took it into the house. It was a very hot day and all the family were thirsty; the fat wife had perspired freely in the car, much to Kisi's disgust and she grasped the first bottle and drank noisily and thirstily, as did the three children. They were all dead in less than a minute. Kisi picked up the empty bottles, replaced them in the crate and took the crate back to the car. She shut the bonnet, got in and drove to the British High Commission accommodation compound. The gates were wide open and she waved cheerily to the guards as she drove in.

*

'Hello.'

'Amanda, it's Mabel,' who was the receptionist at the British High Commission. 'I've had a call from your maid in the compound who says that a pipe in the wall appears to have burst and has done rather a lot of damage to the things in your sitting room. She's asked if you could come quickly.'

'I'll phone and tell her I'm on my way.'

'No, don't try that. Afi thought you might phone and she said that the water has damaged your phone and she had to phone from another flat. She said to say that she's gone back to your flat.'

'Very well, I'm on my way,' and Amanda put another call through to Arthur Russell, the works supervisor in the accommodation compound, and arranged for him to meet her in the flat. Amanda cursed; if things weren't already bad enough with her on her own, not a word from London and now everything in her flat ruined by a burst pipe. She put all the files away in the safe, closed it and spun the combination. She locked the door behind her, put the keys into the combination blister, spun the dial on that and then left the building. She got into her Peugeot 204 and drove to the compound, parked it outside her block and went up the steps to her flat on the second floor.

She had her keys in her hand, but the flat door was open and she went in, preparing herself for the worst. Visions of everything ruined by flooding water had crossed her mind on the drive to the flat and she'd been mentally composing a letter to her insurance company and wondering if the FCO would allow her to move out to a hotel while all the damage was repaired. She was totally unprepared for the sight, which met her as she opened the door. Her maid, Afi, lay on the floor by the bookcase with a large pool of blood spreading out under her head. On the sofa, where he must have fallen as he was looking at Afi, was Arthur Russell, as though he was peering over the

123

back of the sofa at the dead body beyond. There were two black holes in the middle of his back with small bloodstains radiating out from them. For split seconds, incoherent thoughts raced through her mind from her training at Century House and then she was smothered by the cloying, suffocating smell of chloroform and collapsed unconscious on the floor.

CHAPTER 8

'Colonel Gunn!' Gunn stopped and turned towards the receptionist at the Labadi Beach Hotel. Miles Stockwell had dropped him off at the hotel on the way back from the Shangri La. Mary McLaren had gone back to her house with Penny Briars to get Stuart to make a copy of the tape containing the instructions for the pick-up of the second tape the following day. Penny was to bring the tape back to her house from where it would be collected by Gunn.

'That's me,' Gunn smiled as the law of averages had to be on the receptionist's side as he was the only person wearing uniform in the hotel foyer.

'You were asking this morning where Saville Tailors was in Accra.'

'I was, and you very kindly gave me a card which had directions on the back.'

'That's right, Sir. The manageress of Savilles visits the hotel regularly to give fittings and take orders. It's a Miss Gbedemah and she's out in the Terrace Coffee Shop now if you are interested in having a suit or shirts made.'

'Many thanks, that's most helpful,' and then came the standard response.

'You're welcome, Sir,' but already Gunn had discovered that in Ghana it was a genuine sentiment. He walked through the spacious foyer with its refreshing air-conditioning and then out again into a temperature of 34° on the Terrace Coffee Shop where he immediately spotted Dina. There were a dozen or more people in the coffee shop and he looked around; Dina got up and walked towards him.

'Colonel Gunn?'

'Miss Gbedemah; John Gunn. The receptionist said I'd find you here, but I have to confess that I was looking for someone a little older and certainly not quite so attractive.'

'You flatter me, Sir; suit or shirts?'

'Please, John'll do fine and I was interested in a light-weight suit.' Not even the most professional of observers would have seen anything contrived in the greeting.

'Of course; if you would come with me, I have a small showroom in the shopping arcade, which overlooks the pool, where I can take

125

your measurements.' Dina led him to a boutique with the improbable name of Ladygin's and told the young girl to take a break while she minded the shop and measured up the customer. As soon as the girl had gone, Dina picked up her tape measure and opened her order book. 'You can talk now, John; I check this shop every day and it's clean. I've also checked your room as I've got a set of skeletons to cover all the main hotels in Accra; that's clean as well. Spread your legs a touch while I do your inside leg. How's that, comfortable?'

'That's fine; I'd like a sniper rifle with a minimum times seven scope. How soon could you fix, Dina?'

'I can do you a Colt Delta, semi-automatic, point four five calibre....that OK for your waist?'

'Yes fine thanks.'

'....with a times nine Barr and Stroud scope and a choice of five, twenty, thirty or ninety shot magazines. You can have a choice of.....that enough room across your chest? My, but you are a big lad,' was said as Dina looked at her tape before writing down the measurement. 'Where was I? Oh yes....steel-tipped, armour-piercing or hollow-point bullets, with or without sling and it's zeroed to 500 metres; any use?'

'That'll do nicely; thirty round magazine, hollow tipped bullets and sling.'

'This evening be OK when I come round for your first fitting or do you want it sooner?'

'This evening'll be fine.'

'Two magazines?'

'Two magazines.' The glass door opened and two women came into the boutique.

'That'll be fine Sir; I'll be back in the shop between six and eight this evening for your first fitting. Thank you for the opportunity to be of service, Sir. Yes, ladies may I be of help? I've just brought in a new line from my shop in the Rue Vaugirard in Paris which you might like to see......' and the sales patter continued as Gunn left Ladygin's and headed for his room. He showered, changed into slacks, shirt and desert boots, checked the 9mm Tanarmi and replaced it in its ankle holster. He looked at his watch; 12.15.

Miles Stockwell had arranged for him to have a snack lunch with Richard Outram, one of the two Majors in BMAT who was the chief instructor at the Ghana Military Training School. This had been arranged over the radio when Gunn had told Miles that he wanted to be in a position to observe the pick-up of the tape the next morning. Miles had told him that Richard seemed to spend his whole life out in the military training area which was adjacent to the Shai Hills game reserve and was the ideal person to advise and guide him, should he want that sort of assistance.

So where had he got between his arrival this morning and lunchtime? Gunn sat on his bed and for a moment put the information he had gathered into a logical order. Bristow had disappeared after finding out about the conspiracy to bring down the governments of all the West African Countries. A bank had been robbed of its gold and a ransom note had been received by the general manager of a gold mine. Robbery and extortion; as common a method as any to raise money. Money, presumably to buy arms. He must identify the kidnappers of Graham McLean.

That train of thought made Gunn pause and then he picked up his key and left the room. He turned into the shopping arcade from the foyer and bumped into Dina who was leaving her boutique. 'Hello Sir, can we be of any more help? I was just on my way out to the car, but.....'

'No, that's alright Miss Gbedemah, I'm also on my way out,' and when they were heading across the front of the hotel to the car park, Gunn said; 'when I arrived this morning at the airport, I noticed a 747 painted in IMT's livery. Could you check for me if it's still there and find out what its cargo manifest is.'

'How soon do you want the answer?'

'This evening at my fitting?'

'Will do,' and Dina turned to unlock her car door.

'One other thing, if you can, Dina.'

'Try me, John.'

'Can you find out how often IMT flies to Accra.'

'Consider it done, bye!'

'Bye,' and Gunn turned and walked over to his metallic blue Landrover Discovery. He had read something about IMT, was that it? No, he concentrated as he checked the unfamiliar controls of the Discovery and turned on the diesel pre-heat. Brochures, that's it! When he'd been down with the armourer he'd seen a whole row of IMT brochures advertising the arms which it supplied and providing detailed analyses of weapon capabilities. Gunn drove out of the hotel entrance and turned right onto the last part of the dual carriageway which finished a couple of hundred yards short of the entrance to the Military Training Schools camp. He pulled up outside the Outram's bungalow which was a mirror image of the Stockwell's and was immediately greeted by the Outram's two pye-dogs which, he later discovered, would have been very upset at this description as their owners always described them as Ghanaian smooth-haired terriers.

127

'Hello John, Richard Outram,' and the two men shook hands. 'Come on through to the veranda; what'll you have, beer?'

'Beer'll do fine thanks.'

'John!' and the Outram's steward appeared,' two beers please. We seem to have Johns everywhere,' Richard laughed as he led the way through the drawing room and out onto the veranda. 'Miles has only told me very roughly what you do and what you are here for and I'd much rather not know any more unless you think I ought to. He's told me that you want to go out to Shai Hills to watch someone, but not be seen yourself and you will need to go very early tomorrow. Have I got all that right? Denise, that's my wife, is down at the beach with the kids and I doubt if they'll be back until much later this afternoon.'

'Spot on, except I want to go out tonight.'

'Good, I was going to suggest that. Want the proper kit to wear?'

'Please.'

'Right, bring your beer with you and we'll do that straight away. For my sins I'm the team's quartermaster,' and Richard led the way to some buildings grouped around a small yard between his and the Stockwell's bungalows. Richard explained that the buildings housed the team's Landrover, 165 kva generator, and general, clothing, stationery and accommodation stores. Richard opened one of the doors and led Gunn into an air-conditioned store. He switched on the fluorescent lighting and in quick succession handed Gunn a set of tropical combat clothing, jungle hat and boots, web belt and two water bottles. 'Try that lot for size,' and Richard leant against a packing case sipping his beer while Gunn tried on the kit.

'You've obviously got a flare for this quartermaster thing, it all fits beautifully.'

'Quite easy really; that's the largest size we have in everything so if it had been too small that would have been that. Good, let's go and look at the 50,000 scale map of that area,' and Gunn removed his kit from the store while it was re-locked and then the two of them returned to the veranda. Richard went to his study and returned with a map which he unfolded and spread out on the rattan table on the veranda.

'Quick orientation for you. We're here and the route to Shai Hills goes via Independence Avenue and the airport - with which you'll be familiar - the Tettie Quarshie roundabout and then the motorway to Tema... here,' and Richard was tracing the route on the map. 'At the end of the motorway is another roundabout; first left takes you to Shai Hills, Kpong and Akosombo; second left goes east to Ada and Aflao on the border with Togo and the other two go south into Tema;

128

one into the residential area and the other straight to the port on the east side of the town. Now the route to the training area and ranges is via the road to Ada and then you take a left ...here and follow this track which takes you to a 120mm mortar position and the site that is used for all-arms fire-power demonstrations. With me so far?'

'Fine, Richard; what are these high outcrops of hills,' and Gunn pointed to where the closely packed contours showed steep-sided hills rising out of the flat Accra Plain savannah.

'Ah, that's Shai Hills. If you look very closely at the map, you'll see that there is a boundary fence marked.....here, can you see it?'

'Yes, got it.'

'Now that fence is actually there and it's in quite good nick; it's there, I regret to say, not to keep the wildlife in, but the poachers out.' Richard paused and stood up. 'It's very easy for us to criticise, John; we of the so-called developed world who raped the rest of the undeveloped countries for the raw materials which made us wealthy and now choose to admonish those countries for doing exactly what we showed them how to do. Until Jerry Rawlings took over this country back in 1979, it was in a hell of a mess; nothing in the shops, beggars everywhere and people starving to death on the streets. Rawlings transformed the country; did a brilliant job - even if he was an air force pilot!' and Richard laughed at his prejudice which was shared by all three services the world over in their professional rivalry. 'When your wife and children are starving to death and you know where you can find a nice plump deer, which will feed them for a week, would you care very much for what a rich, healthy and well-fed white man was saying about wildlife conservation? I very much doubt it,' and Richard answered his own question.

'I'm sorry, we're off the subject and I get carried away frequently by my anger at the hypocrisy shown by the developed world. Poor old Africa is in such a mess; however you didn't come here to hear me rabbit on and anyway, from the little I've been told, you've come here to prevent another disaster. Where were we?'

'I agree with every word you say, and to my shame I'm extremely ignorant about all this; we were talking about the high ground.'

'You're right, we were; an appropriate military topic. All over this savannah there are very dramatic outcrops of rock - here's one that Simon....you've met Simon Beazley, the fourth member of the team?'

'No, I haven't.'

'Oh; he's the chief instructor at the Military Academy and he takes the officer cadets out to this place,' and Richard had his finger on a feature which possessed sheer-sided rock escarpments of over

200 feet. Richard Outram moved his finger to another feature marked on the map. 'Now, from what Mary McLaren told you of the instructions on the tape, this is where the second tape will be hidden; here, just to the west of this track. Now if I was the kidnapper, or whatever, I would position myself up here,' and Richard produced a pencil from his pocket and put the tip on the map. 'This feature is covered with old caves which date back thousands of years and were occupied - and sometimes still are now - by the Akan tribes. They're mostly full of bats and stink horribly of ammonia from the bat shit, but with those, the thick undergrowth and the baobab trees, you could hide an army up there and never find it. There are many vantage points along this feature where you'd have a superb view of that drop.... is that the right word?'

'It's as good as any I've heard; is there any feature, say within 500 metres, that has a commanding view of both the drop... might as well call it that, and the position that you would choose on that feature.'

'Yes there is,' Richard answered immediately, but it's a sod of a climb and we've had to ban its use by the officer cadets since one of them fell to his death there last year. Here it is.... on the east side of the track and so has the benefit of the low morning sun which would be behind it and shining into the eyes of anyone on this feature.'

'What's to stop the kidnapper using it?'

'Quite wrongly, I expect, I'm assuming that he's an African; is that wrong?'

'No, that's OK; go on.'

'Africans are marvellous tree climbers and brilliant at many sports, but there're a couple at which they don't excel; swimming and rock climbing. No way will your man choose to go up here, when he can drive his four-track up to the top of this feature. What're you like at rock climbing, John?'

'An amateur; do I gather that you've got the ropes, pitons, carabiners, abseil gloves and so on in your stores?'

'I have.'

'Then that's where we go tonight.'

*

As soon as Charles Mensah and his bodyguard had left the private poker suite, Bradley Tracton turned to Frank Raubenheimer. 'We've still got a quarter of an hour before the game, Frank; see if Nat's outside. I asked him to brief me on the Caramansa arms shipment, which is due out tomorrow.' Nat Cohn was playing poker with Bradley Tracton that evening, and had accompanied him in the helicopter.

130

'Right Sir.' His bodyguard returned almost immediately with Nat Cohn who was carrying a briefcase.

'Right Nat, take me through it; how've you arranged this shipment?' The good humour and banter was one thing, but Nat had been with IMT - and more pertinently, Brad Tracton - long enough to know that if he'd got it wrong he'd be looking elsewhere for his monthly pay-check.

'Right Trax; we have 300, 40 foot containers and 400, 20 foot containers; one tractor can take a mix of one 20 and one 40 or three 20s. We have 340 tractors and an all-up load of 20,000 metric tons to load on the Texas Star. Each country-load will form a convoy and will leave here in reverse order of off-loading in Banjul. Each country-load is in a different coloured container, for ease of identification, and the code on the outside of the container indicates what it contains.'

'Which country gets the biggest shipment?'

'The biggest load is scheduled for Nigeria which will off-load last at Gaya from freight train to lighters and tugs and then go on down the Niger River to Baro.'

'Give me the breakdown of this shipment to Nigeria.'

'Right,' and Nat opened his briefcase and dug out an electronic notebook which he opened, turned against the harsh glare of the lights in the poker room to allow the LCD display to show up more clearly and then punched up the data required by his boss.

'Here we go; munitions and ammo first, weapons second. Two million rounds of 9mm ball, two million 7.62 tracer one-in- five, three million 7.62 ball, 100,000 rounds of .45 calibre ball, 200,000 fragmentation grenades, 100,000 smoke grenades - that's with mixed colours of red, blue, orange, green and white phosphorous - 50,000 anti-tank mines, 10,000 anti-personnel mines, 10,000lbs of Semtex explosive, with fuse and detonators, 5,000 anti-tank missiles and launchers - those are Russian not the much better Limey LAW 80 and 5,000 Stinger anti-aircraft missiles and launchers.'

'Now the weapons; 20,000 German Mauser G3, 7.62 semi-automatic rifles, 10,000 Austrian Steyer double-action 9mm auto-pistols, 1,000, .45 calibre Sokolovsky automatics and 100, 20 litre napalm flame throwers.'

'They'll have themselves quite a barbecue with that last lot; thanks Nat, sounds good. Now when's that lot due to move out?'

'They'll be ready to roll at 1000 hours tomorrow. I've chosen that time because we're expecting Al and his 747 in at about 0945 hours with that cargo from Accra. Just thought it might be worth waiting for that before we commit ourselves to the shipment.'

'Wise move. Do we have an escort for the convoy?'

'Sure; that's been fixed with Sheriff Baxter of the Amarillo Highway Patrol. Each country-load is a special convoy and each convoy has a police escort to get out to the Highway 27 south to Lubbock.'

'Who's going to get this show on the road tomorrow?'

'I was going to give you a call when I'm happy that everything's ready to roll and then you can start 'em off with a wave of your stetson!'

'Do that; I'll enjoy headin' 'em out,' and Bradley Tracton emphasised the point with a cowboy whoop which also brought all the poker players into the suite. 'Right boys, let's play poker.'

*

'Fellow delegates of the Security Council, I've called this meeting so that we can hear your progress reports on the tasks which you were given at our 21st conference. All of you have reported individually to me and so I can open this meeting by telling you that your salaries are assured,' an audible sigh of relief around the table and a smile from Caramansa, 'and the Congressional Investigation will discover a very healthy balance of funds. Now to the detail; Kwajo of Senegal; may we have your report please.'

'Yes, Your Excellency; I had in my possession, fellow delegates, incontrovertible evidence of the Burmese Government's attempt to acquire 200 tons of 105mm shells containing Palytoxin. For any of you unfamiliar with that biological agent, it is absorbed through the skin, it is quick and lethal. The acquisition of 200 tons of that toxin would have been more than enough to remove the opposition to the military junta of the Burmese Government. In return for not passing that evidence to the United Nations, we were given 5 tons of cocaine. The first 200 lbs of that shipment has been cut to produce 'crack' and that shipment has netted us 400 million US dollars.'

'And I should add,' Caramnasa interrupted, 'has produced the down payment for the arms and ammunition for our brothers in the struggle for freedom. Thank you Member Kwajo and well done. Now, Kojo of Mali; your report please.'

'The World Bank funding of 50 million dollars for the hydro-electric dam project on the head waters of the Niger River at Mopti has been invested with ICB.'

'Again, well done Member Kojo. Now Kwabena of The Gambia; your report please.'

'The high-jacking of the 200,000 ton oil tanker, Shell Emperor, in the port of Banjul was unsuccessful...' there was a snort of derision from the Nigerian Member.'

'Quiet! There are to be no interruptions,' Caramansa said with icy calmness. 'Please continue Member Kwabena.'

'Somehow, the ship owners had been tipped off about the intended hi-jack and my team of 15 men were all arrested and are awaiting trial in Banjul. I have to offer my apology to the Security Council for such a failure.' There was silence in the large auditorium and a satisfied smirk on the Nigerian Member's face. All knew the penalty for failure.

'You were betrayed Kwabena; I will deal with that at the end of this meeting. Kobina, Kwaku and Kuuku have not completed their task yet, but all report good progress. Member Yaw of Liberia was killed by the German Police when he and his team were hi-jacking a diamond shipment to Rene Kern, the jewellers at 26 Konigs Allee in Dusseldorf. A new delegate will be elected at the 22nd meeting, meanwhile $100,000 has already been sent to each of their relatives.'

'From Côte d'Ivoire, Ekow reports that ICB now owns three of the major hotels in Abidjan; not a dramatic addition to our assets, but a useful income. From Ghana, I have heard from Kofi that his first task is complete which added $10 million to ICB's assets and plans for his second task are progressing smoothly. Fiifi, your report from Togo please.'

'Merci Monsieur le Président, il faut que......'

'In English Fiifi, not French.'

'Pardon....er, I am so sorry fellow members. We 'ave succeeded in removing from the presidential palace all the stolen state treasures. We think that they will be worth about $5 million. These treasures arrived at this building last night.'

'Thank you Fiifi, that was a well-executed task.'

'Pas du tout, Monsieur le.......'

'Yes, thank you Fiifi. Now we have no news from Kwame of Benin so we'll go straight to Kwamena of Nigeria. I know that your task was most successful. A short account would be helpful please.'

'Yes, Caramansa; after you briefed me I set up this....'

'Kwamena, just the result of your task, please.'

'Very well, if you insist...'

'I do, Kwamena.'

'We hi-jacked a 300,000 ton tanker from Port Harcourt and sold the crude to a brother in Angola for $85 million, killed the crew and scuttled the tanker off Luanda.'

'Thank you, Kawmena, and finally Ato from Burkina Faso; your report please.

'Yes sir; the IMF subsidy of $48 million for the rail link between Banfora in the south-west of my country and Fada-N'Gourma in the east, is invested in ICB.'

'A wise investment gentlemen.' In one week, ICB's reserves had risen from nearly zero to more than $500 million and that was after the down payment had been made on the arms shipment. The meeting came to and end and all knew that after the toast to UROWAS it would be the execution of Kwabena for the failure of his mission. The captain and three of his guards came down from the gallery from where they commanded every corner of the auditorium to carry out the execution.

The waiters appeared with the glasses which were set in front of each member and the bottle of Schnapps was handed to Caramansa who made the libation while he intoned the old Akan words of appeasement and penitence to the gods; all stood with bowed heads. The glasses were then filled to the brim and on a sign from Caramansa, all members picked them up and turned towards the UROWAS flag which had appeared on the wall above them. The UROWAS anthem was played and all glasses were raised in the toast; 'UROWAS!' and the contents was drained in one swallow.

The delegates put down their glasses and turned to witness the execution. Without hesitation, Kwabena went to stand in front of the ceremonial altar, but he never got there and the guards never raised their Uzi carbines. There was a choking, rasping gasp from amongst the delegates and Kawmena, the Nigerian Member, collapsed to the floor, poisoned by the toxin, Ricin, which had been smeared round the inside of his glass. Caramansa's voice echoed round the auditorium from the loudspeakers; he had moved to the rostrum while everyone concentrated on the impending execution.

'That, brothers, is the penalty for betrayal of a fellow member of the Security Council.

*

Amanda Routledge came to her senses lying on a bed; nothing made much sense, but like any dream, it would all clear in a few seconds. She tried to brush away a lock of hair over one eye, but her hand wouldn't move; neither would the other one. There was someone looking down at her. Could it be Afi? No, Afi never came to the flat before nine, long after she was at work. The woman beside her moved and held something under her nose. A sharp, eye-watering smell and instant clarity; she was naked and this woman was staring at her, but worse still was the huge African at the end of

134

the bed. Her legs and arms were spread apart and tied to the corners of the bed.

'Can you hear me, Amanda?' The girl on the bed nodded. 'You work for the Secret Intelligence Service and are the PA to Tony Bristow at the High Commission in Accra.'

'No....I work in the registry at the High Commission.'

'No you don't. We removed Mr Bristow last week and he told us everything before, Kojo... yes that's Kojo standing at the end of the bed,' was added as the girl's eyes focused on the man standing at the foot of the bed. In his hand was a knife and he kept wiping the blade across his hand. The girl's eyes registered her terror and revulsion and Kisi laughed. 'We only need one bit of information from you, Amanda, and then you'll be free to go. Did Bristow send any information back to London about a conspiracy to unite the countries of West Africa.'

'No....' and the girl shook her head. Kisi nodded to Kojo Blood-Dzraku who came round the side of the bed. Amanda screamed before a cloth was forced into her mouth and then taped.

'One more chance, Amanda; listen carefully and either shake or nod your head. Do you understand?' The head was nodded vigorously. 'Do you understand what female circumcision is?'

The head nodded and the eyes went wider still with terror. 'I can see that you do. Unless you agree to answer our questions and stop wasting time I'm going to tell Kojo to circumcise you. He'll do it with the knife he's holding. Do you understand me.' The head nodded. 'I'm now going to remove your gag and you will then tell us what we want to know. Nod you head for yes.' The head nodded. The gag was removed and an ear-splitting scream erupted from the girl's mouth. Kojo's knife plunged to the hilt in the girl's heart, cutting off the scream and her life instantly.

'You fool! you brainless, stupid fool,' Kisi screamed and the big, brainless Kojo stared at her with a hurt expression on his face. Amanda had mercifully died quickly and without telling the Caramansa Conspiracy what it needed to know.

*

Kisi drove out of the High Commission compound in her Volkswagen and turned right and right again to the Sankara roundabout and then left down Independence Avenue. Beside her sat the immobile figure of Kojo, still daubed in Amanda's blood from carrying her naked body into the flat's lounge. He had pressed her fingers around the butt of the Bernardelli .22 automatic which Kisi had used to shoot the maintenance man and the maid and the knife

135

had been pulled out of Amanda's chest and placed in the man's hand. The fingers, stiffening from rigor mortis, were forced round the knife's handle.

Amanda's clothes had been scattered around the lounge. Arthur Russell's trousers had been removed as had his pants. The shirt had to be left on because Kisi's bullets had gone through that. The maid's clothes had been torn off her by Kojo and likewise scattered around the lounge. Kisi's bullet had gone straight between the maid's eyes, so no clothes needed to be left on her body. Both of them had only just left the flat when the man with the two women had arrived.

*

'British High Commission, can I help you?'

'Oh Mabel, it's Peggy Russell; I just wondered if you'd seen Arthur anywhere.'

'Hello Peggy, you've obviously tried his number in the compound; what's the time?' and Mabel looked up at the digital clock in front of her, 'it's nearly twenty past one now, Peggy, and I know that Amanda Routledge spoke to Arthur just after eleven because I put the call through for her. He was in his office in the compound then.'

'Do you know if he went off anywhere, Mabel? I'm asking because we're off to Lomé for a long weekend and he said he'd be back at the flat at 1230 sharp.' The Francophone capital city of Togo, just across the border from Aflao, was a popular weekend trip for the diplomatic community, which was exempt the hours of corrupt wrangling and bribes it took all other expatriates without diplomatic immunity to get across from one country to the other. The border with Togo was a three hour drive from Accra.

'Well, Peggy, Amanda's maid, Afi, had rung a little earlier to ask her to come back to her flat because there was a burst pipe or something. Amanda then rang Arthur and I expect they both went to see what the damage was. Amanda's only in the next block to you, why not give her a ring......no, on second thoughts, that's no use because Afi said the phone wasn't working. Why not pop across and see if he's still there helping Amanda.'

'Thanks so much; I'll do that.' Peggy put down the phone and turned to Vera and Ron Jones who were going with them to Lomé. Ron was the first secretary of the High Commission's management section and his insistence on wearing a very ill-fitting toupée caused great amusement in the High Commission. 'Mabel thinks he's up in Amanda's flat.'

'No wonder he's late,' Vera laughed.

'Come on then,' that was Ron who was sweating freely under his ill-fitting wig and constantly had to wipe his forehead. 'Let's go and dig him out,' and he led the way across from the Russell's first floor flat in Block B to Amanda's second floor flat in Block A. There was no answer to the bell and as Ron turned to solicit advice on their next move he lent against the door and fell into the flat as it swung open. 'What the.....' and then he stopped and quickly turned, trying to prevent the women from coming into the flat, but it was too late. His toupée had fallen across his eyes and in his horror and fright he had replaced it back to front. Peggy was standing perfectly still with her mouth opening and closing like a large gold fish; no sound came out. Vera collapsed in a chair and started to weep hysterically.

Ron made it to the phone just managing to hold down the rising bile in his throat and then remembered that Peggy had been told that the phone didn't work, but there was a clear dialling tone so he punched out the number for the High Commission's security officer, Trevor Banbury. The phone was answered immediately.

'Trevor Banbury.'

'Trevor,' and Ron was having the greatest difficulty in holding back his vomit,' please come quick...it's Amanda's flat,' and then he dropped the phone and dashed for the bathroom where he collapsed in front of the lavatory and vomited. Ron flushed the lavatory and both vomit and wig disappeared down the waste pipe. He washed his face and walked unsteadily back into the flat's lounge-cum-dining room. Nothing had changed except Peggy was now sitting by herself in another armchair and her mouth was still opening and closing, mouthing words, but no sound was emitted. His wife's hysterical sobs had calmed slightly and then he heard the squeal of breaks and seconds later Trevor Bambury came into the flat.

Trevor Bambury had retired from the Military Police as a Class One Warrant Officer and had immediately been accepted into the Foreign and Commonwealth embassy security service. Everything to do with the physical and document security of the high commission and any associated compounds was his responsibility. 'Jesus Chris.....Ron, come on; you and the girls come out of here and I'll take you down to Jean who'll get you a cup of tea,' and Trevor coaxed them all out and down to his flat on the first floor. He left them with his wife who had become used to this sort of crisis during her marriage to a policeman and dashed back up the stairs to Amanda's flat. The phone was still on the floor where it had fallen. Trevor went into the bathroom, pulled some paper off the roll by the lavatory and went back into the lounge. He picked up the phone gently with the tissue paper and returned it to the cradle. He lifted it

137

again and punched the number for the Deputy Head of Mission, Mike Truman, who held the overall responsibility for security at the High Commission.

'Mike Truman....I've got a meeting, can I....'

'It's Trevor, Mike; I'm in Amanda's flat. She's been stabbed to death, and Arthur Russell and Amanda's maid have both been shot.'

'On my way,' and Mike Truman put down the phone, adjourned his meeting with the commercial and development sections and went down the corridor to the High Commissioner's office. He came out with Humphrey Winfield and collected Ian Maskell from his office. The three of them left the High Commission and climbed into the High Commissioner's Range Rover.

CHAPTER 9

Using the road map of Accra, which he'd picked up from reception, Gunn had taken the opportunity to drive around the city and get his bearings. Miles had acquired another radio from the High Commission security officer which he'd given to Gunn and told him to use the callsign B-MAT 5.

The route he decided to take went west along the coast road into the city centre, then a right turn to the north up Liberty Avenue as far as Kwame Nkrumah Circle and then a right onto the ringroad, which he knew would eventually bring him back to the coast road and the hotel. The roads were still packed with traffic and he found no difficulty in identifying the Bank of Ghana as there were quite 20 police cars outside it. The rest of his exploratory drive was uneventful except for a flurry of transmissions on the radio as he approached Kwame Nkrumah Circle.

Two or three of the CHARLIE call-signs were summoned to the High Commission compound and others were asked to ring a number which was passed over the radio. Gunn turned right onto the ring-road and then left at the Thomas Sankara roundabout and pulled into Afrikiko's car park. The beer garden had been pointed out to him that morning on the drive from the airport and seemed like an interesting spot from which to watch the comings and goings of Accra.

Gunn sat at one of the wooden tables and ordered a bottle of Club Beer. At the table on his left were three strapping young American men who could have only been off-duty marines from the US Embassy from their shaven-headed haircuts. With them was a pretty, curvaceous and mildly inebriated woman who could have been Vietnamese, with very slightly slanted eyes. Gunn watched the table with mild interest as the rest of the colourful and cheerful life of Accra flowed up and down Independence Avenue. Gunn looked at his watch; nearly twenty past five. Dina would be at the hotel at six and he had said he would be at Richard Outram's house at half past.

As Gunn watched the activity of Afrikiko, he cleared his own mind on what he had been told and what had happened since his briefing in London. For the last fifteen years, some or all of the countries of West Africa had suffered from various levels of terrorism from its embryo stage of political and commercial subversion, as in Côte d'Ivoire, to full blown military confrontation as in Liberia in 1990. Now BID had received information, which had come from BMAT, and to them via a supposedly reliable source, that all of this terrorism was being orchestrated by a group which was led by someone who called himself Caramansa.

Since his arrival, he'd learnt that the source of information was not the discredited SIS officer in the High Commission, which added to its authenticity. The bank had been robbed of 10 million dollars worth of gold and the son of the general manager of a gold mine had been kidnapped. The coincidence of an IMT aircraft taking off from the airport just after the robbery had to link the US arms industry with the plot. It had to be assumed that if Bristow had become so besottedly indiscreet as to bonk a High Commission colleague's wife in a car park, then it was very likely that he had breached security with things which he had told her about his job. That meant that Lin Aldridge was like a loose cannon, banging - in every sense of the word - around Accra spilling what gems she might have gleaned from Bristow. She had to be watched - and followed, and Gunn made a mental note to get Dina to fix that.

What could he expect from watching the collection of the ransom tape at Shai hills the following morning? Probably nothing, Gunn answered his own query, noting that yet another round of beers had arrived at the table on his left and the noise level had risen a few decibels. The two men on either side of the Vietnamese girl seemed to be taking it in turns to put their hands up her skirt and she was loving every minute of it. If he was able to get the registration of a car, it would be something although the car would be stolen or hired by a third party with a cut out which would lead his investigation nowhere. He must also ensure Stuart McLaren's safety; it would be inconceivable that 'they' would kill the 'goose which would hopefully lay a golden egg' for them, but Gunn had discovered in his short time with BID that lack of attention to the impossible, inconceivable or unlikely made him highly vulnerable.

Terrorising the parents of a kidnapped child had been done before to throw the family even further off balance and to ensure their co-operation. In this case it could take the form of a roughing up of Stuart Mclean by some hired muscle with a caution that they would pay his wife a visit next time if they had any suspicion that he had spoken to the police. Yes, the sniper rifle was an essential part of their equipment as was his idea to take an abseil rope up with them as there was always the possibility that he might need to get down from their elevated observation point in a hurry. The real snag of the kidnap bit was the dual removal of hostages, which meant that they had to move so carefully. Even if he did discover where the McLean child was being held, there was nothing he could do about it until he got the word from Christine that the Canadians were about to move in on the kidnappers of the Mackenzie child. That was another point for Dina; he must have an update on progress in Canada as soon as possible.

'These seats taken?' Gunn was being asked by a girl who could have been no more than 16, accompanied by six other expatriate teenagers of which four were girls.

'No, help yourself; in fact I was just about to go so you can have the table.'

'Oh, please stay, we didn't want to crowd you out.' Gunn was just about to answer when the conversation from the table to his left caught his attention. Possibly because he'd tuned his attention to that table, possibly because it was said so loudly, it sounded loud and clear.

'C'mon, Pete, you ain't goin' to cope with Lin by yourself tonight. Whyn't we make it a threesome? You'd like that, Lin, huh?' The use of the 'Lin' rang so clear as did the unmistakable comment of the marine sitting next to Lin who had his hand up her minute mini-skirt. So this had to be Lin Aldridge – the name and the Asian features matched as did her very evident libido - and at that juncture all four from the table got up and walked, unsteadily, out of Afrikiko, no doubt Gunn reckoned, to put the marine's suggestion to the test.

He finished his beer, gave up his seat to a disappointed teenage girl and followed them to the car park. The foursome weaved their way towards a white Dodge mini-bus with the words 'Property of the US Embassy' stencilled on its side. It was parked two cars away from Gunn's Discovery. As Gunn walked past them towards his car, one of the marines who was not engaged in fondling Lin's various parts, turned and grabbed at his shirt.

'You a pevert, or somethin', asshole. I saw you watching us back there, what's the.....' but he didn't get any further and fell to the ground, stunned by Gunn's side-fisted blow to his temple. Gunn walked on towards the Discovery, but was quickly overtaken by the other two men; the well-handled Lin was left by the Dodge mini-bus. Time was short and Gunn had an appointment with Dina to keep; he didn't bother to wait for the threats and posturing, but turned and hit the nearest marine very hard indeed on the nose with a clubbed fist. The bone broke and blood burst over the man's T-shirt as he clasped his face. The third man took a wild swing at Gunn which he deflected and spun the marine round head first into the side of the

141

Discovery. There was a satisfying thump and the man collapsed on the ground between the parked cars at which stage the marine with the broken nose chose to throw up all the beer he'd consumed. Gunn turned him on his side so that he didn't drown in his own vomit. He examined the Discovery for any damage; there wasn't a mark. He patted the car and turned to the rather forlorn, much-fondled and dishevelled figure standing by the Dodge.

'Sorry to spoil your foursome; there're plenty more back there if you're short of company; g'night.' The reponse from Lin Aldridge, who had just been denied an evening of sexual adventure with some particularly fit specimens, was predictable, if physically impossible, but Gunn had other things on his mind and so would be unable to take her advice. It was just after six when he got back to the hotel and he found Dina on her own in the boutique. He tried on his suit; Dina chalked up a few minor alterations and told him that he'd find the rifle in his room. She handed him some keys and said that the rifle was in a battered Samsonite suitcase on the luggage stand. She also told him that the IMT cargo 747 was on its first visit to Kotoka and the manifest was for unserviceable drilling equipment being returned to the USA for repair.

'Machine parts! that's about as convincing as tractor engines,' Gunn remarked. 'Did you get anything else, Dina?'

'The flight had been scheduled for one week and is due to clear Customs at Dallas before flying on to the company's airfield at Amarillo. I couldn't find anything amiss with the paperwork.'

'Thanks; did you find what time the flight left?'

'I did; it took off at 10.43 this morning and before you ask your next question, twenty wooden crates were loaded onto the 747 just before the aircraft left. I got that from some of the cargo handlers hanging around the loading sheds.'

'Dina, please get onto Christine Dupré at the office..... no, she won't be there,' as Gunn checked his watch. 'Ring her at home and tell her we believe the gold may have been shipped out on that IMT 747. Please ask her to find out everything she can about IMT's operation. If that cargo has got to clear Customs, then you can be dead certain that someone has been bribed. Also, please ask her to get an up-date on the kidnapping of the Mackenzie child in Alberta. It's vital that she lets us know exactly what's happening there otherwise our hands are tied here. I'll be in touch tomorrow. Tonight I'm off to Shai Hills to find a place from which I'll be able to watch the pick-up of the ransom tape first thing tomorrow. Can you also get someone to keep an eye on Lin Aldridge. I want to know where she

142

goes, who she meets, inevitably, who screws her - anything you can get - but the tail must be really good; got all that?'

'Got it,' and he turned to leave; 'take care,' she added as he left the boutique and headed for his room.

Gunn opened the suitcase and removed the rifle; at first sight it looked like the US Forces M16 Armalite - of which it was a derivative - but it had a number of modifications apart from the large Barr and Stroud telescopic sight and a long, heavy-duty barrel. It came with a cleaning kit, two, 30 round magazines and a disruptive pattern canvas carrying case. Gunn put everything back in the Samsonite case and took it out of the hotel's side exit to the car park.

The short African dusk had turned to full dark by the time Gunn reached the Outram's bungalow. Before they had supper, Gunn and Richard Outram listened to the copied tape of the ransom message, which Penny Briars had delivered to the Outram's bungalow. With the map in front of them, they listened to the tape twice through, but were unable to pick up any hints from any background noise on the tape. Richard Outram showed him all the equipment, which would be packed into the rucksacks, including anti-snakebite serum in the first aid kit and the abseil rope asked for by Gunn.

He met Richard's wife, Denise, the three children, the two pedigree mongrels, the two African Grey parrots and was introduced, by name, to all the guinea fowl and chickens by the Outram's youngest, Edward. This was followed by a very pleasant supper on the veranda before the duty parent arrived to take the teenagers to Afrikiko.

Edward had watched all the preparation of the equipment and reappeared after supper with his own rucksack, carefully packed with an assortment of things which he considered would come in handy, which he then proudly and very professionally showed to Gunn. First and most important of all was a bag of gobstoppers which Gunn was told would while away the time if he got bored. Then he was shown a Swiss Army knife, a piece of string, a catapult, a torch and a small anti-mosquito spray. When Edward's father told him that he couldn't come with them, the small boy's disappointment led to tears.

'Listen Edward,' Gunn said very seriously, 'tonight you can't come with us, but will you promise to show me some of the things at Shai Hills another time. I wondered if perhaps you'd let me borrow all those things of yours for tonight.'

'Yes, alright,' was the sad reply, 'but not my Swiss Army knife in case you lose it as you're not a real soldier.'

'Thanks Edward; why am I not a real soldier?'

143

'You would've had your own uniform if you were a real soldier and wouldn't have had to borrow one from my daddy. My daddy has to lend his uniforms to all sorts of people who aren't real soldiers.'

After that perceptive and accurate explanation, Gunn changed into the tropical combat clothing, now abandoned by the young Edward because he wasn't a real soldier, while Richard loaded all the equipment into the sand-coloured, hardtop Landrover Countryman. He waited until Denise was reading in the sitting room and Edward was watching a video film, as he'd announced to Gunn, 'about real soldiers' - Rambo 3 - on the TV, before he quietly slipped out of the bungalow and placed the rifle in the back of the Landrover.

'All set, John?'

'Fine, thanks.'

'Right, let's go,' and they both climbed into the Landrover and Richard drove out onto the laterite track leading to the main road.

The traffic through Accra to the Tettie Quarshie Circle was very heavy and it was forty minutes before they turned onto the Tema motorway. After that it was only another twenty minutes before Richard slowed the Landrover on the long, straight Ada road and turned off left onto a laterite track signed to the training area. As soon as he was off the main road, Richard switched off the lights and after an initial bit of difficulty while his eyes adjusted to their night vision, the Landrover's speed rose to a steady 15 mph along the track.

The track ended at the area in which the firepower demonstrations were held and the Landrover skirted round the edge of a lake while Richard pointed out the pits of the mortar fire position to Gunn. Beyond the lake the track ceased and Richard drove across the flat grassland, interspersed with nim and thorn trees, using his knowledge of the area and the needle on the luminous dashboard-mounted compass to navigate. A three-quarter moon had risen which bathed the whole plain in a pale, green-blue light, depriving objects of their natural colour and contrast, but clearly showed the high outcrops of rock ahead of them.

Every now and then, little rat-like animals ran in front of the Landrover. 'What are those little things, Richard?'

'We call 'em grasscutters.'

'Whatever for?'

'God knows; that's what the Ghanaians call them. I think they're related to the South American capybara and, like I was telling you earlier, they eat them here, like everything else.'

'Then what predators are there in this part of Africa?'

'Only one; man. There are less predators in Ghana than in a suburban town in Britain. That's why you see so many chickens and guinea fowl everywhere.'

Richard swung the Landrover to the left where a low outcrop of rocks and trees cast deep shadows. 'It's shanks pony from here, John,' Richard muttered as he eased the Landrover into the shadow, close alongside the rocks. The two men got out and unloaded their rucksacks and the rifle. Gunn then helped Richard unroll a length of hessian, which completely covered the Landrover and over that they draped a camouflage net. The wire fence was the other side of the low rock outcrop and the two men carried their rucksacks the short distance from the Landrover. The fence was only eight feet high and had no barbed wire; Richard climbed over and Gunn handed over the rucksacks and the heavy 200 foot abseil rope before joining him on the other side of the fence.

It was the end of the dry season, which lasted from January to April, and what would have been four or five foot high grass, was all burnt up and no more than a few inches high. Neither of the men spoke, but Richard just pointed to a feature which, to Gunn, looked much like the rock outcrops of the Arizona desert, so popular with producers of cowboy films. The ground rose gradually to the base of the outcrop, which was surrounded in thick-trunked baobab trees, above which, the rock appeared to rise sheer-sided for, what Richard had said, was nearly 200 feet.

In the distorting effect of the moonlight, it seemed that the outcrop was only a few hundred yards away, but after another forty minutes of walking over the rock-hard ground, it was no nearer; Gunn had volunteered to carry the abseil rope and was bathed in sweat after ten minutes. It was another quarter of an hour before the ground started to rise as they finally came to the plinth on which the outcrop stood. Ten minutes later, they reached the trees where there was much snorting, barking and growling as they disturbed a troop of baboons from their sleep. Richard stopped, took a sip of water from one of his bottles and removed his rucksack. Without saying a word, he unwound the climbing rope, clipped it to the carabiner on Gunn's waistline, slung the rucksack on his back and led the way through the trees and scrub to the base of the rocks. Here, they dumped the abseil rope and attached to it a lightweight climbing rope, which would be paid out behind them as they climbed.

The first hundred feet was no more than a calf-aching struggle up a very steep path. Richard paused after five minutes of this stage and then spoke quietly to Gunn. 'The climbing starts shortly; just a couple of things to cheer you up. The crevices that make the best handholds

145

are much favoured by scorpions. There are two types in this part of Africa; the black scorpion which'll give you a nasty sting and put you out of action for a couple of days and the brown, fat-tailed scorpion which grows to about seven or eight inches and can deliver a massive dose of neurotoxic venom in its sting, which will put you out of action permanently within four hours and a child in seven minutes. Death from a brown scorpion's bite is particularly unpleasant and is preceded by paralysis of the respiratory tract, twitching muscles and your arms and legs turning completely blue.'

'Have you made a study of these delightful insects?'

'I have - in fact all of us on the Team have. It pays to know what you're up against, especially if you have children out here. The children are particularly good at identifying all the venomous creepy-crawlies. This is where I get boring; your first mistake. Scorpions aren't insects; they're the oldest members of the Arachnids - spiders; scorpions have been around for over 400 million years. Arachnids' role on this planet is to keep the insect population in check. All Arachnids are carnivores and the scorpion uses its huge pincers - chelicerae, if you want it in Latin! - to grab its victims. It then kills the insect by repeatedly stinging it and then sucks it dry.'

'Great; I'm really looking forward to this climb. Don't scorpions sting themselves to death if surrounded by fire?'

'I believed that when I saw it in the James Bond film; which one was it?'

''Diamonds are Forever'...I think; it comes in the opening scene when those two gays are collecting the diamonds in South Africa...'

'Oh yes, that's right. No, it's a load of bunkum; firstly a scorpion is immune to its own venom and secondly, it might have up to four pairs of eyes, but it's got no grey matter to reason out that solution to its predicament.'

Any other encouraging tit-bits of advice?'

'A couple! At night, all scorpions are brown ones; OK! The other thing to watch out for are the bats. They won't suck your blood or anything like that as they're all fruit bats, but they'll fly out of little dark crevices with an awful screech and it's inclined to make you loose your handhold.'

'That's nice; anything else?'

'There might be snakes, which is why I brought the serum for the four most common ones. The serum and the syringes are in the first aid kit in my rucksack, all clearly labelled, as I mentioned before we left. The fifth bottle is the one with the serum for a brown scorpion bite. This country may have no big game left - certainly not here in the south - but boy, oh boy! does it have more than its quota of snakes! You name it, it's here; from pit vipers through cobras to kraits. It's most unlikely that we'll come across those fellows as the noise we make climbing will frighten them off. Ready?'

'Sure; you lead the way into this theme park,' and the two men started to climb. Climbing was not Gunn's favourite pastime, but he'd had to do a great deal of it during his time with the commando artillery. Then, he'd been able to concentrate on getting good handholds without worrying about a little welcoming creature waiting for a juicy fat finger to be stuck in its home; neither did he have two recently stitched gunshot wounds. For the first few minutes, Gunn was expecting scorpions and bats to appear from every rock crevice, but after that the strain on limb and muscle of the climb drove out all other thoughts and the sweat poured down his face as they both climbed higher and higher. The only bonus which Gunn could discover to this miserable task was that the higher they went the better the cool breeze from the sea could reach them.

The second hundred feet took them just under the hour to climb, and a shade after ten by Gunn's watch, they reached the top of the outcrop; no snakes, no scorpions and no bats. The top of the outcrop was relatively flat and covered an area of about half an acre, Gunn reckoned. Gunn hauled up the abseil rope, thankful that neither of them had had to carry it up the climb. Richard seemed to know exactly where to go and, indeed, this had obviously been done before as there was evidence of some charred sticks in a solid rock hollow where the light of a fire would be completely shielded from view. 'Go on, Richard, you're about to tell me that you bring young Edward up here on Sunday afternoons.'

'Thought about it, but Denise and I have a difference of opinion on that subject! I've brought Miles up here once before and Denise has climbed it, but I haven't persuaded a single Ghanaian to do it. Time for some hot coffee and biscuits and then we can unroll our mats and mosquito nets and get some sleep. I have an alarm and we won't see anything before 5.30 so that's what I'll set it for.' Richard produced a thermos of coffee and biscuits and then both men spread out their mats and went to sleep.

*

Mike Truman had been struck dumb as he entered Amanda's flat closely followed by the High Commissioner. Humphrey Winfield had gone very pale when he saw the scene of carnage in the flat's living room and told Mike Truman that he was going home and could be contacted there.

147

'Fat lot of help he was,' Ian Maskell muttered to Mike as the High Commissioner retreated back down the stairs.

'Don't be too hard, Ian; some people really can't stand the sight of blood. Can't pretend I'm over fond of it myself.'

'It's not the blood that's upset him. You weren't here then, but last year his car was first on the scene of a real old pile-up on the Kumasi road; a lorry had squashed two cars, which were grossly overloaded with very large Ghanaian women on their way into Accra's Keneshie Market. The carnage was appalling and he,' and Ian nodded in the direction in which the High Commissioner had departed, 'was up to his armpits in blood. Did an excellent job so the account goes, including stopping a haemorrhaging artery on one woman. No Mike, blood isn't his problem today. There's something else bothering him, but that can wait; what the hell are we going to do about all this. Any ideas, Trevor? You were a policeman for many years.'

'Nothing much we can do, Ian, except follow the book and that says call in the local police and if they're baffled we offer to bring in someone from Scotland Yard. How we minimise the PR damage of this I don't know; that's your job, Ian, but this is going to look bloody awful however you dress it up.' He stopped as the door opened and the doctor from the German clinic came in. 'Doctor Siegel, many thanks for getting here so quickly. We haven't touched any of the bodies and we'd be most grateful if you can tell us how long they've been dead.'

'Afternoon gentlemen; yes of course, I will do my best, but only an autopsy will give the exact time.'

'Sure, sure, doctor; fully understood, but even a guess from someone who's qualified to guess would be of great help.'

'Yes, of course, gentlemen; how very unfortunate. Now if you will excuse me, I will get to work,' and so saying the slim, grey-haired and bearded German did just that.

'Any ideas Trevor?' this from Mike to the security officer.

'It's weird; from a purely practical angle, the last one to die had to be Amanda.'

'Why's that?' Ian asked.

'She's got the gun in her hand and Arthur's been shot in the back. Arthur's got the knife in his hand and there's no way that he could've stabbed anyone with those two bullets where they are. One's smashed his spine and the other's gone through his heart, I'll bet a tenner. But why the maid was shot or how for that matter, is beyond me.'

148

'All of us have got shoes on, as has Arthur. Both the maid and Amanda have bare feet. Agreed everyone?'

'Yes, of course, Ian; what're you getting at?' came from Mike Truman.

'That,' and Ian pointed at a footprint in the blood on the marble floor beside Amanda. It was huge and couldn't have been made by any of the men in the room let alone the women.

'Unless I'm much mistaken that is the footprint of a very large male and that male has to be African. Would you agree doctor?'

'What's that?' and the German doctor looked up over the top of his half-lens glasses.'

'That footprint beside the girl; Caucasian or African?'

'Oh that; African; there would be no doubt about that.'

'So there was at least a fourth person here, if not more,' Mike muttered. 'C'mon, Ian, while you're in your Sherlock Holmes mood, what else can you deduce?'

'His accomplice was a woman.'

'How the hell do you come up with that?' Trevor queried the amateur sleuth.

'It's not very difficult; that footprint there,' and he pointed to one by the door which also had traces of blood, 'couldn't have been made by either of the women in here as the person was wearing a shoe and if I'm not mistaken, that is a .22 automatic in Amanda's hand and I've never read in any newspaper of a man using a .22 pistol. My money goes on two people who did this.'

'And if it's any help to your theorising,' doctor Siegel added, 'these two people,' and he pointed at Arthur and Afi, 'died at least two hours before this young lady.'

*

'Hello.'

'May I speak to Mrs Dupré please.'

'Speaking.'

'Christine, it's Ama; a private conversation is needed.'

'Go ahead, Ama,' and both women switched to secure speech on the electronic coding and decoding device into which their telephones were plugged.

'Christine, Dina Gbedemah, I have some instructions from John which you will need to act on very promptly.'

'I'm ready, Dina, the recorder's switched on.'

'Will you speak to the Assistant Director for North America who is responsible for the liaison between BID and CIA and tell him that a 747 belonging to International Machine Tools is in-bound to the

149

States and, according to the flight plan, is scheduled to land at Dallas at about 1600 hours local time. The Bank of Ghana was robbed of 53 bars of the Ashanti gold at 1000 hours this morning and we believe it's concealed in a consignment of unserviceable offshore drilling parts being sent to IMT. John would also like a full rundown on IMT's operation,' and then Dina went on to give Christine Dupré a report of what had happened on Gunn's first day in Accra including the request for information on the Mackenzie kidnap. As soon as Dina had finished her report, Christine replaced the phone, switched off the secure speech mode and dialled another London number.

'Hello.'

'May I speak to Mr Barton please, it's Christine Dupré.'

'Yes, just hold on Christine, I'll get my husband,' and Sheila Barton put down the phone in the drawing room of the house in Richmond Hill Court, which overlooked the sweeping bend of the Thames and Marble Hill Park beyond, and called to her husband. Bill Barton was BID's Assistant Director for North America. He came in from the small, walled garden at the rear of the house, wiping potting soil from his hands.

'Just wanted to get those busy lizzies in, darling; who is it?'

'Work, Bill.'

'Right; hello, it's Bill Barton.'

'Christine Dupré, Bill, I'm switching to secure.'

'Right,' and Bill Barton switched to secure speech.

'Bill, I have a number of requests for assistance from John Gunn who's in Accra . The first one is the most urgent and will require some fast work by you,' and Christine went on to give him the task of getting someone to the arrival airfield of the IMT cargo 747 and checking out the IMT operation. She then went on to give him an update on the situation in Accra and suggested that it might be worth checking to see if the name 'Caramansa' had appeared anywhere, possibly in connection with IMT as there now appeared to be a tenuous link between stolen gold being sent to an arms dealer in America and terrorism in West Africa. All of which was recorded and as soon as the call was finished, Bill Barton put another call through on the secure telephone to David Slattery, his opposite number in the CIA where the time in Langley, Virginia was 2.10 in the afternoon.

'David, it's Bill Barton; we need your help for an operation which has now entered your territory. I'm off to the office immediately after this call from where I'll send you a full brief on secure faxlock.'

'Bill, I got all that; what can we do to help?'

'There's a Boing 747 belonging to International Machine Tools due to land at Dallas International Airport at 1600hours local time, where it will have to clear Customs before flying on to IMT's airfield at Amarillo the next day. We have good reason to believe that it has 53 gold bars in its cargo of unserviceable offshore drilling equipment. Those bars were stolen from the Bank of Ghana in Accra at 1000 hours local today. Our field agent in-country is John Gunn who worked closely with your Doyle Barnes on that conspiracy in Hong Kong a few years ago and it might save a lot of hassle if he was available to link up with us on this operation.'

'You're in luck; I've got Doyle right here listening to your call and he's already phoning through to our office in Dallas. They're an hour behind us so it'll be 1315 there right now. Doyle'll hitch a ride in one of our planes - he's now phoning our guys to get them to fire up the engines - which'll take a couple of hours to get to Dallas...say 1530 local time should see him there which'll give him a half hour before the 747 arrives. That's real neat, Bill; nice to see this coming together like that and thanks for the timely warning. How do you reckon they intended to get this gold past the Customs inspection?'

'No idea at the moment, but the gold's worth $10 million at face value and I'm told that it could be worth five times as much to the insurance market because of its historic significance. There'll be a big bribe somewhere to a very senior politician and, or, an airport or customs official so mind whom you speak to.'

'Got it; we'll get onto it right away and wait for your fax.'

'Many thanks, David; fax'll be on its way in about an hour; bye,' and he broke the connection. He then made another call to Canada to the in-country BID agent to achieve an up-date on the Mackenzie kidnap. He turned to Sheila, 'sorry love, I'll have to go. There's an op running; don't wait up, I expect I'll be late.'

'The last time you said that it was the Gulf War and I didn't see you for eight days, so there's no way I'm 'waiting up' as you put it. Go on, off you go, take care and ring me if you can,' and she kissed her husband goodbye.

*

'Where's Kojo?'

'He's round the back washing the inside of the beetle.'

'Right, Kofi; now we need to do some clear thinking to make sure that no more mistakes are made. Kojo and I only just got out of that girl's flat before those people arrived. That was too close and the British have now been alerted. I'm convinced that Bristow sent information back to London and if I'm right, and after the blood bath

151

in the High Commission compound, they'll have an army of people looking for us.'

'What makes you so sure the information went back to UK?'

'It was obvious that the Routledge girl knew about it by the speed with which she denied any knowledge of it. It follows that if she knew about it, so does London. Now, what are the arrangements for the ransom tape?'

'Kojo will go out a bit later to find a suitable four-wheel drive vehicle which he will keep in a lock-up he's got in Nima. He will leave here at five tomorrow morning in the Datsun pick-up and drive to his lock-up where he will leave the Datsun and then go straight to Shai Hills with the tape. He goes past the main entrance of the game reserve where the hut and ranger are and stops at the next gate, which is always locked. He cuts the chain with his bolt cutters, closes the gate behind him and puts a new padlock on it. He then drives to the west-side of the hill which overlooks the drop. He has done all of this with me, but in reverse. He can take the four-wheel drive vehicle right up to within fifty yards of the position from where he'll watch McLean arrive to pick up the tape. I took Kojo right to the exact spot where he is to hide the tape and even placed the rock there for him under which he has to place it.'

'He's to watch the collection of the tape, but more specifically he is to make sure that no one follows McLean. From the position I chose for him, he can see back down the road in both directions for about two miles. Kojo knows how to set up the radio and if he has the slightest suspicion about anything he will contact me here. He has been told to wait there until it is dark and then come back here tomorrow evening after getting rid of the car.'

'Again you have done your planning well, Kofi, and have accounted for everything, but the one thing we can't account for is how Kojo will react if something goes wrong. You saw what happened today with that girl. No, my mind is made up; I want you to drop off the tape. Take Kojo with you. I will stay here and you contact me on the radio if there's any problem'

'Very well; do you want me to stay in Shai Hills until it's dark?'

'I must leave that decision to you. If there's the slightest doubt in your mind then stay there. If it all goes smoothly, as it should after your planning, then return when you judge the time right.'

'Right; I'll go and speak with Kojo.'

CHAPTER 10

'The High Commissioner wants you to ring him as soon as you can, Mike.'

'Thanks Maggie; did he say what about?'

'I think he's got to go back to London. I'll just pop down the corridor and ask June .....if she hasn't gone home.'

'Would you, please, and then I'll give him a buzz,' and Mike Truman looked with dismay at the mountain of files on his desk which had piled up while he'd been at the compound supervising the comings and goings at Amanda's flat. Colonel Osei-Owusu, the Chief of Police for Accra, had visited the flat with his scenes of crime and forensic staff and had then released the bodies for removal to the morgue; putrefaction of human flesh started quickly in a shade temperature of 35° - not withstanding the air-conditioning. Once the bodies had gone, Mike had left the routine of statements for Trevor Banbury to supervise; as an ex-policeman, Mike had reckoned that his expertise would be invaluable at that stage. Maggie reappeared and stuck her head round the door.

'Sorry Mike, June's gone. Is Ian coming back this afternoon?'

'Yes, later...... Maggie.'

'Yes,' and she put her head back round the door.

'Come in and sit down please,' and a rather perplexed Maggie went into the office and perched on the edge of one of the armchairs arranged round a coffee table in front of the Deputy Head of Mission's desk. Mike usually spoke like that when it was her annual report time, but she'd just had her report so it couldn't be that.

'Maggie, there's been a most unpleasant incident over at the compound. You will see lots of telegrams about it soon going back to London and I'm sure when you go back to your flat tonight, the place will be rife with rumour, so I must warn you what it's all about.' Maggie's mind raced, wondering what little affair had broken up, if one of her friends was pregnant or perhaps someone had fallen over those dangerously low balcony rails which they'd been trying to get raised for ages. Mike was talking, but the words took some time to register.

'Did you get that, Maggie?'

'Sorry; could you repeat it, please?'

153

'Amanda has been murdered; so has her maid, Afi and Arthur Russell.'

'Why.....I mean...' and the tears started to roll down the young Scottish girl's cheeks. Mike Truman came round from behind his desk with a large handkerchief and pulled up another of the armchairs.

'Listen Maggie; have a good cry, but please make a big effort to control yourself for just a while. I'm going to need all the help I can get over the next few days and I'm afraid that self-indulgent tears won't solve the problems facing this High Commission.'

'Sorry,' a loud blowing of her nose and then Maggie wiped the tears and looked up. 'I'm alright now, Mike; what do you want me to do?'

'Well done; please get the High Commissioner on the phone for me and then we'll take it from there.'

'Righto, Mike, I'll put the call onto your phone,' and Maggie left his office. The call came through in less than a minute.

'Humphrey, it's Mike; you left a message for me to call you.'

'Yes, thank you Michael.' Always Michael, never Mike, but that was the same with all the High Commission staff; Humphrey Winfield never used a shortened first name. It was like his anger if anyone dared to mention the word 'Queen' - by itself - within his hearing. In his High Commission, the word 'Queen' was always prefixed with 'Her Majesty The'.

'Sir Peter Goddard and Perigrine Humble want me back in London to discuss the deteriorating security situation in our region. What happened this afternoon in the compound is the first evidence of its spread to Ghana and I consider that it's important I discuss this at first hand with my colleagues. Davina and I are catching the British Airways' - not even that could be abbreviated to BA, went through Mike's mind as he listened - 'flight this evening. You'll keep me in touch, of course, with developments.'

'Of course, Humphrey;' Mike knew that the High Commissioner disapproved of him using his first name. He was the only person in the Mission who could get away with it; to everyone else, Humphrey Winfield was 'Sir'. 'Presumably, Humphrey, you've got Amanda's next of kin details and will want to visit her parents while you are in UK.'

'I asked June to get them for me, Michael, but you might check up and have a note sent to the residence.'

'Very well; Arthur Russell has an old mother who lives in Eastbourne and Tony Bristow's parents live in Essex. Did you ask June for those NOK details?'

154

'Yes of course, but you know how forgetful June is, Michael. Grateful if you would check that she has remembered those as well.'

'Right; how long'll you be away?'

'Week, possibly a fortnight; I'll let you know.'

'Thank you; I'll contact Peter Goddard and Perigrine and let them know you're on your way.'

'No need, Michael; I've already done that.'

'Very well; have a pleasant flight, goodbye.

'Goodbye, Michael,' and Mike Truman broke the connection and pressed the number for his PA.

'Yes, Mike.'

'Maggie, please get me Perigrine Humble,' and then to himself, 'we'll see if he really has spoken to the Head of the FCO and West Africa Department.' Mike started drafting a telegram to King Charles Street to let West African Department in the FCO know what had happened. The phone beeped at him.

'I've got Perigrine on the line, Mike.'

'Thanks.....hello Perrigrine, I gather that Humphrey's spoken with you about the situation here and is coming to London tonight to brief you.'

'That's right, Mike; I'm still a bit confused as to why he's coming back, but he seemed determined to do so. What's happened?'

'I'll send you an 'Immediate' telegram, Perigrine, which will be with you inside the hour. He's going to see Peter Goddard as well.'

'He'll find that difficult. Peter Goddard left London yesterday for Vienna to attend the UN Conference on Human Rights. I'll wait until I get your telegram and then brief you; presumably you'll be staying in the office?'

'I'll be lucky to get away before midnight.'

'Good, because I want only you to see the telegram which I'm drafting. I will phone before it's transmitted so that you can go to registry to receive it. No one, I repeat, no one else is to see it and you are to shred it as soon as you've read it.'

'Understood; I'll wait for your call, bye,' and Mike replaced the phone and then rang June Baker's number in the compound. 'June, it's Mike Truman; what arrangements has the High Commissioner made with you while he's back in London?'

'When's he going, Mike?'

'You mean you don't know that he's on the BA flight this evening?'

'Course not, Mike; I always book his tickets. He hasn't said anything about going back to London. He said it was alright if I went to the Duty Free shop at twelve to get one or two things before they closed and I never saw him again. Why, what's up?'

'I'll brief you tomorrow, June. He didn't ask for any NOK details for any of the staff?'

'No....whatever for, Mike?'

'Not to worry.....a misunderstanding; see you tomorrow, bye,' and he put the phone down thoughtfully. 'Curiouser and curiouser', he muttered as he rang Don Peasmarsh in his flat. The phone rang for some time before it was answered and Mike recalled that the only time he'd seen Don that day he'd looked as though he was nursing a particularly wicked hangover.

'Don.'

'Don, it's Mike Truman. Sorry to disturb you, but I need you in the office right away.'

'I was meant to be....'

'Now, Don; please cancel any other arrangements which you might have.'

'I'll be over as soon as possible.'

'The sooner the better,' and Mike put down the phone in irritation, reminding himself that it was high time he and Don Peasmarsh had a discussion on the latter's career prospects - or the lack of them - in the Diplomatic Service.

*

Wisps of blue smoke burst from behind the main wheels of the IMT Boeing 747 as they met the surface of Dallas Airport's runway 150. The 747 filled the entire field of vision of the binoculars of one of the aircraft buffs on the observation terrace of the airport building. Whilst the other enthusiasts made a note of the aircraft's registration, Doyle Barnes turned away and spoke for the benefit of the concealed microphone inside his anorak.

'International Machine Tools' cargo 747, registration Victor Romeo Charlie 748 landed at 1613 hours on runway 150. I'll meet you in the entrance to the Customs building when it's parked up on the apron in front of the Customs complex.' Doyle left the terrace and went to the open-air top floor of the multi-storey parking lot and stepped into the back of a small panel van. Inside the van was one of his CIA technicians monitoring and recording the reports of all the agents deployed around the airport.

'Jack, initiate jamming of all outgoing comms from the 747. They'll try and get a message out when we search the cargo so be ready for that.'

156

'No worries there, Sir; no one on that plane's going to speak to anyone.'

'Good, thanks for that,' and Doyle took off his anorak and replaced it with his suit jacket with the name tag of the Customs Service Regional Commissioner from Houston, repositioned the microphone, picked up an official-looking brief case, stepped out of the van and closed the rear doors. He got into the Ford sedan parked next to the van and drove it to the airport's cargo entrance where his genuine Customs Service pass was checked.

Doyle parked the Ford outside the Customs building in the slot marked for the 'Chief Customs Officer' and went in through the automatic doors. The layout of the inside of the building had been described to him in great detail and with the confidence of someone who might have worked in the building all his life, he went across to the lift and pressed the button for the second floor. He got out of the lift, turned right and went along a wide corridor to the end office which had a sign above it; Chief Customs Officer. Doyle Barnes opened the door and went into a secretary's office. 'Hello Miss Coplin, I'm Alvarez, Regional Commissioner, will you tell Mr Gideon that I'm going to do a check on the clearances for the last three cargoes to land.'

'Right Sir; will you take a seat please. Mr Gideon's got someone with him. I guess he won't be too long.'

'I'll surprise him, Miss Coplin; you stay right there,' and Doyle Barnes crossed the office and opened the door while a confused Miss Coplin hovered uncertainly behind her desk. The two men in the office looked up in surprise as the door opened; surprise which quickly turned to confusion, through anger to bluff. Doyle watched with interest as these emotions were displayed in the expressions of the two men. They were both on the far side of the desk studying a cargo manifest clearance form. One of them was Gideon, the other Doyle didn't know, but he recognised him as one of the many customs inspectors whose job it was to board the aircraft and open selected items of cargo.

'Wha....'

'Sorry to burst in on you, Mr Gideon; this is an unannounced inspection directed by the Commissioner in Washington. I'm going to check the clearances of the last three cargoes to land.'

'The hell you are.....whoever you are. On whose authority?'

'This authority,' and Doyle removed the document from his briefcase and passed it across to the Airport's Chief Customs Officer. The other customs inspector was slowly sliding the clearance form on the desk underneath another pile of documents. 'What's your name?'

157

Doyle asked the man. The attempt to hide the clearance form stopped.

'Ballard.'

'Right, Ballard; take your hands off the desk and stand back from it,' and then Ballard panicked and did a very silly thing; he made a grab for his radio. Before his hand had reached the radio, the second item to emerge from Doyle's briefcase was his Colt Mark IV, .45 calibre, US Army automatic, which had stayed with Doyle on his transfer from the army to the CIA. 'No, Ballard; I strongly advise against that course of action,' and then for the benefit of the microphone,' send in the back-up; I've a couple here for you to take care of.'

'I don't know what the ....'

'Shut up Gideon and both of you step back from the desk and put your hands in front of you where I can see them.' Both men did as they had been ordered. 'That's better.' There was the sound of raised voices in the outer office, which could be identified as Miss Coplin objecting to another intrusion and then the door opened and two men came in. 'Take care of these two and I'll call you on the radio when you can move 'em out. I think we'd better have young Miss Coplin in here too before she has hysterics.' One of the men collected the secretary from the outer office while the other searched both the men, snapped plastic cuffs over their wrists and gagged them. Doyle went to the desk and picked up the clearance form, which Ballard had tried to conceal; it was for the IMT Boeing 747, registration VRC 748. He put the clearance form and automatic into his briefcase and left the office.

It was no coincidence that Doyle Barnes had been in Slattery's office when the call for assistance came through from BID's Bill Barton. Doyle Barnes and John Gunn had met when the latter was doing a six-month attachment to 82nd Airborne Division at Fort Benning in Georgia. The two soldiers had become firm friends and had kept in touch in the years that followed. Doyle had left the US Army, having been recruited by the CIA, 18 months before Gunn had left the British Army after his recruitment by the newly-formed British Intelligence Directorate.

Both men met again on Gunn's first assignment in Hong Kong, but it was not until after Gunn's second assignment, when a lack of close liaison between the CIA and BID had resulted in the deaths of a British agent, three of the staff at the British Embassy in Beijing and a compromised CIA agent that the liaison between the two agencies was formalised. John Dempster, the Head of the CIA and Sir Jeremy Hammond, the BID Director had set up direct links between the CIA

158

and BID which was run in Langley by David Slattery and in London by Bill Barton. Doyle Barnes had been assigned to David Slattery's department for all joint operations between the USA and UK.

Down in the entrance hall of the Customs building, Doyle met up with another of his men, as arranged earlier on the radio, who was carrying a large briefcase. The man led the way out to a fluorescent yellow van with flashing light and climbed in behind the wheel.

The IMT Boeing 747 was parked on the concrete apron and the Customs ground handlers had the big cargo doors open. There was no sign of the aircraft's crew. Doyle and his inspector climbed onto the freight platform and the operator raised it up until it was level with the cargo bay of the 747. There was a whole assortment of crates, but it took only a moment to identify the twenty crates marked as 'Offshore Drilling Equipment'.

With the help of two of the ground handlers they rolled out the first crate onto the platform. Doyle's inspector opened his bag and removed banding cutters and steel levers. The tensioned metal banding flew apart as it was severed and then the Customs seals were cut and the levers used to prise open the lid of the wooden crate. Inside was a very greasy well-head manifold; inside the wide flange of the manifold was a package encased in bubble-injected plastic wrapping. Inside the wrapping were three bars of gold.

'Paydirt!'

'Can I be of help to you?' Doyle looked up to find that he, the inspector and the ground handlers were covered by two machine pistols held by two of the aircraft's crew.

*

A large python was squeezing his arm while all around him brown scorpions danced on their tails like a scene from Disney's Fantasia; Gunn's eyes opened to find Richard Outram holding his arm as he shook him awake. 'It's just before five and will start to get light in about a quarter-of-an-hour. Sorry if I startled you.'

'Very glad you did as I was having a nightmare about being eaten alive by a python; do I smell coffee brewing?'

'You do; here you are,' and Richard handed Gunn the fitted plastic mug from the water bottle, filled with steaming coffee. He then placed an aluminium container filled with beans and sausages, which fitted over the other end of the waterbottle, on the small metal cooker filled with burning Hexamine blocks. Gunn propped himself on one elbow as he sipped at the scalding coffee. 'What time do you think the tape will be dropped,' Richard asked as he prepared the rest of the breakfast. Gunn could see that Richard was well 'in' to the

159

John Le Carré/Len Deighton spy scene of drops, dead letter boxes, cut outs, pick-ups and all the other language of the multitude of spy novels which had fed off the cold war between east and west.

'The instructions said that Stuart was to collect the second tape at 7.30. My guess would be somewhere around 6.30 we'll see some activity and then that'll give the observer - if indeed they leave someone to observe - an hour to monitor all or any movement along the road and in the game reserve. Excellent coffee, thanks,' and Gunn sat up as he took his share of beans and sausages from Richard Outram. A fine line of grey had appeared out of the darkness and gradually objects around them started to develop shape and substance. As in all the tropical latitudes, and Accra was only five degrees north of the equator, dawn and dusk were rapid events and not the lingering ones of the temperate latitudes.

The thin grey line expanded, turned to the purest pale blue and then the golden orb of the sun burst over the horizon flooding the Accra Plain with light; it was nearly 5.40. The breakfast paraphernalia had all been cleared away, the abseil rope was belayed around an outcrop of rock and coiled, ready to throw over the side of the rock-face if required. Richard Outram had loaded a new film into his 35mm camera and had replaced the 28mm lens with a 210 mm telephoto one. Gunn removed the Colt from its case, checked it thoroughly and added a drop of oil to the moving parts of the gas-operated, recoil and self-loading mechanism. He fitted a thirty round magazine, cocked the weapon and chambered the first of the .45 calibre, hollow-point rounds. He flicked on the safety catch and then took the rifle to the position he had selected. Both men were in the deep shadow of a weathered lump of granite perched on top of the monolithic outcrop and concealed by the sprouts of brush and dried grass growing out of the rock crevices.

The sun was now directly behind them as it started to climb into the sky. Both men had binoculars and had divided the area in front of them so that Richard covered from one o'clock left to nine, which took in the road from Accra, the drop point and the left side of the feature behind it. Gunn took from eleven o'clock right through twelve to three, which covered the continuation of the road towards Akosombo, the drop and the right side of the feature from which Richard believed the drop would be monitored.

'Wind's from left to right, John, off the sea as it usually is unless we have a rainstorm and then it's always from the north-east. Down at the drop, I doubt if the wind can be felt at all, but up here it might be worth a very small left compensation on the scope....say one click left?'

160

'Agreed,' and Gunn twisted the azimuth calibrator on top of the scope one click to the left. He sighted the weapon on the flat rock on the other side of the track along which Stuart would drive and carefully adjusted the focus. The times nine magnification seemed to make the whole scene, 200 feet below, leap towards him; every detail of the drop was clear and he felt that he could reach out and pick up the small rock under which the tape would be hidden. Gunn put down the sniper rifle, wiped his hands and face and looked at his watch; 6.10. Not a single vehicle had used the Accra/Akosombo road yet.

'What d'you think'll happen?'

'Probably nothing......except the pick up of the tape. I'm no expert at this game; sure, I've been instructed in all the techniques and we practised it on an exercise we did in Reading, but I've never had to do this for real and it's my bet that neither has the opposition, whoever that might be. Pound to a pinch of sh.....' but the expression was never completed as both men steadied their glasses on the road from Accra. Gunn looked at his watch again; 6.20.

'It's a car of sorts, but still too far to make out what,' Richard muttered as he removed the binoculars from his eyes and quickly polished the lenses to remove the condensation. 'Could be our man.....looks like a Mitsubishi Shogun... just approaching the entrance to the reserve....no, he's gone past that.....and the next entrance which is always shut....no, he's not our man.'

'It's most unlikely that he'll come in through the main entrance to the game reserve; my worry's that he's selected the same place as us and that any moment 'he' will appear over the lip of that cornice behind us - despite your scepticism about African climbing ability.'

'But he'd have to drop the tape first, which would give us a warning,' Richard rationalised.

'Not if he had an accomplice.'

'True.......Christ, that would put a different slant on the whole business.'

'Here,' and Gunn held out his 9 mm Tanarmi which he'd removed from the ankle holster. 'There's a round up the spout and it's on half-cock. Pull the ring hammer fully back and it's ready to fire. It's got 16 rounds. You keep an eye on this area while I watch out for the vehicle.'

'Right,' and Richard took the automatic.

'Hello, this might be our man,' and Gunn swung the binoculars onto a long wheelbase, white Toyota Landcruiser which was approaching the game reserve from the Accra direction. It went past the entrance and then slowed as it came to the locked gate. 'I think

161

our visitor's here, Richard......he's stopped by the gate....and turned off the road....there must be two of them in the car as someone's getting out of the front passenger door....he's carrying someth.....they're bolt cutters. These are our guys, Richard; forget the area behind us and there're at least two them.' Richard put down the automatic and picked up his glasses.

'ACB 6211; that's an Accra registration plate for what it's worth.' The white Toyota drove through the entrance once the gate was opened and then stopped while the gate was closed and re-locked. 'Whether this is our lot or not, they're up to no good. Look at the size of that man who's getting back into the Toyota; he's huge.'

'Isn't he.....impossible to see if there're more than two. The sun's reflecting off the windscreen.' The vehicle wound through the low grass and scrub bushes, startling a herd of Roan antelopes which scattered and disappeared into a thicket of thorn trees. Just as the Toyota was about to go out of sight as it came towards the dead ground on the other side of the feature opposite Gunn, it turned to the left and skirted round the base of the feature to get onto the track. Again Gunn looked at his watch; 6.43. The Toyota turned onto the track in Gunn's two o'clock position to the right of the feature and then picked up speed as it came towards the drop. The vehicle seemed to be right below them when it stopped and once again, the passenger door opened and the huge African climbed out. Gunn could see him clearly. There was a soft 'click' beside Gunn and Richard Outram lowered the Nikon 35mm camera with its 210 mm telephoto lens.

'That'll do for starters if you have to prove anything or want a mug shot to show around.' Richard went on taking photos as the large man walked awkwardly through the scrub towards the rock. 'That man's never been outside a town in his life, John; there's no way he could've climbed up here. Trouble is we're looking down on top of the car and can't see inside.'

Gunn had put down the binoculars and was now looking at the man through the telescopic sight of the sniper rifle. He could see the sweat on the man's face as he climbed up the rock to its flat plinth. In the middle of the plinth was the flat bolder and the man walked up to it and removed the tape from the breast pocket of his shirt. He bent down with some difficulty and reached under the flat bolder with the tape in his hand. Had Gunn not been using his sniper scope, he might have missed what happened next.

With a violent reaction, the hand was withdrawn from the bolder and the tape fell to the rock. The large man shook his hand in rage and kicked away the bolder to reveal a fully-grown scorpion with raised sting and pincers spread. The arachnid seemed to fill the prism as Gunn watched; the colour was unmistakeable - orange/brown. The man's foot crushed the insect to pulp on the rock before he turned, scrabbled down the side of the rock and stumbled through the scrub towards the Toyota. The driver's door opened and another man got out and went towards the stumbling, larger man.

'Richard, look at both men.'

'Wha...'

'Quickly; just do as I say. Can you see if either's carrying any form of radio. As far as I can see they're not. Quick, or I'm going to lose this opportunity.'

'No...no, I can't see anything. Both men's hands are empty and there appears to be nothing in their pockets.'

'That's what I reckoned.' Both men were now about ten yards from the car and the large one was holding out his right hand gesticulating wildly with the other. 'They mustn't get near the car,' Gunn muttered as he brought the crossed wires of the scope onto the large man's right leg. The sharp 'crack' of the Colt echoed back from the feature in front of them and was followed quickly by three more shots. The heavy, hollow-point bullets slammed into both men's legs, knocking the men to the ground. Gunn put down the sniper rifle and put the automatic back in its holster. He went over to the coiled abseil rope and hurled it over the side of the rock-face.

'Richard; I'm leaving my rucksack. I've got my radio and will use it if I have to, but I'd rather not. I'm taking the morphine and field dressings from the first aid kit. You climb down and go and get the Landrover. Cut the fence and bring the vehicle here and pick up the kit and then meet Stuart when he arrives. I'll leave the tape. Tell him to go home and listen to the tape and to carry on as though nothing had happened. I'll get in touch with him at his house. You go back to Accra in your own time and I'll meet up with you there. Have you got all that?' Richard nodded. Gunn gave these instructions while he slung the fabric carrying case for the rifle over his right shoulder, undid the gate on his carabiner and put the abseil rope inside it. The rope also went over his right shoulder so that the fabric case would reduce the friction burn. 'All clear?'

'Yes; see you there,' came from a subdued Richard who hadn't been mentally prepared for such a rapid and dramatic change to the plan. Gunn slung the rifle across his chest, pulled on the thick leather abseiling gloves and then took hold of the rope. His left hand grasped the rope a couple of feet beyond where it entered the carabiner and his right held a bight of the loose, trailing length which disappeared over the side of the precipitous rock-face. Gunn swung

163

the bight across his chest, which acted as a brake on the rope, and stepped back over the cornice and out of Richard's view.

After three or four leaps, the heat generated by the rope's friction had burnt through the rifle case to Gunn's shoulder, but by then he was only a few feet from the ground and the elasticity in the rope allowed him to let the last of the rope run through the carabiner and he stepped clear of it and the rockface. Gunn turned and looked at the scene by the drop; despite bullets in both legs and the effects of the scorpion's sting, the large man had dragged himself nearly three yards towards the car. The other man hadn't moved.

Gunn ran down the slope of the plinth around the base of the outcrop, across the track and then approached the Toyota from the rear. He removed the Tanarmi from its holster and pulled back the ring hammer to full cock. There was certainly no one visible inside the car and when he wrenched open the rear door there was nothing but a powerful little radio on the back seat with two sub-machine guns. The radio was switched off and the adapter on the power lead wasn't even plugged into the cigarette lighter; there was a telescopic aerial which hadn't been extended. If they had arranged a radio schedule, then that presumably wouldn't start until later.

The weapons were two Scarab Scorpion 9 mm auto-pistols; Gunn removed both magazines and worked the bolts to eject the chambered rounds. Neither of the two men had a weapon. The large man had stopped trying to reach the car and watched Gunn as he approached. Gunn left him and went to the second man; the Colt's bullets had smashed both the man's legs below the knees and he lay face down. Gunn turned him over and the man screamed with the pain. He removed his water bottle and poured some water into the cup, which he offered to the man who accepted it.

'Listen carefully because you get one chance at this. You give me the information I want and I'll see that you are protected from Caramansa' - the use of the name had a dramatic effect and the man turned to look at Gunn - 'You'll want to know that we've got the gold which was taken from the bank yesterday and your contacts in IMT. Your friend over there,' and Gunn waved the barrel of the automatic in the direction of the large man, 'is of no danger to you because he'll die anyway from the scorpion sting. In my pocket here I have morphine and bandages for your wound and you'll be taken to hospital where your legs will be operated on. If you don't tell me what I want to know, I will smash both your arms, then your legs again and finally your genitals. I don't have any time to spare. Have you understood what I've said?' Silence; Gunn unslung the rifle from across his chest and placed the muzzle against the man's elbow.

'Yes,' came almost as a whisper.

'Ah, good; can I have a name?'

'Not while he's alive,' and the eyes moved towards the prone body of the large man.' Gunn turned and shot the large man in the head.

'Name!'

'Kofi.'

'Where's the boy?'

'Accra.'

'Listen Kofi, because you get no more warnings, just bullets. Each time you fail to answer properly - a bullet. Right let's start again.'

'Where's the boy?'

'House in Accra......no! no! no!' was screamed as the muzzle was placed against his arm and the safety catch flicked off. 'Independence Avenue......number 24.'

'Where in the house?'

'In....in the cellar; please let me have the morphine.'

'When I've got the answers.'

'Who will be in this house?'

'No.....er, one woman.'

'Name, damn you!'

'Kisi.'

'Kisi what?'

'Kisi Quartey, she's Cha....er, Caramansa's woman.'

'Whose woman?' and Gunn placed the barrel firmly into Kofi's elbow and took the first pressure on the trigger. 'Mensah! don't shoot! Charles Mensah.'

'Charles Mensah is Caramansa?'

'Yes,' barely audible.

'Anyone else in the house; servants?'

'No, just two servants.'

'Where's the boy in Canada?'

'Don't know....no! please,' as the rifle was placed against his arm. 'I don't know....now I've told you where the boy is in Accra, there'd be no point in not telling you where the other one is. All I know is that he isn't in Canada. He left the country in a private aircraft for England. Please may I have some morphine?'

'What was the radio for?'

'I was to contact Kisi if anything went wrong so that she could speak to the parents. She intends to mutilate the boy if anything goes wrong. She'll do it, you have to believe that. She and Kojo,' he winced with pain as he pointed at the large dead man,' that's Kojo;

165

have already killed Mr Bristow, the girl who worked for him, a maid and someone else at the British High Commission.'

Gunn put down the rifle and removed the morphine self-injection ampoules from his thigh pocket. He opened one packet, removed the needle cover and plunged the needle through the trouser leg into Kofi's thigh and squeezed out the entire contents of the plastic ampoule. The relief it gave was almost instantaneous. He gave Kofi another drink of water, strapped the field dressings round the wounds in his legs and then lifted him into the back seat of the Toyota. He removed the two machine pistols and the radio and put them on the floor in front of the passenger seat.

Gunn's next task was to drag the ox-like corpse of Kojo to the car and heave it through the tailgate into the rear compartment after removing the keys to the gate padlock from the trouser pocket. He walked back to the rock, placed the tape under the bolder and brushed away the remains of the scorpion with the tip of his boot.

Gunn turned the Toyota round and drove it back the way it had come to the padlocked gate. As Gunn got out of the car, his lightweight combat blouse stuck to his side and he pulled it away. He reached out with the key to unlock the padlock to find that his hand was covered in blood. Gunn assumed that it had come from bandaging Kofi's legs and once the gate was open he removed one of the bandages from his pocket, which had not been needed for Kojo, to wipe the blood from his hand. He lifted his blouse and saw that the exit wound in his side had opened. Gunn placed the heavy gauze pad of the field dressing over the wound and bound the bandages tightly round his waist. Still no sign of any cars on the road in front of him. He closed and locked the gate behind the car, climbed in behind the wheel and then turned left onto the main road and headed for Accra. The digital clock on the dashboard registered 7.11.

*

Stuart McLean turned the white Nissan Patrol off the Akosombo road into the Shai Hills game reserve and paid his entry fee at the gate to a warden who had been fast asleep. For the hundredth time he checked his watch; 7.22 - eight minutes to go for him to reach the RV where he was to pick up the tape. He could have screamed with frustration as the sleepy warden painstakingly wrote down the number of his car, dropped the book of tickets, picked it up, dusted it off, blew his nose with his fingers and wiped his hand on the back of his trousers and finally tore off the ticket and gave it to Stuart.

He reset the odometer to zero and with clouds of dust billowing from the spinning back wheels, Stuart drove through the gate and along the laterite track into the game reserve. It was only a short distance to the RV, but he was terrified that a late show might jeopardise his son. He swung the big four-track round the first sharp right-hander, skidded and nearly piled the car into one of the large nim trees. He then calmed down and continued at a more sedate pace, easing the car over the brow of the hill at the bottom of which was the RV. There was a Landrover parked beside the rock. It was the BMAT Landrover.

'Oh no!' Stuart shouted aloud. 'Please don't let anything go wrong.' Richard Outram was standing beside the Landrover and he pulled up five yards away and jumped out of the Nissan. 'For Christ's sake, Richard, what the hell're you doing? They're bound to be watching and you've now screwed it all up and my son's life as well.'

'Nothing's been screwed up, Stuart. Here's the tape. Put it into your casette and we'll both listen to it.'

'But what about.....'

'No one's watching. There were two men waiting to see if you followed your instructions. One's dead and the other's been made to talk and we reckon we know where Graham is...'

'What're you saying.....who...I mean...'

'Listen Stuart please.'

'I'm sorry, Richard....go on.'

'Mary's met the man who was sent out from London to deal with this kidnap. I can't tell you from what organisation he comes, but I'm sure you can guess. He killed one of the men and then interrogated the other one until he found out where your son was.'

'I hope that interrogation was under duress.'

'It was.'

'Good; go on, Richard.'

'He has now gone to find your son. In the mean time he left instructions that we were to listen to the tape and obey the instructions to the letter. May we now play the tape in your cassette player. The Landrover doesn't have one.'

'Yes, sure,' and the two men got into Stuart's car and he inserted the tape into the cassette player. The short message on the tape told them that the Sikafuturu Mining Company should prepare to hand over $100 million dollars worth of gold bars. The drop for the gold would be in North America and further instructions would follow in 24 hours.

'Go home Stuart. Phone Canada and pass that message to your boss. They say that they've got your phone tapped so they would expect you to pass that message, so do so. Got that?'

167

'Yes; thanks Richard......is...is this man from London a real professional. I mean, if you were in my shoes would you have confidence in him.'

'He's the only secret service agent I've ever met so it's difficult to make comparisons. He shot the two men, here, where you and I are standing, from on top of that outcrop.....up there,' and Richard pointed to where he and Gunn had spent the previous night. He seems to be ruthless, thoroughly professional and is a big and powerful character. It would be a great relief to me if I knew he was looking for my little Edward.'

'Thanks; that's an enormous comfort. You never know that your country has these sort of people until you get landed in a nightmare like the one Mary and I are facing. I'll go home and make that call.'

'Do that,' Richard said as he opened the car door,' and I would say nothing to Mary yet. Just say everything went to plan.'

'Yes; that would be better.'

Stuart turned his Nissan Patrol and drove back the way he'd come. Richard Outram watched until he was out of sight and then climbed into the Landrover and drove back across country, through the hole in the fence and past the firing range to the southern road into Accra. He was not prepared to take the risk of the warden becoming curious about two vehicles leaving the game reserve when only one had entered.

CHAPTER 11

'Mike Truman.'

'Mike, it's Janice from registry. We've just had a call from London to say that there's a person to person Top Secret signal ready for transmission to you. Are you free to come up for it?'

'Thanks Janice; on my way,' and Mike Truman put the phone down, left his office and went up to the registry on the second floor. He looked at his watch; 8.15. Hopefully he would be able to let Janice go home after this signal transmission was over. He was still only half way through the pile of files in his 'in' tray, mainly because he found it so hard to bring himself to concentrate on important, but mundane routine matters when he was surrounded by the bizarre and extraordinary situation which had developed in the last 24 hours. He punched out the code on the lock into registry and let himself in. Janice was sitting at her desk reading a Danielle Steele novel and sipping coffee from a large mug.

'Hello Mike; if you'd like to go into the box to call London, I've set up everything for you to receive on machine number two.'

'Thanks; I hope we can all go home to bed after this.'

'No problem, Mike; I only had to break a date with Tom Cruise, but I'm sure he's still waiting for me.'

'So am I, if he has any sense!' and Mike Truman opened the door of the 'isolation' box in which all speech and communication was un-tappable and closed the door behind him. A green light came on to show that the room was sealed. He picked up the secure phone and dialled Perigrine Humble's number in King Charles Street.

Mike Truman was as popular and effective in his appointment as Deputy Head of Mission in Accra as the High Commissioner, Defence Attaché, and First Secretaries Economic - Bristow - and Commercial - Aldridge, were unpopular and ineffective. Mike was on his second marriage and had the children from both marriages with him in Accra. His first wife had walked out on him and her children in preference for a stable lad of 19 at the local racing stables in Oxford. Jean, his wife, had also had a disastrous and childless first marriage and had returned to her original job in the FCO as a personal secretary. The two had met in Canberra and had contrived a dual posting to Bangladesh where they got married. The High

169

Commission was held together by Mike Truman and Ian Maskell and but for these two, would have suffered a wholesale series of resignations from the junior staff who suffered from a total absence of effective leadership, management and career planning.

'Humble.'

'Perigrine, it's Mike Truman in Accra.'

'Thank you, Mike; are you now on your own in the registry?'

'The duty grade ten, Janice, is here.'

'Most grateful if you would ask her to leave the registry while I transmit this signal to you.'

'Yes, of course; ready when you are, Perigrine, and be in touch shortly, no doubt.'

'Indeed; don't hesitate to ask for any assistance from London if you think you need it. I can assure you now that you will get it as a matter of top priority. Bye.' Mike Truman put down the phone, opened the secure door and went back into Janice's office.

'Janice, may I ask you to wait outside registry. It appears that no one's even allowed to be in the registry with me.'

'That's OK Mike; it's one of 'those' signals. I'll take my book. See you in a few minutes,' and Janice departed with book and a chair out of the registry.

Mike Truman went into the cypher room and sat in front of the equipment marked Number Two. The screen came to life and the signal started to appear. When it was complete, Mike pressed the key for a hard copy and the machine beside him hummed into life and spewed out a copy of the signal. He typed in the acknowledgement and the screen went blank. He took the signal into the office and read it twice.

'Bloody hell!' and the signal disappeared into the shredder.

*

'That's a sensible offer and one I can't refuse,' Doyle Barnes replied to the IMT crew member who was wearing a uniform with the rank of a First Officer on his epaulettes and who had made the offer of assistance. Doyle's tone of voice might have been the same had the man asked him the time. 'But I think that it's me who can help you.'

'OK smartass, how'd you figure that out?'

'Very easy; only the best brains are employed in the CIA,' which produced a sneer of disbelief from the crew member. 'Everything you've said or done has been recorded and filmed. I have a mike inside this jacket and the camera, with a 1000 millimetre lens, is behind the window, third from your left, second floor. At the other

170

end of that floor are two snipers, and around this airplane are eight CIA agents carrying a selection of weapons from pump-guns through stun grenades to machine pistols. Above you, but out of sight,' was added as the younger man - not in uniform - glanced up, 'are two F-16s from Wheeler Airbase which will barbecue this 747 on their Sidewinders if you think that you can get away from here and deliver this cargo to Amarillo.'

'Bullshit, smartass, you're bluffing.'

'Let's test that opinion; don't get excited, son. I'll just get all those people show you where they are.'

'Go on then, you ain't fooling no one, right now.'

'No fooling, son;' Doyle bent his head towards the mike, 'all stations on this net show your location. Foxtrot one and two; do a low pass over this airplane.'

Around the 747, ground handlers in overalls stopped what they were doing and turned towards the cargo bay of the 747; all were armed. The windows in the customs building opened and from the left end appeared a man holding a video camera with a long telephoto lens attached to it. At the other end of the building, two men appeared at windows holding sniper rifles, but most dramatic of all was the arrival, with no sound, and travelling only marginally sub-sonic, of the two General Dynamics F-16 fighter planes, barely 100 feet above the 747.

The mind-shattering thunder of sound and the roar as the pilots of the F-16s pushed their throttle levers through the gate into reheat and climbed at Mach 1.2 away from the airport would have allowed Doyle and his CIA inspector to take the two armed crewmen in front of them, who all but dropped the machine pistols which they were holding. Doyle put a restraining hand on his colleague's arm as the jet fighters receded into the sky.

'Right now, you two and the remainder of the crew in this 747 are facing an indictment for your part in an armed robbery, in which at least one man was murdered. You are also facing an indictment for your part in a conspiracy to bring gold into the USA illegally, evading Customs revenue. Your prison terms will range from something like ten to twenty years, depending on how slick your lawyers are - and I bet old Bradley Tracton will hire the best.' The use of their employer's name unsettled the two men even more. The younger one turned to the First Officer.

'C'mon Ben, we don......'

'Shut up, Chris, for crissakes.....I'm thinking. There has to be a way out of this. Trax has always looked after us before.....no call now for that to change. You there!' and the First Officer pointed with the muzzle of the machine pistol at Doyle Barnes, 'Smartass; we'll take you with us and you get it if anything happens to us.'

'No one's going anywhere with you, son, if that's....'

'Don't call me son!' the man screamed hysterically at Doyle.

'You might kill me if you fire that grease gun, but both of you will be dead before I hit the ground. Put the guns down while you both still have the chance to live. Shoot us and I swear that all of you'll be fried alive in 'ole sparky'.' The one called Chris threw the machine pistol away and started to raise his hands.

'That's it, Ben; I'm giving myself up, it's......'

'You bas.......' and Ben swung the machine pistol towards his friend, but stopped before his gun had swung through even a half of its arc as he was hurled to the back of the 747's cargo bay by the impact of the two magnum calibre .357 bullets from the sniper rifles.

'How many more crew in there, son?' Doyle asked the young man.

'The captain and engineer officer, Sir......they were on the flight deck last time I saw them.

'Time to pay them a visit,' and Doyle took his Colt out of the briefcase. 'You come with us,' and the hydraulic freight platform lowered them all to the ground. Doyle, with the inspector and the crew member called Chris, climbed the steps to the flight deck entrance. When they reached the open door of the 747, Doyle shouted, 'this is the CIA; I want both of you to come down from the flight deck with your hands raised, now.' Nothing happened; 'last warning; the grenades come next.' A sound of movement and then both men appeared with their hands raised. 'Search them,' and the CIA inspector checked both men.

'They're clean, sir.'

'Tomorrow we're all going on a short flight to the IMT airfield at Amarillo. You get this wrong and you go to the electric chair if I don't blow you head off first. Now come outside so that the cameras can get a good picture of you and then each of you will state his real name.'

'Control, patch me through to Langley,' Doyle said into the mike.

'Slattery here, Doyle.'

'Right Sir; phase one complete; one casualty for them. Ready to start phase two. Our ETA at Amarillo will be 0943 hours tomorrow. That will be the revised 'L' Hour for phase two. Please advise all units and call-signs of this change, over.'

'Roger, out.'

The crew of the 747 were removed to spend their lay-over at the military base at Fort Worth rather than the Sheraton, as had been planned, while the aircraft, with its cargo of Ashanti gold, was guarded by the CIA at Dallas Airport. The Chief Customs Officer and his inspector were flown to Langley, Virginia where they were provided with equally spartan accommodation by the CIA.

*

Kisi was woken at 6 am by the maid and after her bath went down to the lounge and switched on the powerful transmitter/receiver and tuned it to the frequency on which Kofi would contact her with a communication check at 7 o'clock. Her breakfast was brought in on a trolley by the maid.

'Patience.'

'Yes, madam.'

'You and Soloman may take the rest of the day off when you've cleared up after breakfast.'

'Thank you madam. Will it be alright if we go to our village?'

'Where's that, Patience?'

'Between Accra and Nsawam, madam; only 45 minutes by tro-tro.'

'Yes alright, but make sure you're back tonight.'

'Yes madam.'

'That's all, Patience; you may go now.'

'Very good, madam,' and Patience was out of Kisi's hearing when she added....'mean an' evil witch' and the maid crossed herself and curtsied to the small shrine beside the stove in the kitchen.

Three minutes past seven and nothing from Kofi. Kisi re-tuned the receiver and transmitter and increased the volume, but all this had been checked three times before and she knew that communications between Shia Hills and the house on Independence Avenue worked perfectly.

'Something's gone wrong, I know it,' she muttered, staring at the radio and willing it to burst into life. She had no appetite for the rest of her breakfast and pushed the trolley away. Her brain began to race; perhaps she was already on borrowed time and it would be only moments before the police and BNI arrived at the house. That whole business at the British High Commission compound had been handled really badly and amateurishly. No, there was no doubt that this house was no longer safe and no sooner had that thought process occurred in Kisi's mind than she went briskly out to the kitchen and told Patience and Soloman that they were both dismissed and wouldn't be required any longer. They were given no money and as soon as Kisi left the kitchen, Patience took off her apron, collected her

173

husband Soloman from the front garden where he was weeding and the two of them walked out onto Independence Avenue.

Kisi went up to her room, dressed and packed all her things. Before going down to get the boy from the cellar, she made a thorough check of the house to make sure that there was nothing to connect it to Caramansa. Kisi collected the bottle of chloroform and gauze pad from her room and went down the steps into the cellar.

The house had been very quiet for some time and Graham was both bored and frightened. He had watched all the video films which had been placed in his room and had eaten most of the food which had been in the well-stocked fridge in the small kitchenette on one side of his room. He had seen no one since he woke up to find himself lying on the bed and that must have been on Monday. He had been in the room for four nights, so it had to be at least Friday and possibly Saturday, depending on how long he'd been unconscious. His Mum would be really worried - and this understatement in Graham's thought process almost brought tears; not tears of self-pity, but tears of anxiety for his Mum because he was very close to becoming a young man and childish tears had ceased some few years previously. It was high time that he did something positive about getting out of this place - if anyone came to see him - because he'd already examined the door and steel-barred window and there was no implement in the kitchen drawers which would make the slightest impression on either of those; but there was - what his Mum called - a little kitchen devil. Amongst the very few implements was a small and very sharp, black-handled knife. This, Graham had removed from the drawer and placed inside his sock above the high-ankled Reebok trainer.

Graham had just finished his cup of tea when he heard someone coming towards his room. He checked the knife, which was exactly where he'd put it the day before. A key was put into the lock of his door and Graham stretched out on the bed and pretended to be asleep.

Kisi opened the door and looked into the room; the boy was on his bed asleep and still in his clothes. She walked into the room holding the chloroform and gauze pad. As she reached the bed, the boy leapt off it and made to dive past her heading for the unlocked door. In a rage of self-incrimination for being so stupid, Kisi dropped the chloroform bottle, tripped the boy and as he fell to the ground threw herself on him reaching for the chloroform as she did so. She forced the gauze over his nose and mouth and as she sprinkled the chloroform onto the gauze there was a sudden convulsive move by the boy and Kisi felt a burning sensation in her left side. As the boy

174

lost consciousness, she looked down and saw the small knife buried to the hilt in the left side of her stomach.

Tears of frustration and anger ran down Kisi's cheeks as she got up off the unconscious boy and went to the chair beside his bed and removed a towel, which she held over the wound in her stomach. She knew that there were no bandages in the house so she tied the towel round her stomach while she tore up the sheet into strips and then took off her clothes and examined the puncture made by the knife. It wasn't a pleasant sight as the struggling boy had pulled on the knife, enlarging the wound; it was deep and she knew that there would be internal bleeding in addition to the large amount of blood, which had already stained the floor and bed. Kisi made a pressure pad out of a strip of the sheet and then bound the strips of sheet firmly round her stomach.

She dragged the boy upstairs to the hall and went up to her bedroom where she removed a loose-fitting dress from her suitcase and got dressed in that. She took the suitcase and the blood-soaked clothes downstairs, drove the car round to the front and dragged the boy down the front steps of the house and into the back seat of the car where she tied his hands and feet. Back into the house again to collect the suitcase and put that in the luggage compartment under the beetle's bonnet.

One last look round the house; no time to clear up the bloody mess downstairs - let them think what they like if the house is searched. It would only heighten the misery of the parents who would assume that the blood was their son's and ensure that they paid up the ransom quickly. Any messages for Kofi and Kojo? If they were both still alive and got back to the house then Kofi would know where to find her whereas Kojo wouldn't have the faintest idea which was exactly as she wanted it. Kisi collected a dustsheet from the cupboard by the stairs, closed the front door, got in the car, covered the boy in the back with the dustsheet and drove out onto Independence Avenue.

She would have to get urgent treatment for the stab wound and there was only one place where she could get that. If she went to any of the clinics, her real identity would be discovered in next to no time and she would be straight back to that dreadful room in the interrogation centre of the BNI headquarters. Death was infinitely preferable to that. She had to get to Caramansa's distribution centre on the border of Togo. From there she could get over the border to the mission hospital at Atakpamé. Besides, the distribution centre was a much safer place to keep the wretched child who still lay unconscious in the back of the car.

175

She stopped at a chemist's shop in the main street of Kpando, where the ferry crossed the Volta River, to buy some gauze and bandages for her wound. Her family had lived in the village for three generations, but after her mother's death, her father had taken her to Ashanti region so that he could find work in the mines. Her mother's long illness had drained away what little money her father had saved. In desperation, he had gone to the high priests of the Oracle who had insisted that in return for their prayers for his wife, he must hand over his daughter to be trained in the rites of a priestess. In effect, this meant that she, at the age of fifteen, became the mistress of the High Priest of the Oracle; Charles Mensah. That superstition surrounding the Oracle had kept even the armed forces away from the mist-shrouded hills where weird and unearthly incantations could be heard when the wind stirred around the cavernous entrance to the Oracle as though they were coming from the depths of the underworld.

She crossed on the ferry over the Volta and stopped once more in Zebila for some water where both she and the woman selling her the bottled water noticed that the blood had soaked through her dress. As soon as she arrived on the plateau she was met by the Oracle's guards whose magical appearances from the many concealed entrances to the labrynth of tunnels under the plateau ensured that very few people visited the place. Once they saw who it was, Kisi was carried into the cave, as was the boy. It was only then that she was told that it seemed that she had been followed and there was another car only a few minutes behind her. Charles Mensah had established a highly effective warning system which had nothing to do with drums and voodoo, but relied on ardent and well-paid devotees of the Oracle in Zebila who phoned warnings through to the cave via the cable laid when the Caramansa organization had taken over the Oracle as its headquarters and distribution centre.

Before the establishment of ICB, Charles Mensah had obtained his weapons to foster terrorism in Togo, Mali and Burkina Faso from Libya. The consignments were flown from Marzuq in southern Libya to Niamey in Niger and then went by road through Burkina Faso to Mango in Togo. From there they were collected by Caramansa and taken to Atakpamé where the unsuspecting hospital mission stored them, thinking that they were medical supplies. This belief was excusable as in every consignment of arms was a generous supply of drugs and medical equipment for the hospital. This arrangement also ensured that there was a secure place for hospital treatment for the Caramansa 'freedom fighters'.

The distribution centre was not only used for the provision of arms and explosives to terrorists, but was also the collection point for gold and precious stones stolen from the mines in Ashanti and had a well-equipped laboratory for processing the raw cocaine which came from Columbia and the opium from Burma. The distribution centre was run by Doctor Kwajo Twum-Danso who was a pharmaceutical doctor as opposed to a medical one, but it was he who re-dressed Kisi's stab wound, injected her with penicillin and anti-tetanus and then arranged for her to be flown in the Caramansa helicopter direct to the mission hospital. The unconscious boy had been put into one of the five cells in the centre which were used for re-indoctrination of those brothers whose ardour for the Caramansa cause had waned, interrogation of informers and comfort rooms for the workforce to entertain women brought up from Zebila.

Kwajo Twum-Danso's first priority was to get Kisi to hospital. He supervised the fitting of the stretcher into the German Mescherschmitt 105 helicopter and then stood back as the two, 420 shaft-horsepower Allison turbines built up power. The helicopter lifted off from the west side of the Whispering Hills which lay exactly on the border between Togo and Ghana and turned to the east for the short fifteen minute flight to Atakpamé.

*

Ahead of him, Gunn saw the police control point. He and Peter had passed through a similar one on the other road the previous night on the way out to Shai Hills. The police would probably shoot him on the spot if they saw what he had in the car. The previous evening, he had noted that the moment they saw a white face in uniform, the police were more than happy to let the Landrover through. There was no other course, but to bluff it out; his Toyota was already in sight of the control point and any suspicious behaviour would have alerted them. Gunn removed his jungle hat and wound down the window. Kofi appeared to be unconscious. The control point was now only 100 yards away. There was no sign of movement; under a piece of canvas stretched between four poles was a low wooden table; on the low wooden table were two bodies. Two policemen who were fast asleep.

Gunn leant out of the window and waved as he slowed down; the head of one of the prone bodies turned in his direction and his wave was returned. Gunn drove through the chicane of the check point and gradually accelerated away the other side. He closed the window and turned the air conditioning up to full to dry off the

177

sweat, which made his combat blouse stick to his back. His next worry was the tollbooth at the entrance to the Tema motorway.

He dug some of the Cedi notes out of his pocket and selected a faded, orange-coloured 200 Cedi note. Gunn drove the full circuit of the roundabout and took the last exit onto the motorway. Four hundred yards ahead was the tollbooth, but now there was more traffic on the road and to his intense frustration, two cars ahead of him waiting at the toll. He slowed down; around the two cars were hawkers selling everything from cigarettes to goats. The first car went through. 'For Christ sake have the right change,' Gunn said out loud. Whether the driver had the right change or not, the old Honda moved forward amidst clouds of blue smoke.

Gunn pulled up opposite the booth and handed in the 200 Cedis; he was given his ticket and started to move forward as a woman tapped on the rear window in an attempt, possibly, to wake up the sleeping Kofi. Once clear of the toll, Gunn accelerated away, but there was no commotion behind him, only a nearly empty motorway stretched in front of him leading to Accra.

He drove into Accra on the road, which passed the airport, the military hospital and Afrikiko. Round the roundabout and then he watched the numbers of the properties. Even numbers were on the left of the road and uneven on his side on the right. First came the Canadian High Commission, some more houses, the American Ambassador's Residence followed by two large private properties and then Number 24. Gunn drove past and continued down to the next roundabout at Castle Road and drove back on the other side of the road. He reached down and pulled the Tanarmi from its holster, pulled back the hammer to full cock and put it on the seat on his right.

He turned into the driveway of Number 24 and drove round to the back of the house as he had assumed that the car would be a stolen one and they would hardly leave it outside the house in full view of the main road through Accra. There was still no murmur from Kofi. Gunn picked up the Tanarmi and got out of the Toyota. There was no sign of any life from the house and no other cars parked round the back. Gunn climbed the wooden steps at the rear of the house into the kitchen; no servants.....not a sound. Through the kitchen into a large dining room and from there to the hall; not a sign of anyone. The silence was almost oppressive. In the hall were the stairs leading down to the cellar. Twenty-three steps to the bottom Gunn counted, as he descended as quietly as possible before turning into the corridor which ran the length of the house above.

He paused at the first door which was ajar and pushed it open; a self-contained little suite which had been recently occupied by the look of the rumpled beds and an uncleared meal on the table. At least three people had sat at that table. Gunn went on down the corridor to the next door on his left...also ajar. Another room similar to the other one, but smaller; and then he saw the blood. It was all over the bed, some on the floor, more smeared all over a towel, some on the table. Gunn went to the table and touched the blood stains; they were still sticky. He turned to leave the room and there, by the door, in the blood were three footprints, two of which could have been made by a pair of trainers. He ran out of the room and checked the other doors in the cellar; all revealed empty rooms or stores. He took the stairs two at a time and rushed from room to room through the house; no one...nothing.

Gunn got into the Toyota and shook the recumbent body in the back. Eventually there was a groan and Kofi showed signs of consciousness. 'Kofi, listen damn you,' and Gunn shook him again.

'More morphine....'

'Listen man; the boy's gone. No one's in the house. If you want to live longer than the next couple of minutes, I want to know why and where they've gone.'

'Witch...'

'Which what, man?'

'No...she's a witch......knew something wrong.'

'What the hell are you talking about? Who's a witch?'

'Kisi...Kisi's a witch. All the village knows that... that's where she's gone.'

'Where...where is this village, Kofi. She's done something to that boy and there's blood everywhere.'

'My village.....both from same village .,....Kpandu.....that's on the Volta... my legs, my legs.....morphine please.' Gunn squeezed another ampoule of morphine into Kofi and then lifted him out of the car and carried him into the house where he put him on a sofa in the drawing room. He returned to the car and dragged Kojo out of the back, up the steps and into the kitchen.

The traffic was really heavy and it was another forty minutes before Gunn pulled the Toyota into the side of the road, a hundred yards beyond Dina's shop. He walked back and went to the entrance, which had a large 'Closed' sign in the window. That was hardly surprising, Gunn thought as he checked the time; still a quarter to nine. He went round to the back of the shop where there was a small yard and steel steps leading up to the flat above. Gunn went up and knocked on the door. A curtain was pulled aside, a pause and then the door was opened by Dina.

'Come in, John; what's happened? You're covered in blood.' She led him into a small, but very modern and well-fitted kitchen. 'Coffee?'

'Please, Dina; I'm fine, but you and I have got to move very quickly indeed if we hope to save that boy's life - if he's still alive.' Very briefly, Gunn told her what had happened at Shai Hills and about the two men he'd left at Number 24 Independence Avenue. 'Have you got someone who can clear up the mess at Number 24 and get rid of the Toyota which was probably stolen.'

'That's no problem; where is it?'

'About a hundred yards down the street....these are the keys,' and Gunn placed them on the work surface beside him as he sipped at the coffee. 'Where's Kpandu? Kofi said something about it being on the Volta and do you have a car I can use to get there now.'

'Yes and yes; I'm just going to make a call to arrange the removal of the car, the disappearance of Kojo and medical treatment for Kofi and then we'll go.' Dina went out of the kitchen and Gunn finished his coffee. He looked down at his combat suit; he had to admit that it was a bit gory, but that would have to wait. Beside him on the work surface was a jotting pad and pencil and Gunn pulled it towards him and scribbled some thoughts down and then tore it off and went out to the small hallway where Dina was just replacing the phone.

'Fine, John, that's all fixed.'

'Dina, does the name Charles Mensah ring a bell with you?'

'Too right; he was a counsellor in the Ghanaian High Commission in Ottawa until they discovered that he had set up a bank.....the International Credit Bank, I think......using funds from World Bank loans which were intended for Ghana. His bank has its main branch in Las Vegas and is about to undergo a congressional investigation as it has links with almost every terrorist organisation and drug cartel in existence, but nothing proved to date. Is he part of this?'

'The head of it, I think. He's Caramansa.'

'How do you know?'

'The character I shot in both legs produced that piece of information when I threatened to do the same to other parts of his anatomy. Look,' and Gunn handed Dina his piece of paper torn from the jotting pad. 'I'd be grateful if you'd give Christine a ring and ask her to check on these points, produce a full report on Charles Mensah and identify all his contacts while he was a counsellor in the Ghanaian High Commission in Ottawa.

'Right away,' and Dina punched out Christine's number. Gunn returned to the kitchen. The coffee was most welcome and cleared some of the dust from his throat; he placed the mug in the sink as Dina reappeared in the kitchen, dressed in slacks, blouse and with her hair tied up in a scarf in the local Ghanaian fashion. 'Right, John, that's all fixed and Christine will fax her report through on the faxlock. I'll take you to Kpandu.'

'OK Dina; just stop by the Toyota and I'll remove the hardware from it. What do I do with the keys?'

'Leave them in the car; it'll be removed in less than five minutes.'

Dina opened the garage at the rear of the shop and climbed into a long wheelbase Nissan Patrol, which she drove out into the small back yard. Gunn shut the garage door and then got into the passenger seat. Dina pulled alongside the Toyota and Gunn removed the rifle, radio and machine pistols and put the keys in the ignition. No one in the area paid them the least amount of attention; as soon as Gunn was back in the Nissan, Dina let in the clutch and headed back through the centre of Accra to Independence Avenue to retrace the route, which Gunn had just driven.

As Dina guided the Nissan through the permanently congested morning traffic, she pulled a map out of the pocket on the driver's door and handed it to Gunn. 'Follow the road past Shai Hills, John, and about three or four miles further on you'll see a village named Khasi - most English people can remember that name! In the centre of that village is a crossroads. The left turn is little more than a track and leads to some small villages, but the right turn is a metalled road and goes north-east towards the Volta.'

'Got it; if Kisi went this way, then she must have driven right past me.'

'There really is no other route, so she must have. Follow that road, John and where it reaches the Volta, you'll see Kpandu. The road stops there and there's no crossing point, but the village operates a ferry which can just about cope with a couple of lorries or half-a-dozen cars. Its engines frequently break down and the ferry ends up miles downstream, so it's a bit of a gamble. The proper bridge is at Kpong.'

'How many people in this village?'

'Oh, it's very small....about two thousand at the very most. It's a bit of a dead place since the bridge was built at Kpong. There's no reason to go there. At one time there used to be a large sugar-processing factory....it's marked on the map, just to the left of the road and about a mile or so before the village.'

'Spotted.'

181

'That's now derelict and occupied by squatters.' Dina paid her 200 Cedis at the tollbooth and drove due west along the Tema motorway. 'How do you want to play this when we get to Kpandu.'

'What language will they speak?'

'Evé.'

'And you can speak that?'

'Yes, that's my natural tongue, second to English.'

'Then I suggest that I keep out of sight and you go and make enquiries as to where this Kisi Quartey lives, or if anyone's seen her, and a boy.'

'How do you intend keeping out of sight?'

'I'll climb into the back luggage space and sit with our small armoury of weapons.'

'Any idea what you're going to do?'

'No - to be perfectly honest. I'm sure that we're fast running out of time and that as soon as Kisi discovers what's happened, young Graham's as good as dead. This car's unknown and so are you and I in Kpandu. Is there a main street in the village?'

'Yes; it's the only one and runs parallel with the river bank and the village - what little there is of it - is on either side of the road. It's some time since I was there, but I doubt if it's changed much.'

'Just drive along the main road, Dina, until either you see someone you think might help us or we spot something. We can't be that long behind her, assuming of course that she's here. That blood was still wet and in this heat blood must dry in minutes.'

'What's made her rush off like this? Presumably you're not going for this witchcraft bit?'

'Always ready for surprises, but I really can't understand why she's harmed the boy before the tape had even been collected. Neither of the men could've spoken to her and the police really don't have the slightest idea what's happened. I'm an eternal optimist, but if we are successful in saving this boy, I'll lay you long odds in favour of a very simple explanation.'

'Hope you're right; Khasi and the turn off are about a mile ahead......in fact you'll see Khasi as we come over the next rise.....there. How are you going to keep this Caramansa thing from finding out about Graham McLean and then starting to mutilate the three year old....I've forgotten his name.'

'Ian.'

'Yes, Ian...in Canada?' and Dina slowed and turned right off the main road. The village, if it could be called that, was spread around the crossroads and a filling station which boasted two, hand-cranked pumps. Children, dogs, chickens and goats scampered around the crossing and vegetable and fruit stalls were laden with produce for sale. The red laterite dust was everywhere and the car and windscreen had a thick coating all over. Dina reached for the wash/wipe switch on the right-hand lever on the steering column. Gunn interrupted her move with his hand.

'Can you leave the dust; it makes it much harder to see into the car which is to our advantage.'

'OK.'

'I don't think Ian's in Canada and there's been something nagging at the back of my mind since we learnt of the double kidnapping and my visit to the High Commission. If I've got it wrong, then I'll have the death, or mutilation of at least one, if not two boys to live with.'

'Is that what those questions for Christine were all about?'

'Yes; is that Kpandu?'

'It is.'

'Right, I'll get into the back,' and Gunn climbed over the seats into the luggage area at the back of the station wagon.' The windows of the car were thickly coated with dust, making it very difficult to see much of anything in the car, and quite hard to see out, as well. The Nissan came to a 'T' junction; straight ahead was the mile wide Volta, left and right was the high street of Kpandu. Dina turned left.

'The main part of the village lies to the left: here we go.'

The little village was bustling with activity, but even in the first few hundred yards, it was noticeable that the village was populated by either the old or very young. The working age group had gone to the city or the bigger towns where the money was. Dina stopped the Nissan outside a tiny chemist's shop. She left the engine running and went into the shop. Gunn had replaced his jungle hat and pulled it well down over his eyes and rolled down his sleeves to hide the light-coloured skin. Dina reappeared and got into the car.

'Owners of chemist shops the world over are the best-informed gossips in villages. One of the many similarities between Ghana and its old colonial ruler! I asked the lady who owns the shop if any other cars had been through the village in the last half-hour. The answer was three; two of those were vans, but the third was a Volkswagen, which stopped right where we're parked. The lady from the car bought cotton wool, gauze pads and white spirit - doesn't sound too good, does it - and then drove off. I asked her if she recognised the lady and gave her Kisi's name. The old madam's eyes rolled a bit - still a tremendous amount of belief in witchcraft and witch doctors in my country - and she then pointed across the river.' Dina turned the Nissan round and headed back towards the ferry.

'Kisi's crossed the river, so I suggest you come back in the front and I'll wash the windscreen so that we can see where we're going.' Gunn accepted the suggestion and climbed back into the front of the car.

'How the hell did the old lady know where Kisi was going?'

'How much of the Ghanaian beliefs and culture do you know?'

'Virtually nothing; only what was in the brief which Christine gave me.'

'Here comes a very quick burst of beliefs and culture which will help you understand why the old lady knew exactly where Kisi was going. Can you pay the man for me please?'

Dina had stopped the Nissan at the foot of the ramp leading onto the ferry and payment was now required for the epic crossing. Gunn viewed the prospect with some alarm as the contraption in front of them looked as though it was incapable of keeping itself afloat, let alone having any more weight added to encourage the sinking process. Gunn held out a thousand Cedi note and was given 800 change; everything seemed to cost 200 Cedis. Dina drove the Nissan Patrol onto the ferry, which creaked and swayed alarmingly. A cloud of black diesel smoke - no doubt caused by injectors that had long passed their terminal 'clean by' date, Gunn reckoned - poured from a rusty exhaust stack as the mooring lines were hurled on board. The gap between the riverbank and the ferry widened and then the current caught the ungainly craft and the crab-like crossing of the Volta commenced.

They both climbed out of the car and walked to the front of the ferry; it had neither bow nor stern and was nothing more complicated than a floating rectangle with an engine driving a propeller which was reversed for the return journey. Gunn's combat blouse had stuck firmly to the blood on his right side and he eased it away as they stopped at a point where it seemed safer not to go any further forward.

'You're bleeding aren't you? You silly man; why didn't you tell me. Come with me, there's a first aid kit in the back of the car and some sterile cleansing solution.' Dina opened the back of the Nissan and produced a holdall full of medical paraphernalia, which looked to Gunn like a 'Do-It-Yourself' operating kit. By this time, Dina and Gunn had attracted an audience of some twenty of the ferry's passengers who joined in with oohs! and aahs! as Dina lifted up Gunn's combat smock and cleaned the dried blood from the bullet wound. Having done that she gave him an injection of anti-tetanus and then promptly, and much to Gunn's amazement, proceeded to re-stitch his wound. 'And before you ask, yes, I am a qualified nurse as well as a fashion designer and was trained in London if that sets your mind at rest.'

'Any other talents?'

'That's none of your business; now, hold that in place,' and she put his fingers over a gauze pad covering her stitchwork, 'while I dig out a bandage.' A very large bandage was produced and wrapped tightly round his middle. 'There; that might stop you leaking for a bit,' which was greeted by applause from the audience.

'Thanks; you were going to tell me about the beliefs of your country.'

'Get in the car and I'll start the engine so that we can have the air-conditioning on. I can't hear myelf think with this noisy audience which you and your bloody wound has attracted.' They both got into the car and Dina started it and switched on the air-conditioning. The ferry had just reached the point of no return and Gunn was grateful for something to concentrate on other then his conviction of the impending submersion of the ferry in a river well known for its 'crocs', hippos and barracuda.

'The Akans, who represent the largest ethnic grouping in West Africa, believe in a Supreme Deity and the sanctity of the mother of that Deity; just like the Christian belief in Christ and Mary Magdelene. The most important person in a tribe is not really the Chief, but the Queen Mother, who personifies the mother of the Supreme Deity. Does that make sense?'

'Absolutely; go on.'

'The Akans believe that the moon is the symbol of the Deity and the origin of its tribe and the whole universe. This belief is given tangible form in the shape of the Akuaba doll, which you'll find everywhere in Ghana. The head is in the shape of a disc, which represents the moon and the body can be either triangular or cylindrical in shape with out-stretched limbs. This represents the sky, the earth and the underworld over which the head, or Supreme Deity reigns.'

'All that part of the Akan belief is very respectable, but what follows has led those of the developed countries to make accusations of voodooism, animism or paganism. Below the Supreme deity, there are many other lesser deities which are called Asuman. The power of these lesser deities follows set patterns and these are displayed on charms, beads, bracelets, designs carved on stools and so on...oops!' was added by Dina as the ferry lurched over in a list as something struck it. 'Playful hippo, I expect,' she smiled with as little concern as if she was commenting on the weather.

'Didn't know there were any in this stretch of the Volta, between the dam and the sea.'

'Oh yes; they reintroduced both the crocodiles and hippos some three years ago and they've done really well.'

'I'm really pleased about that. Go on, I'd hate to miss any of this paganism bit by becoming breakfast for a hippo.'

'The Akan belief is identical to Christianity in the belief that man has both flesh and a soul. The flesh comes from the mother and the soul from the father. Now we come to the relevant bit. These beliefs form the basis of an Akan religion known as Tagare which is hallowed in the infamous and much feared shrine, known as the Oracle of the Tongo, at a place called Zebila which lies about fifty miles to the east of us. The shrine is up in the hills where there is a symmetrical grouping of three hills, called the Whispering Hills of Tongo.'

'Come on, Dina, this gets more and more like Rider Haggard's 'King Soloman's Mines' by the minute. Are you serious?'

'Absolutely; from where do you think Rider Haggard got his ideas for that and many other books about Africa which he wrote.'

'I always thought that came from East Africa; Kenya, Tanzania, Uganda and so on.'

'So do most other people, but tell me that at least you knew that Edgar Rice-Burroughs based his character Tarzan in West Africa.'

'I would love to be able to reassure you, but my conscience prevents that. So how do we know that Kisi has gone to these Whispering Hills?'

There's a fetish priest at the Oracle. When you visit the Oracle you have to take a bottle of white spirits with you.... gin or schnapps is the usual gift..... so that the priest can make a libation to the gods and Oracle. Not only did the old lady recognise Kisi as one of the priestesses of the Oracle but she sold her a bottle of white spirit; I thought she meant medical white spirit because she said it in the context of cotton wool and gauze pads. I'm sure it's been stamped out by the police and local administration, but not that long ago it's rumoured that human child sacrifices were made at the Oracle.'

The ferry bumped against the far bank of the Volta, Dina let in the clutch and drove the Nissan Patrol up the ramp and onto the laterite track, which stretched into the distance through the scrub and thorn trees to Zebila and the blue Whispering Hills beyond.

CHAPTER 12

'Tower, Victor Romeo Charlie 748 outbound for Amarillo, ready to taxi.'

'Tower, roger Victor Romeo Charlie 748, you are third in sequence behind American Airlines Airbus 320, November 756, on runway 330. Taxiway Sierra 50 Alpha, flight level 31, contact Amarillo on 146 decimal 5.'

'Sierra 50 Alpha, flight level 31, 146 decimal 5, Victor Romeo Charlie 748,' and the IMT 747 rolled forward from its parking bay in front of the Customs building and turned right onto taxiway S50A behind the Airbus 320. In the left-hand seat of the flight-deck sat Captain Dave Graydon, Boeing's chief test pilot who had been seconded to the CIA for the flight to Amarillo. In the right-hand seat was Captain Alvin Bartolsky, IMT's senior pilot. In the unlikely event thet IMT was monitoring the air traffic control frequencies, all transmissions were spoken by Bartolsky. The time was 0903 hours; the IMT 747 was three minutes behind schedule as it turned onto the taxiway. In the engineer's seat sat another of Boeing's employees; on the upper deck of the cargo 747 was the remainder of the IMT aircrew, watched by Doyle Barnes and the CIA team from Dallas.

While Doyle and his team had gathered at Dallas Airport, an airborne armoured brigade group of the USA's immediate stand-by Rapid Reaction Force had been deployed by Lockheed C-5 Galaxies to the military airfield at Gruver, 42 miles to the north-east of the IMT industrial complex. This deployment had caused no concern to the local population as the infrequently-used airfield at Gruver was in the middle of a military training area. All of the units in the armoured brigade had come from the 82nd Airborne Division stationed at Fort Bliss in Atlanta and after landing at Gruver airfield, had deployed under the cover of darkness to the high ground to the west of IMT. All the units were in position before first light with the exception of one infantry battalion which was waiting at Gruver airfield with twelve, CH-47D Chinook helicopters for the main body of the battalion and Bell 214s and Cobras to take in the assault company and provide its firepower.

Stacked at 12,000 feet to the east of Gruver was a flight of four F-16 Falcons from Wheeler Airbase with a Boeing 707 refuelling tanker in attendance. Fifty miles to the north of IMT's complex and at 88,000 feet, a two-seater Lockheed U-TR 1A - a greatly up-rated version of the U-2 spy plane shot down by Soviet missiles over Sverdlovsk in 1960 - cruised gracefully in the thin violet half-light of sub-space as its sideways-looking, synthetic aperture radar, sensors, EW equipment and cameras watched every movement in the IMT industrial complex.

It was the navigator of this aircraft, cocooned in his astronaut's clothing, who had reported the unusual activity inside IMT's complex. This information was then relayed to Doyle Barnes who, in turn, passed it to the Brigade Commander. As soon as the information had been evaluated by the Brigade's intelligence cell, a company of M-180 reconnaissance vehicles, armed with 30mm canons and M-60 machine guns, was re-deployed to a position astride the road leading south out of the IMT complex to Route 54. The redeployment had likewise been completed before first light. The time was now 0922 hours; in less than twenty minutes, the pilot of the IMT 747 would start to make his descent to IMT's airfield. It was time to speak to IMT as the aircraft would have been on their screens as soon as it reached cruise altitude after the climb out from Dallas.

Dave Graydon checked the frequency; 146.5 and then called Doyle Barnes into the flight-deck. 'Ready to make contact, Doyle. D'you know if there was any pre-arranged code between this guy,' and he jerked his head in the direction of the co- pilot, 'and IMT.'

'All he's told us was that Bradley Tracton told him to make contact when he was in-bound from Dallas to IMT. If friend Al, here, has got it wrong then he can look forward to a ten year extension to his stay at Uncle Sam's expense. Right, go ahead; punch in today's code into the scrambler and make contact. If you alert them, I promise you, Mr Bartolsky, they'll throw away the key when you go down.' The co-pilot punched in the code and then pressed the transmit button on the yoke in front of him.

'IMT tower, this is VRC 748 in-bound from Dallas, flight level 31 with an ETA of 0951 hours. Patch me through to Tracton.'

'IMT, roger VRC 748, reduce to flight level 26, IMT altitude 3335 feet, patching you through now.....wait.....wait, you're through to Mr Tracton.'

'Tracton, it's Al, in-bound from Dallas; should be with you in 'bout twenty minutes.' There was no answer to this transmission, but Doyle's CIA communication and cypher engineer, who had monitored every transmission during the operation at the airport, appeared on the flight deck and handed Doyle a small sheet of paper and then returned to his equipment on the upper deck. Doyle glanced at the paper and then at Bartolsky.

'Our records show that you have a wife and two children, Bartolsky; is that right?'

'What's that to you?'

'Just this, Bartolsky; our records also show that you are very fond of your wife and family. You're a good father and provider - particularly on the salaries that Tracton pays. Oh, incidentally, Bartolsky, when did you start calling your employer by his surname.'

'I don't know....'

'Yes you do, Bartolsky; you see we've been monitoring IMT's transmissions for some time now and 'though we haven't cracked all your codes, our decypher computer has managed more'n 75% of it. One thing we do know is you always call your boss 'Sir', never 'Tracton'.'

'That's not.....'

'Listen Bartolsky; for an intelligent man you're being very dumb. I'll tell you when it's your turn to speak again. Your last transmission went nowhere except in back of this airplane to my comms engineer. That was him returning your call from the tower at IMT's airfield. I mention all this and the business of your family, 'cos you won't be seeing them again until you're an old man an' by then I reckon your wife will've married someone else. You won't be getting bail; in fact the only thing you'll be getting shortly is your wife's lawsuit filing for divorce. Now have I got through to you?'

'What do I get if I go along and help you?'

'Nothing, Bartolsky; you get nothing, but I might just be persuaded to recommend to the judge that he take a year or two off your sentence. Then again, that'll depend on how you perform over the next fifteen minutes or so. Now get on that radio and transmit to IMT's control tower. Time's run out for the Bartolsky family.' There was a momentary pause while Alvin Bartolsky weighed up his future and then he pressed the transmit button.

'IMT tower, this is VRC 748, in-bound from Dallas, flight level 31 with an ETA of 0951 hours. Patch me through to Mr Tracton.'

'IMT roger, VRC 748, reduce to flight level 26, IMT altitude 3335 feet. Switch to 152 decimal 8 and insert code Bravo for talk-through to Mr Tracton. Come back on 146 decimal 5 for glide path; IMT tower.'

'Flight level 26, altitude 3335 feet, 152 decimal 8, VRC 748.' Bartolsky changed the frequency, punched in the code for the scrambler, pressed to transmit and spoke. 'IMT this is Al Bartolsky, is the boss available, Joanne?'

'Hi Al, just hold it and I'll get him for you; he's expecting the call......OK Al, go ahead.'

189

'Hello Sir, it's Al; we're in-bound from Dallas with an ETA of 0951 hours.'

'Thanks for the call, Al; you sound a bit pissed off. Any problems with the cargo or maybe you just didn't make it with any of the broads in Accra; hey, was that it?

'No problems, Sir; cargo's fine. You're right, I don't feel so good; maybe something I've picked up in Africa.'

'That so, Al; well you check in to the medical facility as soon as you've cleared the cargo. Don't want anything from Africa being spread around IMT do we?'

'No Sir; I'll see to that as soon as I'm through with this flight. Nice talking to you, Sir.'

'Thanks Al, bye.' Seconds after the transmission finished, Doyle's engineer appeared again with fist outstretched and a raised thumb.

'Seems like my boys think you did alright, Bartolsky. Now let's see what happens when we get this plane on the ground. Over to you, Dave; I'll go back with the rest of them and get ready for the welcome committee.'

*

'So what's so infamous about this particular shrine, Dina?' Gunn asked her as she changed up through the gears on the winding laterite road. The Nissan threw up clouds of laterite dust which hung in the hot, still air behind them. Apart from the thorn and nim trees, the flat scrub was filled with termite castles, some rising 15 or 20 feet above the ground. Well back from the track were small groups of wattle and palm frond thatch huts and along the side of the road small groups of women carrying huge bundles of kindling wood on their heads while naked children scampered around them, only pausing for a moment to stare with wide, round eyes at the Nissan. Above them in the clear blue sky, the buzzards circled, every now and then falling like stones on their abundant prey of voles, grasscutters and snakes.

'It's all a load of dreadful superstition, but if you believe in it fervently, as the tribes in this area do, it really does affect their lives. Once the witch doctor or fetish priest places a curse on a person they just give up the will to live and really do die.'

'No, don't get me wrong; I'm not cynical about all this voodoo and black magic. Let's face it, if one of these people was to be taken into one of the churches in Europe, where a form of 'high church' is practised, of whatever religion, they would see little different from their form of worship with all the burning of incense, throwing about of holy water, using a string of beads to pray with and genuflecting

190

all over the place. I need to understand what's behind this particular belief or dread so that we can predict Kisi's behaviour.'

'Alright, this is the limit of my very sketchy knowledge of the Oracle of the Tongo. The shrine is on a sort of plateau out of which rise three hills. These hills are inhabited by the Talensi tribe which claims that its people rose up out of the ground - from a sort of underworld, I suppose. Any pilgrim wanting a sickness cured or a wish fulfilled must climb to the plateau and present a gift or make a sacrifice. The area of the plateau and the three hills is riddled with deep caves and it is these that give the place its name of the Whispering Hills, because as the wind changes direction it produces sounds which really do sound like some form of unholy incantation.'

'What a place! And Kisi's going there to be healed or get a wish fulfilled. I've assumed all along that the blood I saw in that room in the cellar was young Graham's, but why shouldn't it have been Kisi's? He's fifteen and from what his mother told me, big for his age and pretty sharp. Could he have attacked Kisi?'

'It's possible, but that line of deduction leads us to a pretty horrible conclusion.'

'The sacrifice of the boy to heal her; you're right, but I've always found it far better to assume the worst rather than closing your mind to such a possibility. Is it my imagination or are we starting to climb?'

'No, it's not your imagination; we leave the savannah when we get to that line of deep green vegetation and then the track climbs pretty steeply through rain forest to the town of Zebila. After Zebila the road gets worse and worse and is quite impossible in the rainy season as it turns into a torrent of water, but this machine is pretty rugged and we should be able to make it to the plateau. How's that wound of yours?'

'Fine thanks; what about this man Mensah? What's driving him to turn West Africa into another turmoil of bloodshed and genocide.'

'I don't know a great deal of detail about him, except that he personified everything that makes it so hard for Africa to develop normally. Mensah comes from this area and is therefore of the same tribe as Kisi. He was well educated by devoted parents, went to university in Accra where he studied law and then to Harvard in the States. He joined Ghana's diplomatic service where he rose rapidly through the grades and was tipped as a future Ambassador in Washington. This track's getting really bad,' Dina interrupted her account of Mensah as she weaved the Nissan around some real tank-traps of potholes and concrete hard ruts. 'Where was I?'

'Mensah as Ambassador in Washington.'

'That's right; well, the temptations to get rich quick must have been too great because he became involved in every form of corrupt practice you can think of; you name it, he was taking ten percent of it. The International Credit Bank was the peak of Mensah's corruption where he diverted desperately needed aid funding to provide drinking water for the Northern Region into his own account. Since then, John, it's the same old story; more money, more power.'

'Why Caramansa?'

'Oh, that's easy; I can't think of a more suitable name for him. Back in the 15th century the Portugese had to deal with local chiefs and gave them the title of 'Mansah'; that's a Mande word and means 'leader'. The all-powerful chief of Eguafo State - which covered nearly all of the coastal area of West Africa - was known as 'Kwamena Mansah' and it looks as though 'Caramansah' came from that source. Whatever the origin of the title, he was an appallingly corrupt leader who sold his own people into slavery in exchange for weapons and merchandise brought in by the Portugese, Dutch and British slave traders. You'll find supposedly accurate historical accounts in the Accra library which recount how the slaves were forced to swallow nuggets of gold so that Caramansa could smuggle the gold past the colonial administrators in the castles to the commercial trading companies. If the slaves didn't pass the nuggets quick enough by defecating they would rip their bowels open on the ships while the men were still alive. In many cases the poor creatures couldn't pass the nuggets because they were either so large or so numerous that they jammed up the small intestine or the colon.'

'Christ, we don't have much to be proud of?'

'Oh....oops,' and the Nissan bounced over a pothole, 'it's almost impossible to be the judge of what happened in those days; different attitudes, beliefs, superstitions and even then it's difficult to judge who was the most depraved - the colonial slave traders or those who sold their own people into slavery. What I'm sure about is how appropriate the title of Caramansa is to this man Mensah. Right, now we leave the savannah and it's rain forest from now on to Zebila.'

Within less than a hundred yards the scenery completely changed; gone was the open plain and canopied thorn trees to be replaced by ever thickening jungle which grew higher and higher around the track. Gone also was the clear blue sky to which Gunn had awoken at 5.30 that morning; that had been replaced by a thick black line of clouds to the north and a dull, overcast sky above as the track wound through the dank jungle.

Zebila was a town, which was fighting a losing battle with the jungle. Like Kpandu, the young workforce had transmigrated to the cities, leaving behind the very young and old, neither of whom had the energy or will to keep the tropical vegetation at bay. The town was little more than a village and was based on a central square, which boasted a church and a market. It was a few minutes before twelve when Gunn and Dina drove into the square. Dina stopped the Nissan Patrol at the first market stall, from which any vehicle arriving in the town could hardly fail to be seen, and took out her purse. Gunn also got out of the car to stretch his legs.

Dina had gone over to the stall and had selected some oranges, a melon, papaya and a large bottle of Coca Cola. During the selection of the produce she kept up an animated conversation with much arm waving and pointing, back down the track by which they had arrived and eastward to, presumably, where the track continued on into the jungle-covered hills. The people of the market looked at Gunn with ill-concealed fear; Dina had told him that this would be caused by a combination of his skin colour, the uniform and his size. Gunn looked around the market; whatever their beliefs and superstitions, none of these people were going to die of starvation as there was an abundance of food everywhere.

'She's ten minutes ahead of us and it's Kisi who's bleeding. The woman never saw a boy so she's either killed him and dumped him somewhere - unlikely, I think - or he was drugged or perhaps asleep in the car. Any changes to our plans?'

'None; let's get going. You happy to go on driving or would you like me to take over?'

'Would you; even with the power steering, I find this dreadfully heavy. I think I'll switch to one like your Discovery.' Gunn climbed in behind the wheel, shunted the seat back as far as it would go and then threaded the Nissan through the market to the track leading up into the hills.

The jungle canopy had started to sway with the wind driving the black rain clouds down from the north and they had barely gone more than a couple of miles before the first big drops of rain splashed against the windscreen. Now there were very few people and when they turned off right to climb the zig-zagging road to the plateau of the Whispering Hills they saw no one at all. The rain became heavier and heavier and soon, just as described by Dina, the track turned into a torrent of rainwater.

The Nissan bounced and slewed over boulders as they ground their way up the steep track until after nearly half an hour with the wipers at full speed, the jungle thinned and the track eventually levelled out onto the plateau, above which rose the three conical Whispering Hills. Great swathes of cloud now drifted amongst the

193

three hills, driven by the northerly wind. Gunn stopped the car, switched off the engine and wound down his window,which was on the lee side of the car. The track petered out some twenty yards further on into nothing more than a narrow footpath leading towards the centre of the three hills.

Barely ten yards in front of the Nissan was the Volkswagen. Gunn removed the Tanarmi from its holster and got out of the car. The rain had reduced to little more than a stinging drizzle driven by the wind. The Volkswagen was empty, but there were dried blood stains on both the driver's seat and the back seat. The keys were still in the ignition, which Gunn removed and placed in his pocket. Up above him, the caves in the hills were clearly visible, as the clouds veiled and unveiled the shrine of the Oracle of the Tongo while the wind, funnelling through and across the caves, seemed to fill the air with the moans of souls in torment.

'What a bloody awful place,' Gunn muttered and turned back to the Nissan Patrol to get Dina, but Dina had gone.

*

'Yes, Joanne.'

'It's Nat...for you, Sir.'

'Thanks, put him through.'

'Hello Trax, it's Nat; that convoy's checked and ready to move out. Wondered if Al had contacted you yet with a confirmed ETA?'

'Just put the phone down. His ETA's 0951 hours and there're no problems. He says he picked up something in Accra and doesn't feel too good. He says he kept away from the dusky maidens while he was there so let's hope it's nothing catching or fatal! Told him to check in at the medical facility after the cargo's all dealt with.'

'That's good; d'you have time to come and check over the convoy before it rolls?'

'Sure do; just going to put you on hold to check my schedule with Joanne,' and he pressed the hold button already knowing that Nat would have checked his schedule with Joanne before offering the invitation. 'Joanne....Nat wants me to go and check the arms shipment. Do I have any appointments?'

'None other than the arrival of VRC 748 in eleven minutes time, Sir.'

'Right, I'll have Frank with me and you can get me on the mobile if anything comes up.'

'Very well, Sir,' and she pressed the button which sounded the warning buzzer in Frank Raubenheimer's office.

Frank was waiting outside Brad Tracton's office as he emerged and walked with him to the front entrance where a Chevrolet Charger and driver were waiting. Tracton and his bodyguard got into the back and the station wagon was driven round the perimeter road to the north side of the IMT complex where all the loading of containers onto trucks was carried out by overhead gantries and controlled entirely by computers.

When they arrived at the freight make-up area, Brad Tracton could see little else but row upon row of gleaming trucks, hooked up to flatbeds loaded with one long or two short containers. Parked in front of these were fifteen police cars from the traffic branch of Amarillo PD. The head of the Police Department, Sheriff Bob Bannerman was there, stetson set at just the right raffish angle and one high-heeled cowboy boot resting on the cab step of the leading truck. He had lost heavily at poker with Brad Tracton the night before at Caesar's Palace; he could afford to lose on the pay-offs he got from IMT's President.

'Mornin Trax,' he greeted Brad Tracton with deference having touched the brim of the stetson and removed his boot from the truck step. 'Got yourself a real fine convoy; biggest ever to roll outa here, heh!'

'Sure is, Bob; your boys ready to see it safe onto the highway?'

'Ready when you say the word, Sir,' even more deference to his real paymaster. The Sheriff, his wife and four children had just returned from a two-week holiday in Florida where the entire tab had been picked up by IMT. Nat Cohn came up to escort his boss on an inspection of the convoy.

'So this will be for Nigeria,' and Brad Tracton nodded towards the front truck of the convoy, which was a huge 8 litre, turbo-inter-cooled General Motors Truckmaster which had more chrome-work on it than IMT's plating plant.

'That's right, Trax. Each convoy has a police escort, which will take it out to Highway 87 south of Amarillo. At that point the Sheriff of Lubbock takes over and runs the convoy through to Highway 20, west of Abilene, where the Dallas PD take over and sees it out onto Highway 45 south to Houston. Our boys in Galveston will meet the convoy at Huntsville and take it through Houston to the Texas Star at Pier 12 in the port.'

'Sounds real neat,' Brad Tracton commented and then they all looked up as the sound of the IMT 747's engines drowned the noise of the convoy's engines. 'One minute to go; that's how I like to see things planned.

*

195

Barely three miles from where Brad Tracton was standing, the Brigade Commander of the Armoured Brigade from 82nd Airborne Division was also looking at his watch. He turned to his operations officer. 'Assault company, move now!'

'Right Sir.' The order was passed and immediately the Chinooks and Bells lifted off from the airfield at Gruver preceded by their escort of Cobras.

*

'B-MAT 1, this is CHARLIE 02, over,' and Mike Truman released the transmit button of the base radio transmitter in the High Commission.

'B-MAT 1, send over.'

'CHARLIE 02, are you free to come to the High Commission. I have some rather important matters to discuss with you, over.' It was very rare that Mike ever imposed on Miles to drop everything and come to the High Commission and the Commander of the Military Team realised that for 'rather important' was meant 'very important and urgent', but there was no point in broadcasting that sort of information to the monitoring system of the Bureau of National Intelligence.

'B-MAT 1, I'll be with you in ten minutes, out.'

Mike Truman replaced the microphone in its clip by the transmitter/receiver and returned to his office. That morning, he had already gathered all the UK-based staff into the High Commissioner's office, which was the only place large enough to get them all in at one time. Rumours had been spreading like wildfire and varied from one extreme of the mass slaughter of all British people in Accra to a sexual deviation group in the High Commission Compound. Mike allayed all this by explaining that a robbery had gone very badly and tragically wrong and there was no cause for alarm, but certainly a great deal more vigilance was required and all staff were directed to be particularly careful about inviting people other than High Commission staff into the compound.

He had summoned Don Peasmarsh to his office after the meeting and told him that his performance was below that expected and would be reflected in his annual report unless a considerable improvement was shown in both his professional performance and his social behaviour. Mike Truman had told him that he was drinking excessively and unless the improvement materialised, a recommendation for his return to London would be made. Don was leaving Mike's office when he had paused and turned.

'I brought a woman back to my flat the night before last, Mike.'

196

'There's nothing wrong with that, Don, except the dreadful hangover you brought into work the next day.'

'No....it's....well...'

'Come back and sit down and get it off your chest,' and Mike Truman came from behind his desk and indicated an armchair to Don Peasmarsh. He sat down on the edge of the chair and looked extremely embarrassed. 'Right, away you go.'

'We were all drinking at Afrikiko that night and I...well, I had had a few too many. Oh Christ, I was stupid......'

'Look Don, if it's any help to you, nearly all of us do something bloody stupid at one stage or another in this business. What separates the sheep from the goats is those who have the guts to admit their stupidity and declare the mistake so that any damage can be limited.'

'You see, Mike, I think I might have been partly, if not wholly, responsible for Amanda's death...and ...and.. that's not all as I think I might also have risked getting Aids...' the young man was almost in tears of remorse and self-pity.

'Right, let's have it all; what happened at Afrikiko?'

'Well we were all chatting away in a pretty light-hearted way when this girl....woman asks if she can join us. Said she was American and had just arrived to do a project for the Peace Corps.'

'Black or white woman?'

'Black.....she was very pretty and friendly and interested in what we were doing.'

'And what were you doing?' the conversation was painful, but Mike Truman knew that it was the only way to find out what had happened.

'We were having a wake for Tony Bristow.....I..I told her that he had drowned at Ada, also.....oh God why... I told her that Amanda worked for Bristow. She came back to my flat... I can remember her taking my clothes off and then I think I puked ....no, I know I puked because it was all over the bathroom floor the next morning. Jesus what a mess.....then I can't remember anything else except waking up naked and the whole bed soaked in water. She...she'd gone....and....and...' then silence.

'Yes, what else had gone, your wallet?'

'No, one of the keys from my key ring....nothing from the wallet. That wasn't touched.'

'Was this woman in your car?'

'No...no, had her own...er..a Volkswagen; a green beetle.'

'She drove that Volkswagen into the compound?'

'Yes.'

197

'Just hold on a second.' Mike Truman picked up his phone and pressed the buttons for Trevor Banbury's extension. He waited and then Trevor answered. 'Trevor, can you get hold of the two night watchmen who were on duty at the compound the night before last and bring them up to my office please as soon as possible.' He replaced the phone. 'Anything else?'

'No...that's really everything. I don't know how I'm going to live with it if I was the cause of Amanda's death.'

'Well that's something only you can show if you've got the guts and character to put right the mess you've made so far. In the meantime, pull yourself together, get down to the clinic and get them to test your blood for HIV infection - I've no idea if it will show up so soon after the event.' Don Peasmarsh left his office. There was a knock and Trevor Banbury asked if he could bring in the two night watchmen. The three of them came into the room and the two Ghanaians looked thoroughly uncomfortable.

'Right gentlemen, you know what has happened in the compound?' The two men looked at each other and then nodded. The night before last; did another car come into the compound with Mr Peasmarsh's Suzuki jeep?'

'Yes Sir,' in unison.

'What sort of car was it?'

'A Volkswagen, Sir.'

'Who was in it?'

'Lady, Sir.'

'Ghanaian or British?'

'Black lady, Sir....like us.'

'Did you see that car again?'

'Yes. Sir; next morning, same lady and large man come into compound.'

'Did you see where they went?'

'Accommodation Block B, Sir.'

'Did they go into the block?'

'Yes, Sir and came out with carpet.'

'What time was this?' For answer the senior night watchman produced his log book. Mike's hopes rose at the thought that they might just have logged the car number.

'First or second time, Sir?'

'The car came in twice that morning?'

'Yes Sir, first time at 1030 and second time at 1320, Sir. Bring carpet back second time.'

'And take it up to a flat?'

'Yes, Sir.'

'Registration of the car?'

'Yes, Sir; ACB 4381.'

'Well done both of you. Is there anything else that you can tell me?' Both heads shook. 'Thank you; thanks Trevor,' and the trio left the office as Miles Stockwell appeared. Mike Truman had decided to gloss over the fact the two guards had allowed the VW into the compound twice when it was not accompanied by a member of the High Commission. A small piece of the extraordinary puzzle was beginning to take shape.

'Come in, Miles, sorry to keep you,' and the Commander BMAT came in and took the chair recently vacated by Don Peasmarsh. 'Rather than talk in this office, Miles, I'd like you to come up with me to the box.'

'Sure,' and Miles got up from the chair which he'd just occupied and followed the Deputy Head of Mission up to the next floor where they went into the isolation box and Mike closed the door.

'Miles, I received a signal late last night from the FCO which has clarified a number of matters for me. The signal came from the Head of West African Department - Perigrine Humble - who earlier in the day had been summoned to the Intelligence Directorate. I'm, of course, well aware of all the changes that have taken place in our Secret Intelligence Service and the reasons for the removal of the SIS officer from the premises of embassies and high commissions. I have to say that I consider that the measures are, perhaps, an over-reaction to the leaks and breaches of security for which, I know, the FCO has been responsible and it is my hope that in time we will be able to revert to a collocation. Having said that, I also realise that the Tony Bristows of this world did a great deal to contribute to this situation and the FCO's become the victim of its own, over-liberal interpretation of the security vetting procedure of its personnel and the blind eye which has been turned to extra-marital relations which made its personnel vulnerable to blackmail.'

'The signal, Mike?'

'Yes, I'm sorry, I'm wasting time. The signal informed us that there was a BID agent in Accra who was here to investigate the disappearance of the SIS officer and information, which had been reported by BMAT of orchestrated terrorism to overthrow the legitimate governments of West African countries. It said that the robbery at the Bank of Ghana was part of this and that there was a kidnap and extortion of a huge ransom, which was still on-going. It said that I would be contacted by the BID agent at the discretion of that agent. I wasn't told the name of the agent. It is my

199

understanding, Miles, that you might know who this agent is and I do need to get information to him ....or her.'

'The day before yesterday, Don Peasmarsh made a complete fool of himself at Afrikiko while much the worse for drink and told a very inquisitive and pretty black woman with an American accent that Amanda worked for Tony Bristow....'

'Oh no!'

'Yes, I'm afraid so......Amanda was murdered the following morning....that's yesterday, as was her maid and Arthur Russell; those two seem irrelevant, but must've got in the way of the murder of the intended victim. It is my belief that Amanda was tortured before she died...'

'Dear God; were there marks......'

'No, there were no marks on her body other than some pretty severe bruising around her throat and upper torso, but we know now, after checking with the guards, that she was removed from her flat and brought back two hours later....dead. I have to assume that she told them whatever it was they wanted to know and was then killed to ensure her silence. We got the number of the car which was used - a Volkswagen - but when we checked with the Accra Licensing Authority it transpired - perhaps predictably - that the car belonged to a car hire company. The person who hired it paid in cash in advance and gave both a false name and address which gets us precisely nowhere.'

'You asked me to come to the High Commission, Mike; what is it you want me to do?'

'Three reasons for getting you here, Miles; firstly I need someone to whom I can talk and bounce ideas and theories off and we've both done that often enough in the past....'

'True...'

'And secondly I think its time that the BID agent was appraised of these latest murders in the compound. I have to add that I would very much like to meet this agent......'

'That makes sense....'

'And finally, I need to confide in someone that I'm very concerned about the behaviour of Humphrey Winfield.'

'What's up with him?'

'He's been behaving in a very distracted manner......really for the past ten days or so ....and then dashed off to London on the BA flight yesterday showing no concern at all that four employees of his High Commission had been murdered, booked the flights himself, told me that he'd been summoned to London by Sir Peter Goddard - which was untrue and said that he intended to visit the next of kin of those that had been killed which was also untrue.'

'How do you know that?'

'He said he'd asked June - his PA - for NOK details. She knew nothing about that, nothing about his intention to go to London and had nothing to do with booking the flight.'

'How very odd; I'll tell you what I know,' and for the next quarter-of-an hour Miles Stockwell told Mike Truman what had happened from the time John Briars had informed Bristow about Eddie Twintoh's information to Gunn's departure the night before to Shai Hills.

CHAPTER 13

'Right, Melanie, is everyone here?'

'Mike Parker's on his....ah! here he is; that's everyone, Sir.'

Sir Jeremy Hammond, BID's Director waited while Mike Parker, the Assistant Director for Sub-Sahara Africa took his seat and looked round the table. There was Christine Dupré, John Gunn's controller, Bill Barton for North America and Canada - and liaison with the CIA, his Deputy Director for Overseas Operations and Espionage, Miles Thompson who was sitting next to his opposite number, Sir Jeremy's Deputy Director for Domestic Counter-Espionage and Operations, Paul Manton, and then down at one end of the table was Mary Panter from Finance and John Stevenson from Transport.

'Right everyone, let's get on with business. Mike, you've briefed me and initiated this meeting so that all those who need to know what's happening in West Africa, the USA, Canada and in this country, have all the information currently available. All of you know already that John Gunn was sent to Ghana to investigate the disappearance of the SIS officer, Bristow, and the then unsubstantiated rumours that there was a mastermind behind the terrorism in West Africa. This was supposed to be a sinecure for John Gunn while he fully recovered from the gunshot wound he received in the Channel Islands, but now seems to be turning into a very active operation which, as you all know, spreads across three continents. Enough from me; Mike.'

'Right, Sir; it's now known that there is a conspiracy to overthrow the legitimate governments of the countries of West Africa which is being masterminded by a man called Charles Mensah. Charles Mensah is a well-educated Ghanaian who was sacked from his country's diplomatic service for embezzling World Bank and IMF aid funds for his country when he was a counsellor at the High Commission in Ottawa. With the embezzled funds, he set up the International Credit Bank which has its headquarters in Las Vegas and some hundred branches in capital cities throughout the world, but particularly in the developing world.'

'Charles Mensah has given himself the name 'Caramansa' which comes from a 15th century West African chief who ruled nearly all the Sub-Sahara area of West Africa. It seems a realistic assessment that his aim is to use his bank to fund terrorism to overthrow the governments of the countries of West Africa and then unite them into a huge republic under his presidency.'

'That part of Africa was carved up by the colonial powers with boundaries which cut across ethnic and tribal cohesian and the scheme to unite it once again is not as hare-brained as at first it might sound.'

'To help him achieve his goal, Charles Mensah has gathered around him, at least a hundred and probably more, expelled West Africans who've fled their countries to escape justice or persecution - rather depending from which perspective you judge their predicament. I've strayed into Bill's area because some of this information has come from the CIA which was alerted to the presence of Africans who meet regularly in the fortress-like building in Las Vegas which houses the International Credit Bank.'

'This orchestrated terrorism has been simmering for some time now and broke out openly in Liberia, Mali, Togo and Nigeria in the late eighties before dwindling through lack of funding. Just like the collapse of the Bank of Commerce and Credit International in 1991, the ICB started to fold as its sources of illegal funding dried up and the recession bit deep in the industrialised nations. Some time in the last three or four months, Caramansa decided to boost its rapidly waning assets through theft and extortion on a grand scale for two reasons; firstly because it was threatened with a US Treasury investigation and secondly, to provide arms for its terrorist campaign in West Africa.'

'We know that Caramansa has struck a deal with International Machine Tools - the Texas-based, squillion dollar arms manufacturer and dealer and from various reports around the world from Burma through Africa to Europe, there have been reports of extortion, theft and embezzlement organized by expelled nationals of West African countries. That is all background.'

'John Gunn discovered that a gold robbery from the Bank of Ghana had been air-freighted to IMT. That information uncovered the IMT deal. A very quick follow-up by the CIA resulted in the arrest of the IMT Boeing 747 carrying the gold and in about four hours from now, when that 747 lands at IMT, an armoured brigade group of the US Rapid Reaction Force will assault the Fort Knox-like defences of IMT. John Gunn is now also involved in preventing another fund-raising activity of Caramansa in Ghana which was to kidnap the son of the MD of Canadian Sikafuturu Goldmines. At the same time as that kidnap took place, the grandson of the president of the parent company in Edmonton was also kidnapped and, we think, flown to this country. That seems to be the right moment for me to hand over to Bill who will bring you up to date on his part of the world.'

'Thanks Mike; I will keep you all informed on the operation in Texas, but have no news yet on our investigation by our in-country agent and the CIA into the leads suggested to us by John Gunn to follow up in Canada. I will now hand over to Paul Manton who will cover the operation in this country.'

'Thank you, Bill; like Bill, the information passed to us about the connection to this country of the kidnapping in Edmonton is being investigated vigorously, but as yet I have nothing to report to this meeting, Sir Jeremy.'

'Many thanks Paul, Miles and all of you for that up-date. Mike, is John Gunn fit to continue with this operation or does he need another agent in-country with him?'

'He hasn't asked for help, sir.'

'No, and neither would he. Please find out as a matter of urgency from the in-country agent what his physical condition is and Christine will you prepare yourself to go to Ghana please. Any questions, anyone?' There were none. 'Right that's it; let's get to work. Thank you everybody.'

*

Gunn walked back to the Nissan Patrol to see if Dina had got back into it or if she'd nipped behind some of the scrub bushes for a quick pee after that long drive. Gunn considered these possibilities while he refused to accept that she had been spirited away whether they were at the Oracle of the Tongo or not. But there was no Dina in the Patrol and she didn't reappear from the undergrowth. He opened the rear door of the Patrol and removed one of the Scorpion machine pistols, inserted a magazine and cocked it. He replaced the Tanarmi in its holster, shut the door, went round to the driver's door and locked all the doors on the central locking.

Dina had told him that the whole of the feature was largely limestone and riddled with caves through which the wind funnelled. If it was limestone and there were caves then there would also be tunnels. Which direction to start his search? The small plateau which he was on at the moment or climb up to the caves above him? The decision was made for him. Gunn caught sight of movement right on the edge of his peripheral vision and turned raising the stub muzzle of the Scorpion. Between him and the Nissan were some twenty men; completely naked and daubed in some form of white paint which gave the exact effect of skeletons against their jet black skins.

Each carried a spear and a club with an enlarged rounded head to do the clubbing. They stood perfectly still. More movement; Gunn turned his head slowly and there were about the same number of men behind him.

Even with a 32 round magazine on the Scorpion and the 16 rounds in his Tanarmi, they would still overwhelm him with numbers. He bent down and placed the machine pistol on the ground and straightened up. Somewhat ludicrously, Gunn felt the urge to ask these men of the Talensi tribe, always assuming that's who they were, to take him to their leader. After they'd stared at each other for a few more minutes without anyone moving, one man came forward from the group between him and the Nissan and using his spear as a pointer uttered the clear and unmistakable instruction, 'go!'. Gunn went; surrounded by his painted and naked escort, they walked towards the caves in the hill above them.

After only fifty yards or so, the procession rounded a buttress of rock, which extended out from the high ground in front in the form of a spur. On Gunn's right was a substantial stream which was swollen from the torrential rain which had fallen earlier. Once they were the other side of the buttress, Gunn saw that the stream curved round to the left in front of them. The procession walked beside the stream, which emerged out of the rocks from a cave through which Gunn could have driven the Nissan. The stream flowed towards them down the right-hand side of the cave while the procession, with Gunn in the middle of it, walked along a well-worn path on the left side.

The whole scene was so reminiscent of those that Gunn had seen in the re-runs of films like 'King Soloman's Mines', 'Where no Vultures Fly', 'Tarzan' and 'Daktari', that he expected any minute to bump into Stewart Granger, Ava Gardner, Johnny Weismuller, John Wayne or any other Hollywood star of that era - perhaps even the ubiquitous Humphrey Bogart dragging the 'African Queen' along the stream. The thought made Gunn smile, but that illusion was brought to an abrupt halt. The ambient light from the cave entrance had gone and was now replaced by artificial light; not a burning torch - the sort that in movies never burned down or went out - but a simple electric light bulb inside a round reflector with a metal grid to protect it. So much for the Hollywood illusion, Gunn thought; back to reality and this was the first indication that the Oracle of the Tongo might be a very useful cover for something completely different.

This suspicion was confirmed in the next few seconds when the worn mud path beneath Gunn's feet changed to a concrete one and after a further hundred yards opened out into a large cavern. The procession had passed through a set of steel doors at the end of the tunnel which were closed behind them by men wearing overalls, finally shattering any vestige of illusions about King Soloman's Mines.

Gunn judged that the cavern was approximately circular and about fifty metres in diameter. It seemed to be some form of reception or loading area and trolleys were being pushed across it towards Gunn's right as he was led across. Gunn's machine pistol had been picked up after he had placed it on the ground, but no one had made any further attempt to search him and the Tanarmi was still in its holster on his right ankle. Why such a silly oversight? he wondered, or were they so supremely confident in superiority of numbers that it didn't matter. That didn't make sense, but what made more sense was the fact that he was dressed in British Army combat clothing with the same badges of rank - virtually - as a Lt Colonel in the Ghana Army and British officers didn't carry concealed automatics in ankle holsters.

No one knew of his presence in Ghana and his and Dina's arrival on the plateau, whilst immediately, no doubt, connected with the arrival of Kisi and a British school boy, must have caused some thought and doubt about what action to take. Whatever action was taken, now that both of them - and he presumed that Dina was still in the present and not the past tense - had seen this place, it was unlikely that they'd be allowed to live. The problem, Gunn decided, which was facing whomever ran whatever was going on inside this mountain was how much was known and by whom. Once that had been established, goodbye Dina and John. On reaching that comforting thought he was led into a square chamber, hewn out of the rock, about ten feet square with bed, basin, light and a bucket and the door was slammed shut and bolted.

*

The computer-enhanced photos being taken by the cameras in the Lockheed U2/TR1-A which had descended from 88,000 feet to 75,000 feet to achieve better definition, not only showed all the activity involved in preparing the arms shipment convoy at IMT, but also clearly identified the presence of the Amarillo Police Department. It was hoped that the surprise show of overwhelming force would prevent resistance by Bradley Tracton and the workforce of IMT and the inevitable casualties, but to involve the unsuspecting Amarillo Police in the middle of a fire-fight was out of the question.

The Brigade commander was informed of the new development and ordered the assault battalion back to Gruver Airfield. He could see, as could those on the ground, the Boeing 747 making its approach to IMT's airfield. In the Boeing, Doyle Barnes had removed one of the gold bars from the packing case, which had already been opened once and re-sealed.

The group of men standing by the lead truck of the convoy watched the 747 turn for its final approach and then Brad Tracton turned to Sheriff Bob Bannerman, took off his stetson and with a loud whoop told him to 'head 'em on out!' The Sheriff climbed into his car and with sirens wailing and lights flashing the convoys started to roll. Great gouts of black diesel exhaust belched from the chrome stacks of the tractors as the drivers started up the big eight cylinder engines. One after another, the convoys and their police escorts drove past the president of IMT who was enjoying it hugely. Fifteen minutes after the first truck had moved out behind the Sheriff, the last police car went through IMT's gates, which closed behind it.

'Right Nat, let's see what Bartolsky's got for us,' and Brad Tracton walked to the Chevrolet followed by Nat Cohn and his bodyguard. The 747 was just turning off the taxiway onto the apron in front of IMT's above-ground storage warehouses. Inward goods stayed in this above-ground storage for the minimum of time possible before they were either taken to where they were needed in the factory and machine shops or taken below ground for storage. The ground handling equipment was all pre-positioned in the parking bay allocated to the Boeing and the nose wheel of the 747 was exactly on the yellow line, which ended in a circle. Just back from the circle was the controller with ear protectors and fluorescent batons who was directing the pilot of the aircraft.

The nose wheel entered the circle and stopped. The whine of the engines died as steps were driven up to the forward aircraft door and the freight-handling equipment was positioned by the large freight doors. The Chevrolet Charger stopped at the foot of the steps and the three men got out. Brad Tracton shielded his eyes as he looked up to the top of the steps. The door swung out and folded back against the side of the 747. There was a pause for a few moments and then Al Bartolsky appeared in the door with his thick pilot's briefcase in his left hand and a bar of gold in his right.

'Godammit! will ya take look at that, boys. Ain't that one of the purtiest sights ya ever saw,' was uttered in a tone of reverence and a very exaggerated Texan drawl, to which the President of IMT was prone in times of great success, stress or excitement. This was certainly one of those occasions, but just how stressful it was about to become, not even the marvels of IMT's Information Technology could have forewarned its President. From 75,000 feet above IMT every detail of the reception was recorded and from a great deal closer, inside the aircraft, both video cameras and highly sensitive directional microphones recorded every movement and word.

As Al Bartolsky reached the foot of the steps he handed the gold bar to Bradley Tracton who accepted it with both hands and then all hell was let loose. From over the low ridge of foothills in the San Juan mountains burst a flight of four F-22s at supersonic speed and no more than 100 feet above the ground. Everything rocked, resonated and vibrated with the deafening thunderclap as the fighters shattered the sound barrier. Inside the 747, Doyle and his CIA team had been prepared for the noise and were wearing ear-protectors, but even they were dazed by the onslaught of brain-numbing sound.

Outside the 747, Bradley Tracton had dropped the bar of gold and had been thrown to the ground by Frank Raubenheimer who had a gun in his hand and was desperately looking for something to shoot at. He didn't have long to wait. Following close behind the F-22s came the Huey Cobras shooting in the assault company in their Bell Iroquois 205s. Canon rounds ricochetted off the concrete but none were aimed at anything or anyone. Behind the Bells came the Chinooks with their double rotors thrashing at the hot, thin air. Even as their tail wheels bounced on IMT's runway the main body of the assault battalion poured down the rear ramps and took up fire positions as base-ejection, 105 mm artillery shells burst overhead, scattering smoke canisters which engulfed the whole scene in dense, blinding smoke.

By the time the smoke cleared, the aircraft was surrounded, the guards at the gatehouse had been rounded up, the convoy had been halted by the armoured reconnaissance squadron and the search of IMT's complex had begun. There was only one casualty of the assault and that had been Frank Raubenheimer who had been the only employee of IMT to draw a weapon. He had been shot by Doyle Barnes who replaced the large Colt .45 automatic in its holster, walked down the 747's steps and retrieved the bar of Ashanti gold from a stunned Bradley Tracton.

*

John Mackenzie had called in at his father's house on the Cedar Park Estate on the south-west suburbs of Edmonton before going into work at the head office of the Sikafuturu Mining Company on Rupert Street in the centre of the city. He had felt that he could no longer just sit in the house waiting for the phone call, letter, tape or whatever, which would produce the ransom note and conditions for the return of their son. The only news which the RCMP had been able to give them about the kidnap of little Ian was that a ransom note was about to be picked up in Ghana which would spell out the procedure for the return of the two children. The family had also been told that any overt approach to the police after the receipt of the ransom instructions would result in the maiming of one or both of the boys. Mary's parents had come to the house immediately that they'd heard of the kidnap and had said they'd stay until it was all over - one way or another. John was unable to do anything positive about the kidnap and so, to release his frustration and anxiety, had decided to visit his parents and call in at the office.

John left his parent's house, walked across the gravel to his British Racing Green Jaguar XKR and drove out of the gates; it usually took about twenty to twenty-five minutes to get to the office. The quality of life was considerably better than when he had been at the company's office in Ottawa where the drive into work in the rush hour could take as long as an hour or even more. He crossed over the river, skirted round the university campus, back over the river again and then turned right into Rupert Street and drove into the underground car park below the company building.

As the executive vice-president of Sikafuturu, John Mackenzie used his key to open and then operate the private lift to his suite of offices on the twenty-fourth floor. He was thankful to be out of Ottawa, particularly during this crisis in his and Mary's life, and back in Edmonton where they could rely on the support of the family and their large circle of friends which they'd had since childhood. He had disliked Ottawa, not only because of the time it took to commute from house to office, but also the never-ending round of diplomatic parties where he was constantly being asked by counsellors of commercial sections in embassies and high commissions to accept visits from trade and industry ministers. It wasn't the visit itself, which bothered him as that was always good for business, but it was the meaningless entertainment. Mary had seemed to cope much better than he had and had developed some close friends in the various diplomatic missions.

He was an expert at what he knew most about which was metallurgy and mining and if it had to be admitted, and he did, as the lift smoothly came to a halt on the 24th floor, he was probably a bit of a bore and didn't have the easy social graces possessed by Mary - which, of course, was one of the many reasons he'd found her so attractive. John walked out of the lift and into his suite of offices, acknowledging the greetings of his staff. As he reached his office, he was met by his personal secretary, Merilee.

'Good morning, Sir.'

'Morning, Merilee.'

'Could you give Doctor Campbell a call; he rang about ten minutes ago.'

'Yes, sure; did he say what it was for?'

'No, Sir; just asked if you could call him. Shall I get him for you?'

'Please,' and John Mackenzie sat on the edge of his desk and looked out through the ceiling to floor windows at the view over the sweep of the Saskatchewan River as he waited for the call. His phone buzzed.

'Doctor Campbell for you, Sir.'

'Thanks........Angus?'

'Hello John, Angus here; sorry to bother you. Any chance of you having time to come in and see me?'

'Today, Angus?'

'Only if you've time. I'd like to go over the tests we did last week.'

'Sure, no problem,' and John looked at his watch and then at his desk diary which was open in front of him. 'How's about right now?'

'That'd be fine; see you in about ten minutes then.'

'Will do; bye,' and he put down the phone and buzzed Merilee. 'He wants me to call round at his surgery a couple of blocks away. There's nothing on my schedule, Merilee, so I'm going there now.'

'Very well, Sir.'

He left the office again and went down to the street where he walked the half-mile or so to the surgery where he was met by the receptionist and taken straight into Angus Campbell.

'Hello, John; take a seat and I'll come round and join you.'

'That doesn't sound too good. I do that when I have something difficult or personal - or both - to discuss with my people.'

'Everything that I do is personal, in my profession, and sometimes bloody difficult,' and he didn't say out loud - 'just like this meeting.' He sat down opposite his lifelong friend with whom he'd studied at school, college and university.

'Of course it must be, Angus. Go ahead.'

'How's young Ian?'

'He's fine,' John lied, fervently hoping that it was the truth.

'What'd he be now....five?'

'Nearly five.....birthday's in two weeks time; May 2nd.'

'Right...so what made you decide to come to me for a sperm count, John.'

'We thought it was time Ian had a companion. Mary and I'd like another baby. We've been trying hard, but so far no success. I read an article that all sorts of things can cause temporary impotence in men....stress, worry, over working, diet and even wearing the wrong type of underwear. Anyway, before Mary goes off to have all those tests and things, I thought it'd make sense if I nipped in and had the quick once over from you.'

'Absolutely right,' and Angus Campbell shook his head with despair.

'Come on Angus, what's up? You found I got cancer or something?'

'No John... no, nothing like that. We've been friends for a long, long time and I don't want that to end, but I owe it to you to tell you this. You're right in your fears; it's not a matter of temporary impotence. I have to tell you that you're sterile. You don't have a sperm count at all, John, and you never have had one. You are unable to father a child. You could not have been the natural father of Ian. Please tell me that you and Mary agreed to artificial insemination or surrogacy or something John.....please.'

'You're saying that Ian's not my son?'

'He couldn't have been. Please, please let me help you.'

'You have....you have,' and John Mackenzie got up and walked to the door.

'Please John... please listen to....'

'Bye Angus; many thanks,' and John Mackenzie walked out onto the street.

*

The receptionist opened the door of 33 Upper Wimpole Street, which was the address of a group practice of three gynaecologists. She found two men on the doorstep, which was unusual, given the specialisation of the practice.

'Good morning, gentlemen; may I be of help?'

'Yes you can,' said the elder of the two men who had produced his Metropolitan Police warrant card which he showed carefully to the receptionist making sure that she read it rather than glance at it. 'Detective Chief Superintendent Halpin from Scotland Yard. May I see Doctor Martin, please? My colleague is Detective Sergeant Collins. Doctor Martin should be expecting us.'

'Yes, of course, gentlemen; won't you come in,' and the receptionist led the way into a very pleasant waiting room where the pastel shades of the decor were no doubt chosen because they were unlikely to cause offence or stress. The two policemen were studied with considerable curiosity by the two women already in the waiting room and then, with irritation, as they were called by the receptionist and escorted through to Doctor Martin.

'Good morning, gentlemen; I've been expecting your visit. How can I help you?'

'I would be most grateful Doctor if you would read this letter from the Home Office,' and Detective Chief Superintendent Halpin handed over the letter which he'd removed from his briefcase as he spoke. 'You will see that it authorises me to ask you to reveal information about one of your patients. May I assure you that what is revealed to us will be kept as confidential as possible, but is required to assist in the investigation of a very serious crime indeed.'

'Yes, I quite understand that, Chief Superintendent; who is the person?'

'A Miss Moss who we believe would have visited you for a consultation in 1980.'

'Right, please wait a moment,' and the doctor pressed a button on his phone and then asked his nurse for the relevant file, which was produced within three minutes. The doctor opened it and looked up. 'What is it you want to know, Chief Superintendent?'

'Why did Miss Moss consult you, doctor?'

'Infertility; she and her husband - she used her maiden name for the consultation and I have no record of her married name - had been married for two years and had had no success in having a baby. I gave her a full examination at our clinic in Richmond, which involved her admittance as an in-patient. I'm sure you won't want me to bother you with medical technicalities - I will if you require it?' and he looked up over his reading glasses at the two men.

'No doctor, layman's terms will do fine.'

'Very well; Miss Moss was incapable of having children... ever; she suffered from a congenital disorder which is not uncommon, but as yet, for which there is no cure. I recommended that she and her husband consider adoption and offered to put her in touch with the appropriate authorities. Anything else, Chief Superintendent?'

'No thank you, doctor; you've given us the information which confirms what we had suspected. Thank you very much and I apologise for interrupting your work. We'll see ourselves out.' The two men were shown out of the gynaecologist's consulting rooms in Upper Wimpole Street by the receptionist. The elder man hailed a taxi and the younger walked to Regent's Park Underground Station where he caught the west-bound train on the Bakerloo Line to Paddington Station. Having bought his ticket, he only had a three minute wait before the 0950 to Oxford via Reading pulled out of the station.

*

'Vice-Chancellor,' the door into Doctor Edith Morrison's office opened and her secretary stood at the door.

'Yes Mary; is that my visitor?'

'Yes, Vice-Chancellor; Mr Pennington from the Oxford Regional Health Authority.'

'Please ask him to come in.'

'Very well, Doctor; Mr Pennington, would you come this way please,' and Mary Tremlett, secretary to the Vice-Chancellor of Girton College at Oxford University, stood to one side to allow the visitor to enter the wood-panelled room with its arched, mullioned windows with square leaded lights.

'Good morning, Mr Pennington. My secretary tells me that you are from the health authority. Please sit down and tell me how I can help you.'

. 'Thank you Vice-Chancellor for sparing me some of your time when I am well aware of the pressure of work on your appointment.'

'Are you, Mr Pennington?'

'Yes indeed; I graduated from Magdalen eight years ago,' James Pennington replied.

'Did you indeed,' and from this moment on, Doctor Edith Morison decided that her visitor could tentatively - unless of course proved otherwise - be treated as a reasonably intelligent member of the human race.

'Perhaps I may show you this card, Vice-Chancellor, which establishes my identity as some of my questions are about the background of one of your graduates from this college. You will see that it is my task to make some inquiries about couples who wish to adopt children,' and James Pennington returned to his seat.

'And who is the person about whom you are making inquiries?'

'You would have known her by her maiden name, Doctor; Miss Davina Moss.'

'You're right, I would, and you've done your homework well Mr Pennington because we graduated together. We both got Firsts, but she was far cleverer than me. In fact she was brilliant and should have taken her PhD, but went into research work and drove herself to a nervous breakdown. What a waste; it was really bad, Mr Pennington and for her own safety she had to be committed to an asylum. A private and very expensive place at Stanford-in-the-Vale, where she eventually made a complete recovery. I think I'm right in saying that she married a man in the diplomatic service who is now an ambassador, but the name escapes me.'

'Winfield.'

213

'Winfield; that's it. However, if you've done your homework, Mr Pennington, you would also know that I have been approached before by your people who were seeking to establish Davina's suitability as a mother to adopt a child. She was turned down the last time; sad, but I have to say I would agree with that decision. Is her application being reviewed? I would have thought that Davina - who must be the same age as me - was a bit too old to adopt.'

'All cases of unsuitability are reviewed, Doctor, particularly if there is another application.'

'I see; anything else I can do?'

'No thank you, Doctor; you really have been most helpful and I won't take up any more of your time.'

'Not a bit; tell me, because it's been bothering me and I fervently hope that I'm not losing my memory, but who would Magdalen's Vice-Chancellor have been in '84.'

'Dr Maurice Williams - a fanatical Welsh rugby player and a blue himself. He trialled for Wales, but only made the reserves.'

'Of course; an unforgettable character.'

'Yes Doctor, unforgettable; goodbye and thank you again. You've been most helpful,' and when he was a out of her hearing and crossing the paved quadrangle to the porter's lodge added, 'you cunning old witch.' Tom Courtney - alias James Pennington - of BID's counter-espionage directorate, caught a bus outside the college which took him to the station where he caught the 12.52 back to London.

The cunning old witch put down the phone having made her call to the regional health authority where she was told that Mr Pennington was away on a visit, but would she like to leave a message. She had no message.

214

The door to Gunn's room opened and he was invited to 'come' by two men who were not armed - as far as Gunn could see. He was led along a tunnel, up a flight of very steep steps where there was a constant stream of water running down the rockface beside it. At the top of the steps the tunnel opened out again into a fairly smart reception area, not disimilar to that of any hotel. He was taken through a door where he was met by a grey-haired African who introduced himself as Doctor Twum-Danso.

'Good afternoon, Sir, and may I know why you have come to visit the Whispering Hills? It would seem to be rather far removed from the area of interest of the British Military Team in Accra.'

'Quite right, doctor; my name is John Gunn, but I'm not a member of the Military Team; I've been visiting it from the Ministry of Defence in London and am hoping to take some leave after my official commitments are finished.' During this introduction process, the doctor had led the way into a simple, but spacious apartment, which appeared to be only partially inside the cavern. There was a large expanse of glass in the ceiling and all of one wall was glass through which the late afternoon sun filtered through the thick jungle canopy of the Whispering Hills. The apartment had modern furniture and the rock walls were decorated with opened bolts of brilliantly coloured Kente cloth. The doctor took a seat and indicated that Gunn should do likewise. The two guards, minders or whatever their function was, remained in the room.

'And what has brought you to this rather isolated part of our country which is well off the beaten track of most of the tourists?' Gunn had been trying to think of a rational and believable explanation for his and Dina's visit and could easily have found one if it hadn't been for the wretched Scarab Scorpion machine pistols. There could be little doubt that Dina and he would have to be removed now that they had both seen this place in the Whispering Hills. He had to try and feign ignorance of the Graham McLean kidnap to prevent any mutilation of either or both of the kidnapped children. If possible, his explanation had to buy time for him to find both Dina and Graham. Had they interrogated Dina already and would now see how his explanation differed? Certainly, that's what he'd have done if the roles were reversed.

'Oh well, here goes,' Gunn thought to himself and then out loud, 'it may help, doctor, to explain my presence here if you'll let me explain the purpose of my visit to Ghana.'

'Please do, Colonel, I'd be most interested.'

'The department in the Ministry of Defence in which I work is responsible for all the military training teams which the British Government sends all over the world to countries which request that form of assistance. These military teams are usually part of an aid package to developing countries and the team in Accra has been here for about twenty-six years. Now on this visit I had a dual role. Another branch of the Ministry of Defence, known as the Defence Export Services Organization, is responsible for assisting British defence equipment manufacturers with the export of their products. These sales are often tied to proven responsible behaviour in the area of human rights - if he believes that bullshit, he'll believe anything,' Gunn thought as an aside.

'The two machine pistols which were in the back of the Nissan are Scarab Scorpions made and patented in the United States by Armitage International which is a subsidiary of International Machine tools. The weapon is built under licence in the UK by Enfield, which is a subsidiary of Royal Ordnance which, in turn, is owned by British Aerospace. Sorry, doctor, about this detail, but it might help a little.'

'On the contrary, Colonel; don't apologise. This is all most interesting.'

'I hope so; we manufacture the Scorpion in the UK under licence. It is used by our special forces along with a host of other weapons like the Uzi and the Heckler and Koch machine pistols. The Ghanaian Armed Forces have expressed an interest in the weapons used by our special forces for their own Force Reserve Battalion - with which I'm sure you're familiar.'

'I am, Colonel.'

'On this visit of mine, I have brought a selection of these weapons - the ones I've just mentioned to you - and the British Army's Enfield SA80. There's also a sales team in Ghana at the moment and a firm called Hunting Engineering are demonstrating their latest anti-tank missile. This was all taking place at the military ranges near Shai Hills this morning. Oh, incidentally, Miss Gbedemah, who was driving me, is our in-country agent for the sale of defence equipment. She owns a number of dress shops and boutiques, but uses her international financial backing to set up these visits and the exchange control guarantees for arms sales.'

'By their very nature, arms sales are both sensitive and controversial and the agents who act for governments, like Miss Gbedemah for the Ghana Armed Forces, do their utmost to keep their identities as confidential as possible. I have no doubt, if indeed she's here, as she vanished just before I was confronted with your very fierce group of warriors, and you've had a chance to speak with her, that she would have been very reticent to disclose her connection with me. By telling you all this, I have little doubt that I've compromised her agency and will be very unpopular.'

'So why have you told me all this.'

'Well, doctor, if I was in your shoes and someone trespassed on my property and they were in possession of loaded weapons, I would need some considerable convincing that their intentions were benign rather than hostile.'

'Keep going, Colonel, you have my interest, but why are the loaded pistols here and not back at the ranges?'

'Good question and I'd have asked that', Gunn thought and then again out loud, 'both a simple and rather stupid answer to that, doctor. The stupidity is mine. At the end of the demonstration this morning, General Amanfo said that he was not interested in the Scorpion as it was no better than the Uzi or Heckler Koch. He is interested in the Enfield SA80 and Hunting's LAW 80 man-portable anti-tank missile. I agreed to take the two Scorpions back with me and Miss Gbedemah will arrange the air-freighting of them back to UK. Silly of me not to put the pistols in their crate and equally silly of me, but perhaps forgivable, to have taken the pistol out of the car when Miss Gbedemah vanished.'

'We have spoken with your Miss Gbedemah and you are right, she was very reticent about her role, but she did say that she was responsible for taking you wherever you wished to visit. So why here?'

'Thank God, Dina was alive, but how had she been questioned?' and then aloud Gunn answered the question; 'after the demonstration on the ranges this morning, there was some light refreshment and then I was due to return to Accra with no further engagements for today. This is my first visit to Ghana - West Africa in fact - and I had expressed an interest in two aspects of the history and culture. I wanted to visit some of the coastal forts, which I understand are in a remarkable state of preservation and also learn about the shrines and ethnic religious beliefs.'

'Miss Gbedemah told me that we could visit Kpandu which was the original crossing point over the Volta because it was just up the road and she had a friend there who owned a chemist shop. I agreed and we went to Kpandu where we met the friend who owned the chemist shop and learnt that there was another car heading in this direction a few minutes in front of us. In Zebila we bought some fruit and drink for lunch and the plan was to come up here, have a picnic lunch and then drive back to Accra.'

'And you asked about the car in front of you when you bought your fruit in Zebila.'

'Yes, that's right and were rather surprised to be told that the woman, who I think was driving, had been injured. Miss Gbedemah was trained as a nurse and we wondered whether she might be able to help in some way.'

'What do you think of this place, Colonel Gunn?'

'Very impressive, what's it for, doctor?'

'We import and export goods through this place and thereby avoid the corruption and bribes of the Ghanaian Customs and Police and the exorbitant import tariffs imposed by our government. That's it; we slightly enhance the superstitions about this place and that ensures that we are left alone.'

'Very neat and none of my business. We train the Ghana Armed Forces and on this trip have demonstrated some weapons with a view to a possible sale.'

'Perhaps you and Miss Gbedemah would have supper with me this evening; I'm sure that she has told you that our Acan culture directs that no male visitor to a house can leave without being given food and - you may have heard - being offered sexual relief with the woman of the house. I can't offer you the latter, but I can offer the former. I must insist that you stay the night here because we have a very delicate deal going through at the moment and I cannot risk even an inadvertent remark which might direct the interest of the Armed Forces, Customs or Police in this direction. I'm sure you'll understand. And now perhaps you'll join me in a drink,' and before Gunn could answer, Doctor Twum-Danso turned to the guards and in English ordered them to go and get Miss Gbedemah.'

'Yes, that'd be nice.'

'What'll you have, Colonel Gunn?'

'Beer?'

'Excellent choice; Club or Star?'

'I think I rather prefer Club.'

'Quite right; our Club brewery was set up by the British whereas Star relies on German brewing techniques. Ah! Miss Gbedemah;

218

thank you for joining us.' Gunn turned and still determined to continue with the charade however flawed it may have been, showed his relief at seeing her again.'

'Hello Dina, where on earth did you disappear to? I was really worried. I much regret that I've probably compromised your agency for defence sales in my explanation to the doctor, here, for our arrival with those two machine pistols.' Gunn tried to see if Dina had been mal-treated, but if she had it didn't show either physically or in her spirited and relaxed response to him.

'Hello John...Doctor; well, these things can't be helped and I doubt if it's the end of the world for my agency. I'm paid by the British Government to look after their defence sales interests in Ghana and visitors from both the MOD and commercial companies.'

'And were you pleased with the demonstration this morning, Miss Gbedemah?' There was no possible way that Gunn could communicate to Dina the pack of lies he'd told Twum-Danso and this he'd been prepared for. He judged the sequence in which he would need to take out the three people in the room and moved his position slightly by topping up his beer glass from the bottle on the glass coffee table so that he had a clear shot at the minder who was closest to Dina.

'Not bad, doctor; it could've been better. The General was unimpressed by the machine pistols, but thought that the other equipment was most effective.' Gunn nearly choked over his beer. How the hell had Dina been able to read his mind? and she was smiling now, obviously enjoying herself. It seemed that her answer had convinced Twum-Danso who offered her a drink and dismissed his two minders. He then pulled on a tasselled cord and a steward appeared with whom he spoke while Gunn and Dina, who had also chosen beer, animatedly discussed the marvels of the place in which they now found themselves - all for the benefit of Twum-Danso.

The light from outside quickly faded and was replaced by a chandelier and hidden lights in cornices hewn out of the solid rock. 'Doctor, I'm intrigued by your abundant source of electricity. Am I allowed to ask if that comes from the national grid or do you generate it yourself?'

'Yes, of course you may ask, Colonel Gunn. The answer is the latter; we generate our own power, but not perhaps as you imagine. Both of you come with me; supper will be about another hour and a half and I will show you our generating system of which I'm rather proud. I must also apologise for your very spartan accommodation on arrival. I've directed my steward to arrange for you to occupy guest rooms next to my own apartment.' The doctor led the way

219

from his apartment and they were immediately joined by the two minders.

They were led across the reception area and stopped outside a lift, which Twum-Danso summoned by pressing a very ordinary button. All five of them entered the lift and it went down for about twenty seconds before halting and then the doors opened. The first thing that struck Gunn was the noise, but even that was catered for because the minders removed two sets of ear protectors from hooks on the wall and handed them to Gunn and Dina.

Twum-Danso led the way towards the noise and the short corridor opened out into a large generating room, which had three turbines side by side in the centre. Around the walls of the underground chamber were all the associated transformers, switching gear and cabling. Three large steel ducts carried the water from what must have been a substantial subterranean river to the base of the turbines, which in turn drove the generators. The spill-water from the turbines was then carried away in other steel ducts and left the cavern as the river which he'd seen when he first arrived, Gunn reckoned. He also noted the bypass valves, which would divert the water from any selected turbine so that it could be shut down for servicing. There was a very simple lubrication system for the generators, which pumped oil to the generator bearings from a large reservoir.

From the turbine room, Gunn and Dina were led through to an auxiliary generating room where there were two, 150 kva diesel generators with all their associated transformers, switching gear, cables and heavily insulated ducts for the diesel exhaust. Between the main and auxiliary generating rooms was a small switch room from which the required power could be selected and then fed into the mains.

Right inside the core of the Whispering Hills, Caramansa had a limitless supply of power from the hydro-electric turbines and their back-up diesel generators. All the time, Gunn was looking for an opportunity to speak to Dina, but the two of them were closely watched. Gunn knew that all he'd done was negotiate a possible stay of execution, which might just give them a chance to find the boy. They would have to get away as soon as possible because it would be only a matter of time before his story was proved to be just that. Indeed the 'phone calls had probably already been made.

The conducted tour was now finished and the doctor led the two of them back the way they had come to the lift and up to the accommodation level. Once they were out of the lift, Doctor Twum-Danso escorted each of them to new rooms where they were offered the opportunity to freshen-up before supper. The minders positioned themselves outside each door. They were told that supper would be in one hour at 7.30.

Gunn went into his room which would have rated five stars at any international hotel and was considerably larger and more luxurious than the one he had left in Accra the previous evening before going to the Shai Hills game reserve. In the bathroom were all the accoutrements for shaving and bathing. Surely they must have run out of time. Their 'host' was not expecting to see them for an hour, during which time his fabricated story could be thoroughly checked and then either before or after their 'last supper', the two of them would undoubtedly be killed. No, time had run out; it was now time to act and Gunn stooped to remove the Tanarmi from his ankle holster, but he hastily stopped and straightened up as the door opened.

Dina walked into his room and closed the door. 'Sorry, John, I would have been quicker, but my guard was very persistent.'

'Where are the two guards?'

'They're dead, so we don't have more than a few moments to compare notes before we must find that boy and get the hell out of this place.'

'How the hell were you able to follow my story about the demonstration?'

'You need to know Ghanaian men to understand that. If there is one thing that exceeds a Ghanaian man's libido, it's his conceit about it. My guard was easily seduced with the promise of laying me - I should apologise that I took your name in vain and told him that you were useless as a lover and could he remind me what a proper man was capable of. After that comment and a little bit of mild titillation, the blood and any sense he possessed drained from his brain to another part of his anatomy, taking with it all caution and it really was very easy to learn what had been said during your interrogation. I have to say that for instant improvisation, that story would've convinced me.'

'You're amazing Dina; how many more talents do you have?'

'Perhaps a couple you haven't seen yet.'

'How did you get rid of the guards?'

'I keep a knife strapped to the back of my thigh - the guard nearly found it when he was groping me down in those cells. He thought the strap was a garter, which heightened his arousement!'

'That behaviour matches their neglect in searching me; I still have my gun. Dina, the Doctor will rumble my story any minute now. Find Graham McLean and get out as fast as possible?'

221

'Can't think of a better plan. Do you know where he is?'

'No, but I intend to start at the cells we were in. There were more than two. This time we stick together as it would be too easy to get lost or separated in this labyrinth. Come on, let's get the hell out of here,' and Gunn removed the Tanarmi from his ankle holster, opened the door and the two of them crossed the reception area to the steps which led down to the loading area and cells below.

They met no one as they descended the steps to the lower level, which was explained as they approached the loading area, by the hive of activity. A shipment of some sort had arrived and trolley after trolley of hessian-bound bundles were being dragged across the loading area. The cells were on their left, in view of the workforce. Gunn and Dina knew which cell each of them had occupied, but that still left three to choose from to find the boy. All the cells were kept locked by a bolt on the outside - no keys required.

'Raw opium.'

'What?'

'Those bundles; that's raw opium. I'll wager you that's the reason for a doctor here and I'll bet a month's salary that there's a processing laboratory in this cave complex. That lot'll be refined to produce heroin. You're looking at a street value of billions of dollars of the stuff. How the hell are we going to get across to that tunnel with all this lot around.'

'With great difficulty or not at all has to be the answer. In the generating room there was a tunnel where those large steel ducts disappeared. That tunnel must be wide enough for someone to go down it as it would have to be possible to repair that steel ducting. Wait here and cover me.' Gunn gave the Tanarmi to Dina and went to the closest door, pulled back the bolt and opened it. Empty; the next had been his and the one next to his, Dina's. The one beyond was almost out in the loading area. He walked to the door; no shouts or alarms. He opened the door and there was a frightened 15 year old boy sitting on the bed with hands and feet still bound.

'Graham Mclean?'

'Yes, I'm Graham; who're you?'

'My names's John; John Gunn. I'm a soldier from England and it's my job to get you back to your Mum and Dad.' While Gunn was explaining this, he undid the cord binding the boy's hands and feet. 'Can you walk, Graham?' The boy stood up and hobbled a bit as the circulation returned to his feet.

'Think so; where are we going?'

222

'As far away from here as possible. Listen Graham; when I take you out of this room, turn to your right and walk towards a Ghanaian woman whom you'll see waiting for you...'

'Is it...'

'No, it's not the woman who brought you here. Got that?'

'Yes.'

'Right, off you go,' and Gunn opened the door and gently urged the boy through, placing himself between the boy and the activity in the loading area; still, no attention paid to them. Graham walked up to Dina who took his hand and then the three of them retreated back along the corridor, up the steps and into the reception area. Dina gave the Tanarmi back to Gunn who led the way across the reception area to the lift. It was now just before 7 pm; still a half-hour or so before they would be summoned to supper with Doctor Twum-Danso.

The lift was still on the reception floor and the doors opened immediately when Gunn pressed the button. When the doors re-opened down on the generating level, Gunn handed the ear protectors to Dina and Graham and then went ahead of them into the turbine chamber. The duty engineer was busy working on the lubrication pipe on the turbine furthest away from Gunn. The man neither saw nor heard Gunn who hit him across the back of the neck with the Tanarmi and then dragged the unconscious man into the diesel generator chamber.

Gunn cimbed down into the well into which the steel ducting for the three turbines went and where they joined into one large steel duct which disappeared into a natural tunnel in the limestone rock. There was no lighting in the tunnel, but the duty engineer had had a torch in his tool kit. Gunn climbed back up into the turbine chamber and removed the torch from the toolbox and flicked the switch; it worked. He beckoned Dina and Graham over to the well and indicated that they should climb down. He gave the torch to Dina and then held up three fingers. Dina nodded and she and Graham disappeared down into the well. Gunn removed a large pipe wrench from the engineer's toolbox and went into the diesel generator chamber. Underneath the generators was a thin layer of sand in a drip tray to catch any oil spillages or leaks. In the corner of the chamber was a box of clean sand to top up the drip tray. Gunn twisted off the cap from the oil-filler on the top of both engines and put three or four handfuls of sand into each engine. Using the heavy pipe wrench, he smashed the diesel feed pipes to both engines and then went back into the turbine room and disconnected the lubricating oil feed to the bearings of all three turbines. By the time

223

he had disconnected the oil feed of the third turbine the temperature gauge of the first turbine was into the orange sector and climbing towards the red.

Time to go; Gunn climbed down into the well, took the torch from Dina and led the way into the tunnel.

*

Marcus Ransby continued reading the Times until the crush of rush-hour humanity had forced and jostled its way through the gates at Waterloo Station and then he folded the paper, placed it in his briefcase and left his first class compartment. He walked across the station concourse and down the steps into Mepham Street. He crossed York Road on the footbridge, went through the Shell Building and then over Westminster Bridge via Jubilee Gardens and the London Eye. He arrived at the entrance to the Foreign and Commonwealth Office in King Charles Street at 8.52 and walked into his office at 8.58.

His PA greeted him as he came through her office and she followed him into his office with his cup of Earl Grey tea and slice of lemon. He was looking forward to a quiet day in the office, lunch with his solicitor at the club to discuss the wretched business of his divorce from Moira, away from the office by five and the opera at Covent Garden with Elaine followed by the night spent with her at his flat in Kensington.

The day followed its planned pattern exactly until 4.34 in the afternoon when absolutely everything went wrong. It started with his PA, Shirley, coming into the office to tell him that he had a visitor.

'That wasn't on my programme, Shirley.'

'No, Marcus; Mr Collins arrived ten minutes ago.'

'Then he'll have to come back on Monday,' was said in a petulant rebuttal of anyone or thing which disturbed the Head of the FCO's Overseas Estate Department. 'Mr Collins is a detective from the Metropolitan Police and will not be able to wait. He told me to say that if a quick meeting with you now was impossible you would be required to go to the police station in Old Scotland Yard the other side of Whitehall later this evening.'

'I shall do no such thing; I've a busy programme this evening.'

'Mr Collins or his boss has already spoken with Sir Peter Goddard who told them that you would make yourself available for a meeting this afternoon. I was asked what was on your programme by Sir Peter and I told him 'nothing' after your lunch appointment with your solicitor.'

'Oh, very well, I suppose I must; what is this Collins - a sergeant or something?'

'I have no idea. I'll go and get him,' and Shirley left his office closing the door and then stuck her tongue out at it, which made her feel a lot better. She found Mr Collins out in the corridor examining prints and paintings of British Embassies and High Commissions dating back to the year dot. 'Ah! Mr Collins....Mr Ransby will see you now, if you would like to follow me.'

'Shouldn't think he was too happy at having me barge in at this time on a Friday afternoon, was he?'

'Oh no, that's alright; what made you think that?'

'Because I heard his comments from out here.'

'Oh! I'm sorry Mr Collins.'

'That's OK; I'm used to it,' and he followed the PA into the Head of OED's office.

'Marcus, this is Mr Collins from....er'

'From MI5, Mr Ransby.....counter-espionage; I have some questions which I need to ask you about some events which took place at the High Commission in Ottawa between 1989 and 93 when you were a First Secretary in the Commercial Section.'

'You're what?....but I thought...I mean, you're not a policeman?'

'No, Mr Ransby, I'm not a policeman, but frequently we have to make use of our Metropolitan Police warrant cards when interviewing people. For someone as senior as yourself in government employment and subject to the Official Secrets Act, we can declare our real employer. Needless to say perhaps, Mr Ransby, my name is not Collins, but if you would care to ring that number, with which I think you might be familiar, you will receive confirmation of my appointment to interview you today.' Marcus Ransby took the card from 'Collins' and then turned to find Shirley still in the room with a huge grin on her face.

'That'll be all for now, Shirley.'

'Very well,' and she closed the door behind her, but didn't let it click shut.

'I would be most grateful Mr Ransby if you would phone the number on that card; correct procedure in a matter like this.'

'Oh yes...yes of course' and Marcus Ransby phoned the number and mumbled some 'yeses' and 'noes', replaced the phone and handed back the card.

'Collins' removed two small tape recorders from his briefcase and placed them on the table between the two of them. 'I shall record this interview, Mr Ransby, on these two machines. At the end of the interview, you may keep the tape out of either of these machines. All clear?'

'Yes....Mr Col.... yes, quite clear.'

'OK then, here we go,' and 'Collins' switched on both the tape recorders. 'For this interview my name is Collins and I'm interviewing Mr Marcus Ransby, the Head of the FCO's Overseas Estate Department in his office on King Charles Street. The date is Friday the 15th of April 2004 and the time is' and Collins looked at his watch, '16.42 hours. The reference code for this tape is BOX 500/137/94.'

'Mr Ransby, what appointment did you have in the diplomatic service from 1989 to 1993?'

'I was a First Secretary, Grade 7, in the Commercial Section of the British High Commission in Ottawa.'

'Who was the head of that section?'

'Humphrey Winfield.'

'Were you accompanied by your wife on this appointment?'

'I was.'

'Were you invited to many of the same social functions as Humphrey Winfield in pursuance of your representational duties.'

'I was.'

'Did you meet a John and Mary Mackenzie at many of these functions.'

'I..I can't remember all the names....Mr..er...Collins. There were so many people,' and then to himself, 'dear God where were these questions leading? Surely....surely...he'd been so discreet.'

'Did you meet a David and Elaine Dalton. They were a Canadian couple, like the Mackenzies, and he worked for Canadian Pacific Railways.' Marcus' worst fears were realised; this man knew everything and was just playing with him. This had been such a wonderful day when it started and was now turning into the worst possible nightmare.

'Er..' and Marcus Ransby clered his throat, 'yes, I met them.'

'Who, Mr Ransby, the Daltons or the Mackenzies or both?'

'I met both of them.'

'Frequently?'

'Frequently.'

'In your judgement Mr Ransby, did Humphrey Winfield and Mary Mackenzie form an attachment?'

'I....I really don't...'

'But you and Elaine Dalton and Humphrey and Mary Mackenzie spent at least one weekend together at the High Commission's cottage at Lake Maurice. Didn't you Mr Ransby?'

'Er...yes...yes we did.' That was it then. Goodbye any appointment as an ambassador or high commissioner. He'd be lucky to keep his job here. Christ! how much more did these people know?

'Were you aware that Mary Mackenzie became pregnant by Humphrey Winfield?'

'Yes,' very quietly.

'Louder please, Mr Ransby, so that the microphone can pick it up,' and me, mouthed quietly by Shirley who had her ear welded to the crack in the door and whose eyes were out on stalks at what she had just heard.

'Yes.. yes I was.'

'Thank you Mr Ransby and was it Humphrey Winfield who introduced you to the surgeon, Mr Myers, who aborted Elaine Dalton's child fathered by you?'

'Yes, it was.'

'And now Mr Ransby, would you tell me in your own words what happened to the baby which Mary Mackenzie was expecting.'

'Mary desperately wanted a baby because after something like five years of marriage, she and her husband had failed to produce a child. Mary had been to a gynaecologist who had confirmed that she was perfectly capable of having a baby. Having been told that, she decided to find out if her husband was also capable of fathering a child. I don't know how this is done, but apparently she'd taken a swab after intercourse with her husband, John, and took it to her doctor who'd confirmed that he was sterile. The whole purpose of her affair with Humphrey was to become pregnant without having to let her husband - whom she clearly loved very much - know that he was incapable of fathering a child. She had absolutely no idea of what Humphrey's ulterior motives were and, understandably, believed that his motives were the same as Elaine's and mine - to dabble in a casual affair and extra-marital sex. This all happened at one of those weekends at the lake cottage.'

'But there's still worse to come, isn't there, Mr Ransby?'

'Oh yes,' to his surprise, Marcus now felt quite calm. It was an enormous relief to get all of this off his chest. 'Yes, there was far worse, as you say. There was another person whom we all met at nearly every function.'

'His name?'

'Charles Mensah, the Commercial Counsellor at the Ghanaian High Commission. Somehow he discovered that there were some pretty wild parties and weekends at the BHC cottage. Someone who'd had too much to drink told him or he overheard it. Anyway, he bugged our cottage and the next time the four of us were there, he turned up with the tape and played it to us. It was, of course, blackmail. He wanted $250,000 from each of us.'

'But Humphrey came up with his own blackmail.'

'Yes, how he knew of the account into which Mensah had embezzled nearly two million dollars of Canadian Overseas Development Aid prior to its transfer to a bank in Las Vegas - I've forgotten the nam...'

'International Credit Bank.'

'Yes, that's it....I'll never know. Anyway it was what's called a Mexican stand-off, I think; each pointing a pistol at the other man's head. I have no cause to be judge in this affair, but Humphrey's performance thereafter amazed me. To this day I couldn't believe that I'd been party to such a deal. I wasn't, in fact.....I'm not making excuses, but all Humphrey wanted was a witness to the deal.'

'And that deal was...?'

'The tape was destroyed and Humphrey handed over the evidence incriminating Mensah with the embezzled aid money. Humphrey knew of his next appointment as High Commissioner in Accra and agreed to help Mensah in his conspiracy to foster terrorism and destabilisation in that region, if the latter arranged to have the Mackenzie child kidnapped - supposedly killed - but actually handed over to the Winfields. Of course, Mary Mackenzie knew nothing about this.'

'Do you have any idea, Mr Ransby, of the enormity of the crime of which you are a willing conspirator or the people who have already died because of this unholy conspiracy and your silence about your knowledge of it.'

'No...I don't think....I mean.. no.'

'I've no idea what will happen to you, Mr Ransby, but if I had anything to do with it I'd hang you for treason. As it is I expect that you'll be locked up and they'll throw away the key. That's you and Humphrey Winfield,' and Collins leant forward and switched off the two machines. He flicked one open and ejected the small cassette onto the coffee table where he left it for Marcus Ransby. He put both machines in his briefcase, got up and walked out of the office. It was nearly twenty past five.

Marcus Ransby stood up and looked out of the long windows at the view across the corner of Horseguards Parade and St James' Park. The clocks had changed to British Summer Time just a fortnight or so before and already the evenings were getting longer. The long summer evenings reminded him of the river where they still kept their boat and the fun that he and Moira had had with the children.

228

That seemed like another lifetime. What had happened to it all? The answer was easy to find; he had destroyed it.

His ambition, his selfishness and his casual affairs had destroyed the happiness of a family. The children had grown up and he no longer saw either of them. The divorce from Moira would leave her with the house in Burnell Avenue by the river in Teddington. What would he have? The flat in Kensington and Elaine Dalton. He didn't even like her any more. The relationship was entirely physical and both of them fooled each other that they shared the same interests. Who on earth did they both think they were fooling? That was something else that he'd destroyed. The Dalton's marriage would have survived its temporary dullness if he hadn't lavished attention on Elaine, bringing excitement at a time when her children had left home and her husband was required to spend a great deal of time away.

Marcus left the office by his own door without saying goodnight to Shirley and walked back to Waterloo where he caught the train to Kingston Station, collected his car from the station car park and drove home. He left the car in Burnell Avenue outside the house and walked down to the river where the boat was moored. The name of the boat was the cruellest irony of all and it stood out, bold as the brass of its lettering on the stern, mocking him; Ourmoney. A not-so-subtle play on words; the vast amount of money which the boat had cost - or so it had seemed in those days when they were very strapped for cash - and the 'harmony' of a young and happy family. It was still shrouded in its tarpaulin cover, and the thought occurred to him that it was time to take it off and give the boat its Spring clean and fresh coat of varnish ready for those long summer evenings of sun and laughter while they watched the swans around Trowlock Island.

Silly thoughts; he'd be lucky to get anything less than 15 years for his complicity in the conspiracy. What was he now? 49. He'd be over sixty when he got out having brought disgrace to his profession, his family and all those who had once been their friends. He walked along the bank towards the lock and the pathway that crossed over the Thames beside the TV studios. Laughter, like he remembered, came from a rather scruffy and varnish-bare little motor cruiser where a father and his two teenage children were in the process of casting off for an evening potter along the river. The children's mother appeared from the small cabin with cups of coffee and they waved to Marcus as the small boat turned out into the river and headed up-stream. Happy days gone forever.

The Thames River Police found the body of Marcus Ransby below the weir at Teddington Lock after it had been spotted by a small boy crossing over the river on the footpath. Seats M11 and M12 in the centre of the balcony at Covent Garden were not occupied for the performance of Rossini's opera L'Italiana in Algeri on the evening of Friday 15 April.

CHAPTER 15

For the first few yards of the tunnel, they could see where they were going by the reflected light from the generating chamber, but gradually this faded to leave them with only the light from the torch which Gunn had taken from the mechanic's toolbox. The metal duct carrying the water away from the turbines was about five feet in diameter, with metal flanges which stood proud of the casing. These, Gunn presumed, were not only to join each section of the duct, but also provided it with a measure of rigidity. He could feel the duct vibrating with the pressure of water inside it and if that wasn't indication enough of the harnessed, brute force of the underground river, the increasing tumult of noise in the confined space of the tunnel was made far worse by the lack of any light except that from the torch which Gunn shone in front to see the way and then behind him to guide the two following.

The tunnel through which the steel ducting ran was fairly spacious in some places with stalactites reaching down from above. In others, the three of them could only just squeeze past the protruding ridges of the steel duct. Gunn judged that they had probably gone about seventy or eighty yards along the tunnel when his torch reflected off water around their feet. He stopped and Graham and Dina bumped into him. Any form of verbal communication was impossible; it was even difficult to concentrate with the constant hammering roar of sound all round them. Gunn bent down and looked at the rock on which they were walking; it was covered in water - flowing water - and it was coming from behind them. Already, his jungle boots were soaked.

The tunnel had been completely free of water only a short distance further back because he'd shone his torch all over it. Where the hell was this coming from? Gunn answered his own question as it was a glimpse of the blinding obvious; there was only one place it could come from - the generating room. The intense heat of the unlubricated turbine bearings must have caused the turbine shaft to disintegrate. The rev counter on the switch panels had shown that the turbine shaft speed was between 5,000 and 7,000 rpm. Collapse of the bearings and then the shaft itself, at that speed, would have released similar destructive energy to that of a chemical explosive compound. It would seem that the steel ducting had been ruptured by the explosive force of the turbine disintegrating, the well for the ducting manifold had filled up and now the river was reverting to its old course down the tunnel. Even as Gunn paused, the water level rose.

The three of them hurried on as fast as possible with the water sloshing around their ankles. Gunn shone the torch alternately in front to see what lay ahead and then down at the swirling water around their feet to guide the two behind him. In front, the torch reflected off the sides of the tunnel, the steel ducting and the stalactites and then.....nothing. On Gunn's left the steel casing had stopped and there was just a solid, five foot diameter spout of water arching out into inky blackness. He shone the torch at his feet and barely a yard or so in front of him, the water disappeared over a ledge, likewise into the same inky blackness.

Again Graham and Dina bumped into Gunn as he stopped. He shone the torch at what he'd just seen and held up his hand like a policeman on traffic duty to indicate that the two of them should stay where they were. Gunn got down on his knees and crawled through the river to where it disappeared in a waterfall over the floor of the tunnel. He shone the torch down into the darkness to the right of the waterfall. The woefully inadequate beam showed an almost vertical rockface which vanished into the darkness some five yards below him out of the range of the torch beam. Gunn crawled back to the others and holding the torch above his head to cast some sort of light on the scene, pointed to himself, then to Graham and finally at Dina. He handed the torch to Dina, indicating that she should hold it while he and Graham climbed down; she was then to pass the torch down to him via Graham and he would hold it while Dina climbed down. With the water around them rising by the second, it was the best Gunn could come up with and anyway, he rationalised with himself, without wings what the hell else could they do?

The three of them moved forward to the edge of the tunnel and Dina positioned herself so that she could shine the torch down the rockface. Gunn turned and let himelf down over the edge, searching with feet and hands for footholds and handholds on the wet and slippery rock. Gunn had never rated climbing as his favourite pass-time and certainly not in the dark; on two successive nights he'd had to climb; up the night before and now down into the blackness of Hades. It wasn't quite as bad as it had first seemed from above because the face was a few degrees out of the vertical which allowed him to lean against it. He judged that he had reached the limit of the torch's beam, stopped and waved.

Without any hesitation, Graham came backwards over the edge and climbed down to Gunn, taking the torch from Dina before she was out of reach. He passed the torch behind him to Gunn who then held it to illuminate the rockface and, hopefully, not blinding Dina. Gunn noticed that Dina had removed her shoes and with cosiderable agility, followed Graham. As soon as she reached him, Gunn handed the torch to Graham who directed its beam onto the rock face below for Gunn's next descent and so it continued.

Gunn wasn't certain whether it was spray from the waterfall on his right or sweat which ran into his eyes. As he concentrated on testing the footholds before putting his weight onto them, he tried to imagine the size of the huge subterranean cavern into which the outflow of the turbines and river disgorged. Although the level of noise was far more bearable in the cavern, there was still no indication by noise of how far below them the water hit the base of the cavern. Then his worst nightmare was realised; he lowered his right foot, searching for a foothold and there wasn't one. He raised his foot again and ran the toecap of the boot down the rock until, with a slight lurch which nearly made him lose his grasp of the rock, his foot went out into space.

Gunn waited until the other two had gone through the process of climbing down to him and then tapped Graham on the leg. The boy lowered the torch to him and very carefully Gunn shone it along the rock face below him. Directly below him, the beam showed nothing. For all he could tell, he might be perched above a one foot or one thousand foot drop. To his right, the beam dimly lit the waterfall, but it did show that it was running down the rockface. To his left, as far as the beam of the torch could illuminate, the rock face appeared to disappear. Gunn shone the torch to his right at the waterfall and passed it back to Graham in that position. The fifteen year-old boy understood the significance immediately and the beam steadied on the rockface to Gunn's right.

Slowly, foothold by foothold, Gunn traversed across the rock face to his right until he was in the waterfall and there was rock below him. Drenched by the water cascading down from above, he started to climb down once more and then stopped to allow the other two to join him. Progress was painfully slow, but gradually the rock face became less and less vertical until it seemed that it was no more than about 45 degrees to the vertical. The waterfall now ran over the rock rather than down the face of it. There was the gravest danger of the torch slipping from their grasp as it was carefully handed from one to the other amidst the torrent of water. Were they at the bottom of the cavern or was this merely a ledge? Again, Gunn tapped Graham on the leg and the torch was carefully placed into his hand.

Gunn turned over onto his back and shone the torch below him. The beam showed that the slope on which he lay with the river all around him levelled off only a short distance below his feet where the river had returned to its old course along the base of the cavern. On his right, the disappearance of the rock face was explained when the beam showed a concave section which would have certainly resulted in at least two broken legs if he'd slipped over the edge. Gunn stood up and shone the torch for the other two to come and join him. The three of them followed the river until the torch revealed where the spout of water from the turbine outfall landed. There was spray and water everywhere, but as all of them were soaked to the skin this mattered little.

Gunn led the way through the spray and once beyond it there was a noticeable diminution of the level of noise. They stumbled along the edge of the subterranean river until it tumbled over a small ridge into a lake. By shouting into Dina's ear, Gunn told her that they would go to the right first to see if they could find where the river continued - it had to, otherwise, Gunn tried to convince himself, the cavern would fill right up. The answer was quickly revealed by the torch beam which was getting dimmer and dimmer; the water flowed into a depression which formed the lake and then out into another tunnel. They had reached what seemed to be the end of the cavern and what might well be the end of their escape route.

Gunn climbed down into the river where it flowed out of the lake; the water came up to his waist. Both Dina and Graham followed him into the water and he led them to the mouth of the tunnel. The gap between the surface of the river and the top of the tunnel was about eighteen inches and so Gunn, Dina and Graham had to go down on their knees and crawl through the water. The sides of the tunnel were almost as smooth as marble, having been scoured by the water for hundreds, if not thousands, of years which at least meant that there weren't stalactites and other projections to scalp them as the torch became dimmer and revealed fewer and fewer of the hazards.

After some twenty or thirty yards of very slow progress, two things happened; the fast-waning energy of the torch batteries revealed that the top of the tunnel and the surface of the river met two yards in front of them and after this revelation, the torch went out. Utter and complete darkness; so dark and black that Gunn felt that he could touch it; not the faintest glimmer of any form of light. However, the mind-shattering roar of the water had gone and having reached around him and found the other two, Gunn was able to speak quite normally to them.

'Graham, you OK?'

'Yes, I'm fine; what happens now?'

'Hang on a sec; Dina, you alright?'

'Fine, but I swear that I'm giving up water for Lent next year. What happens now?'

'I think this is what cavers call a sump; very similar to the 'U' bend in a lavatory bowl. The problem is very obvious; how long is the 'U' bend and will we be able to hold our breath long enough to get through it? In fact there really isn't a problem because we can't go back and if we chose to try and find another way out, without any light, we could stumble and grope our way around the cavern behind us until we all went mad. As I see it, there's only one thing we need to be clear about before we press on; we must assume the worst case that this sump goes on too far for me to hold my breath to find how far it is and then come back to you. I think the current is also too strong for me to make my way back. I'll go first and keep going until I find air to breathe. I think I can hold my breath for about 40 seconds - thereabouts anyway. I want the two of you to wait for a minute after I've gone and then Graham comes next followed by Dina. Anyone got any suggestions?'

'I think I can hold my breath longer than 40 seconds,' came from Graham. 'We have competitions at school and I usually win. I can hold my breath for over a minute.'

'Excellent, then you might have to pull me out of this place. Will you look after Dina after I've gone?'

'Yea, sure.' With that sort of confidence there had to be a way out of this dreadful place, Gunn thought. The current in the river was very strong making it quite difficult to avoid being dragged under the lip of the sump. It was Gunn's hope that if he, any or all of them lost consciousness, the river might spew them out the other side. There was also little likelihood that this river was the one he'd seen when he'd been led into the cave. They must have descended at least 200 feet or more, including the lift ride down to the generating cavern and moved forward two or three hundred yards, so this river had to have a different out-fall from the mountain.

'See you both the other side; bye!' and Gunn hyper-ventilated two or three times, took a deep breath and dived under the surface of the river.

The moment his knees were clear of the riverbed rock, Gunn was carried forward at great speed by the combination of the current and him swimming. He tried to swim only just below the surface and with his left hand stretched above him 'felt' for an airspace between the water and the top of the tunnel. To Gunn's relief this space became evident after only a few seconds and he surfaced with about a foot between the surface of the river and the rock above. He gulped in the rather damp and foetid air and then positioned himself on his knees, facing into the current with legs and arms spread as wide as possible to catch young Graham.

Graham appeared within about half a minute and Gunn pulled him to the surface where he gasped and spluttered to get his breath back. Competitions at school were one thing; swimming under water in complete darkness was something else entirely! Gunn steadied the boy on his left side to act as a barrier to prevent Dina slipping past. In the event, he caught Dina on his right and pulled her to the surface. Once all of them had steadied their breathing, Gunn moved forward again with the current. Within ten yards he came to another sump and the three of them repeated the procedure four more times before Gunn surfaced and was unable to touch the top of the tunnel above his head. Not only that, but the air was fresh and while he was waiting to grasp Graham, something bounced off the water beside him.

Graham surfaced, followed by Dina and all three of them dragged great gulps of the comparatively fresh air into their lungs. There was a smell which was familiar and then the relief which came from the realisation of what it was and what had bounced off the water beside him, made Gunn want to shout with glee; bats! The funny ammonia smell came from their droppings on the ledges of the rock where they must hang in this cave. If bats could fly in then there had to be a way out; at least there was air for them to breath and even as this relief dawned on him, Gunn also realised that the total blackness which had enveloped them when the batteries finally packed in had given way to a lesser shade of darkness, if that was possible.

Gunn looked at the luminous figures and hands on his watch; 8.45. It would be full dark outside, but if there was a moon then it would account for the fact that he could now see his hand in front of his face and the outline of Dina who was holding onto the boy and kneeling close beside him in the water. The current was still quite strong. Gunn bent down and with his head close to the water, looked along the surface of the river in the direction of the flow of water and there it was! a sort of semi-circle of paler darkness above the surface of the river. Gunn moved towards it still holding on to Dina's hand. He reached it much quicker than he'd expected as it was totally impossible to judge distances. Not only did the current sweep all of them towards the aperture, but the air was suddenly filled with the fluttering, clicking and squealing of hundreds of bats leaving the cave for their nightly feast of fruit.

One moment Gunn was tumbling in the rushing surge of water towards the venturi leading out of the cave and the next he was falling through space. All he had time to think about as he fell was the marvellous purity of the air and what it was like to be smashed to pulp on the rocks below. No rocks and no pulp; the three of them plunged into a deep pool at the foot of the waterfall and all rose spluttering to the surface. They swam to the side of the pool and dragged themselves out onto the sand. All round them, the dense, moon-lit rain forest dripped with the spray from the falls, but for the moment it was the best sight - dark as it was - that Gunn had seen for years.

*

The phone on the desk rang and Kwajo Twum-Danso picked it up and listened. He grunted a retort a couple of times and then put down the phone. He sat in silence for a moment and then looked up as the lights dimmed and then came back to full power.

'Well, Colonel Gunn, or whoever you are, so you told me a pack of lies did you. I think it's time we found out how much you and Miss Gbedemah know. The boy will make a very useful tool to speed up the process of gathering that information.' He looked at his watch; 7.28. He pressed out the number for the reception telephone, but no one answered it. That was strange; the first forebodings that their smooth and seemingly unstoppable operation was unravelling urged the doctor to his feet and out into the reception area which was quiet. The lights dimmed once again... for longer and then came back up.

Twum-Danso walked across to Dina's room and tried the door; locked. The Colonel's door was also locked. He went back into this apartment, collected his own set of keys and went back to Dina's door. The lights almost went out before regaining their normal brightness and he heard voices coming up the steps from the loading area. He unlocked the door and went in. Worst fears realised; both guards lying on the floor with their throats cut. Back out into the corridor to meet his senior foreman from the loading area and two of his lab technicians who greeted him with a babble of hysterical questions.

'Quiet!' the doctor shouted and then in a calm voice, 'follow me.' He led the way to the lift and pressed the button. It seemed like an age, but the lift doors eventually opened and they all climbed in and Twum-Danso pressed the button for the generating level. The lift descended rapidly and then stopped with a violent jolt. The doctor pressed the over-ride button, but nothing happened at first and then the lights dimmed and went out. Pitch blackness for thirty seconds and then the dim emergency, battery-powered lighting came on. The mains had failed and that meant that the doctor and his three companions were stuck in the lift until someone went down the emergency exit staircase to the generating level and started up the diesel generators. Well, they all knew the emergency procedure so it was just a matter of waiting until power was restored, the doctor thought as he tried to dismiss horrific thoughts, which invaded his imagination.

These nightmarish thoughts were translated into reality as Twum-Danso suddenly realised that all of them were standing in about half an inch of water. The lift shaft was filling with water. That meant that the entire generating level was flooded; there would be no return of power. The doctor reached up and pushed open the escape panel in the top of the lift.

'Come on you three, lift me up,' which they did without any further encouragement having now seen the rising water in the lift. Twum-Danso climbed out onto the top of the lift and then reached down and helped to pull up the other three men. Once they were all on the top of the lift, the doctor led the way by stepping onto the steel rungs embedded in the rock-shaft and started to climb up. By the time the last of the four men had started to climb, the water was over the top of the lift and blind panic urged them up the hundred foot climb to the accommodation level.

Gasping and trembling with fatigue, Twum-Danso reached the door at the top and forced back the locking mechanism to open it. One by one, they all stepped out into the reception area where they paused to regain their breath. The doctor was the first to collect his thoughts. He spoke to his foreman.

'Kwame, get all the men together; hunting weapons and body paint. Take the two machine pistols as well. Go and find the man, woman and boy. They must not get away. Understood?'

'Yes, Sir.'

'Go, then; you two,' and he turned to his two lab technicians, 'find the portable generating sets and get some lighting fixed up.' The two men followed the foreman down the steps from the reception area. Doctor Twum-Danso returned to his apartment, which was dimly lit by the emergency lighting.

'Damn! damn! damn!' he shouted at the dimly lit walls. 'Damn you, Caramansa; why couldn't you be content with being a millionaire. If we don't find those three people, we're all dead.

238

John Mackenzie had no idea how long he'd been walking or where he'd been since leaving Angus Campbell's surgery. He had walked south from the city centre towards the river. A walk which he and many inhabitants of the city frequently did as the Saskatchewan River valley was the city's most outstanding natural feature. Apart from all the bridges which crossed the river, both banks had been developed on either side of the terraced Convention Centre with high-rise apartments and the much-sought-after city residential areas which then gave way to golf courses and woodland trails, through which John had walked when he was at university.

His mind had been in a turmoil of emotions since Angus had delivered the numbing news that someone else was the father of his child. For the hundredth time since he'd left the surgery he asked himself the question...who? It was a silly question because Mary had obviously been very discreet and he'd been unaware of any affair. After initial emotions of anger, betrayal and humiliation, he had started to rationalise his thoughts. He was certain about one thing; he loved his wife and son more than anything else. Did Mary love him? Well, if she didn't, she was a real good actress because she gave a damn good performance of love and loyalty to her husband.

With only a fraction of his attention, John noticed that he had turned east along the north bank of the river and was following the road through the high-rise residential area. As soon as he and Mary had been told what had happened to little Ian, Mary's parents had come to stay with them to give support and he had only gone into the office that morning, via his parents, to do something other than sit around the house waiting to hear what the ransom demand and its conditions would be. Now, yet another bombshell for him to cope with; to confront Mary now with the knowledge he possessed would turn a near disaster into a total disaster from which their marriage was unlikely to emerge intact.

Let's face it, John thought, if he'd discovered his inability to have children earlier in their marriage, he and Mary would have discussed all possibilities as they did with any problem and this would have covered adoption or some form of intra-uterine fertilisation. So what had Mary done? After nearly five years without producing a child, she must have gone to a doctor and found that she was perfectly capable of producing a child. That, of course, cast doubt on his ability to father one, but she would have had to be certain. After making love, she must have managed to retrieve a sample of his semen, which had proved that he was sterile. In her highly practical way, Mary had decided to deal with the solution to the problem herself and had found someone to father their child. Rational thoughts or wishful thinking? Perhaps a bit of both, but the promiscuous role was completely alien to Mary's character so there had to be some sense in his line of thinking.

The walk had done him a great deal of good and now that he'd cleared his mind, it seemed that all their problems could be solved if only the wretched kidnappers would get in touch and they could get the whole business finished. John waved at a taxi cruising through the high-rise residential area with its 'free' light illuminated and asked to be taken back to his office on Rupert Street. Once there he went up to his office and collected his briefcase; Merilee met him and said that Doctor Campbell had phoned twice, asking for him. John told her that he'd call the doctor from his home, left the office and picked up his car. He turned right on the one-way system and pushed one of his tapes into the cassette player. Yes, he thought, Mary and he would beat this crisis together.

*

'Emma darling, could you answer the phone; I'm washing my hair,' Penny Briars called to her daughter as she wrapped a towel around her head in turban style.

'Alright Mum, I'll get it,' came from her son Richard who went into their living room and picked up the phone which was a party line shared by the four BMAT houses. 'Hello!'

'May I speak to Colonel Briars please; I'm phoning from London.'

'My Dad's away playing golf. Will Mum do?'

'Yes, your Mum will do fine; its Christine Dupré speaking.

'Hang on a sec then and I'll go and get her,' and Richard met his mother in the doorway. 'It's a woman from London who wants to speak to Dad, but says that you'll do,' he announced, disappearing back to his room and the brain-numbing sound of 'Coolplay' in quadrophonic reproduction.

'Hello, Penny Briars here.'

'Mrs Briars, it's Christine Dupré; I work with John Gunn. Does that make sense to you?'

'Oh yes, yes it does; what can I do to help? I'm so sorry, but John - my husband - is playing golf, but should be back in about an hour.....that's if he doesn't get caught at the 19th hole.'

'No, Mrs Briars...'

'Penny, please.'

'No, Penny; I just need some information and I'm sure that you'll be able to do that.'

240

'I'll try,' Penny answered praying that'd she'd be efficient as she grabbed a pencil and pulled the telephone scribble pad towards her.

'Do you know where John... that's John Gunn...is, as we are unable to raise his colleague in Accra to get that information?'

'Last night, John went to Shai Hills with Richard Outram...Richard's another officer with BMAT. They had planned to stay......oh crumbs!' Penny suddenly said in horror, 'I've no way of knowing if you are who you say you are.'

'No, Penny, that's right and I can't prove that to you with some ludicrous code-word or by telling you that I know he has a mole on his right buttock, as they do in the best spy films! We haven't heard from John or his colleague for nearly 24 hours. We have some information for him, but more important than that we are concerned about his condition. He was quite badly injured about a week before he went to Accra.'

'Then why on earth was he sent here? He's never stopped since he arrived and I know that last night he climbed to the top of a rock escarpment which is at least 200 feet high. I've heard from my husband that John Gunn shot two men this morning, then jumped off the escarpment on the end of a rope - I can't remember what that's called - threw the bodies in a car and disappeared. We haven't seen him since, but know that he went to search for the McLean's boy.'

'When was all this?'

'John Gunn left the Shai Hills reserve at about six thirty this morning.'

'So nothing's been heard for about 12 hours.'

'Not by any of us, Christine.'

'Thanks; perhaps I might ask one more favour of you which I would normally get our contact in Accra to arrange.'

'Yes, of course,' Penny agreed, cursing soundlessly as the point of the pencil broke because she'd been scribbling patterns so furiously on the telephone notepad.

'Let's see; we're now an hour ahead of you as we've changed to summer time. I'll catch the BA flight tonight from Gatwick which gets in at about 6.30 your time in Accra. Can you book me a room in a hotel - preferably the same one John Gunn's in - please.'

'Why don't you stay with us. I'll meet you at the airport with my John tomorrow morning; you can't miss us - he's large, round and bald and I've got red hair. We all know our way around this part of Ghana and it would mean you could use our cars and Landrover without anyone taking the slightest bit of interest.'

'I ought to go to a hotel, because it's unfair to involve you in this sort of thing.'

'Nonsense; we're all involved already. I'll meet you tomorrow at Kotoko Airport and you'll stay with us. If we've heard anything by then I can tell you over a decent breakfast in our house after you've had a bath and unpacked.'

'That's kind and very convenient; I accept gratefully.'

'Excellent; see you tomorrow, bye.'

'Bye, Penny,' and Christine put down the phone.

'You'd better go and pack. I'll fix the chopper to take you to Gatwick,' Mike Parker offered.

'Thanks, that'd be a great help. What the hell can have happened to both Dina and John?'

'I've no doubt that you'll get that answer in Ghana. Go on, off you go and pack and then come back straight to the helipad at the top. Everything'll be fixed by then.'

*

The TV licence detector van turned off the A329 in Moulsford through the weathered brick-pillared entrance of the Elizabethan house. The house stood well back from the road and with grounds surrounding it which reached as far as the banks of the River Thames to the east of it. It was five minutes to ten and an ideal time for the visit of such a van because of the popularity of the BBC's ten o'clock news. The occupants of the van weren't in the slightest bit interested in TV licences or the nine o'clock news. As the passenger in the front seat got out of the vehicle, the rear door opened and four men and a woman made their way quickly and silently round to the side and back of the house to seal off any exits prior to making a forced entry. Lights showed from five windows and the fluorescent glow of a TV screen was visible in one ground floor room. The uniformed TV licence inspector went up to the front door and rang the bell. The door was opened by a middle-aged lady who was pulling on a cardigan against the chill of the April night.

'Good evening madam, are you the owner of this house.'

'Oh no; I'm the housekeeper and my husband's the gardener. Mr Winfield owns this house, but he and his wife aren't here.'

'I'm a TV licence inspector Mrs.....'

'Edmonds.'

'Mrs Edmonds; I've an instruction here which directs me to inspect your house and requires you to produce your TV licence. Here is my identification and you will see that there is a phone number on it which you are encouraged to ring if you are concerned about the authenticity of the order.'

'Oh gracious no, Sir; this house is watched by the police because Mr Winfield's a very important man. He's an Ambassador.'

'Thank you Mrs Edmonds, but even Ambassadors have been known not to pay for a TV licence.'

'I'll have you know, young man, that he'll hear of that remark when he returns,' the affronted Mrs Edmonds threatened.

'You do that Mrs Edmonds, but perhaps you could just get your licence for me,' the unperturbed inspector replied.

'I'll do that, but don't you come in off that front step, young man,' and Mrs Edmonds disappeared in the direction of the room from which the inspector could hear the voice of the presenter of the ten o'clock news. As soon as she'd gone, he looked at his watch; six and a half minutes. His colleagues had said they needed ten minutes to do the search. Take your time Mrs Edmonds, he muttered to himself. Eight minutes and he could hear her voice raised above the newscaster asking her husband where he'd put the licence. It seemed it had been put in the drawer of the table on which the TV stood. Reappearance of Mrs Edmonds; nine and a half minutes.

'There you are young man and it's valid for another six months.'

'Thank you Mrs Edmonds; would you allow me to come in to the light so that I can write in my book. That will ensure that you don't get troubled again.'

'Come in then if you must.' The inspector walked in and while he wrote in a small notebook, the pager at his waist bleeped.

'What's that noise mean?' the housekeeper asked.

'I'm wanted on the mobile phone in the van, Mrs Edmonds. When will Mr and Mrs Winfield be back?'

'Back? Lord knows young man. He's the Ambassador in Accra....that's in Ghana.'

'You mean he's gone back there tonight?'

'Where else would he go; caught the plane from Gatwick this evening,' and she looked at her watch through screwed up eyes. 'Took off three minutes ago.'

'Both he and Mrs Winfield?'

'Yes of course; and the little boy they've just adopted.'

'Thank you Mrs Edmonds, you've been most helpful,' and the inspector returned to the van, climbed in and slammed the door. 'They've got the boy and the flight's taken off for Ghana.'

'Don't know about the flight, Dave, but we found a fully equipped little boy's room which seemed odd for a couple with no children,' the girl from BID's counter-espionage department commented.

243

'It all fits,' Dave muttered while he dialled up the number on his mobile phone. He explained what had happened to his assistant director at Kingsroad House after which he listened making no comment until he broke the connection.

'What was all that about?' the girl asked.

'I have to hand it to those cowboys; they've already got an agent on the same plane as Winfield. How the hell did they know he'd be on that flight with the boy?'

'Does it matter,' the girl replied. 'I'm looking forward to an early night tonight,' as the driver turned onto the M40 and headed back to London.

*

After a delay of only twenty minutes, the huge convoy of arms from IMT was on its way again, but instead of heading south on Highway 287 to Amarillo, it turned east onto Highway 54 to Gruver Airfield led by the Armoured Recconnaissance Company Commander in the lead police car. As the convoy pulled onto the large concrete aircraft dispersal area, it was confronted with thirteen lanes marked out with traffic cones into which each country convoy was directed. As soon as each convoy had stopped, cranes removed the containers from the flatbeds and the tractors drove them away to a designated parking area.

At this stage of the operation, a swarm of fork-lift trucks then moved up to the containers and removed the entire arms shipment which was cross-loaded into other containers. Once each container was empty, it was refilled with crates from another part of the airfield, which contained compacted scrap cars from dealers in Amarillo, Lubbock, Abilene and San Angelo. The operation had been controlled throughout by the commanding officer of the 82nd Airmobile Logistic Battalion of the US Rapid Reaction Force. He had hired the heavy lift equipment from construction companies in the same towns from which the scrap had been gathered to fill the containers. Two and a half hours after arriving at Gruver Airfield, the convoy was once again back on the road and this time it did turn south onto Highway 287 to Amarillo on its way to load onto the Texas Star in Galveston.

While his battalion had swapped the contents of the containers, the commanding officer had gathered all the truck drivers and had briefed them on their task. All would receive full payment for delivery of their containers, but each tractor would have a co-driver/minder from the battalion just in case any of the tractor drivers should be tempted to augment their pay packets by offering information about the cargo switch. None of the tractor drivers had ever heard of Caramansa; they had been contracted by IMT to deliver a cargo to Galveston and the terms had been the going rate for the job. Provided that they were still going to be paid, they showed no concern that they had become part of some military/police operation.

By alternating drivers and cutting refuelling and refreshment halts to a minimum, the convoy had covered 400 miles by midnight on 15th April; it was twenty miles south of Fort Worth and only one hour behind the original schedule planned for the convoy. By 10.45 on the morning of Saturday 16 April, the first truck of the convoy drove through the dock gates at Galveston with its local police department escort, which guided it to the Texas Star in berth 12 on the southern extremity of the container port. The driver of the lead tractor stopped his vehicle under the container-lift gantry alongside the ship at 10.55 - five minutes ahead of schedule.

At 22.30 on the same day, the code flag 'P' was hoisted on the signal halyard and at 15 minutes before midnight three short blasts on the ship's foghorn preceded the Texas Star's departure astern from berth 12 in Galveston's container port.

*

Dickie Shepherd, the Captain of the British Airways Boeing 747, G-950D, Flight 079 from Gatwick to Accra via Abidjan in Côte d'Ivoire, took the fax from his engineer officer and read it while he sipped his coffee.

'I wonder what all this is about, Ted? You've read it?'

'Yes sir; it's from our Security Branch and says that the information comes from the Home Office - that's usually a euphemism for the police or MI5 or whatever it's called these days......the James Bond bunch.'

'Yes I'd got all that, Ted,' and then Dickie Shepherd read it allowed; 'Personal for Captain Richard Shepherd from Director of British Airways Security Branch. Once you have read this message, please pass it to Mrs Rachel Davies, Club World passenger in seat 11B. Message reads: Mr and Mrs Winfield are in First Class seats 2A and B and Ian Mackenzie is in seat 2E. Please be aware of this, but take no, repeat no, action. Malcolm, you have control.'

'Roger Sir; I have control,' the First officer replied.

'Ted, it's time I did my PR bit with the passengers. I'll take this note with me and have a look at Mr and Mrs Winfield.....of course! how bloody stupid of me. He's the ruddy High Commissioner......pompous ass.. I'm expected to genuflect in front of him anyway. I'll then go and give this Rachel Davies the once-over as well.'

'Right Sir.'

Dickie Shepherd unbuckled his harness and climbed back out of the front left seat of the flight deck. He put on his jacket and hat and then went back through the door and down to the First Class section of the 747. He spotted the Winfields immediately and feigned instant recognition, which obviously boosted their egos enormously.

'Evening High Commissioner.....Mrs Winfield; pleasure as always to have you aboard our flight,' Dickie Shepherd said obsequiously and then to himself, 'Jesus, the things I do to preserve my salary!' and then bending down beside Ian Mackenzie said, 'and who are you young man?' Before the child was able to answer, Mrs Winfield interrupted.

'This is Ian for whom we're acting as guardians on the flight to Accra where he will be met by his parents.' The small and very tired boy was surrounded with toys and was trying to cope with the silver service trappings of the First Class dinner, presumably because his guardians were unfamiliar with the system of ordering children's meals in advance.

'Would you like something else?' Dickie asked him. The little head nodded. Dickie looked up and caught the eye of the senior stewardess. 'Susie, take all this away and see if there's something else for this fellow,' he said quietly so that it was not heard by Mrs Winfield.'

'Yes of course Sir; no problem. One of the unaccompanied children has just refused its child's meal so I'll have a go with that.'

'Thanks; please enjoy your dinner High Commissioner,' and Dickie Shepherd moved on smiling and chatting with his First Class passengers who represented the jam on the bread and butter of maintaining a profitable cash flow for the airline. He pulled back the curtains and went into the Club World section, glancing to his right to identify the woman in seat 11B. If he hadn't known that the film star had died two years previously, he would have sworn that he was looking at something like a forty-year-old Audrey Hepburn. 'Mrs Davies?' The large eyes looked up from the Langoustines Provençales, which had just been served with a dry white Côte du Rhone wine.

'Yes, I'm Rachel Davies, Captain,' and Dickie Shepherd had seen the alert eyes note the four stripes on his sleeve before answering.

'I've a message for you,' and he handed over the fax, which he'd removed from his jacket pocket. 'If there's anything that you need to do... like answer this, then please let the stewardess know and she'll bring you to the flight deck.' Mrs Davies' eyes had glanced at the fax and assimilated it instantly.

'Just one favour, Captain.....'

'Richard Shepherd,' he answered holding out his hand, which was taken and shaken in a surprisingly firm grasp.

'Captain Shepherd; may I use the toilet in the First Class section please?'

'Of course; I'll speak to the stewardesses,' and he returned to the First Class section. Once he'd gone, Christine Dupré, alias Rachel Davies, removed her tray into the empty seat beside her, folded the table into the armrest and then got out of the seat and went forward into the First Class section. None of the stewardesses took any notice as she went forward to the port side toilet without glancing at any of the other passengers. When she came out three minutes later she identified the Winfields and the little boy as she returned to her seat in Club World section.

CHAPTER 16

'How's that bit of stitching I did on you, John?' Dina asked as the three of them sat on the bolder-strewn sand beside the pool into which they'd been spewed by the subterranean river.

'Feels fine, thanks. How're you, Graham? Ready to move on?'

'Yes thanks; I'm OK. Why did you need stitches,' the boy asked.

'Someone took a pot shot at me about a week ago and the hole hasn't healed up yet.'

'Have you still got the bullet in you,' was asked with a boy's blood-thirsty desire for gory details.

'No, it went right through.'

'Wow! Did it hurt?'

'I think it did...a bit. Now, unless I'm much mistaken, the Doctor will have a hunting party out searching for us. It's now over two hours since we left him and an hour since that turbine must have blown up, cutting off the power supply to his distribution centre. It looks as though it's all downhill to Zebila and as that jungle looks pretty impenetrable my instinct would be to try the river. Unfortunately, that's exactly what the Doctor's men will expect us to do - whether they know we've gone down the river tunnel or found some other way out, they will expect us to go down. Does that make sense Dina?'

'That's what I intended to do. What are you suggesting?

'That we go back up.'

'What! Not through those dreadful tunnels.'

'No way, but the Doctor's men must know this area well and will find us in no time. If we go back up it has two advantages; firstly, they won't expect it and secondly, there must be some sort of transport up there - even if they've disposed of your Nissan and Kisi's VW, they must have some transport of their own up here.'

'Well.....'

'Shhhhh......' came from Graham. They had been talking in a loud whisper, but had not heard what he had. 'I'm sure I saw a light and heard voices over there,' and he pointed to the other side of the pool. Gunn eased back into the water motioning the other two to follow him. He lowered himself down in the water amongst the rocks around the edge of the pool with his head just above the surface.

Dina and Graham did the same, the former wiping the sand clear of their prints as she slid back into the water. Less than a minute later, the first of a group of almost naked, painted hunters appeared silently out of the jungle on the other side of the pool. Seven of them gathered by the pool and spoke softly to each other.

To Gunn's amazement, one of them cupped some water in his hands, tasted it, spat it out and pointed with his spear downstream. Surely thay weren't capable of tasting their presence in the water, Gunn reasoned, but he'd removed the Tanarmi from its holster in case the search party came in their direction. The men disappeared back into the jungle, heading downstream; that meant that they now had the doctor's men between them and Zebila - and for all they knew, on the other side of the river and between them and the Doctor's subterranean headquarters.

'I think you're right,' Dina mouthed close to Gunn's ear. 'It's up, not down.' Gunn held up his fingers to his lips. He had sensed rather than seen the man standing on their side of the pool. He stood still as a statue and if it hadn't been for the white paint on his body which showed up clearly in the moonlight, Gunn would have got out of the pool and walked straight into him. Silently as shadows, four other men joined him, one of whom urinated into the pool.

'Yuck!' came very quietly from Graham beside Gunn. The four other men urinated in the pool and then drifted off silently downhill on the right bank of the river. Gunn eased himself slowly out of the water and waited, crouched amongst the rocks. He beckoned to Dina who followed and then Graham and quietly led them to the point in the jungle from where he'd seen the four men appear to join the first one. It was a jungle track of sorts which went up the side of the rock face out of which their river spouted in a waterfall.

The three of them stumbled up the track pausing every few yards to listen. All Gunn could hear was their own laboured breathing in the thick, humid air and the inevitable squeaks, shrieks, rattles and scuffles that are the constant background noise during nightfall in a jungle. Gunn looked at his watch during one of these pauses; three minutes after midnight. There would only be four and half more hours of full darkness.

It was one of these pauses which saved them all. They had stopped for what seemed like the hundredth time when Gunn distinctly picked up the smell of tobacco. It was gone in an instant. He motioned the others back into the dense foliage on either side of the track and put his mouth next to Dina's ear. 'Knife,' he breathed and he felt the knife placed in his hand; Dina had obviously been holding it ready for any eventuality. He placed the automatic in his

249

belt and started to move forward step by step, never allowing his weight to come on the leading foot until he was certain that there were no branches to break or twigs to snap. The tobacco again, and this time he saw the smoke in the moonlight. It was blowing towards him down the path.

Gunn was downwind of the smoker and had the moon behind him. He spotted the glowing tip of the cigarette first and then identified the shape of the man. This one was fully clothed and stood in a small clearing in the jungle. One of the Scorpion machine pistols was slung over his shoulder. Gunn slowly pushed himself back into the foliage on the right side of the track. He turned his watch on its stainless steel bracelet to the inside of his wrist to hide the luminous glow from the face. The track up the hill had been littered with rocks and stones which had made it so difficult to move quietly; now, these were exactly what Gunn wanted. The man had his back to Gunn and threw down the butt of his cigarette which he ground out with his booted foot.

Gunn bent down, selected two stones and slowly straightened up. The man stood with legs apart and hands on hips, evidently very disgruntled with his task as a long-stop should they do exactly what they had done. This made Gunn remind himself not to underrate the Doctor and his men as this was a professionally organised search. The first stone hit the man in the middle of his back and the second stone rattled down the track to Gunn's left. The man spun round and dropped the machine pistol, the packet of cigarettes and his lighter which rang like a bell as it hit a stone on the track. He retrieved his machine pistol and cocked it. The organisation of the search had the stamp of professionalism, but not this searcher who'd been standing on guard with an uncocked weapon.

He came towards Gunn, tripping and stumbling over the uneven surface of the track. On the edge of the small clearing he stopped, afraid and unsure about going into the darkness of the track. Both men stood still. Gunn could smell the sweat and body odour of the man, but the latter would still be incapable of smelling anything else other than the nicotine of his own cigarette. The dark of the track was too much for him and the man turned to go back into the clearing. It was most unlikely that he ever felt the knife as it plunged into the back of his neck. His knees buckled and without a sound, Gunn lowered him to the ground. He withdrew the knife and wiped it on the man's clothes, listening all the time to see if there was a companion. Gunn dragged the dead man into the undergrowth and returned slowly back along the track. He would never have seen Dina if she hadn't put out her hand and stopped him.

Dina and Graham came out onto the track and the three of them crossed the small clearing and continued up the steep track. They had gone about another fifty yards when Gunn realised that the track had stopped. It had been very indistinct since they first started up it, but now there was nothing. Gunn looked at his watch; 12.45. He took a cautious step forward and disappeared up to his arm pits in a hole with all the attendant noise of a baby elephant falling into the proverbial trap.

'Shit!' seemed an appropriate epithet, if only whispered while Dina did her best to stop laughing and she and Graham helped to pull Gunn out of his hole. When he was sitting on the edge of it and had confirmed that nothing was broken, he examined the hole; it was but one of what must have been hundreds of entrances to the labrynth of tunnels and caves. Gunn climbed out, whispered to Dina and Graham to stay where they were and went back down the track to the clearing. It took him no time to find the packet of cigarettes and the lighter was right beside it. He put the lighter in his pocket and rejoined the other two. His logic seemed reasonable to Gunn; if the Doctor's men had come out of this hole then it must lead back into the distribution centre.

Gunn lowered himself down the hole and once inside, thumbed the catch on the small disposable gas lighter. Under his feet was a reasonably gradual slope inside a wide tunnel which levelled off some twenty feet further down. There were many footprints in the soil around his feet. Gunn stuck his head above ground and beckoned again to the other two. Holding the lighter above his head he led them down to the bottom of the slope where they were all able to stand up. The little lighter was getting red hot. Gunn let go of the catch and shook his hand and then realised that he could see the other two without the aid of the lighter. Light was filtering along the tunnel which meant that they were close to the distribution centre and that the Doctor had some reserve source of generating power.

Gunn put the lighter in his pocket and removed the Tanarmi automatic from his webbing belt. Once again, the three of them made their way slowly forward towards the light. After twenty yards the floor of the tunnel became a concrete path and after a further twenty yards Gunn could both hear and identify what he had called the loading area. The loading area was lit, not by electricity, but by high-pressure paraffin lamps. There was the unmistakable noise of a small generator running somewhere, but the loading area was deserted. Gunn motioned to Dina and Graham to stay where they were and then moved out into the loading area towards the rubber doors through which they had seen the trolleys loaded with raw opium being pushed.

He reached the doors and pushed through them. Outside was an area of about 100 yards by 70 yards which was lit by a lighting set strung out from a small Yamaha portable generator. On the left side of the area, closest to the rock, were parked four Mercedes panel vans. On the right side of the area, on a raised portion of hard-standing was parked a helicopter with a man in black overalls refuelling it and another removing what looked like a stretcher from inside it.

Gunn cursed quietly and vowed that he'd get himself trained as a rotary wing pilot on return to England. Fixed wing was no problem, but he'd never gone on to rotary. If he'd been on his own he'd have taken the risk as he'd sat beside countless pilots during his military service when he was a Forward Observer with his artillery regiments. Many of them had allowed him to take the controls and he was familiar with the feel of the cyclic and collective sticks and the starting procedure for the turbines, but he couldn't risk Dina's life and certainly not young Graham's. No, regrettably, it would have to be the Mercedes.

Gunn pushed back the rubber doors and returned to the loading area. Still not a sign of anyone. He walked across to the tunnel entrance and found Dina and Graham five yards inside the tunnel in the deep shadow.

'Any success?' Dina whispered.

'Yes; we're OK for transport. There're four Mercedes trucks out there. There's also a helicopter which has just been refuelled, but I'm not qualified to fly one so we'll......'

'I am,' Dina said.

'Well, I'm buggered. You're an ace; come on, you'd better take a look and see if you can manage it.'

'Of course I can manage it; I've been flying the things for over six years. Lead me to it John and let's get the hell out of this place.'

'Great! Are we going in a chopper?'

'Looks like it, Graham; do you trust lady pilots?'

'No, not really, but I think Dina's alright.'

'Thanks for that enthusiastic vote of confidence. What are we waiting for?'

'Nothing; follow me,' and Gunn led the way back across the loading area to the rubber doors. He peered round the doors; not a soul in sight; no one by the helicopter and no one anywhere else.

'That's a German MBB 105. I've never flown one, but it's most unlikely to differ from any other twin turbine chopper. Let me go ahead of you two and have a couple of minutes on my own. Is that possible?'

'Why not? I'll cover you. Signal when you're ready. I'll come and sit on your right and try to be useful. Graham, you dive straight into the back and strap in. Got that?'

'Sure; my friends at school will never believe all this when I tell them. Did you kill that man back in the jungle?'

'Yes I did.'

'Cool!' from the young boy said it all.

'Right Dina, off you go,' and she ran bare-footed to the starboard door of the helicopter, opened it, got in and shut it behind her. With the door shut and the reflection of the lights on the perspex dome of the cockpit, it was almost impossible to see Dina inside the helicopter. And then their luck ran out. From somewhere beyond the four Mercedes trucks, the two men who had been working on the helicopter reappeared and headed towards it. They were twenty yards from Gunn and the young boy. Gunn raised the Tanarmi at the full extent of both arms and fired twice. Gunn and Graham were running for the chopper before the two men hit the ground. The boy remembered his instructions and went for the near side, rear door while Gunn ran round the chopper to the starboard cockpit door. The rotor blades started to turn as they both got in.

'This machine has only been shut down for about twenty minutes; turbines are still warm. Have you airborne in a sec,' Dina said without taking her eyes off the instruments as her hands darted over the switches. Gunn kept his door open and waited to see what would happen. The rotor blades had reached 50% of power and revolutions and the needles on the instruments had moved from the red to yellow sectors of the dials.

Twum-Danso appeared from behind the Mercedes trucks with a puzzled expression on his face, which rapidly changed to one of desperation as he spotted the two men whom Gunn had shot. Gunn fired and the bullet ricocheted off the bodywork of the truck beside which the Doctor was standing. Dina had the cyclic stick in her right hand and the collective stick in her left; her eyes never left the instruments. The needle showing turbine combustion chamber power was nearly into the green sector and the Mescherschmitt helicopter swayed and vibrated on its metal skids. Twum-Danso rushed from behind the furthest truck and scrambled into the driving cab. Gunn's shot whined harmlessly off the bodywork again.

It wasn't difficult to see what the Doctor intended to do. There was only a slight rise in the hard-standing where the truck was parked, up to the helipad. A burst of black diesel smoke appeared at

253

the rear of the truck. Gunn swung his automatic onto the driver's position in the truck, but Twum- Danso was obviously crouched below the dashboard, because nothing was visible above the top of it. Gunn fired and the windscreen crazed over into an opaque blind as the panel truck swung clear of the other three and accelerated towards the helicopter. Gunn glanced across at Dina and then down at the instruments....85% power...and now the front of the Mercedes was filling their entire view in front of the helicopter.

Dina raised the collective stick, which tilted the aerofoil rotors and at the same time eased the cyclic stick to the right and pushed down on the right rudder pedal. The swish of the flattened blades rotating above them altered to a throbbing beat as the aerofoils bit into the air. The helicopter lifted clear of the pad and side-slipped quickly across it's surface out over the precipitous side of the hill and the thick jungle canopy below. Twum-Danso had aimed the truck from his position of cover below the dashboard and in that position was unable to make either quick corrections to the truck's direction or to operate the brake pedal effectively.

The Mercedes hurtled past the helicopter, burst through the crash barrier on the side of the helipad and somersaulted out into space over the side of the rock face before being enveloped by the jungle canopy. Gunn saw a crimson ball of fire rise out of the darkness below the helicopter as the fuel ignited and then nothing more.

Dina swung the helicopter round to the south side of the hill and then pushed the cyclic stick forward, dipping the machine's nose as she increased its airspeed, westward, back to Accra.

*

John and Penny Briars stood on the concrete apron in front of the terminal at Kotoko airport waiting to catch the first glimpse of the British Airways 747 as it approached Runway 175 from the north. All aircraft came in north to south as there was a permanent on-shore wind the year round. John Briars had used both his Diplomatic Corps pass and his uniform to take Penny airside to meet the BA flight from London. Whilst multi-party democracy had come to Ghana without bloodshed, that democracy was permitted to exist by the power of the armed forces and of those armed forces, the power rested with the army. An army officer's uniform was the best pass in Accra.

John's sharp eyesight picked up the 747 first and he raised the small radio to his mouth and spoke into it. 'B-MAT 1, this is B-MAT 2, British Airways flight two minutes ahead of schedule. We should be with you for breakfast in about half an hour, over.'

'B-MAT 1, roger out.' John Briars made a half-hearted pass at a small lizard, which skittered off across the concrete, which was already beginning to absorb the heat of another roasting day at the end of Ghana's dry season. The rains would start in May or June and then the red laterite would turn to a quagmire.

'D'you think she'll look like a Mata Hari, with biceps like a Sumo wrestler and a....'

'Shhh.....control your sexual fantasies. I bet she's wearing specs and looks like Popeye's Olive Oil.'

'Dear God, I hope not. No, I've more faith in John than that. I think she's going to be really sexy, just like Pussy Galore in Goldfinger.'

'Really John,' and Penny was having to shout now as the 747 was turning towards the apron, 'in matters of sex you really have never matured.'

'That's not what you said last......' and the handbag caught him across his large backside with a hefty thwack. The engine noise died and conversation was possible again.

'Bet you 10,000 cedis I can spot her before you.'

'Rubbish!'

'Bet you.'

'Oh alright; 10,000 cedis it is.' The two sets of steps had been positioned in front of the opened doors and the first passengers were emerging from the First and Club World sections. 'Oh Jesus, it's HC and Lady Muck; I'd better chuck up a salute, bow or, far better, wave two fingers.......'

'Shhh John; they'll hear you. What's that little boy doing with them?'

'Dunno....probably belongs to somebody else.'

'Then why's Davina holding his hand?'

'Odd, I agree........morning Sir....Davina. Have a good flight?'

'Yes thank you, John, but you didn't have to go to the trouble of meeting us. Is our car here?' Humphrey Winfield asked.

'No idea Sir; we've come to meet one of Penny's family. You appear to have acquired an admirer from the flight,' and John indicated the small boy.

'Yes...er...he's our new adopted son. Come on my dear; there seems to be no one here to meet us.' Penny and John looked after them in stunned amazement.

'Did I hear right?'

'You did, but you'll lose your bet if you don't watch the rest of the passengers.'

'Look at that; now that's what I call class.' Christine Dupré had just emerged from the front door of the aircraft. She watched the Winfields disappear into the passenger terminal with Ian Mackenzie. She had already spotted Penny and John and now descended the steps, looking as immaculate as John Briars had described, dressed in skirt and blouse and large dark glasses.

'Is that your choice?'

'Nooo.....sadly; have to be another.'

'Right, I'll plump for her then,' and at that moment Christine looked straight at them and waved.

'10,000 cedis please.'

'Paid, with pleasure...this I'm going to enjoy. I think I'm in love already.'

'Oh shut up; you wouldn't know how to spell that word. Now promise you'll behave.'

'Promise....scout's honour.'

'Hello Christine! I'm Penny and this is my husband John.'

'Hello and thanks so much for meeting me.....thank you..John,' as he took her hand baggage.'

'We've just been stunned by seeing Humphrey and Davina Winfield with a little boy they say they've adopted. I....'

'No Penny....sorry, can we keep moving quite quickly as I must try and keep the Winfields in sight.'

'Sure thing,' and John Briars led the way to the front of the immigration queue. They'll have gone through the VIP lounge, but we'll catch up outside the terminal. What's up?' As the Ghanaian immigration official languidly started thumbing through Christine's passport while John Briars steamed with suppressed frustration.

'That little boy with them is Ian Mackenzie; the son of the Mackenzies in Canada......'

'Jesus Christ on a bicycle!... what the hell are the bloody Winfields up to?'

'Shhh John,' Penny cautioned as the three of them went through to the baggage claim area where the carousel had just started to clatter into action bringing in the aircraft's hold baggage. While they waited, Christine went on to explain the recent developments.

'You both knew of the double kidnap.'

'Yes,' John and Penny said together.

'Very quickly then; Davina Winfield is unable to have children. She also spent two years in a private asylum hospital after a very serious nervous breakdown. This debarred the couple from adoption. In Canada, he had an affair with Mary Mackenzie and made her pregnant. Ian Mackenzie is the child from that pregnancy.'

'But why....'

'Hush dear, let Christine finish.'

'Right... oh! That's mine, John.'

'The Louis Vuiton one?'

'Yes...thanks,' as John lifted the case off the carousel onto a trolley and led the way through Customs. He produced his Ghana Armed Forces ID card and the three of them walked past the Customs official who had already spotted much richer pickings in the form of his returning fellow countrymen and women with bursting, string-tied brown parcels of goodies bought in England. Once outside the terminal, John discarded the trolley and carried the cases to the Military/Diplomatic car park where he and Penny had left their battered Nissan. Penny climbed into the back and John opened the door for Christine after putting her bags in the back. He climbed in beside her in the front. 'Go on Christine, this is the most amazing story I've heard for years.'

'I wish it was a story; the tragedy is that it's real life. We don't know exactly what arrangement was made; whether it started as some sort of surrogate birth which went wrong, or whatever, but we do know that Humphrey Winfield arranged the kidnapping of that little boy in return for tacit co-operation with this man Caramansa who wants to turn the whole of West Africa, by means of terrorism, into a Republic with himself as its leader.'

'He must be off his rocker.'

'You mean Winfield.'

'Yes...both of them.'

'Well, you're probably right. Inability to procreate has tipped the balance of sanity or rational behaviour many times before.'

'There they are!' came from Penny in the back as a dark blue Range Rover pulled out of the VIP car park, cut across the one way circuit and headed for the airport exit.

'I shall have to get in touch with London to confirm how they want this handled,' Christine voiced her thoughts aloud as John Briars raced after the Range Rover with engine screaming and gears grinding and crashing. 'Please don't alarm them John.'

'For heaven's sake, John! Try and be a little more subtle,' came from a very uncomfortable Penny who had been hurled around in the back of the Nissan as John weaved his way through the Accra traffic in a fair imitation of a stock car race.

The two cars parted company south of the Military Hospital roundabout as the Range Rover turned right towards the Residence. The Nissan continued on down to the coast road and at a little after 7.10 ground to a halt with squealing brakes in a cloud of red dust outside Miles Stockwell's bungalow in the BMAT compound. The Commander of BMAT was waiting for them, as was a wriggling and excited Shemma who rushed up to Christine and planted two red paw marks on her immaculate navy blue skirt.

*

Joanne crawled out from under her desk where she had dived for cover as the building shook from the sound-barrier over-pressure created by the F-22s. The plate glass of the windows had shattered and the false panelled ceiling which concealed all the electrical and fibre-optic cables and plumbing had collapsed in many places. There was dust, ceiling panels and broken glass everywhere. Two minutes before, Joanne's world was neat, ordered and very well paid; now it was a shambles. But there was worse to come. As she crawled out from her place of cover, she was confronted by a pair of boots; boots which led up to army disruptive pattern combat dress and a soldier with an M16 carbine held loosely across his chest.

Joanne kept telling herself this was all a dream. The company sold weapons to other countries; those weapons weren't meant to be used against them. However many times Joanne blinked her eyes, the soldier wouldn't disappear and what was worse, she realised that there were many more in the offices, pulling open drawers and removing files. Reality came with a rush as she saw a soldier wearing sergeant's stripes start to remove all the floppy disks. She staggered to her feet, shouting, 'no!' but was held firmly by the soldier standing beside her desk. What was worse still, the strong room was open, which contained all the records of every arms sale. Too late again; Joanne saw a trolley of files, floppy disks and microfiches appear from the strong room. The soldier in front of her spoke.

'Please pick up any personal belongings, lady, and go out of the door over there.' Joanne obeyed, collecting her bag and then left the office and went out into the reception area. A worse scene confronted her there. Not only the mess caused by the damage to the building, but there was her boss and her lover, Nat Cohn, handcuffed to the wrought iron work around the ornamental gazebo in the centre of the reception area. Scores of their employees were disgorging from the bank of six elevators which serviced all the underground levels. She was led by her escort soldier to the entrance where there was a long row of buses into which all the IMT employees were being led. Camera flash bulbs constantly flickered from every direction as photos were taken of every item and where it had been found before it was likewise taken out of the building to another line of panel trucks where it was all being placed into steel containers.

258

Joanne climbed into the third coach from the front, but not before she saw Bradley Tracton and Nat Cohn escorted into a police department car and driven out of the IMT compound.

'What'll you be doing with this place, Mr Barnes, once all my men have left?' the one star Brigadier General who had commanded the airborne cavalry assault on IMT asked Doyle Barnes.

'It'll continue much as before but under different management, General. The majority of the workforce weren't involved in the illegal deals, which Tracton set up. The documents will reveal, I've little doubt, who was being bribed on Capitol Hill and the distribution plan for this current shipment to West Africa. We'll pass all the distribution information to the governments of the thirteen countries involved and they'll be able to catch all the terrorists red-handed - so to speak. This factory provides skilled labour and housing for a number of wet-backs from across the border, but we'll turn a blind eye to that, regularise their immigration into the States and set them to work again. Tracton will have the best lawyers that money can buy, but they're not going to beat this rap. Tracton and Cohn will be lucky if they escape 'ole sparky' with their proven complicity in the murder of the bank guard in Ghana when the gold was removed.'

'Right then; that about wraps it up. Not one casualty - my medics are looking disappointed.'

'There was Tracton's bodyguard, General.'

'Yea, well I reckon the world's a better place without scumbags like that. I'll move this lot and my men out. A neat job, Barnes,' and the stocky, shaven-headed General strutted off to give the appropriate orders.

Doyle Barnes watched the retreating figure and shook his head slowly. Two professional killers; one a 'scumbag' and the other a soldier - just as he'd been a few years before. What a strange old world, Doyle mused, but nothing would get done if he allowed his thoughts to wander along that line of doubtful discrimination or self-justification. There was much to be done, not the least of which was the next stage of the operation. This would be the removal of Caramansa and his men and the closing down of the International Credit Bank; for that Doyle hoped to be able to get John Gunn's assistance, if for no other reason, it had been a long time since the two of them had drunk cold beers together and swapped lies.

*

John Mackenzie turned into his driveway and parked the Jaguar behind his father-in-law's Dodge station wagon. Mary was standing on the doorstep waiting for him.

'Your father's just called, John. Stuart McLean phoned him earlier from Accra to say that he'd picked up the cassette tape with the ransom instructions.' John went indoors out of the nippy April air followed by his wife. He took off his coat and went into the large sitting room on the right of the entrance hall. A fire was blazing in the wrought iron basket of the inglenook fireplace and the room felt rather over-heated after his invigorating walk by the river.

'Any news of Ian?'

'No, just instructions for us to have $100 million worth of gold bars ready to take to an RV somewhere in North America.'

'Jesus, that doesn't tell us much. Mary, can you get your coat and come for a walk.'

'Sure, if you want. Will we be gone long?'

'No... just a few minutes.'

'Go on darling, you go off with John. I'll get some lunch,' Mary's mother offered getting up from her chair where she'd been reading a newspaper.

'Thanks Ma; won't be long,' as she pulled on a well-worn sheepskin coat. John led the way across the grass to the private road through the Cedar Park estate with its views over the Saskatchewan. When they were on the road, Mary took her husband's hand. 'What is it John? Do you know something more about Ian, which you didn't want to say in the house?'

'I think the answer to that is 'yes', but not about his kidnap,' they had now reached a path which led down to the river which was a favourite dog-walking place. 'I had an appointment with Angus Campbell this morning,' and he sensed rather than felt the tenseness in his wife. 'He told me that I'm not Ian's father.' John had stopped and turned to face Mary who had her head bowed. 'I spent an hour walking beside the river, beyond the convention centre, while I sorted myself out and got rid of a whole lot of pointless rage which was mostly about my own deflated ego.'

'John....'

'No, Mary....just hear me out and then if I've got it all wrong....and even if I haven't, you have your go. You see I'd figured it out that you found out I was incapable of fathering a child and so went about a solution in your own way so as not to upset my macho views of my own virility. Am I far off track?'

'No,' was accompanied by a small sniff and he saw that large tears were rolling down Mary's cheeks. 'You never have a hankie.....here,' and John passed her his. Her hand gripped his tighter while the other dealt with the tears and nose blowing.

'I guessed that you identified some guy who'd been flirting with you at one of those many parties we used to go to in Ottawa and then fixed it so that you got pregnant. Am I way off beam?'

'No,' and Mary turned and hugged her husband. 'Is it my turn yet?'

'Yes, sure.'

'I've been longing to tell you this. It happened exactly as you say and I thought that I'd managed the whole thing perfectly. The man.....he was from the British High Commission....only seemed to want casual sex.....he said his wife was frigid or something. We...we made...we had sex four times and then my period was late so I told him that it was finished. He hadn't wanted casual sex at all, John. He wanted the child that was in me. His wife was incapable of having children and so he'd decided to do this. He said that unless I handed over the child, he'd tell you of the affair. I told him he was welcome to do that and to go to hell. He then offered....he offered to buy the child, John. One hundred thousand dollars is the value he placed on little Ian. I told him that if he bothered me once more, I'd go to the police. He told me that he'd get the child and I never saw him again after that.'

'Who was it, Mary?'

'Winfield; Humphrey Winfield... he was the head of the commercial section of the British High Commission in Ottawa. You had a number of meetings with him in connection with the sale of some British mining machinery which you were thinking of buying.'

'I remember him......where did he go after leaving Ottawa?'

'Back to London, I think. I tried to put the awful man out of my mind and had almost succeeded until all this happened. You don't think this has anything to do with him. This is all connected with your mines in Ghana isn't it?'

'I thought so, but this puts a different angle on it and....' but John didn't say what had come into his mind because he had no wish to cause any more anxiety. What he'd been about to say was that it didn't matter what they paid, if this man Winfield was a party to the kidnap it meant that they would never see their little boy again.

'And what?'

'Another train of thought,' and he looked at his watch. 'I've got a contact in the British High Commission still and I think I'll give him a call.'

'You won't do anything to let the kidnappers think we've contacted the police, will you?'

'No way... nothing like that.'

'Will you ever forgive me?'

261

'Right now, I'm not sure that you've done anything that requires forgiveness, but if you think you have then you know that I'll forgive almost anything except if you decided to leave me. I should've spent a great deal more time talking about things with you instead of trying to increase the company's profits. Come on, let's get back to the house,' and the two of them walked briskly up from the river.

There was another car parked in the drive, which was unfamiliar to both of them. Once in the hall, they could both hear Mary's mother talking in the lounge to the visitor. They went in and a short, stocky man in a rather ill-fitting suit got up and looked at them.

'Mr Mackenzie?' the English accent was as clear and sharp as ice. Mary's heart raced.

'Yes, that's me.'

'Patrick Smythe; I'm the Honorary British Consul in Edmonton. I have this fax for you from London. I was told to deliver it immediately and to no one else but you. There! That's my duty done and now I'll not bother you any longer. Goodbye; I'll see myself out,' and the Consul hurried out of the house, glad to have been able to complete his instructions to the letter.

CHAPTER 17

'Any idea what the air-defence radar surveillance coverage is like in Ghana, Dina?'

'Yes John; Siemens/Plessey upgraded all the radar and ILS equipment at Kotoko a couple of years back and the air traffic control for both commercial and military aircraft is good.'

'Are there any fighter aircraft on the military part of the airfield?'

'From what I can remember, the Ghanaian Air Force has a mixed bag of Italian Aermacchis. I think it was about six at the last count.'

'Any idea of armament and speed of deployment from Kotoko?'

'They've got a couple of the up-dated 339s; they're single-seat fighters armed with 30 mm canons - more than enough to deal with us, if that's what you're thinking. As far as speed of deployment is concerned, I can only quote you an incident which happened a couple of years ago when an unidentified boat appeared off the coast - almost smack opposite the Christianborg Castle - and the air force ops room was phoned alerting them, it was still an hour before the Aermacchis were airborne.'

'That's encouraging; no, my line of thought was that the arrival of this helicopter at Kotoko - with no registration marks......'

'Damn! I never noticed that.'

'Hardly surprising under the circumstances; anyway, it could cause us both a lot of hassle. Neither of us wishes to become the focus of the attention of either the military or civilian bureaucracy of this country and landing an unmarked chopper with no flight plan will raise everyone's blood pressure - particularly if they fail to spot it on the surveillance radar.'

'You've got a point.' Dina was concentrating on her instruments as she flew the helicopter over the dense black jungle canopy below them. Despite, or perhaps because of the intense excitement of their exploits over the last five or six hours, Graham had fallen asleep on the bench seat in the back of the MBB 105. Gunn looked at his watch; 1.35, and then at the ground speed indicator; 230 kph.

'How far to Accra, Dina; 120 miles?'

'Perhaps a little more...say 150.'

'If the guys operating the radar in Accra are switched on - and the kit is as well - then we should be on their screens. Dina; please come

263

down to a height just above the canopy and head due south for the sea. Once you reach the coast, the surf will provide a good reference point and I want you then to come right down to sea level.'

'Would you like me to do a loop and barrel roll as well?'

'Later,' Gunn smiled as he pulled the life jacket out from under his seat and examined it as the chopper banked to port, the nose dipped and the airspeed indicator increased as the machine dived down until it was skimming across the jungle canopy. 'We'll all put on these things, Dina, and then I'm going to get you to ditch this machine in the sea off the firing range near Labadi Beach. Does this have an autopilot?'

'No.'

'Is it possible to jam the controls so that the chopper will hover long enough for the pilot to jump?'

'I expect so.'

'Right, this is what happens. We follow the coast at wave-top height until we get to that deserted part of Labadi Beach opposite the military camp. You will hover the chopper at about ten feet or so and I will hold it while you and Graham jump into the sea. As soon as you've both gone, I'll jump and we'll leave the chopper to ditch itself in the sea.'

'No.'

'OK, what's your plan, chief?' Gunn smiled at the greeny-yellow reflection of the light from the instruments on Dina's expression of stubbornness. She was now flying both by instruments and sight and probably by the seat of her pants, Gunn reckoned. Her eyes darting from the instrument panel up to the perspex dome in front and then to left, centre, right and above them as the helicopter hugged the contours of the ground below where the jungle was thinning and turning to coconut palm and paddy with the occasional light from a dwelling which flashed past under them.

'I agree with all of that except the last bit; I'll hold the chopper and you go out with the boy. You don't know how to fly this thing. It's not too hard to jam the controls, but as the weight of the last person leaves the machine, it'll go crazy. I'm half your weight and I know what I'm doing. No more argument.'

'I was hoping you'd do your heroic bit, as I had no intention of being the last one out.'

'If I hadn't got both hands fully occupied, I'd.....ah! here's the sea,' and the helicopter banked hard to starboard and flew even lower as it raced across the deserted dunes and marram grass and then out over the sea.

'How much longer?'

'That's the Volta Estuary below us and the lights to your right are Ada. It's about 50 miles to Accra and at this speed,' and Dina glanced at the air speed indicator,' we'll be at Labadi in about 15 minutes. Time for you to put those jackets on Graham and me. I've no intention of hanging around at Labadi; we'll stop in the hover and then it's all over the side.'

'Right,' and Gunn turned and gently shook Graham awake. He explained what was about to happen and the young boy soon had the life jacket on. Gunn pulled the toggles on the small CO_2 bottles, made sure that the jacket inflated properly and checked that the straps were tight. He then undid Dina's shoulder harness and placed the lifejacket over her head. While she sat forward in her seat, he clipped the straps into the buckles and pulled them tight.

'Once you've got your's on, John, the next thing is to get rid of the doors.'

'OK,' and Gunn tightened the straps of his life jacket. Ready.'

'On the hinge side of the door, you'll see those tags attached to yellow and black-striped pins; seen?'

'Seen.'

'Hold the door handle, pull out the bottom pin first and then the top. Swing the handle up through 90 degrees and push. The prop-wash of the rotors and our airspeed will do the rest. Do both of the rear doors first and leave Graham's lap strap fastened until the last moment. Then do my door and lastly yours. Eleven minutes to go. Get rid of the doors.'

'Roger,' and Gunn turned and checked Graham's lap strap first and then discarded first the port and then starboard rear doors which spun away below them into the bands of white surf which stretched in front of them like phosphorescent lines guiding them to Accra. Dina swung the chopper out to sea as the lights of the port of Tema appeared in front of them. The cooling air from the blades and their airspeed buffeted around inside the cockpit. Dina swung the helicopter back to the beach as the lights of Tema disappeared behind them. Gunn leant across her, released the pins and pushed away her door after checking that her lap strap was secure. Last to go was his door which spun away into the surf below.

'That's Teshie Village in our two o'clock position. One minute to go.' How far off the beach do you want to ditch?'

'No more than 50 metres.'

'Right; here goes. Get ready everyone,' and she ripped off the headset and mike as the nose of the chopper came up and it sank into a hover over the sea. Lower and lower and then the machine levelled. Dina looked all round. 'Right, John,' she now had to shout as she unclipped her lap strap. Gunn turned and undid Graham's lap strap and shouted at him to jump. No hesitation, and he'd gone. The helicopter lurched and steadied; Gunn stepped onto the metal skid and jumped clear.

They were only about six feet above the water and Gunn quickly picked up Graham's light on his jacket. He swam towards it as he saw Dina leap from the machine. The helicopter rose, steadied for a moment and then banked to port. The blades hit the water and it cartwheeled across the surface before diving in upside-down. All noise stopped except the sound of the surf on the beach. The strong current was carrying them to the east, but both Gunn and Graham swam with it, angling slowly towards the breaking surf.

Gunn's feet touched the sand and then both he and Graham scrambled out of the undertow onto the hard sand. They were almost exactly opposite the spot where Graham had been fishing at 5.30 the previous Monday morning. Dina appeared out of the surf a further 50 yards down the beach and both of them went to join her removing the lifejackets as they went. Gunn went in and helped Dina from the surf and then removed her lifejacket. The three of them walked up the sloping beach to the scrub beyond. Gunn glanced at his watch again. Just before two.

'Where are you going?' Dina asked as Gunn led the way towards the Labadi Beach Hotel.

'We can't get into the military camp where the BMAT houses are because there're guards on the gate and even if they are all fast asleep we can't take the risk of letting them connect us to the ditched chopper. I've got a room in the hotel, a car parked outside and you've got a shop there, Dina, where you can get a change of clothes. They keep all the beach towels locked up in a hut and it won't be difficult to get that open. First, we need to get rid of these life-jackets and we'll do that in the mangrove swamp over there,' and Gunn pointed to where a particularly evil part of the Africa Lagoon reached to within 50 yards of the beach. If we all wrap towels around ourselves and walk into the hotel no one will bat an eyelid, or even if they do it doesn't matter.'

'There's a certain crazy logic in that. Reception keeps a spare set of keys for the shop. They have to; it's part of the hotel's fire regulations.' They threw their life-jackets into the swamp and crossed over the overspill from the Africa Lagoon which ran across the beach and followed Gunn to the beach hut which dispensed umbrellas, towels and loungers.

There was no one around, but they could hear music coming from the hotel, which was still a blaze of lights. The beach hut door was firmly locked. Gunn stripped off his clothes until he was left in a very wet pair of underpants. He removed the ankle holster and then placed the barrel of the Tanarmi against the lock. He placed a wadge of his wet clothing all round the automatic and pulled the trigger. There was a muffled 'thump' and the door swung open. Gunn went in and found the towels. The other two stripped down to their underwear and then wrapped towels round their bodies.

Gunn piled up all their sodden clothes, rolled them up in a towel and led the way across the beach to the small ornamental bridge across the pond between them and the hotel gardens. They went through the gardens, past the two-tiered swimming pool and up to the terrace. There were still some people in the Terrace café and the noise of the Friday night/Saturday early hours disco came from the hotel's nightclub. They walked through the glass doors of the Terrace café and John told Graham to go up to his room while he and Dina went for their keys. No one even glanced at them and the duty night staff on the reception desk were in no mood to notice the dress of Gunn and Dina as the keys were handed over. Dina took her keys and then arranged to come up to Gunn's room for a bath when she'd collected some clothes from her shop.

Gunn went up to his room where he found Graham waiting. He opened the door and told Graham to take the first bath. By the time Dina arrived, Graham had finished and she took over the bathroom. By the time she had finished, Graham was fast asleep in one of the twin beds. Dina declined the offer of a bed and said she would go down and grab a taxi to her home. She agreed to be back by seven that morning when they would all go first to BMAT and then return Graham to his parents. Gunn set his alarm, removed the bandages and had a scalding hot bath.

Gunn was awoken by the alarm and had no sooner switched it off than there was a knock on his door. Dina came in carrying an armful of clothes, which she said might fit Graham. She woke the young boy who was still dead to the world while Gunn showered in the bathroom. Dina had decided that it would be better if she didn't go with them as there was no necessity to announce her presence in Accra to any more people. She also told Gunn that there had been a number of messages for her on her secure answering machine, not the least of which were those from Christine expressing concern about Gunn and another from Mike Parker informing her of Christine's arrival in Accra on the same flight as the Winfields and Ian Mackenzie.

'If the BA flight was on time, Christine should already be at BMAT, so that will fit neatly if you go there now. I'm sure she'll brief you on what's to be done with the Winfields. Mike Parker's instructions are that the boy is to be returned immediately to London - preferably on the return BA flight which leaves at 1100 today. I'll get onto Dennis Motram, the British Airways Manager and make the reservations for you, Christine and little Ian. There's more detail about the arrest of the Winfields, which you are to effect with the Deputy Head of Mission present. The instructions then direct that we leave the FCO to sort out their own mess and the removal of the Winfields from Accra.'

Gunn and Graham had been dressing while Dina briefed them and were now ready. 'What happens, Dina, if someone other than you presses the playback on the answering machine?' Gunn asked as he reloaded the Tanarmi's magazine and replaced it in the ankle holster, watched with fascination by Graham.

'That's a very simple device; if the correct code for replay isn't entered into the machine, the tape is wiped clean. Didn't they show you that in London?'

'No; probably reckoned that it was too technical for an ex-soldier. Come on, we'd better be off.' They were just about to leave when Dina glanced out of the window, which overlooked the beach.

'They've found the chopper; look.' There were about six or seven fishing boats all milling around an object which stuck out of the sea. It was one of the chopper's rotor blades. The receding tide had revealed the submerged machine and approaching the beach was one of the Ghana Navy's patrol vessels.

'Come on folks; we've overstayed our welcome,' Gunn remarked. The three of them walked down to reception and then out to the Landrover Discovery which had been returned to the hotel by Richard Outram. Graham hugged Dina and then jumped in beside Gunn. It was a shade after 7.15 as they pulled out of the hotel and turned right on the road to BMAT. The drive took no more than five minutes and Gunn turned off the road through the military camp into the BMAT quarters and left again into the driveway of the Stockwell's bungalow. Dina was correct; Christine had just arrived at the Stockwell's bungalow and she, the Briars and the Stockwells were standing outside on the red laterite. All of them turned as Gunn drove into the driveway.

They were greeted with expressions of amazement as Graham jumped out of the Discovery and ran across to greet the Stockwells' two girls, Sarah and Anna. Christine walked across to the Discovery brushing laterite dust off her skirt and followed by the playful Shemma who was also delighted to see her tummy-tickling friend back.

'How are you, John?'

'I'm fine, Christine; Dina stitched me up again. She's listened to all your messages and has passed them to me.'

'Where's she been?'

'With me; it's quite a story, but I think it will have to wait. I think it would be appropriate if Graham was taken home now by the Briars as they're close to the McLeans. I gather that I'm required to remove the boy from the Winfields, arrest them and hand them over to the High Commission's Security Officer.'

'I hadn't heard that part as your arrival beat my call to London. But, yes, that all makes sense. When do they want us back?'

'On the return BA flight so we've got to get a move on; first to pick up the Deputy Head of Mission and Security Officer from their houses and then to the Residence. We ought to have Miles, here, with us.'

'Agreed.'

Gunn walked over to Miles Stockwell and explained what was required. The BMAT Commander readily agreed. At this stage, Penny Briars could no longer contain her excitement and rushed over and kissed John Gunn. She was followed by John Briars who shook his hand and apologised for his wife's exuberance and then they and Graham climbed into the battered Nissan and drove off to the McLean's house. Miles collected his radio from the bungalow.

'This might save us a bit of time.' He pressed the transmit button. 'CHARLIE zero two, this is B-MAT 1, message, over.' He had to repeat the call twice before Mike Truman replied.

'CHARLIE 02, send, over.'

'B-MAT 1, on my way to your house. Could you contact SIERRA two zero and get him to come to your house to meet us, over.'

'CHARLIE 02, roger out.' And almost instantly from an alert Security Officer, Trevor Banbury, came the acknowledgement.

'SIERRA 20, roger, I heard that. On my way, out.'

'OK, let's go,' and Miles Stockwell led the way in his car and Gunn followed with Christine who had transferred her suitcase and hand baggage from the Briars' Nissan to the Discovery.

They turned right at the 'T' junction beyond the Labadi Beach Hotel and went north towards the airport. Just beyond the entrance to Burma Camp, the main military barracks in Accra, Miles turned left, went over an intersection and then through a set of gates which had been opened by the watchman. On the left of the driveway was an expanse of lawn with every species of tropical tree providing ample shade. On the right was a large house with a drive-through portico where Miles stopped. Two men were standing on the steps.

269

Miles did the introductions and all of them went into the cool, air-conditioned lounge.

Before Gunn explained what was to be done, Mike Truman confirmed that he'd had a call from Perigrine Humble, the Head of the West African Department at the FCO, who had instructed him to assist in that morning's operation. Gunn then explained that the over-riding priority was the safety of the child. It seemed likely that the boy would be asleep after the flight from London, but it also seemed sensible that Mike Truman should go into the house first to confirm where the Winfields were, either by locating them or by asking the Residence staff. Once that had been established, Gunn and the security officer would go in and remove the boy.

Mike Truman led in his car with Trevor Banbury, Gunn followed next and Miles brought up the rear. As Mike Truman turned and stopped in front of the gates leading into the Residence, Gunn pulled into the side of the road by a fruit stall and he and Christine got out. Miles Stockwell did the same and the three of them walked through into the Residence driveway when the gates were opened for Mike Truman's car. Trevor Banbury got out of Mike Truman's car and joined Gunn as the Deputy Head of Mission drove up to the covered portico of the High Commissioner's Residence.

The glass doors of the Residence were opened by the Ghanaian steward and Mike Truman went in. As Gunn and Trevor Banbury reached the portico, the former stooped and removed the Tanarmi from its holster and stuck it behind his back in his trouser waistband.

'You don't think you'll have to use that, do you?' expressed a worried ex-policeman.

'No point in wondering about that when it's too late. The boy has to be rescued and I wouldn't hesitate to shoot both of the Winfields - and anyone else, for that matter - to achieve that.'

They went in through the front door and Gunn heard voices in the room to the right of the hall. He heard Mike Truman and then both of the Winfields. Gunn went up to the door, which was ajar and looked through the crack. The Winfields were having breakfast and Mike Truman had been offered a coffee. No small boy. Gunn quietly retreated and beckoned to Christine who had just come through the front door.

'Go upstairs with Trevor and get the boy,' he whispered. The two ran up the curved staircase in the corner of the hall. In the curve of the staircase was a grand piano with the lid open and music in the stand above the keyboard. Gunn walked over and looked at the music as he listened for any movement from the dining room. Miles quietly came into the hall and stood by the door. The music in the stand was the score from the 'Sound of Music'. 'What a tragic mess,' Gunn muttered as Christine and Trevor reappeared; the latter carrying the small boy who was still fast asleep. Miles opened the door and Christine and Trevor went out. Trevor handed over the boy to Christine and then came back in through the glass doors.

Gunn removed his BID identity card from his back pocket and pushed open the dining room doors. Trevor and Miles followed him into the room. The Winfields turned and Mike Truman stood up. 'Mr and Mrs Winfield, on the instructions of the Home Office and your Foreign and Commonwealth Office, I'm arresting you both for your part in the kidnap of Ian Mackenzie, and conspiracy with Charles Mensah in the murder....' there was a gasp from Davina Winfield, 'of a security guard at the Bank of Ghana and the theft of the Ashanti gold and the murder of Mr Bristow, Miss Routledge, Mr Russell - all from the British High Commission - and Miss Routledge's maid. Anything you say will be recorded for evidence. Ian Mackenzie has been taken away....' Davina Winfield's head dropped and she sobbed loudly. Humphrey Winfield sat like a carved effigy and hadn't moved apart from turning when Gunn had entered.

When he did move, it was with remarkable speed; he dived past the three of them, throwing Miles Stockwell out of the way with maniacal strength and then ran across the hall and out of the glass doors. Christine was some fifty yards away holding Ian's hand as they both walked towards the gates and the parked cars. She turned as Winfield ran from the house in their direction. Gunn was split seconds behind Winfield as the glass doors burst open on the end of his foot as he held the Tanarmi in both hands. He shouted one warning of his intention to fire, but Winfield was beyond hearing, heeding or understanding that warning. Gunn fired twice. His own momentum and the muzzle velocity of the soft-nosed 9 mm round bowled Winfield head over heels towards Christine and the boy where he fell, five yards short of them, quite dead.

Gunn put the automatic back in its holster as Trevor Banbury joined him. 'Bloody hell; I see what you mean,' said the security officer and then walked towards the prone body of the High Commissioner. Gunn overtook him and knelt down by the body and felt for a pulse in the neck. There was none. He stood up and handed the Discovery keys to Christine.

'Take the boy back to the hotel and I'll join you there. My room number's 208.' Christine nodded and led the boy out through the gates towards the Discovery.' Gunn walked back towards the house.

He stopped beside Miles Stockwell. 'Be very grateful for a lift back to the hotel a little later, Miles.'

'Yes, of course; sorry I failed to stop him.'

'We all failed,' and Gunn went into the house where Mike was still sitting with Davina Winfield. He looked up as Gunn came into the dining room. The question was in his eyes. Gunn shook his head.

'Can you just stay with her for couple of minutes while I speak to my wife, Jean. We'll get some of the wives to come up here and look after Davina. I'll fix the Ghana Police. I think we'll have to send Davina back to UK as a medevac,' and both of them glanced at the woman leaning on the table who was moaning like a soul in torment.

'Sure, go ahead Mike. I'll stay with her.'

Mike Truman reappeared three minutes later and told Gunn that Jean Truman was on her way to the Residence. 'Go on, John you go with the boy. Does he have a passport?'

'No idea.'

'Right; we'll have a search around for one. If we can't find it, I'll get my Consular Section to have one ready for you at the airport in time for your departure. I'll ring them now and someone will come to your room at the hotel with a polaroid camera.' He looked at his watch. 'It's a quarter to nine; you'll need to be at the airport in about an hour so there's not much time. I'll see you at the airport. Bye.'

'Bye,' and Gunn went out of the Residence. A tarpaulin had been draped over the body of the High Commissioner. He got into Miles' car and eight minutes later was dropped off at the Labadi Beach Hotel. When he got to his room, Christine was in the bathroom taking the opportunity of a bath before the return flight to London. Ian Mackenzie was asleep. Gunn picked up the phone and dialled Dina's number. She answered immediately.

'Hello, John; success?'

'Yes and no; we've got the little boy and he's in good shape. Winfield's dead. Can you contact London and get them to contact the Mackenzies in Canada. Mrs Winfield looks like an asylum case and will be medevac'd later today. Winfield will no doubt be returning in a pine box at some stage. Christine, Ian and I will be on the BA flight and the BHC is fixing a passport for the boy. Could you get the office to fix a car to meet us, please?'

'Got all that. When are you leaving the hotel?'

'In about forty minutes.'

'I'll be there to say goodbye,' and she rang off.

*

272

John Mackenzie awoke out of a deep sleep to the sound of the persistent buzzing of the phone beside their bed. Mary was still fast asleep, curled up on the other side of the double bed. He turned on the light as it occurred to him that this might well be instructions for the ransom for little Ian.

'Bugger! no pencil and paper,' John cursed and jumped naked out of bed and grabbed his notebook and biro off his dressing table. He then picked up the phone. 'Hello.'

'John Mackenzie?'

'Yes, that's me.'

'I'm phoning from London, Mr Mackenzie, and I work for what most people call the British Secret Service. Your son, Ian, is safe and will be delivered to your doorstep by us later today. He is currently on his way from Ghana to London where he will transfer to a flight to Ottawa and then to Edmonton. He will be escorted all the time. If you can refrain from celebrating his return for a further 24 hours, we'd be grateful, as we have one or two loose ends to deal with. As soon as he arrives in London we will ring you again and you will be able to talk to your little boy.'

'How do I know all this is for real?'

'Did you get a message from the British Consul, telling you that we'd located your son?'

'Yes...yes I did...a few hours ago.'

'Good; well the rescue of your son went without a hitch and he's in excellent health, if a little tired. I'm delighted to be the bearer of such good news.'

'Thanks....thanks; I don't know how to thank you enough,' and rarely for him, John Mackenzie found himself close to tears.

'You just have, Mr Mackenzie. We'll be in touch again in about six hours' time. Bye.'

'Goodbye,' and John stared at the phone in his hand.

*

The Head of the BHC's Consular Section had arrived in Gunn's room accompanied by his opposite number from the Canadian High Commission and complete with polaroid camera and briefcase full of equipment to produce an instant passport. Ian Mackenzie had been woken, his photo was taken and within ten minutes a brand new Canadian passport was in Christine's possession.

No sooner had the consular officials gone, than Dina arrived to say goodbye and said that she'd drive them to the airport in the Discovery and then return it to the manager of Landrover in Accra. Dina told Gunn that the message to Ian's parents had been sent and that Bill Barton, who had passed it, had told her that they would be met at Gatwick. Ian would be taken off their hands by a courier who would take him back to his home in Edmonton. Christine would be driven to London and Gunn was to catch the Virgin Atlantic flight to Miami where he would transfer to an American Airlines flight to Las Vegas where he would be met by Doyle Barnes.

They drove to the airport, checked in the baggage and waited in the executive lounge which was marginally less hot and humid than the rest of the building and then were called out to board BA flight 078 to Gatwick. The 747 took off four minutes late at 11.04, by which time Ian Mackenzie was fast asleep once more.

CHAPTER 18

The automatic doors of the monorail, connecting the north and south terminals at Gatwick, closed and Gunn waved goodbye to Christine and Ian. The flight to Gatwick via Abidjan had been totally uneventful, except for strong high altitude northerly winds which had increased the four minute late departure from Kotoko to a forty minute late arrival in England. This had reduced Gunn's transfer time across to the North Terminal and the Virgin flight to twenty-five minutes. Gunn had abandoned his hold baggage and transferred with only his hand baggage. His Tanarmi had been left behind in Accra to return with the next Queen's Messenger to London.

His name was echoing around the departure lounge of the North Terminal as the announcer made the final call for boarding the Virgin flight to Miami. Gunn was the last person to board the 747-400 and went up to his seat on the upper deck. The doors closed and the 747 was rolled back from the boarding tunnels, the engines were started and it took off at 20.30. It landed at Miami International Airport at 02.15 local time on Sunday 17th April and the American Airlines Airbus A-300 took off at 04.00.

The Airbus landed at McCarran International Airport on the southern side of Las Vegas at 03.05 local time, by which stage Gunn's body-clock was totally jet-lagged. As he walked wearily from the disembarkation tunnel into the terminal, in direct contrast to his own lack of sleep, the entire airport was wide awake, full of life and every gambling machine imaginable to remove money from any new arrival before experience provided enough wisdom to avoid them. Aircraft schedules were shown on the TV monitors, departing and arriving 24 hours a day; the city never had to worry about noise pollution from aircraft as the sound of spinning wheels on one-armed bandits and roulette tables, the non-stop music from chorus lines and discos, the clatter of silver dollars in jackpot trays, accompanied by the shrieks of ecstatic winners drowned anything that General Electric, Pratt and Whitney or Rolls Royce could do to interrupt a city that never slept.

Doyle Barnes' smiling face to greet him restored Gunn's spirits and the suggestion of a few hours rest in the Gambler's Paradise Motel at the junction of Sunset and Eastern was accepted with alacrity. In the airport parkng lot, Doyle handed him a Browning Hi-Power 9 mm automatic with four, thirteen round magazines and a carton of 9 mm shells. In the car, they chatted about mutual friends and things, which had happened since they last met at Langley three years previously. Doyle told Gunn that he would return for him at nine to take him to the briefing for the operation to close down Caramansa and his International Credit Bank; the briefing would be at Nellis Air Force base on the north-east side of the city. Within five minutes of showering in the en-suite bathroom of the motel room, Gunn was asleep.

At 06.05, the sun spilled over the Virgin Mountains to the east of the city and quickly eclipsed the man-made electric sun, which had lit Las Vegas through the hours of darkness. It lit the peaks of the horseshoe of mountains which encircled three-quarters of the 'Silver State's' largest city, by turning the Black Mountains to the south, golden - in defiance of the name given to them - and the 12,000 foot, snow-tipped summit of Charleston Peak in the Spring Mountains to the west, pink.

At eight o'clock, Gunn was awoken by room service informing him that his clothes had been washed and pressed and would be delivered in a few minutes together with his breakfast. A couple of minutes after the call, a knock on his door revealed a pretty girl in a mini-skirted uniform and hat who handed over his cotton slacks, shirt and anorak together with underwear and socks. Gunn greeted her in the towelling dressing gown which went with the room and which was the only form of clothing he had. He and his attire met with a look of approval from the bearer of his clothes and underwear. His breakfast was pushed into his room on a trolley, the clothes were hung up in the fitted wardrobe and he was asked, without any form of subtlety if there was anything else he wanted. Gunn declined the offer, managed not to wince visibly when he was told to 'have a nice day,' and parted company with his mini-skirted provider of food and clothing.

The chilled fresh fruit juice, warm rolls and piping hot coffee sharpened Gunn's appetite which had become jaded by successive plastic-packaged, tasteless airline meals for the thirty hours it had taken to cover 14,000 miles from Accra to Las Vegas via Gatwick and the mind-numbing performance of the US Department of Immigration at Miami. Doyle arrived promptly at a few minutes before nine in a Mercedes 290 rented from Hertz. Gunn put his bag in the back, climbed into the front and Doyle drove north on Eastern Avenue to the intersection with the dual-lane freeway of Russell Road where he turned west, heading for the Las Vegas Strip.

'Seen this place before, John?'

'Countless times on the silver screen, Doyle, but never for real.'

'We leave the freeway in about a mile on the east side of the airport. We'll head north on Paradise and then take a left onto Tropicana, which'll bring us to the intersection with Las Vegas Boulevard; that's where the 'Strip' starts.' There was little point in Doyle giving a running commentary because once they had turned north onto Las Vegas Boulevard, each hotel, casino, golf course, entertainment park or palace vied for the most noticeable or outrageous sign to attract clients.

On the left side of the dual-lane road through the centre of the strip, Gunn spotted the better known names of the Dunes Hotel, Caesar's Palace, Stardust, Holiday Inn and Westward Ho, but like a spectator with a side-on view of a tennis tournament, he glanced from left to right to identify the Tropicana, Aladdin, Flamingo, Sands, Desert Inn, Wet'n Wild and Sahara on his right. There were twenty or thirty more of which he'd never heard before.

'Sahara Avenue, right ahead of us, running west to east, marks the northern extremity of the 'Strip', and the start of the business centre of the city. The next intersection we come to is Charleston Boulevard and in the south-east quadrant of that intersection - which'll come up on your right - is the ICB Tower. It's that tower you can see in your two o'clock position with the large plate glass windows at the top reflecting the sun....got it.'

'Got it. Why's Caramansa having a meeting of his exiled UROWAS delegates on a Sunday?'

'Nothing unusual about that; the meetings have increased in frequency as this conspiracy gathers momentum. He thinks he's got a ship-load of arms on the way to West Africa and he wants to boast about it to his fellow conspirators......possibly to ensure that they retain their ardour for terrorism. The meeting is due to start at 11.30 and will then adjourn at about one for lunch. At Nellis, we'll show you how the operation is planned and then you might like to come in with me behind the 'Seal' boys. Most of the units are in position already and the building has been under constant observation and electronic surveillance for the past 48 hours.'

Their road went past city hall and then joined up with Main Street where they soon picked up the signs for Nellis Air Force base. The base was five miles from that junction and ten minutes later Doyle turned right off the dual-lane highway onto a two-way road and then stopped at the guard post at the main entrance to the base. His ID was checked and cleared before they were allowed in.

'They fly the NATO 'Red Flag' exercises from this base. The range is 'bout a hundred miles to the north-west of the base out by Quartzite Mountain and Stonewall Flat,' Doyle waved vaguely to a range of hills that shimmered in an indistinct blue haze in the distance to the north as he drove around the airbase to the operations briefing centre. They came to a row of twelve, dual-finned fighter interceptors, still carrying the five-pointed red star of the Soviet Union.

'Those look remarkably like MiG-29s.'

'That's 'cos they're meant to; they're F-15 Eagles with slight cosmetic alterations to make them more like the Mig-29s. Some of our guys reckon that Red Flag's more dangerous than the real thing. Our boys and yours used this range before Desert Storm in '91 and the gulf war last year. Parts of Death Valley - that's to the west of the firing range - are identical to the desert in southern Iraq. There!......beyond the Soviet MiG-29s...can you see those ones with the red, white and black rectangles on the fins?'

'And green stars?'

'That's it; those are more F-15s, tarted up to look like the old MiG-25 Foxbats used by the Iraqi Airforce. In the event, of course, they all did a runner to Iran before the aerial bombing began. Here we are,' and Doyle stopped the Mercedes in a parking slot outside a very deserted looking building. 'C'mon, John; this won't take more'n a few minutes and then we'll go back downtown to join in the fireworks.' Doyle led the way into the building, which was pleasantly cool from the air-conditioning. There were two flights of stairs up to the next floor and in the centre of the corridor was the operations and briefing room. This room had been primarily designed for the Red Flag briefings and was able to hold about a hundred people in comfort in, what looked like, a small cinema. There was an Air Force police sergeant on duty outside the door who checked Doyle's ID and then opened the doors for them both to enter.

Just inside the door were two men; one was an Air Force corporal who transpired to be the projectionist and the other was a man who was only a half inch or so shorter than Gunn and was dressed in black combat uniform. 'John, this is Major Isaacs who'll command the Seal operation. David, John Gunn from the British Intelligence Directorate which busted the ICB conspiracy.' The two men shook hands and then Doyle led the way to seats at the front of the small auditorium and David Isaacs went up to an enclosed lectern; the lights immediately dimmed.

'Gentlemen, I'll start with the Situation,' a street plan of greater Las Vegas appeared on the screen behind Isaacs and a bright spot of laser light identified Nellis Air Force base. 'This is where we are now and the International Credit Bank is at the junction of Charleston and Las Vegas Boulevards.....here,' and the spot of light illuminated the bottom right quadrant of the intersection. 'This is the building,' the street map was replaced by a slide of the ICB, 'which is thirty-five storeys high with a chopper LP on the top. Floors thirty thru' thirty-three are taken up entirely by a large auditorium where this Caramansa character holds his UROWAS meetings. The thirty-fourth and fifth floors are Caramansa's penthouse. Floors one thru' twenty-nine are the offices of ICB; most of the first, or ground floor, John, as you call it in England, is a banking hall. There is a basement level which contains the back-up generators and two levels below that for staff and customer parking.'

'We know that the building is fitted with a state of the art security system which, if not neutralised by us, will automatically destroy all the bank's records; records which will be needed by the Treasury Department to bring a successful prosecution against ICB and close it down for ever. We know the company which fitted this system in the building and we know how to neutralise it. The delegates will start arriving in about an hour... that's at 1100 hours and will go into the General Assembly - the terminology is Caramansa's and apes that of the UN - at approximately 1125 hours. That's the situation, gentlemen; any questions before I go through the mission quickly and on to the execution of the operation?'

'Yes, a quick one, David,' came from Gunn; 'in your slide of the ICB building, it showed a helicopter on the landing platform on top of the building. Is there one there now?'

'Thanks; it is and it's caused us some bother, but I'll cover how we intend to deal with that in a moment. What the slide also didn't show is that he's got a radar up on that building too. We've done a couple of over-flights and we've got the frequencies of his radar. There're two, in fact; a surveillance radar and a target acquisition radar. On both over-flights, Caramansa's target acquisition radar locked on to our aircraft. Anything else, gentlemen?'

'No, that's very clear, thanks.'

'Right; the Mission is to capture the building and all its documents intact with the limitation that we cause the minimum possible casualties. That limitation led to a significant deduction during our mission assessment of the operation which means that we'll be using overwhelming numbers and firepower to render any form of resistance suicidal.'

'Execution;' the Mission disappeared from the computer-driven display. 'General Outline; this will be an operation executed in five distinct phases as follows; Phase One is the insertion of Seals into the bank; this will be the task of Team A. Phase Two is the assault on the auditorium by the Apache attack helicopters; this is the task of Team B supported by Team A on the inside. Phase Three is the removal of the Bell Jet Ranger from the LP; the task of Team C. Phase Four is the assault by the main group - Team D. Phase Five is the clear-up which is the task of Teams A and D.' Again, the screen scrolled clear to be replaced by the heading Tasks and Organisation.

'Tasks and Organisation; first, Team A; its tasks are to remove the delegates, whom they've replaced, into safe custody - that has already been done; enter the ICB with the other delegates at 1100 hours, take over the electronic search equipment, prime the charges on the back-up generators in the basement level and neutralise the other delegates in the auditorium in conjunction with Team B's CS rocket assault. Organisation; Team A will be organised into three squads; Squad One of three men has the task of fixing the generators; Squad Two with three men is the search team and Squad Three of eighteen men neutralises the delegates in the auditorium.'

'Team B's task is to assault the auditorium from both sides simultaneously launching CS rockets through the plate glass of the auditorium. Its organisation for this task is a flight of four McDonnell Douglas Apache attack helicopters. Team C's task is to remove the Bell Jet Ranger and the organisation for that is two Sikorsky CH-53s. Team D's task is the assault on the building through the penthouse and the clear-up afterwards in conjunction with Team A. The organisation for Team D will be a platoon of 32 men in the third CH-53.'

'Gentlemen, you will know that there's lots more under the communications and logistic headings, but I'll spare you all that. It may help if I run through how we hope to see this operation go.' The screen went blank and David Isaacs came out from behind the lectern as the lighting in the briefing room brightened. 'Twenty-four of the delegates and security staff have already been replaced by our men. The men who operate the search equipment, through which all the delegates must pass, will also be operated by us. Team A will be the last of the delegation to enter the auditorium and is armed with Intratec 9 mm machine pistols, stun grenades and equipped with respirators; these are in their briefcases. As part of the opening ceremony of each Assembly, the room is plunged into darkness to dramatise the arrival of Caramansa on his throne. At that precise moment, signalled by our men inside, all mains power to the building will be cut off and the building's emergency generators will be destroyed. The security system which would then destroy the documents, using stored battery power, will also fail because the circuits were neutralised yesterday during a routine maintenance visit by the security firm.'

'Once the radar is down and the security system is neutralised, Team B of four McDonnell Douglas Apache attack helicopters will strike, launching CS rockets through the plate glass of the General Assembly auditorium. That will be followed by the stun grenades of Team A inside the auditorium. Following the Apaches will be the three CH-53s of Team C; the two leading choppers will have a steel hawser slung down in a loop between the two of them which will be used to drag the Bell Jet Ranger off the LP. Once the LP is clear the third CH-53 will land with a platoon of Seals who will enter the building from the top. Both of you will be in that chopper with me, which becomes my command post as soon as the Seals have gone.'

'That's it gentlemen. Now if you'd like to get dressed in these two sets of combat uniform, there'll be no risk of confusion for my guys. We're providing you with two 9 mm Intratecs with taped magazines; each magazine holds 36 rounds; the machine pistol is semi-automatic with an enclosed bolt which fires bursts of four rounds. Any questions?' There were no questions. Doyle and Gunn changed into the black uniforms, picked up their machine pistols and left the briefing room with David Isaacs. They got into the back of Isaac's Hummer which headed off across the airfield to a line of closed hangars on its far side.

The Hummer stopped outside the furthest of six, arched roof hangars which must have achieved some sort of structural engineering record for an unsupported roof. As they stopped, the fifty foot high, armour-plated doors started to roll open on steel rails embedded in the concrete apron. Inside the hangar was the entire Seal strike force, less Team A, which would have already entered the ICB building; it was 11.07.

At the front of the hangar were the four Apache attack helicopters. On the hard points of the two stub wings on either side of the helicopter were two, 18-round pods of 70 mm CS rockets. Slung below the co-pilot/gunner's forward position was a 30 mm Hughes chain gun which was remotely aimed by the gunner using an integrated helmet and display sighting system which enabled him to acquire targets simply by moving his head. Both pilot's and co-pilot's positions were surrounded in boron armour and the multi-spar, stainless steel and carbon fibre rotor blades could withstand hits from shells up to 23 mm in calibre. Throughout this explanation of the Apache's attributes to wreak havoc and mayhem, Isaacs constantly glanced at his watch. He completed his introduction to the Apaches by telling the two men that the attack helicopters were capable of 200 mph fully bombed-up. In their matt-black paint and drooping rotor blades, giving the impression of a monstrous insect, they seemed the very embodiment of a killing machine to Gunn.

Behind the Apaches were the two CH-53s with the steel hawser connected to the lifting strop beneath each machine. At the back of the hangar was the CH-53 with the Seal platoon standing beside it. As soon as they entered the hangar the platoon enplaned. All four pilots in the Apaches were watching Isaacs who, in turn was looking at his watch. He raised his fist with the thumb up and immediately the two 1,536 shaft-horsepower General Electric turbines on all four machines fired up. Isaacs handed ear defenders to Gunn and Doyle as the noise increased and the rotors started to turn.

The rotors of all seven machines made the air vibrate in the hangar and then all four Apaches moved forward, cleared the hangar, and with no pause, lifted off the apron and accelerated across the airfield at minimum altitude. The CH-53s followed and lifted clear with the 200 metre hawser hanging in a loop below and watched by the two dispatchers from open cargo doors. David Isaacs led the way to the third CH-53 and the three of them went up the steps into the interior and took their places on the canvas seats at the rear of the compartment. Right at the back of the CH-53, Isaacs had his small command post operated by one of his men. He passed headsets, with integral boom microphones, to Gunn and Doyle. His order to the pilot to 'move now' came clearly over the intercom circuit and the large helicopter taxied out of the hangar and lifted into the hot blue sky. It was 11.18.

*

'Has there been any word from Twum-Danso or Kisi?' Charles Mensah asked as he donned the robes of a supreme chief in his private dressing room at the back of the General Assembly auditorium. The question was addressed to his two bodyguards.

'No sir; but there's nothing unusual about that. The satellite lines have been down to Accra more times than up, so no worry there. The Texas Star has sailed with the arms and by the end of this year you'll be able to take your rightful place on the gold Ashanti Stool as Caramansa, Supreme Chief of Eguafo State and the home of the Akan People.'

'You're right; the overall plan is running like clockwork and I mustn't allow myself to be distracted by minutiae, but it's a shame that for the first time the Antumpans will not play today. Time?'

'11.26, Sir; the guard at the entrance to the hall has reported that all except about twenty of the delegates have taken their seats. The Members of the Security Council are all ready to make their entrance.'

'Excellent! This is a great day for UROWAS, my brothers. Our re-funding of the bank has met with only minor set-backs and our freedom fighters will soon be equipped with state-of-the-art weapons.' The small portable radio came to life and Charles Mensah's bodyguard listened.

'All the delegates are in, Sir, and the guards have closed and locked the doors. The Donno drums are playing.'

'Very good; come, brothers, let us watch the entry of the Security Council.' Charles Mensah's bodyguards led the way along a minor labyrinth of corridors under the tiered platform which rose up to the base of the screen where the UROWAS flag was displayed. In exactly the same way that lifts rise up to trap-doors on a stage to allow actors to appear and disappear, so the group of three men stopped in a small room where just such a lift with gold-painted stool and Caramansa seated on it, rose up and appeared in the General Assembly when all the lights went out. On the far side of this small, chamber was a one-way window through which Charles Mensah was able to watch the proceedings in the auditorium before his dramatic appearance.

In the auditorium, the lights had dimmed and the Security Council members were now taking their seats to the accompaniment of the Donno drums. Any moment now the lights would be extinguished and Caramansa would make his entrance. Charles Mensah took his place on the stool and one of his bodyguards put out his hand for the button, which would activate the motor to drive the lift up to the platform above. The auditorium was plunged into darkness and the bodyguard pressed the button.

The lift didn't move, but the auditorium was rent apart by blinding and deafening explosions as the plate glass walls appeared to cave in. The whole area was instantly filled with billowing smoke, some of which seeped into their observation chamber, making their skin burn and eyes pour with tears. One of the bodyguards grabbed Mensah by the hand, wrenched him from the stool and dragged him back along the corridor to another lift. The CS gas had not penetrated that far and all three were able to see and breathe with less difficulty.

There was a contingency plan for just such an attack on the building. The plan specifically allowed for the sacrifice of the people in the auditorium to divert attention from Charles Mensah's escape route. There was a hidden lift shaft, known only to him and his bodyguards, which connected the penthouse to the auditorium and then non-stop to the basement garage where his cars were parked. The corridor was lit dimly by battery-powered emergency lighting. The bodyguard pressed the button to summon the lift; nothing happened. Undeterred, he took a key from his pocket and opened a metal door beside the lift shaft, which revealed a small room with a diesel generator. He pressed the self-starter on the generator, which fired and then steadied to its governed revs. The sound of automatic fire came clearly from the direction of the auditorium.

The bodyguard shut the door of the generator room, locked the door by turning the key counter-clockwise twice and then once clockwise. He stepped back smartly from the door and pressed the button to summon the lift. There was a sharp explosion in the area of the lock on the steel door of the generator room, which effectively welded the door shut. The lift doors opened revealing a small elevator just large enough for the three of them. Charles Mensah had recovered slightly from his inhalation of CS gas and pressed the basement button himself. The doors closed and the lift descended at stomach-jerking speed to the underground portion of the building where it stopped with knee-jarring suddenness.

The doors opened and they were confronted by two masked men in black combat uniform. Both bodyguards fired simultaneously and the two Seals were thrown back from the lift as Charles Mensah and his two men dashed for the big Lincoln limousine. Smoke spilled out from the back of the car as the tyres left burnt rubber on the concrete while it lurched and skidded round the basement to the ramp up to the street. Both of the Seals dragged themselves to their knees and before inspecting the damage to their body-armour and bruising to themselves, one of them thumbed the transmit switch on his radio and sent a contact report to the command post in the chopper on the roof of the building.

CHAPTER 19

'Five...four...three...two...one....now!' Gunn heard the countdown on the command net in his headset and at the same instant, through the windows in the side of the CH-53, saw the four Apaches sweep in from either side of the ICB tower and launch their missiles before flicking over through ninety degrees in a 3G turn away from the target. The sliding doors on either side of their CH-53 were opened as the pilot dived the machine no more than a half mile to the rear of the two CH-53s in front of them.

The steel hawser slung between the two leading CH-53s hooked neatly under the rotor blades of the Bell Jet Ranger on the LP and, much like a fly flicked off a tablecloth, it was thrown from the roof of the ICB tower. At the instant of it falling over the edge of the building, the hawser was cast off by both choppers and it hurtled 400 feet to the road below where it burst in a ball of orange flame and black smoke. The nose of their helicopter rose as the descent slowed and then the wheels bounced on the LP and the Seal platoon exited.

The first man out dropped to one knee, raised an 80 mm anti-tank missile launcher to his shoulder and fired. The roof entrance to the penthouse disappeared and the Seals poured through the gaping cavity into Charles Mensah's apartment.

Gunn and Doyle were just about to leave the helicopter when Isaacs raised his hand to stop them and indicated that they should replace their headsets. Once they had done this he spoke: 'Mensah's escaped using some form of private lift shaft. His black limo's just left the basement car park and turned south on the dual-lane Las Vegas Strip. I've got one of the CH-53s coming in to pick you two up while the other one keeps tabs on the limmo. It'll come in and put its landing gear on the edge of the building...over there,' and Isaacs pointed. 'Take these two radios and two of those anti-tank missiles at the front of the chopper. Good luck!'

Gunn and Doyle Barnes removed the headsets, clipped the radios to their belts, picked up two missile launchers and stepped out of the CH-53 as the other one thundered in, almost standing on its tail rotor as it stopped over the edge of the building and steadied. The dispatcher helped both of them into the machine and after a brief shout to 'hang on!' the chopper side-slipped over the edge of the building and dived to gain maximum air-speed. The despatcher offered them two safety straps and belts with quick-release buckles. Both side doors were wide open and once Gunn had his belt on, he was handed a headset. The co-pilot in the right seat looked over his shoulder and as soon as Gunn had his headset on, spoke: 'the limmo's heading south down the strip an's just taken the connect road to Highway 15 south out of Vegas. It'll be clear of the city in a couple of minutes and then the highway climbs up into the McCullough Mountains. The trouble is, it's Sunday an' there'll be more cars on that stretch of road than weekdays. Here goes, we've spotted the limmo, 'bout a mile ahead of us. You both get all that?'

They both acknowledged the information as the chopper dived lower now that it was clear of the city. The six-lane highway was not over-crowded with cars, but any attempt at destroying the Lincoln, now some 500 feet below the CH-53, would almost certainly have caused injury or death to other car drivers and passengers on the highway. The limmo was being driven with reckless ferocity, weaving in and out of the traffic and careering across the lanes. The pilot kept the machine above and to the left side of the car; Gunn saw that this manoeuvre prevented the front seat passenger from achieving an aimed shot at the helicopter and as soon as Mensah appeared at the rear window with a machine pistol, the despatcher drove him back inside the car with short bursts from his M16 carbine.

The highway left the mountain-encircled bowl in which the city of Las Vegas was still spreading its suburbs and started the climb into the McCullough range of mountains. The wide highway swept in curves around the increasing gradient; to the west of the highway were the pine-covered slopes of Spring Mountain and to the east, Crescent Peak rising to over 6,000 feet in the Lake Mead National Park. Ahead of the Lincoln lay the bleak landscape around the dried-up lakes of Peach, Ivanpah and Mesquite and the inter-state border with California. The commentary on the striking landscape all round the CH-53 was coming from the co-pilot. Once again, Gunn's headset clicked and the unruffled and laconic voice of the US Marine pilot, who might have been acting as tour guide on a Women's Institute Sunday outing, warned them that the first exit from Highway 15 was coming up 5 miles ahead.

'Route 161 leads up into the thick pine forests of Spring Mountain National Park. There are any number of cabins and picnic places in that area an' it'll be hard to follow this guy if he takes that exit. If he does, we'll set you down 'bout a mile ahead of him and then let you take it from there. Problems?'

'None,' both Gunn and Doyle answered, as the Lincoln swerved across in front of a family station wagon, forcing it into the carriageway barrier and then skidded sideways to the exit onto route 161. The helicopter banked to the right and accelerated ahead of the car below and into the dead ground of a ravine, which hid them from the occupants of the limmo. The pilot took the CH-53 at tree-top height up the ravine before he spoke over the intercom.

'Any moment now, you guys; you'll have only a couple of minutes before the Lincoln's onto you.....here we go!' The thump and beat of the rotors increased in volume as the blades braked the descent of the helicopter and the wheels touched the verge of the road where it swung round the edge of the spur which had concealed them from the car. Gunn and Doyle jumped from the chopper which immediately rose and then side-slipped back down into the ravine to conceal its presence from the Lincoln.

Gunn chose a position beside some large boulders out of which stuck a sign welcoming drivers to the Spring Mountain National Park and scenic picnic place. Doyle had chosen a position in the trees on the other side of the track leading off the road. Both positions would give them a head-on shot at the Lincoln as it came round the corner. Gunn extended the launch tube, flicked up the sights, cocked the Winchester-like trigger guard which powered up the firing circuit chip and was rewarded with a green 'GO' light and a bleep. A Chevrolet Commander station wagon came round the corner, slowed and then turned down the track where Gunn and Doyle were hidden. The driver spotted Gunn and slowed, but accelerated away in a cloud of dust when shouted at by Doyle whom he hadn't seen.

Gunn heard the Lincoln before he saw it; the squealing of spinning tyres on tarmac heralded the approach of the car which then slewed into view round the corner, canted hard over on its nearside suspension. The Lincoln appeared in the rectangular frame of Gunn's sight and he squeezed the trigger. The 80 mm missile burst from its launcher, stabilising fins spreading as it accelerated out of the tube, followed split seconds later by Doyle's missile. Both missiles struck the Lincoln in the radiator grill going straight through into the solid cast-steal block of the 6 litre engine behind it. The kinetic energy of the impact stopped the 2½ ton car, but carried the engine block back through it, leaving little recognisable in human form of the two bodyguards. The rear doors burst open and Charles Mensah was ejected from the car milli-seconds before the engine block occupied his seat.

To Gunn's amazement, Mensah appeared to be unscathed by the destructive deceleration of the car or by the dual impact of the

287

missiles.   The Lincoln, minus both front wheels and barely recognisable as a car, stopped by the side of the road, burning fiercely.   Charles Mensah, rolled to the verge, scrambled to his feet and disappeared amongst the pines.   Gunn dropped the missile launcher, caught Doyle's eye and pointed at his radio. Doyle nodded and spoke into the radio. Gunn unzipped the stiflingly hot bullet-proof body-armour of the Seal combat suit and dropped it, the flame-proof mask and the machine-pistol beside the launcher. He removed the Browning from his ankle holster and then followed Mensah into the pines.

It was now a few minutes after twelve and the overhead sun had turned the black, heat-absorbing Seal uniform into a real sweatsuit. Gunn was thankful to be rid of the flak-jacket and mask and to get into the shade of the trees.   Charles Mensah was giving little heed to caution as he crashed through the undergrowth in his efforts to put as great a distance as possible between himself and those pursuing him.   Over to his left on the track through the forest was the Chevrolet Commander with its driver and passengers watching this real-life action sequence.   Even as Gunn saw the four-wheel drive station wagon parked on the track, he realised the danger and at that moment Charles Mensah changed direction and headed for it.   Gunn stopped and fired one shot, but it was impossible to hit the man as he swerved in and out of the thick pines.

Mensah reached the track, wrenched open the driver's door and at gun point, heaved the man out of the car onto the track and whipped the keys out of the ignition before the man's wife had a chance to remove them.   He opened the back door and the three children needed no encouragement to get out of the car.   An hysterical mother ran round from the front passeger's side to her husband who still lay in the dust on the track. As Gunn reached the trees on the edge of the track, Mensah had his left arm round the throat of a little girl who could have been no more than five and used the automatic in his right to fire off a shot in Gunn's direction.

'You come any closer an' she gets it; do ya hear me!' was screamed at Gunn. 'I'm taking the girl an' if you or that chopper comes after me, she gets it! He pushed the girl across the driver's seat to the front passenger seat, holding the muzzle of the automatic against her neck. He then climbed in and reached back to shut the door. Gunn fired twice; the soft-nosed bullets of the Hi-Power blew most of Mensah's head off and the almost headless trunk fell across the wheel. Gunn rushed to the right of the station wagon and lifted the small girl from the front seat and carried her to her mother who was still sitting beside her husband sobbing hysterically. Gunn unclipped the radio from his belt and pressed the transmit button.

'Barnes this is Gunn; it's over. Mensah's dead.'

CHAPTER 20

'Hey mister! You going my way?' Gunn turned at the sound of the familiar voice in the transit lounge of Miami International Airport. Claudine was dressed in some tight-fitting, all-white outfit that was already causing minor passenger congestion in front of the passport-checking booths.

'Hadn't got any specific plans; why, do you have something planned?'

'I do,' she smiled linking her arm through his and leading Gunn out of the transit hall towards where a number of helicopters were parked up. 'That's our taxi,' and Claudine pointed at a Bell Long Ranger helicopter, 'and first stop's 50 miles south at Silver Cay where there's a forty foot ketch tied up with champagne and oysters on ice.'

'Oh, is that all...now I thought you were going to offer something really tempting,' and Gunn just ducked in time to avoid both Claudine's right hook and the rotor blade as both of them climbed into the helicopter.

*

'There can be no doubt about your diagnosis, sister?'

'No, my dear, I regret there's no doubt, but you can always seek another opinion.'

'How long?'

'With care and treatment.....a year...perhaps a little longer; it depends on infection against which you have no resistence.'

'Thank you, sister. I think it's time I went to visit my father.'

'Is that far, my child?'

'He lives and works in Ashanti, just south of Kumasi.'

'Take care, won't you?'

'I will, sister.'

Kisi Quartey caught a bus to Aflao, the border town between Togo and Ghana and another from there to Accra. In Accra, she caught the train to Kumasi and shortly after eleven on the morning of Monday 18th April she stopped outside the small house in Dunkwa where the mining company provided accommodation for its workers. There was no answer from the house and a mother surrounded by three small, naked children next door suggested that she go to the office. From the office she was directed to the medical centre where she was met by the receptionist, Comfort Danso.

'May I help you?'

'Yes, I'm looking for my father; Kofi Anysombe.'

'Ah...at last; we knew he had a daughter, but we were told that she'd changed her name and lef.....oh, something like eight years ago. Is that you?'

'My name was Kisi Anysombe; I changed it to Quartey when I left home. Where's my father?'

'Come with me, Miss Quartey,' and Comfort led her into a treatment room next to the reception area. 'I'm very sorry to have to tell you that your father's dead, Miss Quartey.' The only reaction was the lowering of the woman's head.

'How long ago?'

'His body was found on 21st February in the Ofin River. He'd been dead less than 24 hours.'

'Had he drowned?'

'No, Miss Quartey; he'd been murdered and then his body was thrown into the river.'

'Does anyone know why he was murdered?' There were still no tears or outward sign of grief.

'He was involved in stealing gold from the mine. We have to presume that he cheated on someone who was paying him to steal the gold.'

'Do you have any idea who that was?'

'Not really, Miss Quartey......all we have is some sort of name or title.'

'What was that?'

'Caramansa.'

ALSO BY BRIAN NICHOLSON FEATURING JOHN GUNN

GWEILO

The theft of a birthright has been the motive for murder since Jacob usurped it from his elder brother, Esau. The birthright to the immense riches of Hong Kong will be stolen at midnight on 30th June 1997 from the descendants of the first settlers on that inhospitable, fever-ridden island of decaying granite, as a result of the signing of the Anglo-Sino Joint Declaration in 1984. Not only the New Territories will be handed back to China - acquired by Great Britain in the 1898 treaty - but also Hong Kong Island which was ceded to Great Britain in perpetuity after the first Opium war in 1842, thus forming the birthright of the descendants of those intrepid traders and settlers who had arrived in Hong Kong - 'a place of sweet water' - under the straining canvas of the triangular sky and moonraker topsails of their lean-hulled trading clippers.

In 1986, two years after the signing of the Joint Declaration, the reactor at the Chernobyl nuclear power station exploded. The subsequent meltdown and escape of radioactive material turned the surrounding area for hundreds of square miles into a deserted wasteland of mutant plants and animals and humans riddled with cancer. The world reeled in horror and condemned the corrupt and decaying Soviet Union for its crass incompetence. But one man in Hong Kong, whose ancestor had disembarked from the first of the clippers to anchor in Victoria Harbour and whose father had died for Hong Kong, tortured to death by the Japanese occupation force in 1943, saw the Chernobyl disaster in a different light. It offered the solution to his all-consuming fury at being dispossessed of his inheritance and betrayed by his own country. If he and his descendants couldn't have Hong Kong, then no one would have it - least of all the Chinese.

This is the first of John Gunn's assignments for the British Intelligence Directorate for which he was head-hunted from his SAS induction course because of his fluency in Cantonese and Mandarin Chinese.

292

AL SAMAK

.......is about intrigue, treachery, conspiracy, revenge and violence. It's a story of the flawed and bungled political manoeuvring in the UN before the invasion of Iraq by coalition forces in March 2003. It's the story of Russia's fight to protect its embryo democracy against plotting by die-hard communists. It's the story of Iraq's struggle to achieve a WMD capability to prevent the invasion. It's the story of the desperate measures taken by the intelligence agencies of the coalition to prevent a nuclear holocaust in the Middle East.

It's John Gunn's second assignment with the British Intelligence Directorate, but above all, it's a story.... a story of 21st Century political intrigue and weapons of mass destruction, but this story started as long ago as the 7th Century, as a storm-lashed papyrus raft broke up in the Arabian Sea......but is it a story?....you decide.

FIRE DRAGON

The slaughter of half a million Communists by Indonesia's President in the 1950s is a weeping sore for Arief Sulitsono (Alias Dr Ramano Rusman) the illegitimate son of Aidit- the Communist leader - who is determined to return Indonesia to a Communist Dictatorship. He realises that he can do nothing against the power of the USA unless he and other developing countries of NAM possess nuclear weapons. He therefore enters into a conspiracy with the North Koreans to help them avoid US interference with their nuclear weapons programme.

Fortuitously, he stumbles on the enormous treasure amassed by Admiral Yamamoto and hidden in the islands off Irian Jaya and uses this unlimited funding to build a rocket launch site on Waigeo Island on the Equator. From this rocket launch site he plans to place the North Korean nuclear warheads in geo-stationary orbit out of reach of IAEA inspection and US satellite surveillance and available to any country resisting US interference.

Rusman's plan unravels because there are other clues to Yamamoto's treasure and his launch site is being built on the most likely epicentre of a cataclysmic earthquake. This is John Gunn's fourth assignment for the British Intelligence Directorate in which leads to a confrontation with man-eating dragons in 'the ring of fire'.

THE AUTHOR

Brian Nicholson's life has been almost as exciting and eventful as that of John Gunn. Apart from flying, sailing, scuba-diving, skiing, renovating classic cars and being a talented artist and writer, he has led an unusually exciting and successful life as a soldier. This has varied from active service to negotiator extraordinary in Beijing to rescue the 1984 Anglo/Sino Joint Declaration on the future of Hong Kong. As the personal Military Adviser to Ghana's Flt Lt Jerry Rawlings, he assisted in the planning of the military intervention in Liberia in 1991. As the Defence Attaché in Jakarta, his highly successful expedition to unlock the mystery of what happened to the ill-fated, WW2 Australian commando raid - Operation Rimau - on Japanese shipping in Singapore received wide press coverage at the time.

His first book, 'GWEILO' focuses on a conspiracy to prevent the return of Hong Kong to China. His second book, 'AL SAMAK' is about Saddam Hussein's efforts to acquire WMDs to prevent the invasion of Iraq by the coalition forces in 2003. The third book 'ASHANTI GOLD' uses his exciting exploits in West Africa as a colourful background to a novel that focuses on the famine, chaos and corruption in the African Continent. The author's latest novel 'FIRE DRAGON' uses material from his experience as a Defence Attaché in Jakarta, where he travelled extensively from the remote areas of Sumatra, Kalimantan and Irian Jaya to the troubled Island of East Timor. This provided an ideal backdrop for a North Korean/Indonesian conspiracy to develop a nuclear weapon and the means of delivering it.

He is now writing his fifth novel featuring John Gunn and continues to sail, paint, ski, play golf and restore classic cars.

ISBN 142513354-1

9 781425 133542